The Ba...

By Barrie Condon

Acknowledgements

Thanks to Gary and Emma Gibson for introducing me to the delights of Taiwan, and to Ann, Juanita and Aurora for putting up with my obsessive note-taking on our long trek across mainland China.
I also greatly appreciate the support and encouragement that all the staff at Sparsile have given to me over the years.

1. Elephant Mountain, Taipei, Taiwan

The Son, Benny Hu, and the Disappointing Gifts

Where the concrete of the city ended, the mist—and jungle—shrouded mountainsides thrust their way skyward, surrounding the teeming city like a lush curtain.

Barely two hundred metres up the steep, rock-cut stairway and already Benny Hu's shirt was patched with sweat. It was forty degrees at least and the air was so humid you drank more than breathed it.

Around him the trees had closed in and, though not much more than a stone's throw from a city of millions, it was easy to believe himself lost in endless jungle.

He stopped and turned as though to catch a reassuring glimpse of Taipei through the leaves, but really checking if anyone else was coming up the path. It should be too late on this weekday for early morning walkers.

Uneasily, he saw a single figure plodding up towards him. The man was bowed forward with the effort and all Benny could see of his head was the thick black hair covering its top. He was dressed like everyone else in jeans and T-shirt and sandals. A raised flatness in one trouser pocket revealed a phone, a small irregular jumble in the other a bunch of keys.

There could still be a weapon tucked into the back of his waistband.

Benny watched the slow approach. Maybe it was just the climb or the humidity but his own breathing was laboured. He'd been careful, to the point of paranoia, deploying all the tricks after he'd left his hotel. Even so, Taipei was a busy city, with hundreds always in view, so identifying a watcher would always be a challenge.

He'd ducked into stores big enough to tunnel their way through a whole block and with entrances front and back. Common tactics even in the old days, but even more so now that intelligence services had taken to using tiny, almost transparent, drones. Even they couldn't handle the big store ruse. They could jump over the roof, but the operator would need to know where the other entrance was. By the time they'd figured it out, Benny would be long gone.

There were other tricks. His hotel was near the main station, a blocky iceberg with more going on below the surface than above. Underground malls spread away like the roots of a tree with a score of stairways leading up to the streets. Using these, he'd popped up and down like a whack-a-mole. The Guoanbu, the Chinese secret service, would have needed a team of a hundred to keep tabs on him.

Despite all that, here was someone following him up the mountain. As the distance between them shortened to a few metres, Benny put his hands on his hips and breathed even harder than necessary. He smiled grimly at the man, pantomiming a climber not up to the challenge.

Instead of getting a wry smile in return, or even just the rise of an eyebrow, the other man looked away as though annoyed. It was only as he passed by that Benny noticed his limp. It looked all too real and he guessed this climb was part of the man's therapy. He wouldn't have taken kindly to seeing a fit-looking guy still in his forties making a big deal of being out of breath.

Even so, Benny's eyes followed the man as he climbed away. Shirt sweat-stuck to his back; there was no telltale pistol bulge.

Benny waited until the man had disappeared and then slowly continued up the path. It didn't take long before he caught sight of the viewpoint, a little platform to the side of the stairway.

He might have been comfortable with his own tradecraft, but now he depended on someone else's. The embassy was on the Songgao Road, to the east of the Sun Yat-Sen memorial. Elephant Mountain was only a couple of klicks from there but Benny assumed, and his life depended on it, that whoever had dropped the package had first gone in the opposite direction and into the centre of town. Then, hopefully, they would have ducked and dived for hours to lose any surveillance, before coming all the way back out here with the gifts.

If they hadn't been thorough then who knew what sort of reception might be waiting for him?

He toiled up to the platform and, rubbing a hand over a sweaty brow, walked over to grasp the railing and look out over the city. Taipei 101, a twenty-first century dream of a pagoda, its four sides like rows of dominoes that had fallen over, thrust upward for over five hundred metres out of the city and into the blurry sky. From where he stood, he was afforded views across the mountainside he was on. Here and there, little precariously perched temples poked out through the trees. To his surprise, just to his right, he saw a four-storey building sprouting from the jungle. Each floor had a tiled balcony and on the ground floor there were the tables of a restaurant. From somewhere within came the unmistakable sounds of karaoke.

He checked the path up and down. He checked the sky for movement, the only way he might pick out the little transparent drones. Nowadays, drones as small as a baby's fist could blow your head off. Finally, he turned to look at the trees and the vegetation, only too well aware that the chances of him spotting a camera were insignificant; they could be the size of a screw head.

He undid his fly as though going for a piss. Benny had never liked snakes and he felt a momentary fear as his feet and ankles disappeared amongst the thick green vegetation. Ahead, amongst the yellow blooms of acacia and the rods of bamboo, he spotted the leaves of the single maple tree.

Taking one more glance back, he bent down and groped around the trunk amongst the ferns at its base. His probing fingers found the package. It was heavy but not as reassuringly weighty as he had hoped. If it held two guns, then they certainly weren't big ones.

He quickly shrugged off his little backpack and opened it. He dropped the package in and covered it with his rain mac. Then he stood up and pissed over the maple.

Back at the observation deck and for the sake of appearance, he took one more look over Taipei steeping in the haze, and then made his careful way back down.

The metro, clean and efficient and fairly empty at this time of day, whisked him effortlessly to the Zhongshan station. The place was palatial and he had to make his way up several gleaming escalators to reach the blue-roofed turret of one of entrances, the only parts of the metro station sticking above ground. Beyond its invisible air-conditioning barrier, the humidity struck him in the face like a wet towel.

Heading towards the night market, he ducked quickly down a crowded side street and hid behind a vending machine. This stood proud of an array of exotic vegetables on tables sprawled across the sidewalk.

The metro trip would have foiled any drone and he'd kept a close eye on the passengers who had left the train with him. They'd all headed to other exits except for one, an old lady pulling a two-wheeled trolley with a wicker cage containing what looked like a fox terrier, who had followed him up the escalator. Like many older people here she was still wearing a face mask. Peeking round the machine he watched as she crossed the side street and continued along the main road.

Unless they were watching every entrance of every metro station then he was clear. Nevertheless, for the next half hour he weaved an erratic path through the district until he finally came within sight of the bar off Nanjing West Road.

He leaned against a wall, took out his phone and peered and poked at it, though his eyes were scanning the bar. He watched it for ten minutes through the hordes of buzzing motor scooters and shaky old bicycles. People trudged by on the cracked, white-tiled sidewalk, heads down and lost in the misery of the humidity. Though now in the shade, Benny's shirt was again wringing wet and he had to keep wiping sweat from his brow.

Eventually, and more for the sake of getting some aircon than because his tradecraft was satisfied, he waited until the lights changed and the maelstrom of the traffic came to a halt, then he walked across.

Sure enough, when he opened the door and stepped in, the aircon felt too fierce, the change too sudden, but he knew his skin would soon adapt. The bar was lit by natural light from the many windows and by a potpourri of differently shaped electric bulbs hanging suspended from the ceiling. He much preferred gloom for a meet like this, but to any watchers there might be something disarming about him entering one of the brightest lit bars in Taipei.

Bars were still a fairly recent phenomenon here but, as with anything new, the Taiwanese had adopted social drinking with relish. Behind the wooden bar and above a row of twenty or more beer taps, a blackboard revealed the names and descriptions of a bewildering array of brews.

Far away in one corner he caught sight of Jiang and lifted a hand, then both eyebrows. Jiang nodded his head and chopped a hand across the top of his nearly full beer glass: he was good. Benny nodded in understanding, one man meeting a friend in a bar. It was all so natural that Benny could almost believe it himself.

Behind the bar he saw the waitress was looking at him. Business was light but that wasn't the only reason. He knew he could sometimes, with some women, be a head-turner. He was taller than most other Asian men, with broader shoulders but still with the leanness that many women so prized. With his regular features, and a glint in his eye he had rehearsed to the point where he could turn it on and off like a light bulb, he knew he could be easy to look at.

He gave her a smile and she didn't look away, which by Taiwanese standards made her almost brazen. He glanced up at the blackboard and chose a beer at random. Taiwan had many languages and dialects but, after Chiang Kai-Shek took over the place in 1949, Mandarin had become by far the most common. Benny's own Mandarin was carefully accented to betray Yangtze

9

Delta origins. There were plenty of visitors from China so he wasn't going to stand out. When he ordered, he saw her eyebrows rise in recognition.

"Enjoying Taiwan?" she asked, as she pulled the tap. She was pretty, as so many Taiwanese girls were, and there was a bird-like delicacy to the thin bones of her exposed arms.

"I am now," he said.

Now she did glance away, but she looked pleased. Benny felt an instant of regret that the chances of him ever returning to this bar were exactly zero.

He picked up his beer and turned and headed over to join Jiang. The man gave him a big smile as he rose to shake his hand, but when he grabbed it, he pulled hard so that Benny found himself leaning over the table, their heads barely inches part.

"You took your fakkin' time," Jiang whispered fiercely in English.

Benny was an East London boy himself and at times Jiang's Bermondsey accent could be almost comforting. But right now Benny was in-character, in-country and in-the-zone. "Cao nì yeye," he said in Mandarin dripping with derision.

Angry though they were, they were still managing to smile but this head-to-head couldn't last without people noticing. Jiang let go of his hand and sat back. Now in almost perfect Beijing-accented Mandarin he said: "And if you saw my grandfather, you'd want to fuck him too."

Benny bit back a comment. Jiang had no more known his grandfather than Benny had his. Though ten years separated them, they'd been brought up in the same East London orphanage. When Benny had needed to recruit, it had been the first place he'd looked. Breaking in and perusing the old hard copy filing system had been child's play.

For official MI6 employees the job was almost clubbable; though secrecy and compartmentalisation were paramount, they inevitably met and mixed. They got to know each other, friendships and enmities blossomed.

But not for Benny, and even less for Jiang. Benny was a Deniable, trained by anonymous, nondescript teachers (Ghosts is how he thought of them). Always kept at arm's length.

The story of his life.

And Jiang was strung out even further along this readily broken chain: a Deniable's Deniable. Benny had socialised this understandably bitter, disaffected young man. Had trained him in the dark arts, had praised him when he did well, and slapped him down when necessary. Jiang was the nearest thing to a son he might ever have. He even paid Jiang pocket money, albeit in lavish amounts.

As a result, though Jiang knew who they both worked for, he wouldn't know someone from MI6 if they came and bit him on the arse.

Jiang had been as easy to pull into this world, as Benny had been all those years ago. What was on offer was spicy adventure and lots of money, all catnip to orphans who'd known only a numbing institutional existence. How easy it had been for both of them to take that first step on the long slippery slope to blackmail, bribery and extortion. All for the good of the UK, of course. That still meant something to Benny but for Jiang—not so much.

Benny moved his chair around and sat down so he was next to Jiang, his back blocking the table from the rest of the room. He noticed Jiang's backpack open and waiting on the floor beneath.

From now on it had to be Mandarin all the way or he and Jiang were going to have real issues. Still smiling, he asked: "What's your fucking problem?"

Jiang had a jelled-back quiff that sometimes looked like a horn rising out the front of his head. He had dark brown eyes and a dimple in his chin which, Benny was sure, would make him cute even to London girls who generally didn't favour oriental-looking men.

Jiang narrowed his eyes. "You're late. I was about to crash out."

Benny checked his phone but there was a good five minutes before anything like that would have been necessary. "Bullshit! You're just nervous."

"And you're not?"

Benny didn't bother to answer. He shrugged off his backpack and put it on his lap. Hunching over, making sure nobody could see what he was doing, he lifted out one of the guns and pressed it flat up against the underside of the table. Jiang leaned forward as if to say something and Benny felt the man's fingers slide over his own and take the weight.

Benny was all too aware what would happen next. He'd stolen a quick look into the bag on the metro train and had his suspicions confirmed. Jiang was not going to be pleased and, sure enough, he was treated to a withering look.

Benny heard him shuffle the gun into his pack, then Jiang sat back and grimaced. "What the fuck was that?"

Benny found himself tapping the table in annoyance. "A Beretta Pico.380. Double action, no safety."

"Yeah, I know. A little girl showed me how to shoot one once."

Benny ignored the sarcasm and found himself talking like a Beretta salesman. "It's thin, the thinnest there is, rounded design so nothing to get snagged on when you pull it out. Easy to conceal even if you tuck it in your waistband."

"Yeah, right. Spare mag?"

"No."

Now Jiang really did look incredulous. "One mag, that's it?"

"Hey, nobody is going to do any shooting. These are for effect, even then only as a last resort."

"And what about our friends from across the Strait," said Jiang, pointing with an outstretched hand towards the Pacific, completely the wrong direction. "There could be a score of them. Will they all be armed 'for effect'?"

Benny rubbed a forehead that was beginning to hurt. If this was what fatherhood was like then maybe he should stop regretting never having any kids. Jiang was louche, bolshy and a complete pain in the arse. They could almost be brothers.

Benny had forgotten about his beer. Guys always took a sip within seconds of sitting down but Jiang had rattled him, as usual. He quickly tasted his pint and found it too hoppy for his liking.

Jiang was getting angrier, though his voice was still low and controlled. "And don't bother trying to tell me our friends won't be there. Why else has Six given us these toys?"

As ever when trying to wrangle Jiang, Benny found himself arguing a case he didn't believe in. "They're not toys. They use 9mm and whether that's fired by a Glock or a Colt or a Pico, if you get hit then you're going to know about it."

"But only six shots? What are we, Deadeye Dicks?"

Sick of Jiang's bullshit, he held out a hand, palm up.

Jiang looked at it suspiciously. "What?"

"The money," said Benny. "You're too scared to do the job, so I guess you want to give the money back." In fact, all he'd given Jiang so far was a retainer, barely a tenth of what he'd get when they finished the job, but that wasn't the point.

Jiang sat back and folded his arms. "Boy, you really have taken the Queen's Shilling, haven't you?"

Out of the mouths of babes! Even Jiang could get things right on occasion. Even so, this one wasn't just for King and Country. Benny needed the money badly if he was ever to get out of this terrible, dangerous game. Maybe even lure Lea out of her life and into his. But Benny kept this to himself, just staring right back at Jiang, his hand still open.

Jiang leaned forward. "Look, I'll play along. Just admit this whole thing stinks."

Benny shrugged and withdrew his hand. That was all he deserved.

It seemed to be enough. Jiang gave him a wry smile. "So, when does it all kick off?"

As they discussed their plans, Benny found himself thinking about Jiang. Under MI6's direction, they'd bribed Chinese nationals in Algeria and Zambia, burglarised factories in Taiwan and Indonesia, had set up honey traps all across South-East Asia. Jiang had learned these skills well but was still too wild, too careless for Benny's tastes. Too young, really. Also, like any ersatz son, he liked kicking back at his ersatz father, whether said father deserved it or not.

On the other hand, Benny had to admit he was good to have at your back when things went pear-shaped. The Guoanbu were unflinching when it came to meting out punishment.

"What's wrong?" Jiang's sharp query interrupted his thoughts.

"Nothing."

"Please! How much time have we spent together? How much shit have we had to share? I've got your fucking number, mate, and something's off."

Thousands of miles from home and beginning to lose his way, Benny found himself talking. "Where's this going?"

"What?"

"Us and this game. It was never easy but it just gets harder and harder. Sooner or later we're gonna get screwed. It's inevitable."

Jiang did a double take, theatrical but for the benefit of a crowd of one. "Where did that come from, Mr Buttoned Up Tight?"

"The drones, the face and gait recog, cameras every fucking where. You know how many operatives the Goo have poking away on their workstations? Half a million. A handful of us against one million eyes."

"You're scaring me," and Jiang reached across to touch his hand. "You know I've always looked up to you..."

Benny shook his hand off angrily. "God, what a twat you are!"

Jiang sat back chuckling. "And you're turning into such an old man."

"Something you'll never do."

"Who wants to live forever? Who wants to live for a century by playing it safe? Anyway, the more dangerous it gets the more they pay you and then the more you pay me."

"Not much to spend it on if you're a corpse."

14

"Why now to get cold feet?" Jiang spread out his arms. "This is Taiwan. It's not like Africa. Here there are limits on what the Goo can get away with. No secret cities like under Beijing, no detention and interrogation centres hidden away in the African bush with the locals happy to turn a blind eye. Anyway, what the fuck do we know that would be so important to them?"

True enough in one way but, even so, over time, Benny had figured out quite a bit. What Six knew, how it knew it, how it operated. If the Chinese ever got hold of him it wouldn't be a matter of getting a kicking and then being shot. They'd keep drilling away until they found gold.

Maybe this was how Jiang kept his fear at bay. Ignorance as shield. Good luck with that!

Jiang tapped the table with his forefinger. "If you don't want to do it then fuck off. Introduce me to your bouncer at the whorehouse. I'll do everything."

Somehow this conversation had turned through 180 degrees and it was Benny who was on the back foot and Jiang who was being sanctimonious.

Whichever way you cut it, the man was right. Benny was off his game and getting wobbly.

He shook his head in what he hoped was a no-point-arguing way. "Doing it all with no back-up? Suicide!"

"Worth it if I got your share as well."

Benny looked out of the window. Taipei was humming away as normal, apparently unperturbed. Somehow the people could go about their business even though the People's Liberation Army Rocket Force had thousands of missiles pointed right at them. Taiwan lay like a tiny baby next to a huge mother that might one day roll over in its sleep and crush it to death.

And the Taiwanese weren't even getting paid to take that risk!

"No," he said. "We'll do this together."

2. Shanghai 1895

The Great-Grandfather, Hu Jun, and the Frightened Songbird

On the day that would change his life forever, Jun felt Liu, his anchor in a storm-tossed sea, shaking his shoulder. Not that he had been asleep. He had simply been resting, savouring the one part of the day when life felt entirely under his control. Outside, the ragged, punch-drunk cockerels had long ceased shouting their challenges to the rising sun.

It was time even for a gangster to rise.

"What are you doing, you dreadful woman?" he asked.

"Waking my sack of shit of a husband so he goes to work."

"Let us stay!" and with this he reached out and pawed her heavy breasts. She slapped his hand away and struggled off the straw-stuffed burlap sacks that was their bed and fumbled her feet into her slippers.

"Come back to bed, woman!"

"Go to hell, man! Someone has to make the porridge."

"Try putting something tasty in it for once." He watched her fiddling with the firewood, then became more interested in how her ample bottom stretched the white cloth of her shift as she bent down.

Around him, through the thin wooden walls of the shack he heard the sounds of the village. Dogs barked and couples argued, though in less amiable ways than he did with Liu. She had been insulting him from the moment they met several years before at her cousin's wedding. She seemed uncomfortable on the few occasions when he had indicated even the slightest sentimental attachment.

Liu was a good wife, though she would be mortified if he ever said so. She cooked and cleaned and bound his wounds, berating rather than sympathising every time he got into a fight. Once, however, Jun had caught sight of a rim of moisture in one eye when she had been dressing a cut to his neck which could so easily have been fatal. He had teased her mercilessly ever since for such an unforgivable hint of tenderness.

"Will some marinated pork do you, my Lord?" she called over her shoulder.

"Anything to give your jook some taste." His family had been so poor that nothing had leavened the tastelessness of the rice porridge. The truth was that dangerous work paid. Pork and fish were no longer rare treats.

Jun must have dozed off for the next thing he knew she was shaking his shoulder again. "Your Lordship's breakfast is ready."

He poked his feet into his boots, filched from the rubbish tip of a rich man's house but too big even for Jun, and got to his feet. He was much taller than her and she looked up at him defiantly with her big brown eyes set into a wide peasant face. Despite herself, she ran an appreciative hand over his broad chest. "I am feeding you too well."

He grabbed her and pulled her to him. "You starve me in other ways, woman," and his mouth met hers.

She pulled her head back and grimaced. "Your morning breath is... eugghh! Leave that to the evening! Have mercy and allow me the rest of the day to prepare myself for the ordeal of you rooting at me like an old boar." She shoved him away. "Besides, I have a busy day and have no time for any of your nonsense."

"Drinking tea and gossiping. You poor overworked thing."

"You think our garden looks after itself? You think the cabbage and the corn and the spring onions plant themselves, then pull themselves out of the ground and walk into the house and onto your plate? Anyway, I have to take the Jade Empress to market. She has stopped laying."

The Jade Empress, her name given because she had always seemed like an imperious old lady, was the most venerable of their chickens. Even so, once a bird stopped laying then the inevitable destination was the dinner plate. The only question was whose?

"Why don't we eat her?" he said.

"There is no holiday soon, no festival."

"I know. But things are better than they were, wife. We should enjoy ourselves."

"I must stop calling you Lord. You are beginning to believe it."

He took her rough, pudgy hands in his. She had come from a family as poor as his own. "I am making better money. We can live more..." Words failed him so he waved a hand at the little single-roomed shack made out of boards pillaged from the Shanghai docks.

She looked up at him. "Where? In the city?"

"No. I do not want you there. When I come home, I want to leave my work behind. We will build a new home here, in the village."

"It is a long walk for you every day. Coming back alone so early in the morning, I fear that robbers will kill you."

"They would not dare."

"Perhaps. None of them know how soft you are."

He smiled. "Because it's not true, woman."

She shook her head. "Eat your porridge, fool!"

Old man Jaw-Long looked comfortable enough lying there, but Jun knew all too well how opium dulled pain and discomfort. The customers tripped easily and fell when they were leaving. When smoking their pipes they sometimes rolled off their shelves. Jun had become adept at pulling the spreading lips of their wounds back together with needle and twine. Though the needle was thick and the point dull, the men would look up at him with the same unchanging, empty half-smile as it wove in and out of their slackened flesh.

Jaw-Long hadn't cut himself or fallen but he was slowly injuring himself nevertheless because of Shaw's spite and meanness.

Shaw, the fat, shifty owner of the den, had finally had enough of the lice-ridden straw pillows that cushioned the customers' heads as they drew languidly on their pipes. Shaw's own residence had become infected by lice, his wife claiming he had carried them home from the den. To Jun it seemed more likely the lice had ridden there on the bodies of the owner's arrogant sons who made a habit of sleeping where and with whom they shouldn't.

In a fit of rage, Shaw had had the straw pillows burned and had not bothered to replace them. After they had finished inhaling the sweet fumes of the opium, the customers would now simply lay their leaden heads down on the wooden boards of the many-tiered little bunks lining the walls of the den. Jaw-Long, however, had laid down too near the top, so his head was hanging over the side, the edge sticking up into the back of the old man's neck. It should have hurt, but despite the pain the old man had fallen asleep. He would wake with raw skin and a terrible crick in the neck.

Sighing, Jun reached up to grab his legs and hauled the old man further down the bunk. Jaw-Long's head bounced up over the edge and thudded down on the boards. He opened his eyes just enough for Jun to peer into their fathomless depths.

"Sleep well, old father," he said. The old man closed his eyes and his half-smile, just for an instant, broadened.

Kang, the frowzy old woman who filled the pipes and was even now tamping away, snorted. "Soft-hearted!" she said.

Jun was employed for his fists and for worse if the need arose. "It cost me nothing and it will save him a sore neck. Why not?" he said defensively.

Kang did not deign to answer. She'd been filling pipes for more years than Jun had been alive and didn't feel the need to explain herself to anyone. Her sons, Green Gang foot soldiers like Jun, had a particular reputation for brutality. Kang did not even fear Shaw and so she had little time for Jun.

Jun, as usual, felt no need to take it any further. He preferred a quiet life, though there was little of that in this thrumming city. Shanghai was drowning in vice. It was the centre of the Chinese opium trade and for the smuggling of women from provinces all over China to service its voracious needs. World-weary European sailors, who should know about these things, often averred there were more prostitutes here than anywhere else in the world.

What made it all worse were the colonial powers who ran the place. The British, Americans and French had entered into a pact with the devil himself. They had been at a loss to deal with a culture they could barely understand so they acted through a ready-made army, the hundred thousand or so members of secret societies like the Green Gang. These gangsters ensured the Chinese didn't rebel and in exchange the colonial powers let them get on with their brothels, gambling, drug and women trafficking.

Jun had an ant's eye view of the whole rotten structure but when people's tongues were loosened by the opium, he listened carefully. His heavy forehead and thick eyebrows overhung eyes that were deeply set. He knew all too well how stupid he looked. However, others found this reassuring and they would talk openly with each other in front of him as though he weren't there at all.

The Green Gang ran nearly a thousand opium dens in the city. Once he had heard one of the 'vagabonds', the name the French gave to the gangsters, talking to a fellow gangster of how the Green Gang had an ancient and self-righteous history. Kang had been absent at the time so, with no one to distract him with instructions or complaints, he had stood filling their pipes and listening.

It soon became clear that evil men had to find their piety where they could.

The Gang had started out as a Buddhist sect about five hundred years before. They had turned to canal building to make ends meet but had then been outlawed by the Qianlong Emperor for their unionising. He had suppressed the sect and destroyed its temples.

Driven underground, the sect had evolved with the times. Its name too had changed, becoming for a time the fragrant-sounding Friends of the Way of Tranquillity and Purity. Again, evil men and their unconscious need for piety, they saw themselves as poor monks, oppressed by an evil overlord and forced to make their way in a cruel world.

These dubiously pious monks had gravitated to Shanghai, that sump hole in the making. At that time, it was a modest sea port but it blossomed as it became a way point for grain as well as an entry for foreign opium. Such was the need for crewmen in a thriving port whose business was expanding like the most malicious of cancers, the word shanghaied came to mean drugging and kidnapping men to man the ships.

It might just as well have been applied to countrywomen forced into prostitution to feed the insatiable appetites of the city. Every day lonely men arrived after many months at sea and with plenty of money. It was only natural that the Gang would cater to their needs.

Jun could hardly complain of being shanghaied into the Green Gang. He had always been big and brawny and good with his fists. He had never been to school so his first job was fetching and carrying for stallholders in the Pudong Market. He would work under the blazing sun, protected only by a broad conical hat of woven straw, the same material that made his knee-length skirt and the wings that protected his bare shoulders and arms like large epaulettes. He would scurry through the food stalls, weighed down by sacks of rice or vegetables, watched from their cages by worried dogs and by the alien eyes of serpents, all soon for the chopping board and the pot. He would bump around trays of stinking fish and offal, cuffed by women out shopping if he obstructed even for a second their poking, pummelling and smelling of the wares so profligately displayed.

As he grew even bigger and stronger, Jun would step in for the stallholders to see off the starving poor, attracted like flies to the market, while the stallholders went for a smoke or to void. Often, however, it was so they could use the cheapest of the market whores in their grimy, curtained bolt-holes. Their exertions would often be watched through the chink in the curtains by puzzled but entranced urchins. City children living rough on the street, sex to them was still a wonder, if they were lucky. For kids like Jun the mechanics were already no mystery, forced to listen and watch as his parents struggled noisily and violently for climax in a single-roomed hut without even the benefit of a curtain.

A couple of more finger breadths in height and shoulder width and Jun had graduated to collecting for the moneylenders who preyed on the stallholders. Where once he had kowtowed to the stallholders for scraps as reward for his back-breaking work, they now kowtowed to him, begging for more time, trying to break his heart with their tales of thievery and deceit. Few men, when faced with others begging for their mercy, do not become seduced by the power and whose hearts do not grow scales. As time went on, the scales grew thicker, or so Jun imagined as his scurrying turned to a swagger and his fists became encrusted with callouses.

Only his wife and old woman Kang seemed to think otherwise, that his heart was softer than it looked. One loved him for it, the other despised him.

Soon Jun was the doorman on this Green Gang opium den on the Fushan Road. Opium users could be fractious before they smoked, though never after. Then, soft and malleable like a child's straw doll, they were never a challenge. Arriving Chinese might forcefully haggle for the price of a pipe and occasionally Jun had to become physical. However, traders and managers and soldiers, overlords from the British and French concessions, could not be touched and had to be handled gently, even if they did give you a swat or two.

Drunken sailors, wherever they hailed from, were a different matter and fair game if they caused trouble. Even so, whole days would now pass without Jun using his fists. With plenty of time on his hands he could indulge a natural curiosity previously neglected when he had been scraping a hand-to-mouth living.

Opium was fascinating. It arrived at the docks from India in tea chests—thick, tarry, and smelling like you'd been buried in a tight coffin stuffed with flowers but all tainted with a hint of decay.

Coffins were always on his mind in the den, for the wooden boards on which the smokers lay were stacked like shelves. Each looked like an open-sided coffin. In the depths of their dreams the reclining inhabitants were as motionless as the dead.

Jun was intrigued by the effect the drug had on people. French traders would arrive harried and sweating under preposterously heavy clothes. Unable to communicate, tetchy, nervous, sick of the sights and smells of a malodorous city and its people, the first lungful of opium, bitter though it might be, smoothed away their sharp edges, softened their features, made their shoulders slump. Abdomens held in would slacken and bulge over tight belts. Some smokers became so relaxed they would void, adding one more overlay to the unforgettable smell of the den.

What happened afterward was more difficult for his Chinese customers. The foreign sailors could go back to sea, where their basic needs would be taken care of. The traders were always insulated by their wealth. However, for the Chinese smoker the only road led to death. Earning a living lost its importance, as did food and everything else but the drug. Sooner or later their emaciated corpses would be found by the roadside before the road sweepers would fling them without ceremony into the Yangtze. There they would bob, an everyday sight.

Though the den was a typically ramshackle affair of coarse wood planks it was next door to a far better-appointed whorehouse that served only Europeans. A gate in the metal railings led through a garden of palms and carefully tended clumps of bamboo. The house had belonged to an Indonesian prince who had fled his country with much of its treasury. Someone, and in Shanghai one could never be sure who or why, had murdered him in his sleep and now the rich shunned it for fear of his ghost. Shaw's brother had taken it over and filled it with whores. As each working day drew to a close and the sun was getting low, the women would emerge twittering away to each other and dressed in the most beautiful silks. Living works of art, they would promenade on the balcony winding around the entire middle floor of the three-storey building. The evening spectacle reminded Jun of the serving turntables in restaurants which revolved to bring a particular delicacy within one's reach.

Not that he had ever eaten in such a place but he had watched enviously through the windows.

Other than the den's skeletal Chinese customers who hardly ever left the place, business rarely picked up until well after sunset. After the pipes had been readied for the evening trade, there was little for Jun to do but stand in the shade of the doorway and watch the brothel's customers arrive. The more discreet arrived on foot or by horse but others, whose wives were far, far away in lands he could not even imagine, arrived in coaches driven by liveried servants.

The men would be regarded shyly by the women from behind shivering fans as they looked down from the balcony. Some of the customers, the traders and managers, would be in their suits as plain and dark as Jun's black riding jacket and long tunic. Some of the men who came were soldiers whose clothing was as lavishly coloured and form-fitting as the dresses and robes of the whores. The French officers favoured bright red trousers and caps with small black brims. Even in the heat they wore heavy blue tunics covered with long white capes.

Tonight, Jun could see three horses tied up by the railings. His friend, the doorman Dong Lei, stood guard. Dong Lei was from the same little village as Jun and they had been friends all their lives. It had been Dong who had made the first introductions that got Jun into the Green Gang. Like Jun he was a heavyset man. Though still in his twenties, his head was as bald as a baby's bottom.

Jun sauntered over and they exchanged nods, before both could not help but turn and watch the kaleidoscope of beauty circulating around the balcony.

"They are like the most beautiful birds," said Dong meditatively.

"Indeed," said Jun softly. "Busy tonight?"

"No," said Dong. "There is a banquet in the French Concession. Even the British and Americans will be there. Only those out of favour will come this evening."

That meant a quiet night for Jun as well so they both leaned back against the railings and lit pipes after loading them up from Jun's pouch. The tobacco was American, one of his few luxuries, and he drew in a first deep, satisfying lungful. They smoked in companionable silence as the blue sky turned to red and night began its stealthy approach.

They watched an ox plod by pulling a dung cart enveloped in a swirling cloud of flies. Jun wrinkled his nose and was about to make a comment when there was loud bang from within the brothel followed by the tinkling sound of ornaments breaking.

Dong quickly opened the gate and started towards the brothel, Jun following. Sometimes the Europeans could get boisterous and he was used to helping Dong calm things down.

They were almost at the front doors when these were flung open and two French officers came bursting out. One looked neat, his blue coat buttoned, but the other soldier's coat was wide open, as was the cotton shirt beneath, revealing a luxurious matting of dark hair.

Jun grimaced in distaste, chest hair being so uncommon in China. One more reason the Chinese considered Europeans little better than animals.

The neatly dressed man was angry and arguing with the other, who was red-faced and sweating. They swept Dong and Jun aside as though they didn't exist. The air was suddenly full of the stench of alcohol. The men stalked to the gate and, just as they turned to the right, the first screams came from the brothel.

Through the entrance doors, Jun found the lobby in uproar. All the whores were already there, their silks so colourful it almost hurt his eyes. Dong and he pushed their way through the cobalt blues and blood reds and canary yellows.

Rooms surrounded the lobby but Jun could see the old lady who ran the brothel was standing at the entrance of one of them surrounded by screaming women. She was looking into the room and trembling with what could be fear or rage.

Elbowing aside the women clustering around the door, Jun scanned the room. The walls were draped in heavy red cloth and red curtains covered the windows but these were now thrown back. Light from the setting sun shining through the slats striped the room. The bed, so fluffy and bounteous compared to the sacks Jun was used to, was covered by white blankets. The poor girl lying on them was laid out like a feast. The robe she was wearing, showing yellow birds nestling in bamboo, was dishevelled enough to reveal the hard red marks where knuckles had been driven into her chest. Though the robe still covered her sex, blood was seeping into the bedding beneath. As they watched she gave one great agonised cough and more blood welled from her lips.

The next thing he knew, Jun found himself racing down the Fushan Road, Dong struggling to keep up. He was sure the Frenchmen would turn onto the first road heading west so they could get across the Huangpu River and into the safety of the French Concession.

However, whatever madness had possessed the red-faced soldier had not abated for within seconds they caught sight of him. The man's riderless horse was galloping away down the road. There was no sign of the other soldier. Perhaps he had left in disgust.

There was a little stall on the corner of Fushan and Shangchen Roads that sold song birds. Jun saw the stallholder cowering behind a barrel. The little bamboo cages were strung like lanterns on a rope at head height. They were jerking back and forth, not because of a typhoon but from the mad soldier frenziedly shaking the line. The frantic birds were trying to fly and battering against the sides of their cages, screeching with alarm.

As Dong and Jun rushed up, a catch broke and one of the little cages fell at the soldier's feet. Without pause he booted it hard, the cage disintegrating in an explosion of bamboo and feathers.

Jun had seen plenty of Chinese men go berserk. A resilient people, Chinese could withstand immense oppression and misfortune but when breaking point finally came, they exploded in brutal bloody violence. He had never seen a European go mad before and could not imagine want kind of pressure the pampered fool might have suffered.

Dong dived forward and got to the man first but then he stopped dead in his tracks. Outrage had brought them this far but now what were they to do? This was a European, protected by the might of the French Empire and by a web of agreements between the French and the Green Gang. The French had made their clan master rich.

Big money balanced against a badly damaged whore: not a judgement either he or Dong were paid to make.

Just as Jun caught up, the soldier wrestled a cage from the line. The little songbird inside was hanging grimly to its perch.

"*Ferme ta bouche!*" roared the man, tearing the little door off and reaching in for the bird. Its brilliant blue wings fluttered in alarm, displaying its delicate yellow and red chest.

Despite many long years of reflection, Jun would never understand why the next thing happened. Just as the soldier's fingers closed over the bird, Jun found he had pulled his knife from its leather pouch under his tunic and driven its wicked little blade deep into the man's belly, sharp side up. Numbed, detached, he felt his muscles bulge as he pulled steadily upwards with all his might. He felt the knife slicing easily up through the Frenchman's flesh until it snagged against his breast bone.

The soldier had been brought fully upright. The two men found themselves looking eye to eye. The Frenchman's face was a mask of disbelief made even more so when his innards began to slough out. His expression was so comic that Jun found himself giving a single strangled laugh as he stepped back.

The soldier was still upright though swaying. Soberly he was regarding the glistening, lacerated intestines that were piling up on his fine boots.

Finally, it all seemed too much for him. He closed his eyes and collapsed.

Jun, just beginning to understand the enormity of what he'd done, glanced round and saw many eyes watching him, all from a safe distance.

Dong was nodding his head. "Run!" he said. "Many merchantmen are leaving today. It is your only chance."

Jun shook his head. "My wife..."

Dong made a slashing gesture with his hand. "The first place they will look. With their horses they would get there first no matter how fast you ran."

Jun still hesitated. Could he find a horse for himself? Could he steal it? Could he ride one even if he did? He'd never been on one in his life.

Dong grasped his arm fiercely, scattering his already fragmented thoughts. "I will look after her. Trust me! You must go!"

Jun found himself being pushed towards the Huangpu River and, after a while, he gave up trying to resist.

It was easy to spot the ships about to leave. Last-minute stores were being hurried aboard by endless streams of dockers.

Jun didn't have time to pick and choose. Retribution from the French was the least of his problems for they would never find him. To them he would just be one of a million black-clad Chinese men. The French joked openly of how similar the Chinese looked to their eyes.

His problem was the Green Gang. They would be falling over themselves to win back the favours of the enraged foreigners.

The gang chiefs would already have been pulled from their dreams. Instead of waking to begin their businesses of the night, they would have immediately organised the manhunt. As Jun slipped from shadow to shadow, he could already sense the hunters at his heels.

A beautiful, stately iron-hulled trader was the closest to departure. The sails on its three masts were even now being unfurled. Painted, polished, ornate it was a bad ship to stow away on. The voyage would be long and he was sure to be discovered. A well-manned ship such as that had no need to put a stowaway to work. All he could expect on discovery was to be hurled from the deck and then a long drift down into the ocean's infinite depths.

He needed another sort of ship. A little further down the dock was a wooden-hulled two-master, its deck curving perkily up at bow and stern. Whereas the iron-hull was polished and painted to within an inch of its life, this ship was not so spick and span, its exterior timbers caulked with tar that had melted and run in the heat. It looked as if the hull was crying black tears.

No upright officers with epaulettes and smart jackets gave peremptory orders to loaders. Instead, the crew slouched at the railings, smoking their pipes and leering at women.

Jun became aware of a rising noise behind him. For an instant he couldn't place its guttural, animalistic intensity, then a cold hand clutched at his heart. A mob was approaching, a stupid brutal organism, easily summoned to life in a city full of poor. A release for the Shanghai Chinese, a focus for all their fear and anger and despair.

And what a perfect target he made for a self-righteous mob. The French, British and Americans gave them jobs, fed their children. Fickle and dangerous though these rich masters might be, their largesse was not to be tested.

The wooden ship was too far down the dock to reach before the mob arrived. They would not know what he looked like, but his size would betray him.

There was only one thing to do. Reluctantly, he crouched down behind some sacks of rice and reached over the side of the dock to get a hold on a wooden piling. The wood was dry but splintery and he felt it bite at him as he lowered himself into the black waters of the Huangpu River.

He couldn't swim a stroke but cross-members of ancient rotting wood connected the pilings, all lashed together with bamboo. Using these he managed to haul himself through the water. Soon he was below the mooring ropes of the iron-hull. He passed under the gangway which creaked and flexed as loaders scurried back and forth.

A little further and his luck ran out. Ahead the cross beams between two pilings had vanished, leaving the bamboo lashings hanging like a European's untied bootlaces. The gap spanned several man-lengths.

Just then, above his head, the mob arrived in full cry. He heard the clumping as they fanned out over the dock. The planks covering it had gaps large enough for a rat to fall through. Sooner or later, someone would look down and see him.

If he could get to the river side of the two-master he'd be hidden from view. The sides of the ship bowed out above the waterline. Even the crew on deck wouldn't be able to see him in the water. He could wait there until the fuss died down then try to climb aboard.

First, he had to get further along the dock. The gap between the pilings was too much. If he tried to strike out across it, he would sink like a stone.

Hands wet with the befouled water kept slipping as he struggled to keep his grip on the last piling. To get better purchase, he brought his leg up out of the water and hooked it over the last intact cross-member.

The Huangpu here was not a fast-flowing river, for how otherwise would large vessels sail up this far. Big ships didn't have room to tack so had to be pulled up by squat, farting steam tugs. Around the confounding shapes of the big vessels and the pilings of the dock, the river slowed even further. Ordure and filth and rotting goods from the docks formed a bobbing, becalmed mat under the pilings. The bloated corpses of animals, tossed in as far upriver as Jiaxing, found themselves eddied into this purgatory. Even now the body of a dog stared up at him, the expanding gases of putrefaction pushing out its eyes as though in a final expression of inconceivable surprise.

Somehow Jun hauled himself up onto the cross-member until he was balancing a couple of feet above the water. He had thought to leap across to the next piling, or at least fall short by less than an arm's length so he could grasp at it. However, the piling he was holding onto was now in the way of any such leap.

Above him he could hear the mob. Their feet were no longer stamping down hard, indicating a slower, more concerted search.

He stood on his precarious perch, no idea what to do next.

A man's voice was suddenly raised in fear and rage and was answered by a visceral roar from the mob. Some big bastard must have been mis-identified. Jun didn't need imagination to guess what would happen next; he'd seen it all too often in life. The mob would be manhandling their prize, binding his hands behind his back. Once helpless they could lay into him with anything at hand.

When he'd worked on the market stalls, he'd often caught thieves and then watched as stallholders had indulged their anger. The posture the man would be made to take brought to mind the figureheads found on the older type of foreign ships. Modelled on big white women, their chests were thrust forward, arms behind them like wings. If the thief had been a woman, then her breasts would be shamelessly displayed just like the figureheads whose bright red painted nipples were worn away by the touches of women-hungry sailors.

The thought of the figurehead gave him an idea. He managed to shimmy round the piling, holding it in his hands behind his back. Keeping one foot on the cross-member for support, he brought the other up to brace against the piling. Now he too was like a figurehead leaning out over the water.

Immediately he felt his grasp slipping so he pushed back hard against the piling. Rather than a graceful dive forward, he fell like a stone, crashing into the water. His wide-open mouth and all the handy pockets in his riding jacket filled with water. His head straining up for precious air, he saw the black waters of the river close over his eyes.

Struggling mightily but uselessly, he sank down, the light from above receding. He kicked and pulled at the water in panic. Something cold stroked the right side of his face and suddenly it felt like he was being pulled by invisible hands.

He made himself stop struggling and let this stronger, deeper current carry him. He opened his arms wide, hoping they would catch on the next piling but there was nothing. The current was pulling him away from the pilings and out into the river.

His mouth stung with bitter, earthy river filth. The sweet taste of air was already a distant memory

Suddenly a hulking shape loomed up before him. His hands came up to fend off the sea monster come to devour him, but instead they scraped across the iron hull.

Scrabbling away with his hands, he felt barnacles tearing at his skin. He got just enough purchase to be able to rise.

His head broke the surface. He spat out the river before drawing in the sweetest breath of his life.

Then, to his horror, he found himself already at the stern of the ship. Unless he could get a hold, the inexorable current would sweep him away to his doom.

He redoubled his efforts but it was no use. Taking a last desperate breath, the ship slipped from his hands, and once again he found himself sinking.

Somewhere ahead lay the two-master. If the current didn't drag him out into mid-stream, he might still find it.

Drifting along underwater was like flying and while there was still air in his lungs it was almost pleasant. He thought of Liu and prayed to a god he didn't believe in that Dong could spirit her away into the country before the Green Gang could exact their revenge.

His outstretched arms crumpled on contact with the hull, his face smacking into it. Immediately he realised the hull of this ship was altogether different. Where the barnacles and other molluscs had been sparse on the Indiaman, here they had built themselves into handy mounds. Now he had things to hold onto. He quickly arrested the effects of the current and pulled himself to the surface.

The air was not quite so sweet as that first precious breath by the iron-hull, but Jun was not complaining. He took a closer look at the encrustations on which his life now depended. The long-standing mounds of barnacles had been smoothed away by the passage of water. Here and there, mussels big enough to eat sprouted from the hull and were garnished by fronds of seaweed.

Fully laden as the ship was, the deck was not far above the waterline. Even so, he was not sure he could climb up to it. The empire of the sea creatures did not extend above the waterline, leaving no handholds.

Desperately weak from all that had happened, Jun looked around in despair. How long could he maintain his grip in this current? He remembered the last look on the mad Frenchman's face, as though life had gotten too much for him. He realised just how the man had felt. Would both of them die this day?

The sun had just gone down and the light was rapidly fading. Out on the river the sampans were heading home, the fishermen pushing their single great paddles back and forth. He lifted a hand to signal one when something big nearly struck his head as it fell into the water with an almighty splash.

Dangling before his eyes was a rope, now being pulled up to bring the bucket back up to the deck. Above him he heard someone shouting. He recognised the clipped, peremptory tones of an Englishman in command. There was a splash as the bucket was emptied and water showered down over the side of the deck. As the deluge struck the river, the sawdust in it separated out and floated away.

The bucket came crashing back down. What dreadful spillage had prompted cleaning of this scow?

Then, just as the bucket crashed down once more, the English voice was raised yet again, this time in righteous anger. Immediately he heard footsteps above him receding as someone went scuttling away.

The bucket remained, its rope just before Jun's eyes. He pulled on it. Whoever had been heaving it up had tied the rope to the railing lest it slip from his fingers and the bucket drift away.

Jun took a firm grip on the line. Barely a thumb's width, it nevertheless felt robust. Was it tied firmly enough to hold his weight?

By now it was almost dark and he determined to take his chances. He started to pull himself up. Somehow, he had not lost his boots and was able to scrabble at the barnacled hull without shredding the soles of his feet. Soon he was grasping the edge of the deck.

Taking a deep breath, he pulled himself aboard.

3. Taipei

The Son, Benny Hu, and the Tea-drinking Sensualist

The golden age of Taipei whorehouses was a distant memory. Nowadays they were recalled only by a few smirking old men and by fierce, cynical women wealthy enough to own their own restaurants and marry compliant men who they could boss around. Once famous throughout the East for its prostitution, at the turn of the century it had suddenly become illegal in Taipei except in 'special zones'.

Trouble was, no such zones had ever been opened. As far as Benny was concerned the Taiwanese, just like the men the ex-whores married, were tiresomely compliant when it came to obeying the law. Elaborate pantomimes of licking, kissing, stroking, smacking and rubbing had been developed with everything being negotiable except actual penetrative sex.

Of course, the real thing was still available, but sources were secret and very expensive. Benny had engineered more than a few honey traps in his time but places like Taiwan didn't make it easy.

Their target, Fu Chonglin, loved the whores. Every day before dinner Benny had followed him from his hotel near the station and out towards Linsen Road and the Combat Zone, as the American GIs from Vietnam used to call it when they'd arrived fully loaded for their hell-bending R&R. Nowadays the alleyways held only a few dingy massage parlours offering all the ingenious alternatives to sex. Beyond that the bawdy houses got bigger, better kept and more closely guarded, catering to select groups of Chinese and Japanese businessmen.

One house, so nondescript as to be almost invisible, had attracted Fu like a bee to honey. As far as Benny could tell it was the only place he went alone, otherwise all the drinking and eating was done in the company of his delegation and in never less than ostentatious circumstances.

The doorman at the brothel had been implacable at first. Even though it wasn't his own money he was using, Benny had felt aggrieved at how much it had taken to bring the man around. The deal was that this time, when Fu arrived, the doorman would show him into a small waiting room near the entrance. That's where Benny would make his pitch.

But right now, Benny was sitting at the window of a small coffee shop across the road from Fu's hotel and waiting for the fun to begin. Stratospherically upmarket, it was in the hotel district south of the main station. Through the plate glass windows he saw the sparkle of lights strung like stars in the firmament around an atrium the size of a small mountain.

He took what he hoped was a convincing sip of his coffee. A full bladder would get in the way of what might be a long day. He glanced to the right down Zhongshan Road but couldn't see Jiang anywhere, which was just fine.

A tiny woman walked by, her back bent so far forward she would never again raise her eyes from the ground. Behind her she was trundling a little trolley with a raffia basket. For a second, he could not help thinking what life must be like for her and people like her, wearing the illnesses and injuries of a lifetime for all to see. It made him think of his mother, and the abyss she had left behind. He had the barest memory of her face and its disfigured beauty leaning over his crib. Perhaps she'd been saying goodbye...

He forced himself to push the thought away and it was just as well for he had almost missed Fu. Short, paunchy and bald but walking briskly, energised with the delights to come, he was already making his way down the sidewalk. Torn between the need for speed and fear of alerting any other surveillance Fu might be under, Benny disguised his hurry as best he could as he made his way out of the door.

He needn't have worried. Every day Fu stopped at the little open stall that floured, rolled, and deep-fried octopus dumplings. There was always a queue for the tasteless, rubbery delicacy.

At least this gave Benny a chance to catch up. He risked a look back and caught a glimpse of Jiang about fifty metres away. As usual, Jiang couldn't have looked more casual.

Benny kept strolling. He was a comfortable ten metres away when Fu collected his octopus balls and started walking, hunched over and munching away.

As they approached the station, Fu dived into a subway entrance and Benny followed him down into the glittery warren of stalls and malls. Taiwan mainline station was a huge solid brown block above ground but, iceberg-like, there was far more of it below the surface.

Though there were quite a few signposts in quite a few languages, the station seemed designed to confound. It was said that even Taipei residents routinely got lost here.

So, when Fu turned left when he should have turned right, Benny wasn't too worried. It was only when the man checked his phone, looked around and then continued in the same direction, that Benny began to suspect he wasn't heading towards the whorehouse at all.

Benny's phone pinged. Only Jiang had this number. *WTF* it said.

Any company he typed

Nope

Jiang may be an asshole but he could spot a tail. He might miss a drone but there would have been a big commotion if something like that had tried to follow them into the crowded subway.

Candidates for any surveillance included the Taiwanese National Security Bureau and, of course, the Guoanbu. Neither favoured MI6 but at least the NSB wouldn't slit their throats.

Fu alone would hardly be a match for Benny and Jiang. Without the Goo in the picture, the gun in his trouser pocket suddenly made him overdressed, like he was wearing a dinner jacket to a grunge gig, but that was fine with him.

Fu was striding more confidently now. He walked without hesitation through the entrance to the metro line heading south towards Taipei Zoo. After carding his way through, Fu descended the escalator into the usual cavernous metro station. With its cleanliness and light, it made the London Underground look like the tunnellings of a mad, cholera-ridden mole.

Benny followed more cautiously now as the crowds were thinning. The metro trains were long, so at the bottom of the elevator he turned in the opposite direction to Fu and queued at the first stopping point. Soon Jiang appeared but he followed in Fu's direction, passing him and going to the other end of the station.

Why had Fu gone off-piste? The man didn't seem worried or perturbed. Rather than looking round anxiously he'd put his hands in the pockets of his fawn trousers and was rocking back and forth on his heels. When the train arrived, he stepped aboard without even glancing around.

The train accelerated out of the station and soon climbed into the light of day before making its sashaying way around apartment buildings and office blocks. The carriages were open and afforded views down the whole length. As the train wove its way through the city it was like being in the gut of a huge snake. A gut full of bright blue plastic seats and a floor that always looked clean and polished despite the heavy traffic.

Soon there was only a few stops left before the zoo. The carriages had been steadily emptying and Benny knew he was becoming easier to spot. He needed to keep on his toes. Fu might wait until the doors were closing then leap through, leaving any followers shanghaied on the departing train.

Instead, Fu stayed on and the steamy jungle hillsides started to press in. When the train arrived at the zoo station, casual as you like, Fu stood up and left the train. He headed towards the exit without a backward glance.

Benny had figured out where he was going and had been quicker. As soon as the door had opened, he'd been off the train and running. He'd crossed the ground between the metro and gondola before Fu had even emerged from the station. There was no queue so he was the sole passenger for the next arriving car. It had a small cab, big enough to seat two or three abreast. Stepping aboard, he was being swept upwards before he realised the floor was clear plastic. He saw the ground fall suddenly away from the rising cable car and his scrotum tightened. He grabbed compulsively at the door handle and tried to calm his hammering heart.

The long climb to the teahouses passed over a series of rising peaks. Clearing the first one, and becoming used to the hundred metre drop beneath his feet, he made himself let go of the handle and got out his phone.

Is he on the gondola?
Two cars behind. I'm in the third.

Benny breathed a sigh of relief. Something had told him Fu wasn't intending to look at any animals and he'd guessed right. Fu was headed for the tea plantations and their excruciatingly cute little teahouses that perched just below the mountain peaks. Was he having a meet there? Had some other intelligence service got to him first?

It was a good job Benny had taken the risk of leaping on the first cable car. If he and Jiang had been left trailing behind, Fu might have vanished by the time their car got to the top. Now at least he could see where Fu was heading when he got off.

The steep ride seemed endless. Soon Taipei was spread out below him with the erect phallus of Taipei 101 just penetrating the lowering clouds. Discrete puffs of mist, or clouds of spores from the trees, clung to the hillsides like little bits of cotton wool. As the car rose, the irregular tree tops of the jungle gave way to what looked like bright green contour maps. This was the tea, each contour line a break between the rows of bushes so the pickers could get at all sides.

The gondola ended at Maokong Station. When Benny emerged from the metal and glass, he was surprised to find a rustic road wending its way across the side of the mountain. Little stone walls separated it from small haphazard vegetable plots. Here and there, little shrines nestled amongst the stones. The air was colder and wetter and he felt the lightest of drizzles, almost like a caress, on his bare arms.

There was only two ways to go when Fu left the station but Benny had no idea which he would take. Looking round to make sure he was not being observed, he vaulted over a wall and hid himself amongst the lower branches of an overhanging tree.

When Fu emerged from the station he stopped, took a deep breath of the moist mountain air then turned to look down over Taipei. He waited so long Benny became worried that Jiang would come blundering out of the station.

Just then his phone buzzed. *What now*

Wait

Finally, Fu, after drinking in the view, turned and headed left, following the little road as it rose higher. Benny waited until he'd turned a corner and was hidden by trees, then he vaulted back over the wall and followed.

Following, your left

Perhaps it was his imagination, for they could not have been more than a thousand feet up from the city, but the extra moisture seemed to make breathing just that little bit more difficult.

Peering round the hedges where the road turned a corner, he saw the next little stretch was clear and he picked up his pace. On the downhill side of the road the little vegetable plots suddenly gave way to the bright greens of the carefully manicured tea bushes. Pickers, with raffia buckets strapped to their backs and coolie hats on their heads, bent over the rows.

At some corners, Benny caught sight of Fu ahead, nonchalantly strolling along.

Have we any company
No. What the fuck is he doing here.

Around the next corner, Benny was just in time to see Fu enter a grandly designed teahouse. It stretched out in rising wooden tiers over the hillside. Each little terrace had polished dark-wood tables and chairs amongst little potted trees and piles of rocks. They were like gardens in the sky. A few patrons sat leaning on the wooden balustrades, sipping their tea and admiring the view.

Fu went in through an arched entrance strung with red paper lanterns but soon appeared on the upper deck making a beeline to a table on the end. A waitress appeared and he ordered.

He heard Jiang approaching. "What's going on? If someone's following, they must be way the fuck back. Too far back to be useful."

They looked across at Fu happily sipping his tea. "Too easy! It must be a trap?" said Jiang.

Somehow it didn't feel like it to Benny. With the journey on the metro, they would have left any drone surveillance behind. If Fu was being surveilled here then the drones would have to be here ready and waiting for them. The drone operators and the attendant muscle would be hiding away on these damp hillsides. It all sounded too elaborate.

Benny didn't say anything and the silence hung like the mist on the jungle.

Jiang didn't like silences. "So maybe you think he's just being a..."

"Tourist?"

"But he's a whore hound."

"People can be both."

The silence stretched. "It always comes down to this, doesn't it?" said Jiang.

"What?"

"At some point, someone has to reach out, expose themselves, lay their life on the line." Jiang looked around. "This is some place to do it. I mean, if Fu doesn't want to know then he's going to call his minders. Can we get off this godforsaken mountain before the goons get to the station down below and set up a nice little party for us? With balloons, cakes and a knife between the ribs."

"There are roads."

"It looks like there's just the one. If the Chinese were on the ball, they'd be waiting for us further down. At least with your precious whorehouse we could have legged it into the streets if it had all gone pear-shaped. Up here we're hanging out to dry." Jiang looked around again, eyes creased in best Clint Eastwood manner, a hard man weighing up the possibilities. "I think we should just turn round and get the fuck off this pile of rock."

Benny shook his head. "This is our last chance. Six reckons the hotel is only booked until tomorrow. After that they're gone."

"It's just too risky."

Benny turned to look at him. "We don't get paid to fish. We only get paid to catch."

"Oh, very Chinese." But Jiang looked away as he said it. He liked moaning but he liked money better. They went through this every time. Even after all these years Benny still wasn't entirely sure what was going on behind those slithery eyes.

"Okay," Jiang said at last. "How about this? I go in first, try to get the table behind him. A couple of minutes later you come in and make your pitch. If he goes for his phone, you rip it the fuck out of his hand and throw it way out into the tea bushes. If he waits to go for his phone until after you've left then I grab it and chuck it."

"Other people have phones. He could borrow one."

"So, I put the fear of God into him first. That's what these shitty little guns are for, right? I tell him there are others waiting to see what he does. He tries to use someone else's phone he'll be killed. Whatever happens we get off this mountain as fast as we can."

Inelegant and half-arsed, but at least it was something. Benny needed the money too. What he needed even more was one little piece of information Lea had promised him if he brought this off.

"Fine," he said at last. "Get in there!"

As he waited, Benny looked down on the noisy city silenced by distance. Why didn't Fu have a minder? If the Chinese trusted him that much then maybe Jiang and he weren't the fisherman. Maybe they really were the catch.

After a couple more minutes he entered the teahouse. The archway led directly onto the top floor. A waitress in red shirt and black apron was bringing a tray of used cups back inside. He caught her eye and pointed to Fu sitting alone by the railing. "Oolong, please. I'll be with my friend."

She nodded. Fu was still paying rapt attention to the view and started in surprise when Benny cleared his throat.

"May I join you? I hope you don't mind."

Before Fu could gather his wits enough to say no, Benny had sat down on the opposite chair. Fu was no actor and consternation, confusion and suspicion played across his face. His phone was on the table, easy to grab.

There hadn't been that many pictures of the man and, though Benny had followed him for several days, he had never been really close to him before. He saw big lips and big teeth. Not a good-looking man but not remarkably ugly. Even so, unless he was very rich, he would never get the good-looking women. The beautiful little Taiwanese whores would have been a feast after famine.

Fu took a deep draught of his tea like he was about to go.

"Money," Benny said.

Fu hesitated, the cup held up to his mouth. "What?"

"Money, more than you've ever possessed. A stream of it, year after year."

"Do I know you?"

Benny smiled. "I hope not."

The man's eyes narrowed. He blinked once and looked quickly around.

Benny shook his head. "You weren't followed, except by us."

"Us?"

Benny ignored this. "We can speak freely and none of this will ever get back to your bosses. We're just two tea-drinkers admiring the view."

"You haven't even glanced at the view."

"I'm looking at something far more interesting. Profit for you, profit for me."

Fu sat back. "What are you selling?"

"Paying, Mr Fu, paying. A lump sum, five times your annual salary. And that would just be the start."

Fu put down the cup so he could make a chopping motion with his hand. "Please tell the Guoanbu I am loyal, and I resent being put to such a test."

"I don't work for the Chinese Secret Service. I'm not even Chinese."

"You sound Chinese. Shanghai, I'd say."

"My relatives were from Shanghai but I was born in a land far away."

"The States?"

Benny shook his head. "We're both feeling our way here, Mr Fu. This is only our first date. Neither of us is going to give the goods away just yet."

Fu nodded. "And you know something, I believe you about not being Chinese. Even just the way you sit: somehow, it's not quite right. Somehow you're not quite right."

A two-edged sword indeed. Sometimes Benny's life depended on fitting in so this was something he didn't want to hear. On the other hand, in this instance, it might help Fu buy his story.

Benny drummed his fingers on the table. Spies lied all the time. When they did tell the truth, they could sell it with a conviction that was sometimes disarming. "This is crazy even for me. I mean approaching you like this, totally cold, this is exactly what I shouldn't be doing. It's like meeting a woman and the first thing you do is ask her to fuck you. No long talks, no dinner, no drinks, no soft music."

"I was thinking the same."

"The trouble is the Goo... excuse me, the Westerners I work for find the name Guoanbu doesn't slide easily off their tongues so they call them Goo which mean something sticky in English.

That's appropriate as the Goo usually sticks to you and people like you. That leaves little time or opportunity for seduction."

Fu nodded, smiling. "So, I'm not a girlfriend, I'm a whore you just want to come right out and buy."

Benny smiled. "This sexual analogy is getting uncomfortable and I wish I hadn't started with it."

It wasn't going right but the man still wasn't leaving. A first cautious ray of hope penetrated the clouds.

Benny sat forward a little. "One question, though, if I may. Why have the Goo let you out unsupervised every day for a week?"

Fu's eyes narrowed. Now he knew that Benny had followed him on other days and so was aware of the whoring. Benny could almost see the calculations going on behind his eyes, like the revolving drums of a slot machine except instead of fruit there were pictures of his wife and kids.

Benny shook his head. "This isn't blackmail. There are no pictures, no sound recordings. This is all just about money."

Fu turned and looked out across the wide valley that held Taipei in its jungled fingers. Benny followed his gaze. Many miles away, on the top of the opposite mountainside, were the sleek buildings of a modern university that must have commanded similarly breath-taking views. Taipei was a remarkable city in so many ways.

"You're wasting your time. I'm not a tech boy. I'm a manager. I can't read a line of code to save my life. And that's why what you call the Goo doesn't stick to me like shit to a dog's hairy arse. I've got nothing to sell so there's nothing for you to buy."

Perhaps it was his imagination but Benny sensed disappointment and his heart beat just a little faster.

"We don't want code. What we want you do know about. We want the bigger picture."

"What 'bigger picture'?"

Benny sat back and folded his arms. This was going to be painful. Admitting weakness always was.

"Let me get another cup of tea and I'll tell you everything."

Benny waited at a coffee shop in Taipei Central Station until Jiang finally caught up with him.

Jiang got a sandwich and clumped down on the chair opposite. Two pig-tailed schoolgirls sitting at the next table watched him wide-eyed as he entered. They smiled and covered their mouths with their hands as they giggled at each other.

Benny put down his coffee. "What did he do after I left?"

Jiang shrugged. "He did a lot of thinking. So much so that his tea went cold and he had to order another."

"No phone calls?"

"Nope."

There was silence for a few seconds as they watched the workers streaming by. Finally, Jiang lost patience. "Well, do you think he'll go for it?"

"This is a crazy job we're doing."

"What's that got to do with anything?"

Benny shook his head. "We're like ants trying to hold back a landslide. People back home don't realise how far ahead of us the Chinese have become, though it's beginning to dawn on them. The thing is the Chinese sometimes don't even realise this themselves. Even they still have some sneaking regard for the West."

"Again, what the fuck has this got to do with anything?"

"Because when I explained what we wanted, and when he understood how little we knew..." Benny sighed.

"What?"

"I got the impression he felt sorry for us."

Jiang was looking perplexed. "Still not following. Are you saying he'll do it because he feels sorry for us?"

"No. Whether he'll do it for the money, I couldn't say. Wouldn't like to be the first one to check the dead drop."

"Amen!" Fu by then would be deep inside the Great Firewall of China. Every electronic post he made on any device would be

45

monitored by the Goo. The only way to communicate would be by physical dead letter drop. If Fu had been a good boy and had reported Benny's approach then whoever went to the drop would never be seen again.

Jiang had finally become aware of the regard he was getting from the two schoolgirls at the next table. He winked and they almost swooned with embarrassment. He turned back to Benny. "Do you think they'll ask us to do it, to play postmen?"

"I certainly hope not. But they might. Fu's our baby."

"That would have to be one hell of a payday to get me to do that. So, I guess that means we're back to the Smoke. Which flight do you think you'll take?" Basic tradecraft forbade them travelling on the same flight.

"I'm staying for a while on some personal business. So are you. I need a guardian angel."

"Are you expecting trouble?"

"No, just playing it safe."

Jiang was used to being kept in the dark but Benny shouldn't have left this to the last minute. Partly it was because Jiang had the curiosity of cat, one of several qualities that might sooner or later get him killed. Benny didn't need his nagging questions right now.

And he could see that one was already coming. "Personal business in Taiwan? You're a dark horse, Benny. Does Six know about this?"

"Six put me onto it."

"I don't understand."

Benny smiled. "Then all is right with the world."

He didn't need to go to the graveyard but he did anyway. Any link to his family's past, however tenuous, was something he could never resist, though it always brought a sweet sort of sadness.

The place wasn't even well kept. The gravestones, all shapes and sizes, lay higgledy-piggledy across the gently rising hillside. Bushes and long grasses had colonised the cramped spaces between and he was worried what might be hiding amongst them. That he'd come all this way to look at a grave was already a stupid idea. That would rapidly escalate to farce if he was bitten by one of Taiwan's poisonous snakes while doing it.

Some gravestones looked like miniature pagodas. Others were half cylinders of concrete and stone. The most common were little walls, curving in at either side, like the seats on an old Wurlitzer at the fairground. At each centre was a little headstone. Usually, a black-and-white image was engraved into the stone. Generations of unsmiling Han faces looked back out onto a chaotic world they would no longer be able to recognise.

Lea, drip-feeding information in her ever-so-frustrating way, had only given him a name, an occupation and an address. Taichung was a city of light industry a little over a hundred klicks from Taipei, the Birmingham to its London. Brighter, more open than Birmingham and its centre was filled with parks where families came to stroll and meet on Sundays. As Benny had walked through, he had seen impromptu pet shows, families bringing their iguanas and birds to be admired. Some brought cats and dogs dressed as leather-clad bikers with shades, or samurai with coolie hats and swords strapped across their backs. The animals looked bemused but everyone else had found them adorable.

It had all seemed so odd, so difficult to describe. Finally, he realised that the word he had been looking for was wholesome. Not something you often heard associated with Birmingham.

The suburb where Marshall had ended his days was as nondescript as a hundred others spread around the city. Trim apartment blocks overlooked rows of little bungalows all surrounded by six-foot walls. Crime was rare in Taiwan but, as in many countries, the fear of it was entirely out of proportion. He had had to push a button on an intercom.

"Yes?" a man's gruff voice eventually responded.

"Hallo. Sorry to disturb you. I'm looking for a Mr Marshall."

"Mah... what?"

"Marshall."

"Never heard of him."

Six may be tight with its information, but what they did condescend to give him was usually correct. "Perhaps he used to live here."

Whatever Benny had interrupted, it must have been pressing for the man's impatience was trumping the usual Taiwanese politeness. "We've only lived here five years. Try next door. They've been here forever. It's the house with the toon tree."

Benny could make out the beautiful pink leaves of a young toon tree just poking above the wall of the bungalow to the right. This time when he rang the intercom and mentioned the name Marshall, he was surprised to hear the lock buzz. When he got to the little bungalow the door was already open, an older woman waiting. Even before she had sat him down on a comfortable sofa, a younger woman was bringing them tea.

The older woman seemed eager to talk. "Mr Marshall's brother was very generous. He set up an account. Payment every month without fail. It paid for my mother to tend his grave up at the Wuji Cemetery until she died, then I did it. My daughter here..." and she indicated the younger woman, "... would be happy to continue for as long as might be required." Bespectacled Mrs Fang was in her forties and had that earnestness which sometimes verged on the naive and which Benny could not help but love in the Taiwanese.

"So, he died here. When was that?"

Mrs Fang hesitated as she did some mental calculations. "Before I was born because my mother had to get Mrs Chan's daughter to tend the grave when she was heavily pregnant. Mrs Chan died in 1980, the year I was born, so a few years before then."

Benny had no idea who Mrs Chan was. "So, late 1970s?"

"Yes."

"Could you find out when, exactly?"

She shook her head sadly. "My mother died over twenty years ago, soon after my father. Only they would know for sure."

"What about the bank, where the money to tend his grave comes from? They'd know when the account was opened. Could you possibly find out and email me the date?" He produced a card, printed for the occasion back in Taipei, giving his name as Tony Deming, senior lecturer in history at King's College in London.

She looked up at him, a hint of suspicion tainting her earnestness. "You are not related to Mr Marshall, I had assumed you were?" To which Benny mentally appended *and so that means you don't send us the money.*

"I'm writing a history of the Royal Hong Kong Police. Did you know Mr Marshall used to work for them?"

"No."

No wonder, thought Benny. "Could you find out the date of his death for me?"

Mrs Fang's natural Taiwanese desire to help came through. "Of course."

"And do you know how he died?"

She sat up straight. "I show you!"

Benny followed her out of the front door and around to the side of the house. She pointed at several large but immaculately clean rubbish bins.

"He died here? Was he in the bin?" he asked in surprise. Bin lorries in Taiwan, for reasons unknown, played the same moronic children's tune at full volume at all times of the day and night. The idea of the dead Marshall being loaded into one was bizarre.

"Not in the bin, by them. And next door on the other side of this wall, but in the same place. Someone had been waiting for him and..." She made a chopping motion.

"He was knifed?"

"No, he was hit with a hammer. Again and again."

"Did the police ever find out who killed him?"

She shook her head.

"What was he like as a neighbour?"

She shrugged. "Quiet, my mother said. Foreigners don't usually live around here. My mother said he did not seem to want to make a fuss."

"Like he did not want to be found?"

She shrugged.

"Did anyone visit him?"

Mrs Fang looked away. "He's long dead," Benny said. "No harm can come to him now."

"My mother said that women came sometimes. Bad women, late at night. They never stayed long."

"Any woman in particular?"

"The last one my mother saw had come to our door to ask about Mr Marshall. A week before he died."

"What did she look like?"

"Well-dressed, in her thirties. Would have been pretty but there was something wrong with her nose."

Foolishly, stupidly, he felt a gushing of competing emotions. Relief that Mary, his mother, had indeed been here but revulsion at what she might have done. Could she really have grasped a hammer and brought it down on a man's skull? And what could he have done to her that had been so terrible?

Now, at the cemetery whose address Mrs Fang had given him, Benny stood looking down at the grave. Some graves had a little red brick house with a shingled roof that was not much larger than a loaf of bread. Benny had no idea what these were for, or the meaning of the Wurlitzer-shaped back walls. However you looked at it, this was an alien place for an Englishman like Marshall to be buried.

He heard someone picking their way through the jumbled graves. He'd only spotted Jiang three times on the journey from Taipei and Benny couldn't help feeling just a little proud. Even so, as Jiang came to stand by him, Benny muttered: "Which bit about guardian angel didn't you understand."

"Trust me, nobody followed you. Anyway, you're a tricky customer. If you hadn't told me exactly where you were going, I'd have lost you myself at least twenty times. The only people who know you're right here right now are you, me and whoever this is." He pointed a finger at the grave. "Speaking of which, who is this?"

Benny kept silent, forcing Jiang to bend down and read the inscription and look at the photograph.

"Your dad?"

"Do I look like I have a white man for a father?"

Jiang held up his hand and waggled it. "You can never be sure. Back home you certainly act like you were English born and bred."

"All I know about this guy is that he was a bent copper in Hong Kong back in the sixties and seventies. Was working for the Gonganbu... you know what that was?"

Jiang rolled his eyes. "The predecessors of our much-loved Guoanbu."

"Right, the Goo's dad. The internet reckons they stuffed Marshall's mouth with gold. High level dissidents fleeing the Great Leap Forward and the Cultural Revolution tried to make it to Hong Kong. Marshall was there to hoover up the ones who thought they'd made it. He'd pass their new identities over to the sleeper agents, deep water fish the Chinese called them, for termination."

"Nasty! And thanks for the history lesson, but what has any of this got to do with you? You're fourth generation British. Did he rat out some distant relative or something?"

Benny didn't answer that but he found he was enjoying the opportunity to talk. He'd only ever discussed this with Lea. "When Marshall was found out, he fled the colony and wound up here where there was no extradition treaty. Still isn't."

"What happened to him?"

"It sounds like his past caught up with him. Someone took a hammer to his head."

"Whoa!" Jiang's eyes were suddenly wide. " Is this the work of Mommie Dearest?"

"Don't call her that! Anyway, I haven't a clue."

"Then why did Six tell you about this guy?"

"Don't know."

Jiang chuckled. "You have a tell, when you lie."

"Do I fuck?"

"Seriously! And I'm never going to let you know what it is."

Benny looked down at the gravestone. "There's one thing I do know: this bastard must have deserved it."

He spat copiously on the headstone and watched the phlegm dribble down the black marble.

4. The High Seas 1895

The Great-Grandfather, Hu Jun, and the Eloquent Shrug

Jun dreamed he was tumbling in the cold waters of the Huangpu. When he tried to strike out for air, he found his arms pinned to his sides. Something coarse scraped the side of his face, taking skin with it.

Light flared and he was rolling across a hard surface, then something caught him a blow on the back of his skull.

Nearby someone roared in alarm. "Jesus, it's a fakkin' Chinky!" More angry shouts from many throats. Jun tried to blink away the stars bursting in his eyes as heavy boots stamped towards him. His arms and legs suddenly freed, he brought them up to ward off their kicks.

Nothing happened.

He slowly lowered his arms and found himself inside a circle of white men standing with their hands on their hips. They were looking down at him with puzzlement, anger and contempt.

Two of the men were shouldered aside as a thickly bearded man in a peaked cap thrust his way through. "Where did 'e come from?"

A red-haired man pointed. "Wrapped himself up in that torn bit of sailcloth, Cap'n. Mr Thompson told me to sew it back up. I just pulled at one end and out rolled matey here, like Cleopatra out of a carpet."

The men leered while the man in the peaked cap raked at his beard. "Not so easy on the eye as that lady, I dare say. I shall have a talk with Mr Thompson about the adequacy of his stowaway search."

"Cap'n, do we..." The red-haired man flicked a thumb at the ocean.

Jun had only a smattering of English but he understood that gesture clear enough. He held his breath as the bearded man considered his fate.

"Get the cook!" he said at last. "And get this man to his feet!"

Jun was hauled upright and coarse hands patted at his clothes. Luckily, he had lost his knife in his struggles with the river. Looking around he found the ship surrounded by water. For the first time in his life, land was nowhere to be seen.

The sun was high and he realised he must have slept for well over half a day. He could just remember crawling into the roll of sailcloth, dumped like so much other detritus all over the crowded deck. He had had just enough time to register the hardness and oiliness of the flax sailcloth before falling fast asleep.

As they waited, Jun took in the ship more carefully. The deck was covered in barrels and coils of rope. Over towards the bow, a pig and a goat stood tethered and dumbfounded as the ground rolled beneath them. Above all this he heard sailcloth crack with each gust of wind. Hot air like a horse's breath blew over him from the stern.

Wooden ships were being replaced by iron-hulled traders. Some said that one day steam ships, no longer constrained to rivers and coastal runs, might replace even the iron-hulled sailing ships. Either way, this wooden ship was nearing the end of the line.

He looked around, considering the examples of British manhood surrounding him and was not impressed. As in China, men were either servants or masters. It was the British masters who had frequented the brothel next door, or who rode by on beautiful horses or in elegant carriages. They were often tall, upright, well-fed, well-dressed and showed some civility to each other, if not to the Chinese.

The men surrounding him now were clearly servants, the runts of the national litter. Stooped, thin, a couple were cross-eyed. They were all grinning at him in an evil way and their teeth, what there were of them, were black. Their rank, unwashed smell was offensive. Chinese peasants might bathe once a month at best, but at least they washed their clothes. As well as their frank human odours, these men smelled of rancid fish oil.

More commotion, more shouldering aside and Jun found himself looking into the eyes of another Han Chinese. Like all the sailors he was shorter than Jun, but with a long, braided pigtail. Across his black jacket and tunic was tied a grimy white apron.

"Ask him how he got here," said the bearded man.

The Han kowtowed. "What is your name and what are you doing here, brother?" he asked in Mandarin. "These men are not kind to those from the Middle Kingdom. They will toss you to the sharks without a moment's thought."

Jun bowed the most docile bow of his life. "I am Hu Jun, a humble docker. I was tired, the day was hot and long and I crawled into the sail for a moment's rest. When I awoke..." He shrugged and pointed at the sea.

The man smiled grimly, his eyes shrewd. Jun noticed that his nose had once been broken and poorly reset. The thin white remnant of a knife slash led through an eyebrow and across a temple. "You are no docker. The knuckles of your hands are calloused, not your palms. But you are big and strong and they need men. Fortune may be yours. This is a bad ship, ill-run by drunkards and fools. Many of the crew fled like rats as soon as we docked. If you do not drown now, you will later. The first storm to strike this ship may be as fatal as a blow to a fragile old widow."

"Then why are you here, illustrious brother?"

"Perhaps for the same reason as you. When..."

"Hey! Enough!" interrupted the bearded man. "What did he say?"

Jun could not follow what was said next. The cook seemed to be arguing on his behalf, though not with great effort. The

54

bearded man nodded a few times, with an equal lack enthusiasm. Jun noticed that some of the other men began to drift away and his spirits rose.

Eventually the Han turned back to Jun. "You live to drown another day."

⊕

Live, it turned out, was an extravagance of speech. Jun was given the most back-breaking job on the ship, labouring on the bilge pump. The barnacle-covered hull had saved his life, but its myriad leaks now made it a misery.

Even the best of timber hulls let in water and it all got worse with age. The Fitzgerald, as this old scow was called, let in a deluge. All this trickled its way down into the bilges deep in the bowels of the ship.

The water had to be got rid of and not just because it would ultimately sink the ship. First it would rise to submerge the water barrels, then the crew's provisions on the first deck, then the precious cargo of porcelain and tea on the next.

Though the captain was most concerned about the cargo, their provisions meant the world to the crew. After a dreadful storm in the South China Sea, the water rose despite Jun's best efforts and destroyed half the flour for bread.

The crew had beaten him soundly.

The bilge pump was made of two hollowed out tree trunks penetrating through all the decks from bilge to main deck. A circular pulley system circulated little buckets. At their lowest point they dipped into the bilges and at the upper point they tipped over to spill their contents onto the deck and hence into the sea. Someone had to turn the crank that worked the system and that person was Jun. Heavy work, four hours on and four hours off, night and day without respite.

With his muscles busy but mind unoccupied, all he could think of was Liu. Though anger and dread ate away at him, he had to admit that Dong had been right. By the time he would have got back to her they would have been waiting.

But what had they done to her when he didn't arrive? Someone had to pay for the dead Frenchman. Slavery, whoredom or even death was all the legacy Jun had bequeathed to her. Even if she survived, she would never want him back. He had brought disgrace to both their families.

Many times, the misery and constant sea sickness had him looking longingly at the grey seas and the oblivion they promised. Why he never jumped, like why he had killed the Frenchman, would remain a mystery for the rest of his days.

Jun had always been big but the hours of labour on the bilge pump only added to his muscles. So much so that his old clothes soon no longer fitted. His tunic split and the sight of his torso, hairless like a woman's, led the Captain to fear for disorder amongst the rest of the crew. He reluctantly ordered the purser to supply a sailor's pea coat, a heavy wool affair, double breasted with broad lapels.

The cook's name was Ping Gen and he took pity on Jun. He would slip him extra rations when the white crew weren't watching. In the second of the dog watches, after the evening meal had been served and darkness was falling, the two would smoke a companionable pipe on the forecastle and talk. Ping took the trouble to help him improve his English.

Jun seized every opportunity he could to learn more of this strange new language but found himself overwhelmed by its complexity. They were half way across the Bay of Bengal before the revelation hit him. It wasn't that English was complex, it was actually stupidly simple.

It wasn't that the tones of the language were so exquisitely modulated he couldn't understand them, it was that these ignorant fools had hardly any tonal control at all. Rather than a symphony revealing fine shades of meaning, Hu realised their language barely rose above the grunting of pigs in a barnyard.

In Mandarin the five tones and their change over each syllable altered the meaning entirely. Tones could rise, or they could fall, or they could fall then rise. They could be constantly neutral or they could be constantly high. Mandarin was like music and so was English but only if the musician had had his ear drums poked out with a long piece of bamboo.

The different and uncertain tones of the crew had little to do with the meaning of what they said. Instead, it depended on where they came from, whether they were drunk or sober, tired or ill, angry or sad.

This restored Jun's faith in Chinese culture which was, after all, supremely ancient and sophisticated and therefore superior.

In the dog watches Ping told his own story which Jun soon realised was as fabricated as his own. It was obvious both were fugitives, though Ping's accent betrayed a more northerly origin.

Months passed and the air grew hotter and heavier. High, frowning white clouds seemed to grow from the sea like mushrooms but the rain when it came was warm. To Jun the Middle Kingdom had been the world, the white people insect-like distractions crawling in from its outer reaches. Now he came to understand that the world was far bigger than he had ever imagined.

The Fitzgerald began sailing up a never-ending coast fringed by dense jungle and sandy beaches. Sometimes the wind from the land brought smells the like of which Jun had never experienced. Sometimes entrancing, sometimes too alien for comfort.

"Why does the land smell?" he asked Ping one day as they stood by the rail, breaking the ships biscuit, displacing the weevils and flicking them to the waiting sea.

Ping smiled. "Spice," he said. "This whole land produces it. Peppercorns and chillies, just as we do in Chung Kuo, but much else besides. The British revere them, especially the pepper and cinnamon. Their food is tasteless without it."

Jun's smile must have betrayed his thoughts for Ping suddenly looked stern. "You thought it was my fault the food was so bad. No, these mongrels would accept nothing else. Once I used Szechuan peppercorns, from my own personal stock. They beat me. Pepper must be black not red, they shouted. Fools! As for chillies—they say only savages eat them."

Finally, they pulled into a port called Vasco de Gama in a land named Goa. Huge warehouses that crowded the docks were filled with pungent sacks of seeds and leaves Jun had never seen before. The docks heaved with half-naked men with brown skins who reeked like the spices. The white men here spoke a tongue twisting, ugly language new to his ears.

"Portuguese," said Ping. "They own this land."

Jun had planned to jump ship at the first port but was too taken aback by the sheer foreignness. He could never survive here.

There was one more brief stop to purchase fruit and water off the coast of Africa, before they rounded the Cape of Good Hope. These were supplied by bumboats, so Jun could not abscond. In any case, the next port would be London, the Fitzgerald bringing porcelain, tea, silks and spices. Jun was still a young man and had a notion of seeing what sort of place spawned these white devils.

Once the Fitzgerald had unloaded its cargo, it would return to India and fill the holds with opium and take it all the way back to Shanghai.

Indian opium, brought by British bandits to enslave Chinese people. This was a strange world that worked in evil ways.

Ping had warned him about the Roaring Forties but it had been of little help. Jun hadn't really believed him when he had described the devil-driven winds and rain blowing eternally eastwards all around the globe. When they came around the Cape of Good Hope, they would supposedly meet these horrors head-on.

The change, when it came, was sudden and shocking, like opening a door to a child's bedroom and finding instead a charnel house. Waves that had been barely more than choppy suddenly rose like cliffs. Unprepared, his hand loose on the pump crank as he stole a moment's rest, Jun found himself upended and rolling bruisingly down the deck. Brought hard up against some barrels, he screamed in disbelief as a wall of water, grey like a corpse, loomed high over the masts.

The bow rose to meet this but seemed doomed to cartwheel back over the stern. He imagined the ship turning turtle, the wave smashing down on its vulnerable exposed belly, driving them deep and drowning them all.

For an eternity the bow struggled up the wave front, the crew hanging like curtains from quickly snatched handholds. At the very last instant the bow punched up into clear air. For a breath-taking moment, the ship perched precariously atop the crest. The timbers of the bow and stern, now unsupported, groaned like an ill-used whore and planks cracked like gunshots.

The Fitzgerald hung, all lives on board in the finest of balances.

Then she fell forwards, plummeting down the wave. Jun lost his grip and fell. The bow crashed into the trough and tons of water pulverised to vapour blasted back over the deck. Suddenly he was the one moving but the ship had stopped dead. He crashed into the forecastle feet first, his legs buckling and forcing his knees up into his face.

Everything went dark. He felt his body rolling again. His sight only returned as the ship was half way up the next monster.

"The sails! The sails!" he heard the captain roaring. Each mast had four sails and all were billowing backwards in the face of the wind. A terrible drag on the ship, only adding to its chances of turning onto its back.

Men weaved like drunkards over the uncertain deck, making for the halyards to lift the lower booms and collapse the sails.

"All hands!" the Mate was yelling. Jun staggered to his feet, launching himself to port to get a grasp on a rail beside the captain. He was aware of Ping emerging from his galley and then weaving over towards them.

The captain was struggling to untie a halyard. Hauling on it would be a three-man job. Jun and Ping waited until they reached the moment of balance on the next crest, then they grabbed it just as the halyard came free.

They all heaved back on the line as the ship crashed down into the next trough. The overshadowing waves took the wind out of the sail and the three men hauled to lift the boom while they could.

Just for a second Jun felt a glimmer of hope but then the ship rose to the next crest. The devils in the wind blew another mighty breath, filling the sail instantly. The halyard was wrenched up, tugging Jun's arms almost out their sockets, tearing the rope from his grasp.

The Captain and Ping lost their grips too, falling to their knees, their hands flattening on the deck to steady themselves. On the other side of the ship, he saw men who had kept hold on their lines being jerked high into the air before pitching over the rail and into the boiling sea.

In the twinkling of an eye an invisible knife slashed right across the sail above them with a terrible ripping sound. Jun saw instantly what would happen next. He thrust forward but found himself moving through air that had become thicker than the waters of the Huangpu. As the suddenly unsupported boom fell, he saw Ping and the captain, getting to their feet, their heads only now starting to look up.

Jun had choice but no time for calculation. He charged, shoulder first, driving into Ping's midriff, impelling him backwards. They both rolled clear as the boom crashed down. The captain had straightened just as the edge of the boom came down on him, smashing his skull, driving his head far down beneath his shoulders.

Those shoulders, now unattached, gave one last eloquent shrug as the rest of the body was pounded to the deck, compressed to an unholy mass of blood and bone and yellow fat.

The other sailors on the deck had turned their heads at the ripping sound and had seen it all.

Now, wonderingly, their eyes bored into Jun.

✦

He was choking on a miasma of evil. The grey waters of the southern Atlantic, now calm after the storm, seemed mixed with Jun's tears as the lash tore the skin from his back. He was naked and could feel the blood crawling down the backs of his legs, just as his wife had idly trailed her fingernails after lovemaking.

Every time the whip landed, he heard blood and ripped flesh spattering to the deck. His teeth were clenched so tightly he was sure they would shatter.

After each burning impact the sailors jeered.

"You're a lefty, aren't you, Jonno?" he heard the Mate call. "Take your turn now and give him a nice criss-cross."

"Bastard rated a Chinee higher than a cap'n. My pleasure!"

Jun's face was against the mast but he knew Jonno to be a burly man, far thicker set than Timmons, the right-handed third mate who'd been laying into him.

Jun would die here, strapped to the mast, as men who had never liked the captain let loose spite they'd accumulated over miserable lifetimes.

The next stroke, coming from the other side, was even more excruciating. He imagined his skin, now cut into diamond shapes, coming away and slopping down bloodily onto the deck.

"Ow!" Jun looked back in surprise. Jonno was rubbing his left shoulder with his right hand. "Took such a swing I fucked me own sho'der," he said in wonder.

That seemed to break the evil spell. "Enough!" said the mate, a small man with much to prove now he was the captain. "Fetch the salt!"

Jun had kept silent throughout, his clenched jaws entombing the roar boiling up from his guts. But now, as the salt, hardly diluted by water, was wiped over his torn flesh and it felt like it had been dowsed in red-hot metal, he could hold it back no longer. His voice was deep for one of his race but as his roar rose from his lungs he heard it break shamefully, like a boy whose balls had just descended.

The sailors jeered with disdain. The leather strap binding his arms was untied and he fell to the deck. He heard the men walking away, leaving him behind, an unworthy creature wallowing in a pool of its own blood.

He felt hands carefully grasping his upper arms, avoiding where the lash had caught them. "The bastards!" Ping whispered. "They're not even allowed to do that to themselves nowadays. But you're from the Middle Kingdom and a stowaway. To you the rules don't apply. But never mind, brother. I have opium." Ping helped him to his feet. "And vinegar for your back to kill infection, then goose grease to soothe. I will care for you and you will recover. I am in your debt forever."

5. London, England

The Son, Benny Hu, and the Pale Shadow of a Ring

Lea was always business first.

The passionate kiss on the doorstep was for the benefit of the neighbours or any other watchers, then she pushed him back into the hallway, kicking the door closed behind her.

As soon as it clicked shut, she shoved him away and strode through the flat. With just the two bedrooms and a lounge it didn't take her long to make sure they were alone. Finishing up in the lounge, she pulled the curtains closed.

And he watched every fluid move of her tall, slender frame and admired the torrent of hair even blacker than her business suit coming almost down to her waist. Once they'd gone running together, her hair in a pigtail that swayed back and forth with every stride.

He'd never seen anything sexier.

"Our Chinese friend has taken the bait," she said, without preamble.

Benny hadn't had much hope for the Taiwan job so this came as a surprise.

Fu Chonglin was now behind the Great Firewall of China and his web usage would be monitored to buggery. Every phone call he made would be listened to; maybe even by humans and not just by AIs searching for keywords. To get around all this, Six had hacked the website of a firm selling obscure gourmet foods. Fu must have signified his acceptance of Six's proposals by placing an order for a rare and expensive chilli bean sauce from a monastery deep in Szechuan province, the monks votively stirring the vats of fermenting beans over the many maturing years. The taste was apparently sublime and just the sort of thing a sensualist like Fu would go for.

Fu must have made his mind up quickly. Suspiciously quickly in fact.

"So why are you telling me this?" Benny asked, though he could guess well enough.

"We need someone in-country. You're the only one he knows. Anyone else rocking up might scare him off."

Benny had worked in China before, just simple pickups from established agents plus the occasional in-country debrief. With Fu they were on untested ground. There was a good chance this was a trap, so anyone Six sent had to be a Deniable with no formal links to the security services.

"Is he really worth it?"

Lea grimaced, the only time her fine oriental features looked anything other than attractive. "He's an assistant to a man who implements strategic decisions. That man steers whole industries into making their security products. Products they use to monitor and suppress a billion plus people. What's more, the bastards are exporting their stuff to every repressive regime in the world, freebies that come with their cancerous Belt and Road Initiative. East African dictators are lapping it all up. We need to know what's coming down the pipe and how far advanced it is."

"And you reckon Fu knows enough about this?"

"He scored top marks in a metric some smart-arsed analyst came up with. Ratio of potential knowledge to personal salary, that sort of thing. The higher this metric, the greater the potential. That's why we started looking at him in the first place."

Benny nodded. "Computer says yes. Not so sure I want to risk my life on that. Especially for the same money you promised me for the Taiwan job."

She gave a bleak little smile. "Check your account; it's there. Be sure you give your little chum his cut. By the way, how much will you pay him?"

Now it was Benny's turn for the grim little smile. "That's between me and Jiang."

She held up her hands in surrender, sharp pointy nails gleaming on long slim fingers.

It was only now that Benny realised they were still standing and he thought he caught a hint of embarrassment flit across her face. Both too focused and intense for their own good, they'd dived straight into business; he'd forgotten the niceties and she hadn't missed them.

"Drink?" he asked belatedly.

"The usual." And she took a seat on a long leather divan. He poured them both glasses of Dalmore eighteen-year-old single malt and sat down beside her.

"Tell me, Benny," she said after taking a sip and casting an unimpressed glance around his spartanly furnished apartment, "what do you spend your money on?"

She was just winding him up. It was a stone-cold fact that Six already had a pretty clear idea.

This shading into the personal indicated that the full debrief could come later. Normally he'd be all for the delights such a change promised but the other matter was bothering him.

"So, what has all this bullshit about Marshall to do with anything? What has a bent Hong Kong copper got to do with my family?"

"It's one piece of the puzzle."

"Oh, come on! Just tell me, for God's sake!"

Benny had hazy memories of his mother and grandmother. Both were grieving women. First one then the other had disappeared from his life and the next thing he knew he was in an orphanage. It was perfectly natural to want to find out more about them and about the men in his family he had never known at all.

Six knew something. It hadn't seemed so at first. He'd been recruited many years before by a nameless man who gave him only tasks and money. Old, crippled by some sort of arthritic condition (he'd maintained it too well over the years to be just good acting,) the man had suddenly disappeared when the simple burglaries Benny had been set broadened out into more significant missions. Lea had stepped into the breach as his handler; her cover was that she was his girlfriend. And, after all the time they spent together, and despite all sorts of strictures against it, the cover had become reality.

Perhaps for both of them the strictures had made the prospect even more attractive.

In those intimate moments, and despite himself, he'd opened up to her, about his life, about his mother.

Inevitably, she'd used this.

When he baulked at some jobs, she'd started dropping dark hints about the knowledge that Six possessed about Mary Hu.

But what information she gave him was in her own good time and that she wasn't replying now to his question meant this was not one of those times.

But he couldn't let it go. "Surely you're not suggesting Marshall was my father?"

"I'm not. And if you haven't worked out what Marshall had to do with your family then I'm disappointed in you, Benny."

Benny tapped his fingers irritably on the table. "My mother was there, just before Marshall died."

Lea's eyes found his and held his gaze. "Your mother hammered his head to a pulp."

Benny found himself swallowing hard. "Are you sure?"

She shrugged. "Probably. She'd long since gone rogue so we can't be sure. She certainly had motive and opportunity. She had the means as well... anyone can buy a hammer."

"But what was the motive?"

She waggled her finger at Benny. "That's enough for today."

"Not if you want me to put my neck on the line in China. Is my mother still alive?"

"As I've said before, we really don't know. Almost certainly not, to be truthful. As well as filling graves, she was hell bent on digging others up. Things that are buried should remain that way."

"Then what information do you have?"

She wasn't pleased but knew him well enough to gauge his mood. "Limehouse," she said.

"Christ, these stupid games. Fine: Limehouse, East London. What about it?"

"It's where your great-grandfather arrived in Britain and where he got up to no good."

"My great-grandfather. Who gives a shit about him? Do you give a shit about your great-grandfather?"

She seemed genuinely taken aback. "Well I..."

"If you don't know what happened to my mother, then what about my father? Do you know who he was?"

She gnawed at her lower lip. "Yes, probably."

"And do you know what happened to him?"

"After you get back from China."

"No! Now or you can get Jiang to do the job."

Benny knew Lea shared the same reservations about Jiang. With that man, parental supervision was always advised. Even so, Lea said nothing and the silence stretched.

Benny banged the table in frustration.

"Calm down, for Christ's sake!" she said but then the look in Benny's eyes seemed to alarm her even more. "He's still alive. Your father is still alive."

Benny blinked. "I've done your dirty work for all these years and you're only just telling me this now."

"Some people wished they didn't have a father," said Lea weakly. "Who is he? Where is he?"

"After the job," she said and this time Benny sensed she meant it.

And suddenly there was a gap, a chasm separating the business and personal. Usually when he came back from a trip, and they hadn't seen each other for weeks or months, they manufactured a way to slip from one to the other.

But now there was no rackety old wooden footbridge handy enough to span this chasm.

The silence stretched. Benny felt anger and desire warring within him.

A whole minute must have passed before she sat upright, said "Fuck it!" and covered his lips with hers.

"It's been too long, Benny Boy." Her fingers slipped inside his briefs. It was a hot day in London and he could smell her sweat under the sweet fragrance dabbed across her neck. He felt her breasts pushing into his own chest and below that the hardness of her athlete's body

"I think you missed me," she whispered, stroking him. Fine Han features over thick sensuous lips, eyebrows arched in challenge.

Hands probing, grasping, fondling, they wrestled each other into the bedroom. He was used to taking the lead but that wasn't an option with Lea. Even when underneath she called the shots, her strong thighs thrusting him up, only for her encircling arms to pull him down. Without such tethering he would have been thrown like a luckless rider from a bucking horse.

When the storm passed and they lay together still partly clothed, the obsessive, unwelcome thoughts eased their way back into his mind. She liked the sun and it showed, the milky coffee colour of her skin turning darker with each holiday. What a Chinese woman on the mainland would avoid at all costs, spending her life under a parasol to keep her skin as white as possible, Lea relished.

It was that love of the sun that had betrayed her. It had left its mark after what she said had been a trip to the West Indies. One day in the blazing Caribbean heat she must have forgotten to take the ring off. He had spotted its faint, ghostly memory when she had returned.

So faint, it would have been unnoticeable had he not been looking for it so carefully.

She was pretending to be asleep. He leaned in and playfully bit her fragrant ear. She slapped him. This time when he leaned in, he licked a chocolate brown nipple.

She pushed him away. "You're not ready yet. Don't promise what you can't deliver."

He put his hands behind his head and lay back on the pillow. She was right, of course. Lovemaking with Lea was full blooded; half measures were not acceptable. Give it another twenty minutes.

She ran a carmine fingernail over his chest. Like so many Chinese his chest was bare. It seemed to fascinate her, almost as much as he was fascinated by her thick black pubic hair. The feel of it against the soft skin of his groin as he moved within her felt like he was being caressed by a thousand tiny fingers.

"Were you a bad boy on this trip?" she asked softly.

He shook his head.

"I don't mind, you know."

He turned to look at her. "Perhaps you should."

She kissed his forehead. "Don't spoil it, Benny Boy."

There was a moment of uncomfortable silence and neither liked those. "So, it seems Mummy might not have been a lady," he said.

She snorted. Lea's laughter, like her lovemaking, was fruity and vulgar. "Newsflash! What were you expecting?"

"I'm not saying she was prostitute or anything, or at least as far as you've told me. What I mean is she was capable of... well, awful things."

"She abandoned you, so what exactly were you expecting? Why do you keep doing this to yourself?"

He sighed. She actually poked him hard in the chest. "Out with it, you laconic asshole!"

He tried to keep his voice even, tried to make it sound as far removed from whining as possible. "You had a family, you don't know what it was like for me."

"Seriously? Father abandons his wife and four-year-old daughter. Some family!" Her story at least was consistent, but he wouldn't have put money on it being true.

"Better than an orphanage," he said.

"Come on! Orphanages aren't straight out of Dickens any more. It can't have been all bad. Was there any kiddy fiddling you haven't told me about?"

He shook his head. "No. The violence was physical not sexual. Anyway, I was abandoned at an East London orphanage so of course it was straight out of Dickens. Except it was an orphanage half full of blacks and half full of whites and one single solitary Chinese. Roses all the way!" He'd learned to fight, even though there were usually too many of them.

She put her hand on his chest, perhaps checking his heartbeat. A player herself, she'd be paranoid about being played.

"Okay, so you had it tough," she said slowly. "It is what it is, but finding out about your family can only bring heartbreak. Parents don't give up their kids for no reason. I wouldn't go looking for my father even if he'd struck gold. I wouldn't want a penny from that piece of crap."

What could he say that didn't sound weak? He had nobody, not even her. Especially not her. Tumbleweed, rootless, there was nothing to stop him blowing away.

He saw what looked like real pity in her eyes and found himself struggling to contain a welter of emotions. Sometimes, for the way she played him, he wanted to hit her. Sometimes he wanted to just sink into her arms, into her spider's embrace.

Later, after they'd made love again, her passion blunted enough for a hint of tenderness to creep in, she had to leave. She always did

He didn't bother walking her to the street where her ride would be waiting. Sometimes an Uber, sometimes a black cab but never the same service twice in a row.

In the early days, he'd accompanied her down a few times and, as he'd leaned in for a final kiss, he'd eased a tracker down into the join between the rear seat and the backrest. Small GPS animal collars, just £50 a pop.

Back upstairs in his apartment, he'd watched her progress on his phone. With all the stopping and starting of London traffic it was difficult to identify when she got out. He'd had to assume it was the point where the taxi veered away from its previous course.

Each time the cabs had headed off in different directions from his flat, each time they'd deposited her at a different underground station, always a big one with several lines and five or more exits and entrances. Even if she were only a few seconds ahead of any follower, she could lose them easily.

He'd toyed with getting Jiang to help him, ready with a taxi to follow her really closely, with Benny catching up so they could follow her as a team.

Involving Jiang was too risky, too revealing and completely against the ethos of deniability. Lea could know all about Jiang but it definitely didn't work the other way. Whatever Jiang found out he might use later, if only to save his own skin.

Not that even a team of two was enough to follow someone who really knew what she was doing.

He should have stopped this affair years ago. With so little affection in his life, he had held onto her like a fool, revealing all too freely his deepest, most exploitable yearnings.

Behind him lay a string of broken relationships. So many, even he eventually saw the pattern. Women got close and then he pushed them away. He'd thought up all sorts of excuses; one poor girl he ditched because of the sound she made eating cornflakes. Looking back, they were all decent women and he had to admit that there was single common denominator behind these failures.

Him.

It didn't take a £200-an-hour psychologist to figure out he had abandonment issues. It might have been worth paying one, though, to bring him out of his self-denial earlier. It had taken him until he was nearly forty before working out that he wasn't just unlucky in love.

And then what happened when he reached this exalted state of self-awareness? He fell for a married woman who was also his covert MI6 minder.

It was all so wrong. He was adrift in a world too fluid to grasp.

With a sigh he went back to his rumpled bed, the smell of her haunting him for the rest of the night.

6. Limehouse, London 1896

The Great-Grandfather, Hu Jun, and the Madness of Sins that Were New

It wasn't until weeks later, after they had passed the Canaries, that Jun had slowly emerged from his delirium. A few more weeks and the bright yellow suppurating pus oozing from his wounds gave way to lighter shades of liquor, and the skin began to visibly reform. Even so, it wasn't until the British coast was sighted that he could bear for any clothing to touch his back. It would be many years before he could afford the smoothest of silks but until then he could never don a shirt or tunic without wincing, if only from the memory.

When the land, at first far to both sides, kept closing in, Jun realised they were sailing up an estuary. Ping told him that this river was the mighty Thames, from which all the British came and which led to the very heart of their country and their empire.

It didn't look so mighty to Jun, not compared to the Yangtze. At one point, after a lazy meander where the river was narrow enough for a man to walk the distance in a few minutes, the ship sailed through a veritable sea of shit. The stench brought tears to Jun's eyes and the sailors quickly placed wet rags over their mouths and noses.

"High tide," said Ping. "The British collect all their shit in two big tanks, in places where only the very poorest live. Then, when high water arrives, they release them. As the tide falls, it carries the ordure out to sea."

Already full of trepidation, Jun began to wonder what other horrors England might furnish. Why would anyone collect their shit in the first place and then just throw it away instead of putting it on the fields? Such perversity!

The river continued to narrow, the docks becoming crowded with ships. Above them all loomed soot-blackened warehouses.

The Fitzgerald finally arrived at Limehouse which had all the filth and squalor of Shanghai but without its colour and hot, dry weather. The pollution from this city of burning coal deprived everyone of a blue sky. The blacks and greys of the Thames blended in with the grimy soot-smeared buildings.

Though not a religious man, Jun decided he had been sent straight to a colourless version of hell.

Within his sight, a hundred ships lined the docks, their masts like a forest of bare trees. Hunched, dark-clad shapes swarmed over them, loading and unloading heavy sacks and chests. They shouted, argued and jostled as they wove around mounds of cargo spread haphazardly over the docks. Burly men with heavy staves stood guard, eyeing every man with frank suspicion. Rats ran hither and thither, easily outnumbering the heavy boots of the men.

"We leave now!" Ping had come up behind him while Jun had been standing at the railing watching this pandemonium. "The Mate says they will not pay you. The money will be sent to the captain's widow."

Jun had expected nothing less. The ship had saved him from the death of a thousand cuts at the hands of a mob back in Shanghai. He was pleased enough.

"We leave now." Ping pulled at the sleeve of his coat. "Quickly!"

Jun had no idea where they would go. Suddenly the Fitzgerald that he had spent months praying to never see again, now seemed like a loving mother whose embrace he dreaded leaving.

"Why must we be quick?" he asked uncertainly.

"I shat in their rum barrel. Maybe they all grow sick and die."

Jun had only the clothes on his back and Ping had already packed his own few possessions in a little canvas bag. They clattered down the gangway and Jun felt solid ground under his feet for the first time in months. To his surprise he felt giddy, a feeling that would not pass for days.

Ping led him out of the docks and into a warren of streets full of men and women who jostled the Chinese aside. They were all dressed in browns and blacks, matching the buildings and the streets and the grey of a sky crossed by streamers of black smoke. The absence of colour was like a hand squeezing Jun's heart.

"What are we to do, Ping?" he asked miserably.

"There is somewhere I know we can stay, cheaply. Do not worry, my friend."

"I have no money."

Ping shook his head and a smile twisted up one corner of his mouth. "I have plenty. I steal. I shit in their rum and I steal." He laughed so hard the miserable faces passing by stopped to stare.

Jun glanced back over his shoulder, afraid enraged sailors might even now be bearing down on them. However, there had been so many twists and turns in the warren since they had left the docks that pursuit would be almost impossible.

Ping led on, passing stalls piled high with vegetables Jun did not recognise. Others held platters of fly-blown meat. They passed taverns where cloth-capped men lolled outside against the grimy brick with glasses of beer held carelessly in their hands, casting looks of frank hostility at passers-by.

"Here we are," said Ping finally, knocking at a plain wooden door in a long terrace of brick houses.

The door was quickly opened but only enough for an eye to peer out. After a few seconds the eye blinked in surprise and recognition. The door was opened wide and a Han in black tunic and trousers stood revealed. "Brother Ping! We thought we would never see you again. What news?"

"You have waited years. You can wait another two minutes. Let us in!"

Jun had to bow as he followed Ping into the low-ceilinged room behind the door, but he already knew what he would find. The smell had given it away immediately.

He had travelled all the way around the world but found himself back in the very same place he had started: an opium den.

Somehow, in the grey hell of London he found himself a vein of glittering gold.

Opium was quite legal in England and, apart from alcohol, it was the only effective means of pain relief. Strait-laced Victorians dosed themselves for everything from simple aches and pains like rheumatism and gallstones, to menstruation and child birth. It quietened teething children.

Jun did not possess the Englishmen's benevolent attitude to opium for it had wrecked his own country. Back in Shanghai, as Green Gang members met to smoke their tobacco pipes, the older ones would tell stories of the greatness of China before Britain broke its back in the opium wars.

Long before that terrible matriarch Queen Victoria was even born, China had sold its goods to the world: its porcelain, silks and tea. The trade had become too successful and the European empires had grown to resent the money draining away to the Middle Kingdom. Only too happy to redress the balance, the British East India Company had grown opium on their farms in India and taken it to China: thirty thousand chests of opium a year, each much heavier than a man.

Successive emperors had fought to resist as the number of addicts in China grew to more millions than there were fingers on your hands. Finally, and in desperation, the Chinese seized supplies and blockaded their own ports to prevent opium-carrying foreign ships from entering.

In response, the British had sent their infernal steam-driven gunboats into battle, splintering like matchwood the wooden sailing vessels of the Chinese navy.

Then, to add insult to mortal injury, China was forced to make huge reparations and agree to allow the British to sell opium in China in perpetuity. And, into the bargain, China yielded Hong Kong Island to the British.

If there was one thing Jun knew about it was opium: its quality, preparation and storage. He was offered work immediately in the Limehouse den, though the money was not enough so he had to take other work as well. For two years he lacerated his hands, losing most of the sensation in them forever, weaving ropes in open, hemp-smelling sheds in the docks of Limehouse and Shadwell. His palms became so roughened and calloused he struck his matches on them.

Then finally, after years of hard work, he had the money to open his own opium den. It gave him a bitter, ironic pleasure to sell opium back to British people. To wreck their lives as they had wrecked his.

At first his den had some competition from other Chinese, though no real gang network had yet developed. Jun rarely had to resort to savagery to quell opposition, but he did if he had to.

And sometimes, as he prospered and his English got better, he would talk to the lost souls who frequented his little corner of hell.

The poet lay becalmed by his first pipe. Soon there would be no sense from him, but for a brief time he would talk with no barriers.

The man's velveteen jacket was wrinkled under the pressure of his body on the wooden shelf and his cravat was askew over a gold patterned waistcoat. Thin, fair-haired and with eyes of startling blue, he looked outlandish in this place, like some mythical creature fished from the deep.

Jun carefully picked up the black top hat that had rolled unnoticed to the floor and laid it at the man's feet.

"Mr Hu—Fu Manchu," said the poet and giggled.

"What you say?"

"Merely suggesting that the sublimity you provide gets such a bad press. Dickens, Wilde, Sax Rohmer—all of them terribly anxious about the opium dens of Limehouse. About lost souls wasting away, of lives blighted, of promise unfulfilled."

"That all true."

The poet laughed again. "Honest Hu—too honest for your own good if you ask me. The thing is that wounded souls, of which I count myself one, need the pipe. Something to mute the poverty and squalor that submerges this appalling city." If you don't like the poverty, thought Jun to himself, then stay away. Keep to your fine houses and theatres and restaurants. What's the point of having money otherwise?

"And the dreams," continued the poet. "Coleridge and de Quincey would have been nothing without their laudanum. Half of our culture comes from this." He held up the pipe.

"What you mean?"

"Even when they don't smoke it for inspiration, hacks like Dickens, Mary Shelly, George Elliot, Wilkie Collins, have their characters use it. Without opium as a plot point, they'd be lost."

Jun had had no idea that the literature of this country depended so much on his humble, though lethal product. "You show me!" he said.

And the foppish young poet did just that in exchange for a few more pipes. Though he usually kept it well disguised, Jun had a sly and darkly humorous strand to what had become a bleak nature. He had a plaque made up and nailed to the inside of the sturdy door of his establishment. It read: There were opium dens where one could buy oblivion, dens of horror where the memory of old sins could be destroyed by the madness of sins that were new.

Every night, as he locked up, he would kiss his palm then lay it on these words of Oscar Wilde.

Over time Jun grew accustomed to the East End of London. He came to appreciate all the things he could buy in the capital of what he had come to reluctantly concede was the greatest empire of the world.

However, and despite all his money, there was one thing he lacked.

The loss of his wife was an ache that never left. He lay awake on countless nights thinking of Liu. Had Dong got her to safety? Jun knew full well the horrors the Green Gang could inflict. Someone would pay for what had happened to the Frenchman. Too much face had been lost. Even Dong, more witness than participant, might have fallen victim to the arm's-length revenge of the French.

There was no way to find out. The Customs Post Office had only recently been opened in Shanghai but that was exclusively for foreigners. In any event, a letter needed an address where it could be delivered, and someone there with the ability to read. His wife, if she still lived, would have neither.

The barriers seemed insurmountable. Reluctantly, he let the memory of her fade.

He was still a vigorous man and he needed a woman. Unfortunately, there were few enough Chinese women in London.

Occasionally they returned from the Middle Kingdom as servants to British masters but they were unapproachable, hidden away in grandiose suburban villas.

Occasionally, when the need became unbearable, he would consort with the doxies of Limehouse with their soft, decaying bodies and their coarse, screeching laughter. They were different creatures from the delicate, gilded, twittering whores in the brothel a world away in Shanghai.

Liu, robustly built though she might have been, had had more femininity in her little finger than the scrofulous London whores possessed in their entire bodies.

The years of loneliness passed slowly and left him little choice but to devote all his attention to his business. It was lucky he did. Another opium-fuelled conversation steered him away from a financial disaster he would never have anticipated.

Most of his customers were British tars who in their travels had become addicted to the fruit of the poppy. However, on occasion, as well as the few dissolute poets and artists, more reputable-looking white men would appear for a pipe or two. He took every opportunity to find out more from these strange creatures.

The conversation had taken place with a man whose white collar may have been grubby but at least he wore one. Though Jun usually paid other people to load pipes nowadays, he packed this man's himself.

The man's name was Herbert. He was tall and thin and had been a chemist but had lost his shop because of an impropriety involving a petticoat and a finely turned ankle. Somehow, between his time dispensing drugs and seducing married women, he had gained a taste for opium.

"Damned thing has got a grip on me," Herbert said, though with little rancour as the pipe had already drained away all bitterness.

Jun nodded. "It's a trap. Always is, always will be."

Herbert had given him a loose, one-pipe smile. "That may well be the case for now but it won't last. Not if Bayer has anything to say about it."

"Bayer?"

"A maker of medicines. They have made a new wonder drug called Aspirin. It kills pain."

"Does it give good dreams?"

Herbert shook his head and the dulling of his eyes meant the period of volubility was ending. "No, my friend. No dreams. It does nothing but get rid of the pain."

Jun was struck by a terrible, startling flash of clarity. Opium was tolerated because of its pain-relieving properties, a necessary evil, otherwise the law would have long since kowtowed to the anti-opium crusaders and cracked down on the dens. Now there would be nothing to stop them.

Within a week he had converted the den into many tiny rooms which he let out to sailors and other indigents. As other dens were closed down by the police, he bought the buildings at knock-down prices and turned them into rabbit warrens for people.

He had been a landlord for several years when his old friend Ping suddenly came to say goodbye. Ping had been working in an eel and pie shop in Southwark. Woe betide any cat or dog that crossed the path of the urchins paid a copper for anything resembling meat they chanced across. Animals of every description ended up under Ping's cleaver.

Ping had finally had enough. Jun was hardly astonished; Ping had never lost his contempt for the British. There was one surprise, however. Though their last voyage had nearly cost Ping his life, it seemed the sea had never stopped calling to him.

Jun laughed when Ping told him that he had signed up on an East-bound trader, but sobered quickly as a thought struck him.

"Will you do something for me, brother Ping?" he asked.

"I owe you my life, brother Jun," replied Ping, bowing deeply.

"And I owe you mine. I would have died but for your care." Jun noted that the roots of Ping's pigtail were turning white, reaching a finger joint's length from his scalp.

"I want you to be my emissary. I would not trust anyone else to do this. I want you to find out what happened to my wife and to my friend, Dong. But you must be careful. If the Green Gang know you are connected with me, then they will torture you to find out where I am now."

After the everyday horrors of Victorian London, perhaps Ping's memory of Shanghai had lightened and taken on a more pleasing hue, for he dismissed these concerns with an airy wave. Jun gave him what information and directions he could.

Years passed and Jun grew richer from buying and selling property but Ping did not return. Jun was saddened but not surprised for those who travelled far in this savage world were often never seen again, their fate forever unknown by those they left behind.

The Chinese community grew and so too did the availability of Chinese women. He finally took one, Ju, as a mistress. They took pains not to ask about each other's past. Though too old to bear him a child, she cooked and cleaned and looked after him in other ways. For once in many years, he began to feel almost at ease.

Then, without warning, she left him. Stunned, he found a note written in English. It was the only written language they could both read. It said she had felt the approach of the final enemy and that she had wanted to return to her family, if any still lived, and die in the Middle Kingdom. She had been saving what she could of the small sums he had given her for housekeeping. Enough for passage, steerage class, on the big passenger ships that now plied the world. She wished him a long and peaceful life.

The tone was civil but unloving and it made Jun realise just how much he had walled off his heart from her, from anyone since Liu. For the first time since he was a child, he found himself weeping.

Then, out of the blue, and long since Jun had given him up for dead, Ping returned, the white in his hair now down to the end of his waist-length pigtail. So much time had passed they seemed like strangers. When Jun found him at his door, they could not bring themselves to embrace.

As Jun's maid, an orphan white girl who had the frightened demeanour of someone who worked for devils, poured their tea,

Jun examined Ping's face more closely. Cooks always got first pick of the food so their faces were usually full, the lines smoothed out, but Ping's looked furrowed.

"You do not look well, old friend," he said.

Ping waved this away. "Two years in a Valparaiso jail."

"Where is that?"

"Chile, off the west coast of South America."

Jun blinked and pointed towards the east. "But..."

Ping again waved this away. "It is a long story. Shipwrecks, seizures of ship and cargo, even a fire that sent one ship to the bottom of the South China Sea."

He sighed and took a sip of tea. "I have been unfortunate in my choice of employers, often finding myself stranded in foreign ports. I had to take what ships I could. I have staggered around this world like a drunken man."

"Did you ever get back to Shanghai?"

"That I did. Getting there was easy, it was the getting back when my troubles began. But never mind that, there is much to tell you." Ping suddenly looked immensely pleased with himself as everyone does when they know so much more than the person needing the information.

"Come, Ping! Do not keep me waiting!"

"You are dead!" cried Ping triumphantly. "A crowd caught you down by the docks. They beat you and cut you and threw you into the river for the fish to eat."

Jun remembered the unfortunate man the mob had mistaken for him. An inner tension, with him so long he had forgotten it existed, suddenly fell away. Limehouse should have been well beyond the reach of the Green Gang but their reputation was so fearsome that some part of him had always expected a sudden knife in the back, or a cudgel crushing his skull in a dark alley.

The danger had increased as more and more of his fellow countrymen came to Britain. Gambling dens and mahjong schools were springing up and the gangs would surely follow. However,

Ping's news meant that even if the Green Gang got this far, they would not be looking for a dead man.

"And my wife?"

Ping spread his hands; this news clearly not so good. "She died of cholera, years ago. Dong married her but..." and he grasped Juns's hands to show his earnestness, "... he did it as a favour to you."

Jun blinked. "What do you mean?"

"Your wife was with child. You have a son!"

7. Beijing

The Son, Benny Hu, and the Fuck-You Airport

It was his first landing at Beijing's new airport and Benny didn't like it one little bit.

The Daxing terminal was like a giant starfish the size of a small country that had splattered down onto the flat Hebei plain. At a million square metres, as the Chinese pilot had boastfully told them on approach, it was by far the largest terminal building on Earth.

Inside it was disturbingly organic as though colossal white mushrooms had sprouted, their broad caps spreading out and melding to form a roof. The whole place gleamed, making Benny feel even more rumpled and sweaty after the long fight.

It was clear the building was designed to make foreigners feel unworthy, like Berlin when Hitler was master, or Rome at its height of empire. It was meant to intimidate, to drive home to any foreigner their inferior place in a new world.

Not so long ago, China had not been like this. Soon after Six had wrapped its tentacles around him, and he was earning good money for the first time, he'd come in as a tourist from the north-west on the Trans-Mongolian Express. The hovels of the Gobi Desert had given way to the grimy concrete unhappiness of the north-western towns and cities. Litter was everywhere, accumulating in drifts or crucified against fences by the wind from the desert. Rusty, oily wrecks of vehicles lay abandoned where they had broken down for the last time. Dingy shops hid behind broken signs, their floors spit-speckled. Everyone looked like their clothes needed a good wash.

Then one day Xi Jinping had said Wait a cotton-picking minute! The new rulers of the world shouldn't live in such a shit-hole (or words to that effect).

Overnight he recruited one million cleaners, usually the old and retired, and told them to tidy the place up. Today, you saw them everywhere in their coolie hats, their old-style straw brooms sweeping away industriously.

Nowadays people spat on the floor at their peril.

And at night the gleaming sky-scraping cities sparkled with vast choreographed light shows.

The Chinese had changed too. Here in the terminal building they wore better clothes, better jewellery and moved faster than even harried Western business people trying to catch planes at Schiphol or Heathrow.

Each time he came back to China the whole damned place had changed, evolving and ascending in great upward thrusts.

It scared the hell out of him.

The West and its fading colonialist attitudes didn't have a clue just how far behind they had fallen. Back home they still held to the comforting conceit that once the Chinese got rich enough, they would demand democracy and China would converge with the liberal world view of the West.

As if!

Barely fifty years ago, during Mao's disastrous rule, the people here had been forced to eat grass and tree bark to survive. Nowadays their biggest headache was deciding which model of iPhone to buy. There was plenty of food, plenty of education, plenty more opportunities for travel. Who needed democracy? Who needed weak, indecisive government?

The immigration officer gave him a look that could have withered stone, and why not? Every foreign intelligence agency had no choice but to use spies of Chinese blood. Every foreign-born Chinese exited interest when they rocked up and Benny knew he would be tagged. The officer didn't even try to hide it when he reached to the side and pushed a button. A camera somewhere above the man's desk would be taking even more images of him. These would be added to his passport photograph as fodder for interlinked security AIs lurking like spiders at the centre of a vast web of CCTV cameras across the whole Middle Kingdom.

The AIs were restlessly on the lookout for dissidents or Falon Gong and even for common criminals, though the latter were given the lowest priority. Internal dissent was the main focus of all this cold but efficient attention.

However, when it came to potential foreign operatives, analysis queues were jumped. Anthony Lam, the name on his genuine British passport, would now be ceaselessly searched for throughout China by a creature with myriad eyes and multiple brains that had never been troubled by a single human thought.

The Daxing Terminal had its own subway station and the train shot him at almost bullet speed into Beijing. It wasn't until he emerged onto ground level in the centre of the city that he had his first taste of unfiltered air.

Beijing air quality was a moveable feast. By some measures it was the most atmospherically polluted city in the world, so much so that sometimes you couldn't see more than a couple of city blocks. However, local weather conditions made this highly variable and today the sky was the clearest blue.

The taxi was well-used but clean and the passenger camera, a little black nubbin on the smooth facia of a door post, almost undetectable. Benny looked out of the window as the twinkling city blurred by. Where once numberless ranks of decrepit bicycles would be parked by the side of the road, now were the forecourts of large car showrooms holding swathes of cars, many foreign, many very expensive.

Everyone used to be poor and looked the part; now the only poorly dressed people were the occasional pensioned-off roadsweeper. Glittering shops displayed clothes of every description. Above the bustling streets, bright electronic displays extolled the virtues of some far-off Chinese city, built from scratch in a heartbeat.

Once upon a time Beijing had a run-down sort of quaintness. Most of the people lived in old-style hutongs, acres of tiled roof single-storey buildings. Communal latrines every fifty metres serviced the needs of the inhabitants. There were no sewers so, once a week, a truck would arrive along with a biblical cloud of flies to empty the holes under the latrines. On sweltering hot summers days, the smell was poisonous.

In the vast burgeoning prosperity since Deng Xiaoping took the dead hand of socialism off the free market in the 1980s, the hutongs had been one of the first targets. Once 95 per cent of the city's people lived in them; now only a handful did.

Anyone flying into Beijing could work out where all the old hutong inhabitants had gone—packed off to hundreds of square miles of featureless, grey, high-rise blocks that surrounded the city like an endless thicket of tombstones.

At least those had sewers.

The taxi delivered him to a tourist hotel only a mile or so from Tiananmen Square, handy for The Forbidden Palace and Mao's pickled corpse. Every year millions of Chinese came here from provinces so far away that even the country's unprecedented new prosperity had yet to percolate there. They queued for hours to look at Mao reposing in his crystal case. They'd whisper to each other at how well mankind's most prolific killer had been preserved. All this despite the persistent rumour that it was a Madame Tussaud's dummy on display and that Mao's fragrant flesh had rotted to pulp decades ago.

The hotel room was larger than most flats in this city. He unpacked quickly, not even bothering to check for hidden cameras; all rooms in tourist hotels had them. Once upon a time, numberless

Goo functionaries would monitor twenty such cameras at a time but nowadays there were too many guests in too many hotel rooms. Instead, AIs had learned to spot suspicious behaviour. Though trained by human operators, the AIs ran by their own fathomless rules. They were certainly smart enough to get perturbed by a foreigner just arrived off a long-haul flight checking every nook and cranny in his room.

The damned things got smarter and smarter. Every time a new spy or dissident was unearthed, the AIs would backtrack, digging out any footage of the subject in hotel rooms or wherever they'd been caught on CCTV. They'd tirelessly re-examine the subject's behaviour, modifying and supplementing their alien methods of discrimination.

In this way they learned to recognise tells that even human observers would have missed.

So, Benny didn't pace or root around under the bed or in the wardrobe. He just watched TV until he fell asleep.

Five days of sightseeing followed, and always he somehow gravitated to pokey drinking holes where old men quaffed tiny glasses of sickly-sweet liquor and munched away at cheap offcuts of barbequed meat. The swine flu epidemic had struck years ago but still pork was too expensive for many blue-collar workers, so the provenance of the meat didn't bear thinking about.

Then, on the sixth day, Benny got up early, grabbed his little backpack and headed for a crowded fish market. A low corrugated iron roof covered the stalls, making it difficult for a drone to follow without someone spotting it and yelling in alarm.

A cramped market alley, its floor silvered with fish scales, led off to the right and to his chosen seedy little bar. Weary old fish porters raised their heads when he came in but quickly went back to their food. Benny ordered and finished off some crab, picking the meat out from legs as long as his forearm, before he retreated to the stinking toilet. It had a proper cubicle and was the reason why he had settled on this scruffy place.

He stripped off his tee-shirt and dug the replacement out of his backpack. Though carefully faded to not draw human attention to its newness, it had a faint motif of the faces of jungle animals, mainly tigers. Plenty of eyes, lots of stripes.

He got out the little hand mirror and his make-up. Applying shading and high-lighting around his eyes lengthened them and an artful dab of eyeliner made the corner of one appear to droop. He thickened his lips using carefully matched lipstick and dipped them down the same side as the drooping eye. The graded shading of foundation on one side of his face layered in more asymmetry. The wig he dug out of his backpack also did this more overtly, forming a bang across his forehead that rose to the right.

He gave himself one more check in the mirror. He looked a little odd, but not out of place in a country notorious for a high salt diet and the strokes that followed. The sides of many faces looked like they had suffered landslides.

He packed all his stuff away and strode quickly and purposefully out of the toilet, across to the door and out into the alley. He caught some quizzical looks from the fish porters but this hardly mattered as he was never coming back.

It wasn't just changes to his hair and face to fool the CCTV cameras and the lurking AI. The first line of defence was preventing the AI from recognising that he had a face at all. The tee-shirt with its confusing multiple eye motifs might be enough for this. If this failed then the asymmetries in his make-up and hair might do the trick. The AI's lingua franca were measurements like the ratio of eye width to separation, nose length to width of mouth and thickness of lips. His make-up altered all of these.

One other factor was on his side. Though the country was up to the rafters in CCTV cameras, many were still low resolution. That would soon change, as would the intelligence of the AI. Benny couldn't even imagine what other countermeasures spies like him would have to resort to in the future. Another compelling reason to get out of this game.

He took a winding course to the train station where the passenger lines were long and security was slow. Benny's carefully forged Resident Identity Card showed an image of him in the same make-up and asymmetric wig so the guard gave him only a disapproving look at his sense of style before ushering him through.

Finally, the high-speed train, streamlining sloping its head back like that of a huge serpent, slid noiselessly into the station exactly on time and stopped exactly where it was supposed to. Chinese were already waiting in lines at the marked spots and stepped directly onto the train when the doors opened. They were quick about it as the doors automatically closed after a few seconds whether someone was in the way or not.

Benny settled himself into his window seat. Around him excitable Chinese families yelled at each other and businessmen opened their laptops and started poking wearily away. As they pulled out of the station a cleaner mopped the passageway between the seats.

Accelerating rapidly, the train passed mile after mile of tower blocks before emerging into a transformed rural landscape. Just a few years ago most farmers lived in hovels, sharing accommodation with their pigs and ducks. Birds and swine, the viral stepping stones to humans and why China was the birthplace of so many viruses.

That was bad enough but a few years back had come coronavirus, again arising from an unhealthy relationship between the Chinese and what they lived with and ate. That had sent the whole world into a downward spiral, blotting China's viral copybook even further.

In almost all other ways life was getting better for the Chinese. China's economic growth over the last twenty years had brought money falling from the sky. Out of the window, Benny saw huge new extensions to the old farmhouses, palaces abutting and dwarfing the original hovels. These older buildings were now like little warts on a healthy body. He hoped to God that was where they kept the damned pigs nowadays, in splendid isolation.

The train zipped across huge bridges and through long tunnels. Paralleling the track, multi-lane highways streamed with little cars, though now and again an inky-windowed Mercedes or hulking four-wheel drive would muscle its way through.

Baoding was less than a hundred miles from Beijing so it didn't take much longer than half an hour before the train was barrelling into the station. So many high-speed lines met there that the size of the place was astounding.

China had built something like 20,000 kilometres of high-speed rail in the last decade and were due to build another 20,000 in the next. By then Britain might have built its first kilometre of track.

If it was lucky.

Benny made his way to the station café. He found it easily enough, a Starbucks knock-off selling a startling range of pastries and teas, though coffee seemed surprisingly popular.

Benny waited, sipping his Americano and nibbling at a lemony cake topped with what may have been plum icing. It was certainly purple enough.

"That looks like a sarcoma." Jiang plopped himself down in the seat opposite.

"Wouldn't know, never seen one."

"You haven't lived."

Jiang was looking relaxed and he cast an appraising look at the slender black-clad baristas behind the counter. Like Benny, he was wearing a patterned T-shirt with an eclectic design of ovals and perpendicular lines designed to mess with any watching AI's pattern recognition. Jiang's make-up wasn't evident unless you looked closely but he'd favoured turning the almond shape of his eyelids into something rounder, while darker foundation at each side of the nose brought it more into prominence, making it appear thinner.

"Like what you've done with your nose," Benny said.

"And I don't like what you've done with your eye and mouth. It looks like you've had a stroke."

Benny took a sip of his bitter coffee. "This is why I got into this business in the first place."

"Why?"

"So I could compare make-up tips."

Jiang snorted. "James Bond: licensed to apply foundation."

Office workers came and went as they took their time drinking their coffee.

"I don't suppose you've got another present for me, like that girly gift you gave me back in you-know-where."

"Yeah, right!" Back in Taiwan, British Embassy staff were subject to minimal surveillance by the local security services. Dropping off the guns had not been a major risk. Here in mainland China, it was a different ball game.

"How am I supposed to guard your back? What am I doing here at all?"

"I think this time I'll be watching your back. Anyway, two pairs of eyes are better than one. Either of us sees something dodgy, we text to abort and we both walk away." Like Benny, Jiang would have bought a phone at the airport.

Jiang shook his head. "If our man has turned against us, we are so fucked."

And this was so true. If Fu Chonglin had turned them in to the Goo then they were walking into a large, elaborate and dangerous trap.

Silence fell as they dealt with unpleasant thoughts.

"Why do you do this?" Benny suddenly found himself asking.

Jiang raised his eyebrows, hunting for the joke. "Easy money, what else?"

"Really?"

"Really. I've already earned more than most people do in their whole lifetimes. And my boss, that's you by the way, is so keen to deny my existence that everything I earn is tax free as I'm not officially paid in the first place. Just like with you and your boss, whoever he or she is." The way he said it, with just the hint of emphasis on the word 'she' was worrying. Had he been watching

Benny's house, did he know about Lea? He hoped he'd been careful. If Lea found out that Jiang knew about her, the shutters would come down.

Jiang raised his hands, palms up. "So, early retirement for me, thank you very much."

They didn't earn that much. Perhaps Jiang could retire early but he'd have to live the rest of his life on modest means. That wasn't him at all.

"You never were good at maths, were you?"

Jiang waved this away, like he knew what he was talking about. "Invest to generate income."

"So, like, you'd buy a hairdressing salon or something."

Jiang gave him a weary look. "I could buy my way into the gangs."

Benny blinked in surprise. What kind of arrogant, overconfident monster had he created? With the Triads you worked your way up, that was the whole point.

Then again, he had to admit Jiang did have a marketable skill set, developed navigating the shadow world between East and West. Also, there were rumours the London based 14K Triad were even taking on non-Chinese nowadays.

Times were changing, so maybe this wasn't as half-arsed an idea as it sounded.

"You're happy with drinking wine mixed with your own blood? As initiations go it's not exactly twenty-first century, is it?"

Jiang shook his head. "Nowadays it's just animal blood." He tapped the table between them with his forefinger. "Besides, we've done much worse in our time, haven't we?"

And they had, and blood too had been involved.

It had been a hot, humid Zambian night. He remembered how he'd almost broken his foot as he'd kicked open the door. Seared in his memory was the Zambian woman, broad-browed like the Han, lying splayed out on the bed, her stomach and one heavy breast red with a vast smear of blood. This trailed across her torso, the bed and the floor.

And also across scared-to-death Ru, just climbing up from the bed and already kneading his bloody hands.

"You piece of shit!" Benny roared and shoved Ru back hard against the bedroom wall. Glancing back, he saw Jiang already at the bed, reaching down, touching poor Jalaila's neck. "She's dead!"

Ru's eyes looked like they would pop out of his head. A weedy little man in his fifties, he'd been wearing his glasses and socks when he'd climbed into bed with her.

Benny could hear Jiang's camera phone clicking away. "Get him over here!" Jiang said, the fury in his voice almost palpable.

Benny dragged Ru to the side of the bed and kicked his legs from under him. Stunned, lost in a world of total confusion, Ru didn't make a move to break his fall. His head smashed down hard, face first, his glasses flicking off and skittering under the bed.

Benny grabbed him by the neck and hauled his head up so it was close to the dead woman's.

"Why did you do it?" he hissed in Ru's ear.

"I didn't. I couldn't. I was drunk," said Ru. Then, belatedly, "Who are you?"

"We're the fucking Guoanbu, who else? We're supposed to protect pieces of shit like you, but there are limits and you've taken one mighty step right over them." Wrenching Ru's arms behind him he slipped on the cuffs.

"Finished?"

Jiang had been pacing around, getting shots of the room and inhabitants from various angles. He nodded.

"Let's go!" Together they hauled Ru to his feet and jostled him out of the door. Several Zambians were climbing the stairs from the ground floor, attracted by the sound of the door being kicked in. They came hesitantly, all looking up, eyes wide and white. Two men and a woman in a grubby chemise, they melted away when Benny reached back and hauled the pistol out of his waistband.

He and Jiang and Ru clattered down the stairs and into the bar area, Jiang too pulling out his gun. A crowd of punters and whores were pushing and shoving through the door, desperate to get out into the street. Left behind was a becalmed barman, dish towel and glass frozen in mid-wipe.

Slowly, no sudden movements, the man subsided below the level of the bar.

By the time they got to the street, everyone else had scattered into the enveloping African night. They flung Ru into the back seat of the Toyota sedan and Jiang climbed in after him.

Benny put his gun on the front seat so it wouldn't dig into his back while he was driving. His nerves still jangled. He released the clutch too quickly and the car screeched into gear and kicked forward.

There were only three street-lights out here beyond the city limits, so they quickly left that little patch of light behind as they charged into the bush. With no moon and with the dust haze of the day still hanging, the stars provided only muffled, diffuse twinkles.

"Where are you taking me?" asked Ru, his voice quaking with terror.

"That's a good question," said Jiang. "Where are we taking him?"

Benny looked in the mirror at the men in the back seat, their faces weakly illuminated by the dashboard lights. He cursed and pulled the car over to the side of the dusty road. In daylight the soil here was artery red but now looked yellow in the car's headlights.

They sat in silence as the stilled engine ticked its heat away.

"What's happening?" asked Ru weakly.

"We're thinking," said Benny.

"Yeah, we're spoilt for choice," said Jiang.

"What do you mean?"

Benny turned to look at him. "Well, we could spirit you away back home to prison and disgrace. Bad enough, but at least it would be a Chinese prison."

Jiang sat back and folded his arms. "Once upon a time we'd do that, when all the big copper and coal contracts give us an 'out'. We could deal with our own whatever they'd done."

"But..." Benny smiled. "Relations between the Chinese and our Zambian hosts have become..." and he waggled his hand, "... unsettled." A few years before a couple of the Chinese managers of one of the mines had been trapped in their office by enraged miners following an explosion that killed a dozen Zambians. One manager had panicked and shot a couple of the strikers. Once regarded as welcome guests by the Zambian hosts, the Chinese were increasingly becoming viewed as parasites stripping the country bare.

"I say we just hand him over to the Zambian police," said Jiang. "That would be the easiest. A brief moment of embarrassment, but so what?"

Benny shook his head. "There's something even easier. This poor guy..." he indicated Ru, "...was overcome with remorse after slaughtering the girl. He came out here in the bush and did the honourable thing and put a bullet through his head."

Jiang smiled. "Yeah! That works. Face is saved all round."

"I didn't kill that woman!"

"Her bloods is all over your hands."

Ru looked down in surprise. Out of his mind on drink and drugs, he hadn't even noticed. In the weak light you couldn't see the red but he started to rub his fingers together, for the first time feeling their tackiness.

"This is the worst nightmare!"

"Saves on paperwork too," said Jiang thoughtfully.

Benny gave a quick nod. "Let's do it!"

Ru let out a piercing wail. Even before Benny had got out of the car, Jiang had reached across Ru to open the back door and had kicked him out onto the dust.

They dragged him a little way off the road, his legs kicking at the dirt, trying to find purchase, but when they dropped him, he stopped struggling.

Benny took out his Glock and chambered a round.

"I'll give you money!" Ru yelled.

"Sure, and then we're the ones who wind up with bullets in the head."

"Please don't kill me. I'll do anything you want."

Benny and Jiang looked at each other then Benny bent down so his head was close to Ru's.

"Anything?"

Jalaila sipped at her beer before clunking the bottle back down on the rust-spotted table. They were sitting in the garden of a bar and across the valley they could see the smokestacks of Kitwe belching crap high into the air. Around them the Zambians were laughing and joking. Everyone was smoking and most were drunk even though it was still early in the afternoon.

Benny enjoyed watching Jalaila move for everything that she did, she did with a languid sexuality. Lots of the long-limbed African women moved like that, so different from the quick, darting movements of many Chinese.

Yet again Jalaila lifted up the collar of her shirt and smelled it.

"You don't smell," said Jiang. "Trust me!"

She looked up, disbelieving. "Trust you! Now that is funny."

Benny smiled. "Jiang's right. It's a clean shirt. No blood."

"That is easy for you to say. I lay there for hours covered in the stinking stuff. What in Jesus Christ's name did you give him?"

This was true enough, they'd been watching via a hidden camera, waiting to catch Ru just as he came to. It had taken much longer than they'd expected.

Benny smiled. "You're the one who slipped it into his drink."

"But you gave it to me. What was it?"

"A Micky Finn," said Jiang.

"Spare me! You think Africans are stupid. What was it?"

Benny and Jiang looked at each other. "We don't know," said Benny. "That's what we were given."

95

She clicked her tongue in the universal African expression of derision and turned her eyes away scornfully.

"But we'll give them your feedback," said Jiang.

"Give them my shoe up their backside!"

Jalaila's attention, never the steadiest, was drifting around with her gaze, trying to catch the eye of the mining execs, always looking for business.

"Are we keeping you?" Benny asked.

"A girl has to work."

"After this big payday?"

She shrugged her slender shoulders. "My country is losing patience with you Chinese. When we kick you out then I'll be stuck with these..." She indicated the execs. "Prices will drop. I need to get their money while I can."

"Then don't let us keep you," said Benny. They all stood and shook hands awkwardly, Benny especially, who just ten hours before had been splashing cow's blood over her naked body.

All the men in the garden turned to watch her bottom as she sashayed away.

"Ever been with a black woman?" asked Jiang as they resumed their seats.

"Ever mind your own business?"

"In this game? Anyway, don't deflect!"

"Why do you care?"

Jiang tapped his bottle on the table. "Someone has to. You're shut up way too tight."

"And you're way too loose. What's your point?"

"Benny..." Jiang began but then seemed to think better of it.

He should have let it go but found he couldn't. "What?"

"You're lost, mate. You're searching for something. Don't know what it is."

Why not say something? thought Benny. I'm getting too old for all this secrecy shit. Besides, the kid did well today.

"My mother disappeared," he found himself blurting out. "I've been trying to find out what happened to her. For ages."

Jiang looked genuinely surprised. He leaned forward. "When did this happen?"

"Back in the late 1970s."

"What!" Jiang sat back and folded his arms. "You had me going there for a second. It sounded like it had happened yesterday, not forty years ago." He stopped as another thought came to him. "That's how you ended up in an orphanage. I see. You were abandoned, like me."

Benny hesitated. Give Jiang and inch and he'd take a yard, but even the little he'd revealed so far had lifted a weight off his chest. "No. She was working for Five at the time."

Either Jiang was a way better actor than he'd given him credit for, or this really was news.

"Until recently Five made the boast they'd never had an operative killed. So presumably she just did a runner?"

"Five never had an agent killed on British soil. Thing is, my mother worked for them in Hong Kong in the seventies. HK was considered domestic in those days so it came under Five. Anyway, nobody in Five or Six know what happened to her, or so they say. She might still be alive somewhere."

Jiang looked as dubious as Benny felt. He shook his head. "Ancient Chinese proverb: never open a can of worms, you prat."

"Don't you ever wonder what happened to your own parents?"

Jiang snorted. "Oh, I know alright. It's a good twenty years since the web made finding stuff out a piece of cake. My mother was a whore, my father probably her pimp. Heroin had done for them both even before my balls dropped."

"So, you did look? So, you do understand how I feel about this?"

"I suppose. My curiosity hit a brick wall when their death certificates came up on the screen. End of story, big time. It seems to me this thing with your mother isn't likely to have a happy ending. What about your father? Who was he?"

"Haven't a fucking clue."

"Let it go, mate. Let it all go."

"Yeah, and what's left then?"

Jiang sighed. "I keep telling you, get out more, stop being so clenched up, so..." He hesitated.

"Self-absorbed?"

"Yeah, couldn't have put it better myself. I mean, do you even have a woman, and not one you pay by the hour?"

"Sort of."

Jiang gave a short, bitter laugh. "Sounds great."

Benny shrugged. "She's a different problem altogether."

"Why?"

But Benny had no intention of going there. Jiang waited but when it was clear Benny wasn't going to say anything, he licked his lips. "This business with your mother is important to you. If you need help then let me know."

He looked completely earnest and maybe he really was.

A waitress was wiping down a nearby table with a dingy cloth, her slow strokes making it into an epic. Jiang held up his empty beer bottle with one hand and two fingers with his other. She nodded then moved away as though she were walking through honey and Benny resigned himself to a long wait. A baking hot country and countless generations ravaged by malaria had sapped the energy from its people.

Jiang batted away a big black fly. "We're like the opposite of mechanics."

"What are you talking about now?"

"Mechanics appear, fix something, then disappear again. We appear, fuck something up, then vanish. Also, mechanics know why they're fixing things, but we don't know why we fuck them up. I mean why did we do that to poor little Ru?"

"Mechanics fix cars but they don't necessarily know what the owners will use them for."

Perhaps the lassitude of the people around here was getting to them because neither seemed bothered to pursue the analogy further, but Jiang didn't seem quite ready to let something go.

"What do you think Ru knows that Six needs to blackmail out of him?"

Judging by the speed of the waitress, they weren't going anywhere soon so for once Benny indulged in Jiang's idle conversation. "What do any of the people we deal with know?"

"They all seem...small fry."

"Well, that's good for us. Any higher up the food chain and they'd have security and we'd never get at them. I think Six operates on a kind of leverage principle. We deal with smaller fish, like personal assistants or accountants. They know a great deal but aren't so well paid. If Six reckons they can be bribed then that's what we do. If not, we blackmail them. And as we know, usually we do a mixture of both."

Jiang laughed.

"What."

Jiang gave him a broad smile. "I guess, like Jesus, we're fishers of men."

Benny shook his head. "You just keep telling yourself that, Jiang."

8. Shanghai 1926

The Grandfather, Hu Bai, and the Sound of Silk on Silk

Bai entered the teahouse and stepped into another world. Left behind were the trams and the carts and the horses, the stalls and their screaming hawkers, the bustling throng. Above them all, standing grand and proud, the solid brownstone European buildings on the Bund had seemed caught in this rising tide of chaos.

Yet inside the teahouse there was only quiet, the atmosphere dull and heavy and steeped in the fragrant aromas of teas from all across the Middle Kingdom.

He nodded at stern Zu, Huang's bodyguard, standing ready at the wooden door. Only a favoured few could enter the teahouse while Huang Jinrong was holding court. Bai weaved his way around the beautifully inlaid mahogany tables, bending his head down under the wooden arches. These formed circular doorways leading to smaller alcoves where customers could meet and plot and flirt. Startlingly detailed paintings of birds and dragons covered the walls and little glass-fronted cabinets held exquisitely carved ivories showing Emperors and concubines, warriors and priests.

Each little alcove had a high steepled roof, giving the teahouse a multi-turreted appearance from the outside. The roof spaces drew up the hot air, leaving behind an atmosphere that, though still moist and heavy, was nevertheless a distinct improvement on the heat and humidity of the Shanghai summer.

Gentle murmurings led Bai unerringly through the branching pathways. He heard a short brutal laugh and his heart sank. He hated Fiori and, sure enough, when he found their alcove, the Frenchman was there. He was being all too friendly with Huang, Bai's boss, both of them leaning over so their heads were almost touching across the table. Huang, his skin scarred and fixed by infant smallpox, could barely smile but was trying anyway, though it made him look like he was grimacing in pain.

Then Bai's heart beat faster as he smelled her before he could see her, her jasmine perfume overpowering the herby aroma of the Yingshan Cloud Tea that Huang favoured. She was over in a corner on a divan, fanning herself, the motion drawing at his eyes. He had to fight the impulse to look.

"Ah, it's young Bai," said Fiori, giving his crooked smile. Bai did not know why this man also could not smile properly; he wasn't scarred and he hadn't had smallpox like Huang, but whatever had fixed his mouth, Bai hoped pain had been involved.

Etienne Fiori was the head of the Special Police Bureau of the French Concession but was also Deuxieme Bureau to the roots of his slicked-back, oily hair. It was said he had a finger in every dirty business in Shanghai but Bai knew that could not be true. Nobody had that many fingers.

Huang did not acknowledge Bai's presence and would never have dreamed of inviting him to sit for tea. Instead, he crossed his arms and sat back slightly. He was the highest-ranking Chinese officer in the Special Police Bureau, as well as one of the most powerful men in the Green Gang, yet Fiori was his commander. Through Huang, Fiori kept the Chinese population in check.

Times, however, were changing.

Huang was a policeman like no other. He used informants, as any good policeman would, but he had an interesting way of solving crimes. He would use these informants to incite others to commit them so he would be uniquely placed to bring the criminals to justice. His reputation as an effective detective was without compare.

Bai stood waiting, head slightly bowed. Fiori took a delicate sip of tea, the cup looking fragile in his swarthy hands. "The communists are up to their old tricks," he said sadly. "We must make an example."

Bai kept quiet. His opinions on the matter were not required.

The Frenchman put his cup down and gently rapped his finger with the gold wedding ring on the side of the table. It beggared belief that such a man could be married. He was far too fond of sampling the 'cargo' his Corsican friends brought from France as part of their Grand Combine scheme. At the thought of this iniquitous trade, warmth pulsed into Bai's face and he felt dizzy, but he kept his face immobile.

Perhaps Fiori's wife was safely tucked away back in France. Or the notion that he was married was perhaps just one more deception in this deceitful city, where it seemed that everyone had multiple aliases and many foreigners travelled under a panoply of false passports.

"Militants are meeting tonight in their Wantz Road rat hole. Delegates from revolutionary groups from all over the country are coming. Shanghai is the only place they can meet with their Cheka bosses, white skins standing out too obviously in the rest of

China. Not so here, of course, because of all those damned White Russians who fled here after the Russian Civil War."

Fleeing White Russians and the Russian security services they were fleeing from, would not make an amicable mix if they met here in Shanghai, Bai thought to himself. A lot of scores there to be settled.

He had heard, or imagined he had heard, resentment in the man's voice. Fiori was swarthy compared to other Europeans and Bai had seen how white people treated those with darker skins, particularly the Lascars on the opium ships from India. Bai guessed the French did not quite regard Fiori as one of their own.

It was said that Fiori had haunted the Far East forever, and always working for the Deuxieme Bureau. He had been here so long he had got into something of a rut. The Russian Secret Service had indeed been called the Cheka once upon a time, but it had changed its name to the GPU years before. The old name had stuck with ancient spies like Fiori.

When it came to China, both the Russians and the French had spent too long hedging their bets. They'd set up schools for spies to train both the Chinese communists and the nationalists. The last Emperor had been dethroned years before and the two groups had since been fighting for the soul of the nation, assisted and confounded by assorted warlords. Sooner or later all the foreign intelligence services would have to place their chips on who they thought would win. Bai had a feeling that time would be soon.

The Green Gang were firmly in the corner of the nationalists whose leader Sun Yat-sen was even now dying of cancer. General Chiang Kai-shek was waiting in the wings to take over his Kuomintang group.

Fiori was sipping his tea again, his attention perhaps waylaid by similar disturbing thoughts. He put his cup down and opened his mouth to speak just as Bai heard the sound that haunted his dreams. The swishing sound of thighs clad in the finest silk stockings moving one over the other. He felt the breath leave him like a swallow from a burning barn.

"... supposed to be in Guangzhou, but the imminent death of Sun is dragging them all here to foment their crazy plots."

Who was supposed to be in Guangzhou? His thoughts had flown away with the sparrow and he had no idea how much of the conversation he had missed. She was driving him crazy.

"We should just kill the fucker," said Huang with a chop of his hand. "We should just kill them all."

Fiori waggled a finger at him. "I know where your sympathies lie, my friend, but we French must be a little more even-handed, for now at least. No, we must simply find where their 'Red Sun', this Mao Zedong, is staying while he is in Shanghai." He leaned over the table and pointed a finger at Bai. "A word to the wise, young Bai. Do not dress like a gangster for this work, though it certainly suits you."

Bai was dressed in his finest, a long black silk robe which he knew hung well on his tall, lean frame. On his head perched a dark, white-banded fedora.

He made no attempt to demur but Huang, usually keen to assuage Fiori, sprang uncharacteristically to Bai's defence. "My instructions. The meeting isn't until late and I need Bai before then. Jingfei's bodyguard is ill. At times like this..."

Fiori nodded enthusiastically. "We must protect the fragrant Jingfei." The look he gave Bai as he said her name could have filleted a cow. Fiori knew, or at least guessed, everything. He was a duplicitous, murdering, whoring monster but he was very far from being stupid.

The Frenchman ran his eyes over him. "Forgive me, young Bai, but where in that rather becoming though restrictive outfit do you hide your gun?"

In one smooth movement Bai bent, pulled aside the edge of the robe and plucked the small revolver from the holster wrapped around his inner thigh. He stood up straight, carefully pointing the gun at the floor.

Fiori nodded in approval. He turned to Huang. "Who better to take care of her?"

Again, Bai's breath fled. Only Huang's impervious self-confidence, the unshakeable belief in his own magnificence, kept him from being suspicious.

But suspicious of what? Of Bai's thoughts, for that is all there was. That and her toasted almond eyes drinking him in from across so many banqueting halls. So much kindling but not yet a fire.

Yes, Bai was definitely being driven mad. If he had been alone, he would have shaken his head to clear away these dangerous thoughts.

Fiori stood and reached into the breast pocket of his black suit. He brought out two pieces of paper and handed them to Bai. "Address and time. Find out what you can!"

Bai held up the other paper and raised an eyebrow.

The Frenchman gave his crooked smile. "A written invitation, no less. The communists are getting more sophisticated by the day. The invitations are handwritten so are laughably easy to counterfeit. Your name will be Xu Dan, you are a docker's leader in Pudong.

"But look here, young Bai! Remember every word this Mao says! We've had our eyes on him for a while. He can fuck with the warlords all he likes but we don't like to see him here in Shanghai."

Fiori bowed to the shadowy presence in the corner. "Delightful to see you once again, Lee Jingfei. You make our friend Huang young again and long may you continue to do so."

Bai stood carefully aside as Fiori and Huang said their goodbyes, policeman and gangster like two old brothers parting. As Fiori passed, he gave Bai one more all-knowing look.

Huang stood there thoughtfully until Fiori had gone. "Cursed Frenchman!" he said, resuming his seat. "Always playing both sides at once. Whatever he says, one thing's for sure. If the communists become the new warlords, then the Green Gang is fucked. This Mao Zedong, you don't have to look for an excuse to kill the whore's son. I think that's what the Frenchman was saying without really saying it."

Bai nodded, confused as that also had hardly been an instruction. He dimly sensed that Fiori was distancing himself from Huang who was distancing himself from Bai. It seemed he had to note what Mao was saying, follow him to where he was staying and if, in the process, he should kill him then nobody around here would be too distraught.

"Can I go now?" The voice from the gloom was low and gentle but it shut out all other sounds from the world.

It didn't seem to have the same effect on Huang. He didn't even look to the alcove but instead pointed a thick finger at Bai. "If she's not finished by six o'clock, then drag her out. I'm holding a banquet for some British associates later in the evening. She must look decorative by then and the devil knows how many hours that will take."

"Decorative? Is that all I am to you?"

"Not quite," said Huang giving Bai a coarse wink. For a second Bai saw Huang's pockmarked face looming over skin so smooth...

He felt sick.

More delicious sounds of silk on silk and then Jingfei emerged from the shadows. Bai cast his eyes down as she passed him, the waft of jasmine washing over him like the bow wave of a ship, overwhelming him and tipping him into churning seas.

Huang signalled and he turned to follow. Her cobalt blue cheongsam dress came down almost to her delicate ankles. He could not help but admire the sprigs of yellow blossoms that decorated the tight dress as they moved across her willowy frame. Her coal-black hair was thick but short and her neck was slender and long so he could see bare skin above the collar of her dress.

Zu gave Bai a weary look as he opened the door for them both. Did everyone but Huang understand how he felt?

Already Huang's open-topped Citroen Torpedo was waiting outside, a gift from Fiori. Huang's liveried chauffeur was holding the back door open, his heavy white uniform making his forehead slick in the summer heat.

Bai checked the bustling street. The front of the teahouse had been cleared of stalls so his view of the Bund was unobstructed. Beside him, Jingfei stepped easily onto the running board and then into the back seat before lowering herself decorously onto the cushioned leather. Even so, she managed to arrange herself so the slit in the side of her dress revealed far more of her smooth calf than was necessary.

Bai eased himself into the front passenger seat. It was an absurd place for a bodyguard to sit, for he had to crane round to see his charge. Far easier to sit next to her, to assess threats from the back as well as the front.

However, Bai was a servant, and servants sat with the driver.

The engine roared impressively to life and they pulled smoothly away from the kerb. The shadows of the buildings were beginning to lengthen in the early afternoon sun and the car passed through regions of light and dark.

Bai turned to the driver. "Do you know where we're going?"

The driver gave him a look that was both severe and weary.

"Of course, he knows," said the voice from the back seat. "We're going to my second home."

They were driving southwest and heading into the French Concession. Soon, plane trees lined the wide streets.

"Tell me, Bai, where are you from? Who are your family?"

He did not dare turn round to look at her. Instead, he made a show of scanning the road ahead, unlikely as it was that there would be any trouble. The rival gangs were never friendly but the British and French and Americans were too rich and powerful to offend. The foreigners preferred peace and so that's exactly what they got. As for the communists, even they weren't stupid enough to strike at the mistress of a senior policemen and gang member like Huang.

"I am from a small village to the north-west. My mother died of cholera when I was only five years old but I was looked after by my step-father, Dong Lei. He runs the social clubs for Huang."

"Ah yes, the houses where they keep the French whores that Fiori's Corsican friends drag here against their will."

Perhaps she was expecting him to respond but, if so, he disappointed her. With Huang and his mistress, every subject was difficult ground.

"You said step-father. What happened to your real father?"

"He died, in disgrace," said Bai flatly.

"What did he do?" Her tone was avid, predatory for gossip.

How he despised her! Despised her so much he wanted to tear the clothes from her fragrant flesh and have her right here, right now.

He risked a glance over his shoulder at a nose so dainty, lips so full and brown irises so large. He saw the high cheekbones tapering down to the beautifully defined jaw and all framed by exquisitely coiffured hair. He saw a face so beautiful it was barely human. He turned back quickly, seeking the safety of the road before them.

Even so, he could not refuse to answer. "He killed a Frenchman."

She had been leaning forward eagerly and now he heard the leather creak as she sat back in triumph. "Your name is Hu! My God, they cut your father up and threw him into the river. The French Concession hasn't stopped talking about it ever since. I never knew your name was Hu, everyone just calls you Bai, like you were a child and now I see why. You are the lowest of the low. And you work for Huang because you are..."

"Indentured, yes," he said as irritably as he dared. "It was the price my mother had to pay for both our lives. First to Qianfan, Huang's predecessor and now to Huang himself and then to whoever comes after him."

"That old bastard could go on forever," she said more softly, perhaps regretting what she had said in her enthusiasm for solving the puzzle. "He may outlive us both."

They drove in silence. "Are you married?" she asked.

"I cannot marry, I cannot have children. Such, and much else are the terms of my indenture." For an instant he remembered all the dirty jobs he had endured over the years. Serving in the kitchens, fetching and carrying until he had grown tall and strong and Huang has assigned him to even filthier work. And always the threat, if he failed, of Dong being sliced open from throat to groin. At least his poor mother was dead and free from such a fate.

This time there was a long silence from the back seat but then, finally, "I am sorry," she whispered.

Large stores now loomed on either side of the wide street. Plate glass windows revealed Chinese and European fashions. Though this was the French Concession, many wealthy Chinese had moved here and the proprietors of the big stores were more than willing to cater for them. The Frenchwomen, seeing the brightly and beautifully dressed Chinese women floating among them, had begun to wear cheongsams and to fill their homes with darkly lacquered Chinese furniture. Or so he had heard.

Bai was not surprised when they pulled up in front of one particularly opulent store. Even before he had stepped out, the old chauffeur had got out and round to Jingfei's door and was helping her to the pavement. Without looking at Bai she made for the entrance that had already been opened by a doorman.

Bai hurried after her as she strode imperiously passed bowing flunkies. The store smelled of a hundred different perfumes. All around, displays of multicoloured silks cascaded like waterfalls of every vibrant colour.

"Miss Lee, how nice to see you!" The matronly Chinese woman was dressed in a black cheongsam with the demurest of floral decoration. "Another banquet?"

Jingfei laughed. "You know me so well, Mrs Jin. What have you for me this time?"

Bai followed the women. Around them eddied European couples out shopping, the men irritable and bored. Without exception the men's eyes all turned to follow Jingfei as she walked by, resting on the sinuous movement of the dress across hips as slender as a snake's.

Bai tamped down his anger, a little surprised for he'd assumed the tastes of European men would be different. He found their own women disconcerting: too tall, their breasts and hips too heavy, their hair too light and all dressed so plainly, like peasant women. No wonder the French females were becoming entranced by cheongsams.

They came to a circular room hung with mirrors and the velour curtains of changing rooms. "You may sit," said Jingfei, pointing to a row of well-upholstered chairs set in a semi-circle for an audience to view the show.

Bai bowed. "It is better that I stand here so I can make sure no one enters."

She shrugged and went to examine herself in the mirror while Mrs Jin hurried away for her wares.

Though he had never been present when a woman bought clothing, the process nevertheless soon became boring. Yes, he could glance at Jingfei in one breathtaking creation after another, but for long periods in between he was left in the room with only Mrs Jin, who ignored him.

Most of the dresses were a good fit and Bai came to realise that Mrs Jin really did know her well. Most looked wonderful on Jingfei and he could not understand why she sent back dress after dress. The minutes turned to hours and, outside, the day would be fading. It would soon be dark and he remembered Huang's strictures about the time.

"Mistress?" he called through the curtain. "We must go."

Jingfei popped her head round the curtain, followed by an arm holding the last dress she had been given. "More, Mrs Jin!" she commanded and the older woman, without even a hint of impatience, took the outstretched dress and disappeared.

Head bowed, hands clasped, Bai implored, "I will be in trouble with Master Huang if I do not return you in time."

Bowing as he was, they were almost eye to eye. She looked at him frankly, one eyebrow slightly raised. He felt himself drowning.

A bare arm came through the curtain, a slender finger pointing at the seats. "Fetch me my purse!"

He sighed and went over. The purse was so small he hadn't even noticed it. By the time he got back to the curtain, she had disappeared.

He stood at the curtain, the purse awkward in his long fingers. "Mistress?"

"Reach it in through the curtain!"

And he did, careful not to let the curtain open too far. He felt the purse pulled from his grasp and heard it fall to the floor. A hand grasped his, pulling it further in and he felt his palm close over a warm breast the elegant shape of a champagne glass. Instead of finding a glass stem, his fingers closed on the stubby thickness of an erect nipple.

He removed his hand as gently but as quickly as he could.

Even so, for the rest of the day, his fingers smelled of jasmine. Each time he caught the scent, he heard the sound of silk stockings gliding over smooth thighs.

160, Wantz Road in the French Concession was an unlikely place for a conspiracy of communists. It was a girls' school, closed now in the evening, whose facade spoke of the wealth the Europeans lavished on their buildings. Bai was expecting the inside to be suitably opulent but the place was austere, the echoing corridors smelling of disinfectant and polish.

A couple of strapping young men stopped him at the entrance to the assembly hall and demanded to see his invitation. The counterfeit proved convincing though he wondered whether these men could even read. They waved him in.

A stooped man with a pigtail offered him a leaflet, the cheap ink smudged, and he entered a hall full of grey-smocked workers, the air above them white with the smoke of poor man's tobacco. A lectern stood on a small, raised stage and he edged his way into the shadows at the opposite end of the hall.

He glanced at the leaflet. A kindly cook at Huang's mansion had helped him learn the basics of written Chinese characters. Later on, this had been encouraged by Huang when he began to understand Bai's capabilities and potential as a spy. The leaflet, written for workers who had little or no education, hardly stretched his powers of comprehension. In it, Chiang Kai-shek and the British and French were called the New Warlords. Much was made of their elaborate lifestyles at the expense of Shanghai's poor.

Bai had seen Chiang Kai-shek in earnest conversation with Huang at a teahouse and he had to admit the communists had a point. The man had a penchant for extravagant military uniforms which he wore at every opportunity.

Bai put the leaflet away in a pocket. For reassurance he smoothed the wrinkles in the grubby smock he was wearing. In the inner pocket of his heavy coat nestled a more substantial gun than had been allowed by the more decorative form-fitting robe he had worn earlier. The Webley Service Revolver was a powerful weapon. He was depending on its deafening roar and startling muzzle flash to cause even a group of angry communists to hesitate long enough for him to get away if things became awkward.

A middle-aged man, sharp-faced and intense, stepped up to the lectern. Bai had been on enough of these missions for Huang to recognise Chen Duxiu, General Secretary of the Chinese Bolsheviks.

Chen cleared this throat and the rasping conversations of the workers rapidly ebbed away. "Comrades," he said, his voice high, almost shrill. "Today we have a brother from Guangdong. We will call him the Red Sun. In Guangdong he is training a group of compatriots to fight the warlords and to smash the landowners who fund them."

The hall was filled with murmurs of approval.

"When I first met Red Sun, he was a laundryman here in Shanghai where he had fled from Hunan province. He had been a history teacher in a primary school there and had led strikes and protests against Zhang the Venomous, the accursed Governor of Hunan. He drove out Zhang and claimed the province for our alliance."

Bai knew the KMT had had a large part to play in that business but Chen certainly wasn't going to acknowledge that.

He felt fingers tug at his sleeve. It was an old man, reeking of tobacco, his head wobbling with a marked tremor. "You know who that is, our Red Sun?" Bai was wondering whether to lie or not but the old man was more interested in telling than listening. "It is Mao Zedong himself! We are honoured!" And with that, contented, the old man turned back towards the stage.

Distracted, Bai had not heard Chen's final words for already another man was stepping up to the lectern. He was younger than Bai expected, perhaps only thirty. Either his hair was receding or he was born with a high hairline for an expanse of ruddy forehead was revealed. He had the sun-baked skin of a peasant or of someone who did not wash. The mouth was sensuous, the eyes widely spaced.

"Comrades..." Mao began then without preamble launched directly into his speech. There were more sounds of approval at his fluent Shanghainese for many here did not speak Mandarin.

A good start but then it all went wrong. The rambling two-hour speech tested Bai's attention. It also tested the bladder of the old man next to him who started to shuffle his feet uncomfortably. Bai had trained himself to remember everything from these meetings but Mao's long, meandering speech proved too fearsome a test despite peppering his words with earthy sexual references (warlords had the insatiable cocks of pigs, apparently). However, buried deep within were some eye-opening statements. These alone would be all that Fiori and Huang needed.

Mao wanted to see the end of the warlords. Nobody but the warlords would disagree with that. However, he also wanted to seize the land from wealthy landlords. Again, this idea was hardly testing this audience. What was startling was his definition of such wealth. Anyone with more than a few acres of land he considered counter-revolutionary.

That was bad enough but later he made it clear these supposed 'gentry' merited only imprisonment or death.

Bai did a rough calculation. By Mao's definition about one in ten Chinese would be defined as landowners, perhaps fifty million

Chinese in all. Bai doubted that all the prisons in China would hold even a million. In Mao's brave future, the gravediggers would be very busy.

Mao was raving mad or was so dangerous the idea of putting a bullet through his head was looking more compelling by the second. The KMT, though revolutionaries in their own way, were often disillusioned military men from the landowning classes. They would hardly want to see their families strangled or bludgeoned or hacked to death. Fiori and Huang had always favoured the KMT over the communists and for once they had been right.

Distracted by these thoughts, he missed the end of Mao's speech and was late to join in the loud applause. The old man next to him was staring at the stage, his eyes luminous with joy. He would hardly notice Bai's hesitation but there might be sharper eyes around.

Already the audience was dispersing and Bai edged his way into a cluster that was heading to the exit. He would lurk in the shadows of an alley until Mao left and then follow him and find where he was staying. If he could get off a clear shot then so much the better.

He became aware of a big man at the door staring at him in a frank, appraising manner. Bai reached in through a slit in his coat to grasp the reassuring butt of the gun.

Men leaving were bunching up at the door and Bai tried to ease his way through the middle so the big men couldn't grab him.

For a second, he thought he was going to get away but then, with a loud grunt, the big man pushed his way into the throng until his reaching hand fastened on Bai's collar. To the protests of the men around him, Bai was dragged out and shoved to the side of the corridor.

"Comrade, what is wrong?" he stammered.

The big man, grimacing fiercely, had hair and eyes that were dark as night. His head came forward until their lashes were almost touching. "Who are you? What is your business here?"

"I am Xu Dan. I lead the men in Number 3 docks in Pudong. I have my invitation here..." But as he reached for his pocket the man grabbed his hand and turned it up. Without taking his eyes off Bai's, he rubbed a finger over his palm.

Bai had worked in Huang's kitchen and had fetched and carried from morning to night, but his hands were soft as snow compared to a docker's.

The man's head were so close that Bai could only draw his own a little further back. Even so, when he jerked his forehead forward and down onto the man's nose, the contact was solid enough to make the man stagger back.

Bai whirled and charged, stiff-arming men aside with his left hand, pulling out his gun with his right.

It had all happened so fast that the workers, stunned by Mao's interminable lecture, were slow to react. Bai pushed his way clear of the crowd and raced down the long school corridor to the entrance. Men there were turning at the sound of his approach. He thumbed back the gun's hammer.

The men quickly stepped aside.

Then he was out onto the pavement. He dodged left, ran a few strides then quickly turned and aimed just as the big man came through the entrance. Bai raised the gun slightly and pulled the trigger, the loud bang freezing the man, the muzzle flash smashing his shadow back against the wall.

The heavy calibre bullet hit the sandstone above the man's head, showering him with fragments.

The man turned back for safety even as others were emerging. He charged, tumbling them all back into the cover of the hallway.

Now Bai really did run but had got barely fifty yards before the first gunshot. He flinched as an angry hornet zipped by his ear.

He ducked into the darkness of an alleyway between two big stores. Hidden objects barked his shins, tripping him, and he found himself cartwheeling his arms for balance.

Ahead the alley opened onto a district of densely packed single-storey buildings. It was one of the many hutongs full of the Chinese who worked in the Concession.

Hutongs were labyrinths and would give him a chance to lose his pursuers.

A second gunshot rang out as he got to the first building. The homes were so small that everything not worth stealing was stored outside. Broken birdcages and lobster traps, handcarts that had lost a wheel and ripped house screens all tried to trip him.

He took rights and lefts at random. The shouting was getting louder and he could hear the sound of many feet clattering through the little alleyways behind him.

He might not know this hutong but some of his pursuers would. They would spread out, sending men down every alleyway and each tiny, rubbish-clogged street.

Already he'd lost his sense of direction and then suddenly he found himself brought up against a high mud wall. With no intention of heading back into the mob's ungentle arms, he was about to leap for the top when he saw the sparkle of embedded glass fragments ready to shred his hands.

Could he climb a roof and wait until dawn? He put this thought aside. Poor man's tiles were loose enough to rattle in the wind so everyone inside would hear him clambering across. They'd come out to investigate and were unlikely to be quiet about it.

He headed left and suddenly the little alley along the wall opened out into something larger and he saw the outline of a building lacking the clear lines of the others. Instead, there were spikes and curves, nubbins and larger sweeping shapes.

A temple! A small one, somewhere even priests would not sleep at night.

Climbing was easy, decorative railings providing handholds. The curved roof tiles were heavy and solid. He could make out three tiers of roof, each tier topped with dragons from whose undulating backs sprang rows of spikes. There were other shapes he did not recognise but were likely to be birds and lions and more supernatural beasts.

He crawled amongst the figures on the first roof line, flattening himself so their shapes hid him.

The sounds of pursuit came nearer, but he could hear noises from all around as the men spread through the hutong. None appeared to have lanterns, having set out for a meeting on a well-lit boulevard in the French Concession.

His feeling of alarm quickly subsided and he settled down for a long night. A thought came to him and he lifted his hand to his nose. Still the scent of jasmine lingered. Erotically charged thoughts surged through his mind.

Even so, he would later be surprised by how quickly he had fallen into a land of moist, warm dreams.

He awoke to a maddening profusion of colour and design. He was lying, like a lover, curled up beside a dragon. Its serpent body was longer than his and made of beautifully coloured porcelain, its upper body sun yellow, its underside white. A green-bearded maw was open to reveal a red mouth and sharp forked tongue. Two whiskers, longer than its head, curved out of the nose and back over the elongated snout and forehead. Somehow, temple dragons held onto their bright colours despite the typhoon season's torrential rains.

It was dawn and, as he lay there, he could hear the hutong coming alive, servants and cleaners preparing breakfasts for themselves and their families before they set out to serve their French masters.

Raising his head just a little, he peered over the roofs. The backs of the higher buildings of Wantz Road were barely a hundred yards away. As he got his bearings, he realised there were many entrances to the hutong from the road. The mud wall that had blocked his way was to deter entry from another walled hutong to the east.

Even if the mob had left people behind to catch him, he doubted there were enough for every entrance.

Carefully, he crawled back down across the roof and lowered himself to the ground. He set off towards Wantz Road. He kept his head down, hands in the pockets of his coat like a weary worker heading towards the drudgery of the day.

Despite his careful survey he still got lost in the maze but then he altered course when he caught the rare sound of a motor car that could only be coming from the direction of Wantz Road.

Nobody was waiting for him there. He stepped up his pace. Huang's mansion was also in the Concession so it wasn't a long walk.

Huang was almost always a night owl but not when missions like this were going on. By the time Bai got back to his little garret in the guardhouse and had washed and changed, Huang would be at breakfast and expecting a report.

At noon in Huang's second favourite teahouse overlooking the Yangtze, Bai was made to repeat once again what had happened at Wantz Road.

Thankfully, there was no distracting smell of jasmine. Jingfei was always late to rise.

Long before Bai had finished speaking, Fiori's crooked smile had vanished and his eyes became hooded under lowering brows. Throughout, he interrupted with questions, needing more details of who was there, what they looked like. Bai's memory was good but he could not match the master spy's fine attention to detail. An account that had satisfied Huang, left Fiori wanting, as did the fact that they still did not know where Mao was staying.

When Bai's story petered out, and with Mao still alive at the end of it, Fiori sat back in his seat and sighed. "So, he's got Chen Duxiu on his side. He's a fierce man and Trotskyist to his core but I never considered him crazy enough to condone mass murder."

Huang wrapped his knuckles on the intricate designs of the lacquered table and the little tea cups rattled. "I keep telling you, Etienne, you can't keep playing both sides. The communists are mad with rage. Too much suppression for too long. China will be a lake of blood if they come to power. Sometimes I don't think you French give a damn about us, Etienne, but consider the matter of business. The Green Gang will be finished and you foreigners will be thrown out of China."

He shook his head angrily. "Stop pissing around! Put your weight behind Chiang Kai-shek and the KMT. Kill this serpent while it is barely out of the egg!"

Bai doubted the Frenchman trusted Huang. He would not have been at all surprised if Fiori had doubted Bai's own account, considering it tainted by Huang's prejudices and motives. Even so, though Fiori had questioned him closely, Bai sensed a leaden acceptance. Fiori had many spies and perhaps Bai's testimony was the final corroborating evidence that tipped the scales.

Fiori picked up his cup, a flicker of surprise coming to his eyes as his lips touched the cold, neglected fluid. He put the cup down. "There's plenty of left-wingers in the KMT. It's not all landowners and businessmen."

Huang made a chopping motion. "Chiang has to purge them otherwise they'll give away the plans. Get them out of the way then he can go for the communists."

Fiori, a brutal man drenched in white slavery, nevertheless shook his head with what looked like genuine sadness.

"It's bloodshed either way."

9. Baoding, China

The Son, Benny Hu, and the Long-Sighted War-Bird

Benny watched Jiang step through the sliding glass doors of the big glittering storefront. Once upon a time, the mannequins draped in stylish clothes would have been European, or at least would have been given relaxed European poses. Now their poses were heroic, ironically mimicking the stances of revolutionary soldiers. Hands on hips they stared off into a floridly coloured but industrious future.

Benny peered into the display windows, trying to act like a hick from some far-off village gawping at an exhilarating new world. Then, as though drawn in by its siren song, he entered the store, narrowing his eyes at lighting brighter than the outside sun. Clothes racks at random angles forced him to zig-zag like an earthworm burrowing into loamy soil.

Three cameras but no sight of drones, though there were plenty of shelves higher up where they might perch, waiting. He swerved back as though to check the window displays from the inside. The street outside was busy but there was still no hint of surveillance.

He was so keen to appear not to notice Jiang that it took him a long time to spot him. He was near the centre of the store looking bemused at some fiercely patterned shirts.

Benny wandered over to the trouser section where cut-offs were trying to breach China's conservative style defences. Good luck with that, he thought.

The three floorwalkers were easy enough to spot. They weren't trying to hide how attentively they were observing the customers.

Everything looked so normal, but still his bladder felt full of ice.

Benny knew Jiang was watching him, albeit occasionally and obliquely. If he made for one of the exits then Jiang would follow, not immediately, but as surely as if his life depended on it.

Benny wasn't one for indecision but for once he felt like a man on the roof of a burning skyscraper. Jump or burn!

If they were caught, there was no limits to what the Goo might do to them.

Get a grip! he thought. He moved over to a circular rack of belts hanging down like dead snakes and fingered the leather.

In the intelligence community legends abounded of Dixia Cheng, a huge bunker city built under the streets of Beijing not far from the Forbidden Palace. Nearly a hundred square kilometres in extent, it had its own light railway to carry Guoanbu staff around the city. Once its function had been to shelter the Beijing population, or at least select members of it, when the bombs rained down. It had its own hospitals, schools, markets and dormitories but nowadays it was the Goo that occupied large sealed-off sections. In this sunless domain they could do whatever they wanted to whoever they wanted. A foreign spy dragged down there was entering a world of terror.

Benny felt sweat prickle his brow. For the millionth time he wondered what the fuck he was doing here. To hell with Lea, to hell with his mother! They'd both betrayed him in one way or another. He should get a proper job, should resign himself to being poor, maybe for once find a drop of happiness in his life.

A movement at the corner of his eye made him risk a casual glance and he had to forcefully still his breathing as he saw Fu Chonglin enter. The man was wearing a bright blue and yellow shell suit as though he cared as little about style as he did about being noticed.

Good boy! thought Benny. Hide in plain sight! Then Fu began to fuck it up with his idea of acting casual. The clothing rack they had chosen was the one nearest to a large pillar holding up the roof high above their heads. Fu's attempts to get to it, stopping now and again to take too quick a look at racks on the way, wouldn't have fooled anybody who was taking notice.

On the target rack hung Paddington Bear type duffle coats. It could get cold in the winter here but, even so, this was another valiant attempt to alter Chinese clothing habits. They were also mildly subversive. Wags had started noting the similarity of President Xi Jinping's self-satisfied smile with that of Winnie the Pooh, though an altogether more sinister version. Xi Jinping, and by extension the Guoanbu, had not seen the funny side and there had been a crackdown on the work of that dreadful subversive A.A. Milne. Paddington and Winnie the Pooh weren't the same but wearing a Paddington duffle coat was pushing the envelope.

Fu had finally got to the rack and was working his way through the coats looking for the first one that was medium size. He lifted it from the rack, regarded it doubtfully and then shuffled into it.

The square pillar had mirrors on each side and he stood before one, hands in voluminous pockets, twisting this way and that. The coat didn't seem to please him.

With a little too obvious show of disappointment, he took off the coat and put it back on the coat hanger. Then, forgetting their instructions, he placed it as the first coat on the hanger rail rather than hiding it deeper.

Benny's heart leapt as he found himself being hustled aside. He spun round to find a tiny old woman looking up at him, brows creased with irritation. She gave a little grunt of disapproval before ignoring him and pawing through the belts. The rudeness was so authentically old Chinese woman that Benny almost smiled. By the time he managed a casual glance back at Fu, the guy was almost at the door, not having bothered to check through the other racks like he was supposed to.

Had Fu lost his nerve? Had he seen something? Benny felt the urge to bolt but he made himself stand his ground. A row of shelves held folded underwear and he reached out to feel the material of a singlet. Taking a deep breath, he took the singlet over to a till where a skinny young Chinese girl with too much make-up gave him a card scanner.

In the mirror behind the counter, he could see Jiang mooch over to the rack with the coats. Leafing through, he kept going until he got to the first large size. He took it off the rack and paraded before the mirror. Too big, so he tried on the medium coat. Finally, still apparently unconvinced, he put that back on the rack then headed off to look at the shirts again.

After paying, Benny let a display of hats catch his attention and began trying them on. He kept this up until long after Jiang had left the store. Nobody seemed to follow him and the Goo didn't come swarming out of the woodwork to check the coat rack.

In the end, Benny bought a red brimmed baseball cap he would normally not be seen dead in and left the shop.

✦

They met in another small camera-free backstreet bar in Beijing to the west of the Olympic Stadium. A weary old bartender grudgingly served bottles of Beijing beer, a gaseous Asahi concoction, while bamboo baskets of dim sum steamed away in a corner. During the day the place was frequented by doormen and cleaners and other poor office workers but now, later in the evening, the clientele looked like pimps and whores readying for the night. Benny and Jiang avoided the mildly interested eyes of the women as they ruffled through Fu's handwritten notes.

Jiang was kneading his forehead angrily. "For fucks sake! What did you fucking tell him?"

Benny was no less unhappy. He folded over the sheets so that nobody else could read them and sat back in his ancient wooden chair, its slats hard against the muscles of his backside.

Jiang back-handed the sheet of paper he was holding. "This is rubbish. A million Uighurs held in re-education camps, cameras on every street in Kashgar, the biometric data of thirteen million harvested, a million Han Chinese staying as unwelcome house guests in Uighur households, monitoring their every bowel movement. Who'd have thunk it?"

The plight of the Muslim Uighurs, a people in south-western China where the land turned to desert, had been an ongoing news story in the West for years but Fu didn't seem to know that. Terrorist incidents had made the government crack down hard on the Uighurs.

"I can't give this to the Embassy," Benny said. Dead-drops were always risky, especially in Beijing and whoever put their freedom on the line to collect this would not thank him for it.

Jiang leaned forward, tight-lipped. "We're not going to get paid for this, are we?"

"Neither is Fu."

"And do you think that matters to him? He's gone totally Uighur on us. This is all he's interested in."

Benny looked away. "I'm not so sure. He didn't mention the Uighurs once when I talked to him in Taiwan and there's nothing on the files about him even being Muslim. He knows its AI stuff we want. Which military departments are ordering quantum processor arrays, the input specs for the learning sets, all that kind of stuff. Maybe he just needs a reminder, needs to know how useless this shit is."

"The next exchange isn't for weeks. Six will have taken us off this long before then."

Instructions for the next meet had been planted in the medium duffel coat. When Fu had pushed his handwritten sheets into the pocket he would, hopefully, have taken out their instructions.

Benny took a deep breath. "So, we talk to him before then."

Jiang nodded quickly, not liking the feel of a payday slipping through his fingers. "Fine, but how do we do that? You're saying we go back to Baoding, walk up to his house and bang on his door bold-as-you-please? What could go wrong?"

Benny shook his head. "Six has been watching him."

Jiang sat back a little. "In-country? How?"

Benny shook his head and pointed upwards.

Jiang leaned in again and said as quietly as he could: "They re-tasked a satellite! Fuck, they must be desperate."

"Not sure it was even our war-bird. My boss got cagey when I asked."

Jiang's eyes widened but Benny held out a hand, palm towards him before he could say anything else. If the Americans were involved it only added to their danger. The Goo, like the KGB before them, had infiltrated the CIA to buggery and back.

Jiang's eyes darted to the side and, just for an instant, Benny almost believed flight would beat fight.

But then Jiang's panicky eyes came back to him. "This is so fucked up!"

"Apparently our little friend goes for a run every evening. At least he wears his running gear and stomps off through a bamboo forest to the north of his house. Goes some way into this then heads east along a smaller track to a large apartment block complex. Stays long enough for, I'm guessing, one not very extended fuck with a mistress, then he's back home."

"Sweatiness explained. Does he go running at the same time every evening?"

"Don't know. Don't know how long Six have had him under observation. It might only have been a couple of days."

"So, when you said 'Every evening' it was, like, a complete over-statement."

They looked at each other for a very long time without speaking.

"I could do this myself," said Benny finally. "I will if I have to."

"With nobody watching your back? Really?"

"Are you offering?"

Jiang moved the tip of his forefinger through the moisture left on the rusty metal table by his chilled bottle of beer. "How long have we been doing this?"

"What's that got to do with anything?"

"Ten years, give or take. What do you know about me?"

Benny tried to smile. "Nothing good."

There was no amusement in Jiang's eyes. "Apart from your sort-of girlfriend, you have no real friends. That's sad. What's even sadder is that neither do I."

"That true for neither of us. We have plenty of friends. You certainly go on enough about the adventures of your mates."

"I overstated it. Shoot me! But come on—if we have to lie all the time to people about what we do, are they really our friends? The really important things—the pressures we face, the risks to our lives—we can't talk to anyone else about that. It's just the two of us."

Benny felt the breath catch in his throat. This had been a day of too many surprises.

Jiang raised a hand to catch the barman's attention. "Our food must be steamed to death by now," he said loudly. The barman gave a dismissive wave.

"The service is almost as bad as back in the UK." Jiang picked up his beer, about to take a swig.

Benny raised his own and lightly clinked it against Jiang's.

They drank in silence, waiting for their scalded dim sum.

10. Shanghai 1927

The Grandfather, Hu Bai, and the Jasmine Valley

The tiger heard him, as it always did. It grunted and snuffled in the humid, heavily perfumed night, sensing one more tormentor beyond its reach. He heard the pad of its paws as it paced the cramped little cage.

It was a frightening beast but he couldn't help feeling sorry for it. At times it was listless and surly, other times raging and roaring at its plight.

Bai knew only too well what it was to be trapped. But while the tiger risked only a lost meal or a poke with a stick if it caused trouble, Bai was risking everything.

He crouched, waiting behind a stand of bamboo by the old stables where he slept. There were lights far away at the gate, but otherwise only a cloud-dappled quarter moon provided uncertain illumination. The grounds were extensive and the guards strolled wearily along the path that wound its way all around the inside of the estate. One guard plodded so slowly he was often overtaken, so big gaps would form between the guards but not in an easily predictable way.

Waiting for his chance was nerve-wracking. When it came, he had to be quick, scurrying unseen across the path and then over an open stretch of lawn.

The guards wore black and only when they passed by the stand of bamboo could he see them and assess how quickly they were moving.

He'd seen cats waiting where the Bund was at its busiest, a moving mass of cars and carts and horses. Waiting for a gap to open so they could dash across to whatever midden was their hunting ground. They'd crouch, licking their lips, their patience wearing thin. Then they'd give up, would just dash, trusting to luck, dodging the hooves and wheels.

Most often they made it but sometimes their mangled bodies would be battered around the street until the sweepers arrived to scrape them up.

Was he any better than those cats? Sooner or later he always grew tired and just ran for it.

The guard shuffling by now was Tan, his withered leg giving him a marked limp. Hongqi, younger and fitter, would be next, the gap between them getting smaller.

Unless, of course, Honggi had stopped, as he did every other circuit, to light another cigarette and perhaps talk to the third guard who would sooner or later catch up with him.

As ever, Bai finally abandoned his hopeless calculations and went for it, scurrying across the path, keeping low. Under his bare feet the hard pebbles of the path gave way to the softness of grass. He dived down beside a bush which in daylight was a bright purple shrub.

He waited, his muscles hard with tension, but no shouts or gunshots disturbed the night. He heard the tiger give another, louder snuffle, then an angry snort.

More grass and a couple of little paths were now all that remained between him and the house, its dark shape hulking around windows reflecting the moonlight. It was designed to be no help to any assassin. Huang had had all the ivy and vines cut down so the brick walls were sheer. A veranda on one side, which would have made a good climbing point, had been torn down years before.

The one thing in his favour was that nobody patrolled the inner paths. He made his way quickly to the side of the house, keeping low so he was beneath the ground floor windows. He waited and listened but there were no sounds from within, the hard-driven house servants already deep in their slumbers

He hesitated for a second, the weight of his madness making him dizzy.

Then he was feeling his way along the side wall, his fingers brushing over the grittiness of the bricks. He thought he must have missed it but then his fingers brushed the rope and he forgot everything else. Before he knew it, he had shimmied his way up to the second storey and grasped the window sill, easing himself up and over.

Slowly, careful not to make a sound, he lowered first his hands then his feet to the wooden floor. The room was dark as tar. All he had to guide him was the fragrance. He crawled over the floor like an animal stalking its prey.

The smell was getting stronger and soon his forehead bumped gently against the softness of a mattress. The scent now filled his whole world and he crawled up onto the bed, centring himself on the silk-covered top.

Edging forward slowly with his head raised, the jasmine scent was overwhelming. He opened his mouth, lips and tongue ready. Strands of hair he knew to be black and thick brushed his lips and he pushed out his tongue, seeking the furrow, seeking her inner lips and the sweet, earthy taste of her. He heard her groan, gently, almost reluctantly but he could tell she had been waiting for him and was ready.

Pushing himself up and over, tugging at the waist cord of his trousers, he freed himself and entered her. Scrabbling fingers hastily pulled up the back of his shirt and sharp-pointed nails, hard with lacquer, scored furrows deep into his skin.

She started groaning too loudly and he covered her mouth with his palm. Now she was safely silenced, he could be more brutal. It was only fair. She was always brutal with him and already he felt the wetness of the blood on his back.

Far away he heard the tiger roar as they toiled to a terrible, shattering climax.

⊛

Only the sounds of their breathing disturbed the quiet of the house. Silent enough that Bai could ponder, undisturbed, the craziness that had drawn him here.

Jingfei infuriated him. Her pettiness, her appetite for gossip, the obsessive attention to her clothes and appearance. Her self-regard, the carelessness and guiltlessness she showed in deceiving Huang. She was absurd, a whore, a coquette.

With dismay, he found himself hardening again.

A month or more of these dangerous night-time expeditions, yet he had never seen her naked. Even a lit candle might bring a servant scurrying to attend to her mistress. Once, three weeks ago, she had opened the blinds. The full moon had been somewhere to the side but it had cast enough light to show her willowy outline: a memory he would take to his grave.

Not that he didn't know her body. His fingers and tongue had mounted long, delightful missions of discovery, his ears exquisitely attuned to the faintest murmur of rising desire.

She, in her turn, had been shameless in discovering, claiming, colonising his own willing body.

Huang, she had assured him, would never disturb them. He was usually out into the small hours with his endless informants. When not pretending to be a policeman, he governed a gang of several thousand whose business was always of the night. Even if he returned before the sun rose, he would not visit her until a few hours later. An old man, he needed the rising vigour that a good breakfast and the morning brought to achieve what he desired.

Bai could never imagine himself being old enough to delay lying with this alluring, infuriating creature.

He felt a lacquered fingernail trail down his breastbone. "Do you love me, Bai?" she asked for the thousandth time.

Love was such a weak word for what he felt. When he tried to think of a better one, the only word that came was tiger.

He kept silent like a masterful lover, pretending to be sure of himself, not deigning to indulge her nonsense.

Not that she would have listened to anything he said anyway for she had other things on her mind. "If he dies, I am done for," she said, "yet while he lives, I am in hell."

Bai allowed himself a smile in the darkness. She had everything she wanted, even a virile young lover to satisfy her in the dark of the night.

Perhaps a movement of his body had given him away for fingers searched for, and found, his earlobe and pinched it hard. "You do not care!" The whisper was fierce and all too audible.

His hand found her chin. "Hush, my love," he breathed. He went to brush her cheek and for the first time felt the wetness of tears. "Has something happened?"

She sighed. "Something is about to happen. When that bastard Fiori comes to the house it's with three bodyguards rather than one. And Huang has become secretive, he does not take me with him to his teashops like he did. Whatever is happening, you must tell me!"

"There is nothing," he lied. He could not trust her not to blurt something out to Huang. The old man would wonder who had told her and under what circumstances.

Irritated, she gave a snort but from her tiny nostrils it came out like the squeak of a mouse. He smiled in the darkness.

"What is to become of us?" she asked.

He needed to steer this talk elsewhere.

"Where are you from, Jingfei? You never speak of it."

She turned away. "There is nothing to speak of and there is little I remember."

"Why?"

She sighed again. "I was young, six years old when my father sold me. I do not even remember the name of my village but it was a very long way from here, far to the west. There was desert and houses of mud shaped like bee-hives."

She hesitated but then something made her continue. "I left my village with nothing but the clothes on my back. They would not even let me take little..." She stopped and he realised she was struggling not to cry.

"Little who?"

He felt her shake her head. "Nothing, just a toy, a little panda. The man who bought me led me for weeks in the direction of the rising sun and into a world larger than anything I could have imagined. The land became greener and full of people. I remember seeing a town for the first time and felt like I was drowning in people.

"The woman I was sold to there said I talked like someone from Mongolia, but she was nasty and cruel and she might have been lying. She thought she was a queen because her husband was a tax collector in Henan Province."

This was so far from her usual empty twittering that Bai was not sure what to say. "The work, what did she make you do?"

"I was just a slave, cleaning, carrying and cooking. Then, when my breasts grew and her husband began to show an interest, she sold me to a whore hunter who carried me away even further east. I was a sing-sing girl in a brothel, singing opera and reciting poems while filthy old men pawed at me. One day Huang came and bought me and I wound up here."

The dead, matter-of-fact way she said this plucked at his heart. He began to wonder if her foolishness, her superficiality, was a comfort, somewhere to hide.

She turned back to him. "Let's not talk of this again. What do you want to do with your life, Bai? Huang will not live forever. Your next master may be even less kind."

When he did not answer he felt her lips brush his cheek. "We are both slaves, my love. Our bodies and lives belong to others."

And perhaps that is what made these stolen moments of happiness so sweet. Just for the night they owned nobody but themselves.

<hr />

Bai sat on the stairs, the brim of his Fedora shading his eyes from the late afternoon sun blazing down on the Bund. The offices of the Europeans were closing for the day and people were hurrying home. Today's teahouse was smaller and dirtier, as befitted the informers Huang was meeting. Sometimes the owners of grander houses resented closing their doors to the rest of their clientele, despite Huang's generous gifts. That had not been the case today.

Bai rarely had problems turning people away. This was just one of the reasons he dressed like a gangster. He usually didn't have to say anything.

So, he was surprised when the old man coming up the steps did not turn away as Bai waved a dismissive hand. It made Bai look at his face more closely.

The big man was staring at him unblinkingly from under heavy brows, a look of frank curiosity and surprise. There was something else in that gaze that Bai found unnerving. The man was Han Chinese, clearly, but his skin was paler, as though it had hardly ever seen the sun. He was wearing a suit, darker, less flamboyant than the present style in Shanghai. Even so, it looked thick-cut and expensive and out of keeping with the man's hands. Hanging down empty by his sides, they were coarse and calloused by what must have been years of hard labour.

"Tea-room closed," Bai said. "Find another!"

The old man shook his head of thick white hair. "I do not seek a tea-room." He coughed wetly and hurriedly brought a handkerchief to his lips.

Bai waited as they regarded at each other in silence. What kind of game was this?

The stranger's eyes never left his face. Bai narrowed his own, a look more than enough to send most people scurrying away.

Instead, the old man just smiled and nodded his head, almost as if he approved.

Behind him he heard the door open and he turned, expecting to see a hurrying informer but instead saw Huang waddling heavily down the steps.

The old man was suddenly a potential threat. Even as Bai stood, he was reaching under the slit in his long tunic to grasp the gun's handle. He turned back quickly but the old man had vanished into the bustling crowd.

"What's got into you?" asked Huang as he stumped by. "There'll be no trouble yet. The mouth of Hell does not open until tomorrow."

Moonlight still rippled on the black waters of the Yangtze but the first filmy haze of light was appearing to the east over the Yellow Sea. It felt cool, almost cold and it made Bai shiver.

Or perhaps it was something else. Evil was in the air and he knew he was part of it.

There were around forty of them. Most were Kuomintang soldiers dressed as dock workers in tunics and baggy trousers, a disguise rendered useless by the heavy swords hanging by their sides. They looked dangerous but absurd.

When they had assembled earlier among wavering oil lights in an old warehouse, he had seen their intense, hate-filled eyes. It was a hatred he could only dimly comprehend. It made him feel like a weightless cork being carried away on a tide of blood.

Now they slunk through the bales and boxes, their feet crushing over-ripe and abandoned fruit, their eyes busy trying to penetrate the shadows. Before them hulked another warehouse, a lean-to hut propped along its entire length.

Kang, the KMT commander, motioned for them to move into the cover of a stack of wooden planks. He was a burly man with a soldier's swagger and heavy fists he had already used to chastise several of his soldiers. KMT discipline was even fiercer than in the gangs.

"Corporal Gan, take your squad to the far end and wait. Catch them when they come running out. Take four soldiers and three of the civilians with you!" *Civilians* dripped from Kang's tongue with disdain.

Gan shook the shoulders of the chosen men and, bent low, they made their way between the mounds of waiting cargo.

Kang glared at all those who remained. "The rest of you will breach the near door with me. If any of the communists move then cut them down. You Green Gang people—just try not to get in the way!"

Bai snorted. There were other, more fragrant, places he would rather be than providing back-up for a bunch of idiot soldiers. However, Huang's and Fiori's orders had been clear. Across Shanghai thousands of soldiers and Green Gang members had been split into hundreds of cadres, and all sent out on this April night with but one intention in mind.

Kang must have heard Bai's expression of disgust but he ignored it. He seemed as uneasy with this forced relationship as Bai. Kang eased his long straight sword from its scabbard, moonlight winking on the steel as he turned it gently, like a man turning the arm of a lover.

He signalled and they were all moving again. With his tall frame, Bai found it difficult to crouch as low as the others and sometimes he had to lay one hand down for support on the reeking dock.

Ahead, a red coal suddenly flared. The men froze. Kang grabbed the soldier nearest him and whispered in his ear. The man nodded then scurried back down their line, a heavy club in his hand, and disappeared into the shadows.

Bai risked lifting his head clear of a bale. The sentry took another draw on his cigarette and the coal flared again. He shuffled idly from one foot to the other. Something the length of a forearm hung from a lanyard tied around his neck, swinging with his movements. Though the blade was dirtier than Kang's spotless weapon, its metal still glinted. Bai guessed it was a cane-cutter's dao. He knew that if properly sharpened, it could sever a man's arm as easily as a stand of cane.

Bai took the Webley out of its holster and gently thumbed back the hammer.

The sentry continued to puff contentedly at his cigarette and Bai's knees began to ache in this crouched position. Then a shadow rose up behind the sentry and Bai saw the club swing through a long arc. It hit the man's head with a loud, sickening thud. The man disappeared straight down, like a nail hammered into wood.

Kang gave a big overhand wave and the cadre swept over and around the cargo like a rising tide.

The soldiers were keen, leaving the gangsters trailing in their wake. Bai saw Kang's thick shoulder slam into the door of the lean-to, its thin wood splintering on impact. Kang's momentum sent him flying into the darkness within.

Bai nearly laughed when he quickly scrabbled back out again. Fighting in a darkened hut where you did not know the layout was a path that rarely led to glory.

Typical landowner's son, he thought. Joins the KMT and automatically gets a commission but doesn't have a fucking clue.

Shouts were coming from the other end of the lean-to. The communists trying to exit there were being met by Gan's squad.

At Bai's end of the hut a face appeared out of the gloom. "What do you want, you whores?" it screamed.

"Everyone out!" roared Kang. "By order of the government."

"Government! You shits couldn't govern a piss-hole."

"Come out now and leave your weapons behind."

"Fuck off, soldier-boy!"

"Fetch oil lamps!" Kang shouted to a group of four soldiers, who scattered away. Turning back to the communist he roared, "We'll burn you bastards out."

The communist was contemptuous. "This place is a tinderbox, you arsehole. Everything here burns. Wood, cloth, oil. Your rich daddies aren't going to like you burning down their precious warehouses."

Kang didn't seem to have an answer to this. He gritted his teeth and began to pace back and forth while his men shuffled uneasily. Bai lit a cigarette and leaned on a packing case, the gun by his hand. He had little time for either side and wished they'd all die.

Gan came back to Kang for further instructions, leaving his squad to guard the door at the other end of the lean-to. Bai was close enough to hear their whispered conversation, or at least Kang's end of it. The man's voice was loud, no doubt from a lifetime of shouting at servants.

"The little bastards are right," he was saying, "but I have a better idea. When the lamps come, we split them. Put them near the doors. The wood of the walls looks thin, made of scraps from packing cases. We'll start firing through them. When the communists come rushing out to attack us the lights will make them better targets."

Bai had smoked a couple of cigarettes by the time the men returned with lamps purloined from the nearest hutong. Under Kang's instructions the soldiers used the cover of the cargo to get as close as they could, then dashed out quickly to place the lamps in an arc round the entrance. Though the head at the door shouted insults, to Bai's relief no shots rang out as the soldiers laid the lamps down. The dockers had no guns!

Gan headed back to his squad while Kang went from man to man of his own. "Guns ready," he ordered. Only a few of the soldiers had revolvers, the rests just had their swords. Kang came to Bai. "That includes you. Any of your men got guns?"

Bai shook his head. Huang had demanded them but Fiori had demurred. Once guns had been given, he must have known the gangsters would keep them. One day they might become as much of a menace to the Europeans as the communists.

Bai placed his box of shells on the packing crate, lifting off the top to reveal brass casings glinting like gold in the oil flame.

Kang did a quick tour of his troops then stood up ram-rod straight. "Aim!" he shouted, loud enough for the face at the hut door to hear. It retreated quickly into the gloom.

"Fire!"

The Webley kicked up hard in Bai's hands, the heavy round splintering an entire wall panel into many pieces. He'd aimed high, no matter what Kang had ordered.

Gunfire crashed around him as he steadied his pistol for another high shot. He had just pulled back the hammer when two men burst from the door, screaming their stupid heads off and with their daos held high. One of them made a beeline for Bai, as though joined to him by an elastic cord.

The high-pitched screams and the oncoming threat made Bai's knees suddenly feel watery and weak. The man was fast and was almost upon him before Bai's suddenly nerveless fingers managed to pull the trigger.

The man's chest hollowed out like he had been punched but his momentum brought him on. Something caught his legs, his torso arcing forward and his head smacking down hard on the packing crate.

The arm holding the dao came cartwheeling over, missing Bai's arm by a finger's breadth and slicing into the wood.

Looking down he saw a large red conical hole staring back up at him, like a huge eye socket in the man's back. Shattered rib bones poked up haphazardly around it like peasant's teeth.

Bai had done bad things before but had never killed. He was awed by the power of the heavy bullet at such close range. The man's heart must have been reduced to mince in an instant. He wasn't even groaning or twitching, his spirit gone as quickly as a candle flame snuffed out by two wet fingers.

Dimly, he realised the shooting had stopped and had been replaced by frightened shouts. Looking up he saw empty hands waving at the door. "Stop shooting, we surrender."

Another body lay by the oil lamps. Not so fast as the other communist, he'd been brought down by several bullets and it looked like red roses were strewn across the back of his grubby grey tunic. Even so, he was still groaning as a wide pool of red was spreading out rapidly from under his body.

Kang was standing, legs apart and hands behind his back, master of all he surveyed. "Come out of the hut!" he screeched. "Slowly now, hands held high above your heads. Leave all your weapons behind!"

The communists began to appear from both ends of the lean-to. There were around twenty of them, in the grubby tunics they worked and slept in. They were all thin. There was plenty of food to steal in the docks but their gang-masters worked them hard. They looked frightened but aggrieved.

The soldiers roughly marshalled them into one spot.

"Bind them!" roared Kang.

Bai guessed the man was having the best day of his life.

The dock yielded plenty of rope. Like the oil lamps, Kang seemed not to have anticipated needing it. Bai and some of the soldiers kept their guns trained on the dockers while the others bound their arms behind their backs at the elbows. The older, less limber dockers found this especially painful.

When the last of the men had been tied, Bai placed his thumb firmly on the hammer then pulled the trigger. He gently lowered the hammer, then holstered the gun and tucked away the box of shells in his pocket.

He walked around the packing case, wondering what Kang would do next. If all the operations over the city had been as a successful there would be thousands of prisoners. Shanghai jails were big but, more significantly, always full.

"On your knees!" roared Kang. Bai did not like the dangerous edge of excitement in the man's voice.

Dockers who hesitated had their legs kicked from under them, soldiers grabbing them and pulling them to their knees before forcing their foreheads down flat against the ground.

Kang strutted up and down, his sword swinging back and forth. He stopped before Gan who, with another soldier, was bearing down on the upper arms of one long-haired docker, pressing his face hard down. The man suddenly jerked back, pulling his mouth clear of the dust. "Whore bastards!" he shouted through gritted teeth.

Kang and Gan shared a glance. Gan leaned back and his soldier quickly did the same. Kang put both hands on the handle of his sword. Stepping quickly forward, his sword came round in a huge arc. The sharp metal made hardly a sound as it scythed through skin and bone before crashing and sparking on the concrete.

Detached from the body, the head flipped over so the eyes were staring at its own back.

Bai had never seen anything so grotesque.

Kang was examining his sword anxiously and gently probing the edge with his finger to feel for damage. Meanwhile, the other dockers had seen what had happened and were trying to struggle to their feet. Fists, feet and clubs rained down on them. The soldiers kept striking until the men lay still. Some were moaning, some were crying.

Kang pointed to one of them then flicked his finger upwards. The two soldiers holding him pulled him to his feet, but still keeping him bent forwards. Bai had never seen a Han's eyes open so wide. His jaw was hanging right down as though preparing to swallow the death so rapidly approaching. He twisted back and forth but the soldiers held firm.

There was no danger now of Kang's sword striking the concrete but the victim's neck was more mobile and a challenging target. Kang was fast but the man was faster, turning his head deep into his shoulder. The sword missed his skull but neatly lopped of an ear.

Kang roared at his men. A soldier stepped forward and smashed a pistol butt against the back of the man's head. Stunned, his head lolled forward, exposing a neck that Kang's evilly sharp sword cut through cleanly. The head dropped and bounced and rolled.

The soldiers cheered; the captives began to struggle again but were swiftly clubbed into submission.

Kang pointed at the next victim. This time a soldier had the initiative to hit him with the pistol before the man was pulled to his feet.

Over-confident, Kang was careless. Rather than severing the neck, the sword bit deep into the skull just behind the ear and stuck fast. The soldiers had to struggle mightily with the spasming man before Kang managed to wrestle his sword out of the bone.

Livid with anger, he jabbed the point clean through the man's eye and deep into his brain.

The horrific pantomime continued. As Kang got wearier and his aim got worse, it now took several blows to detach each head. Once, he missed altogether. Rather than take a moment to steady himself, he swung again, striking the man on the upper arm and severing two fingers of the soldier who was restraining him.

Angrily, Kang pulled his pistol and fired point blank into the docker's head, the bullet blasting clean through and ricocheting dangerously off the concrete.

Gan meanwhile had been collecting the heads and using them to build a small pyramid just within the arc of the oil lamps. The man who had been shot presented a problem. The bullet had made a small entry hole in one side of the head but had blown out the entire opposite side, taking almost all the brain with it. Half a skull would not make a good brick in this pyramid. Not only that but the head was still securely attached.

Gan peered around in a puzzled way and his gaze caught Bai's. Bai realised that neither was in a world they understood.

Finally, Gan sighed and cast his eye down at the dead man, then shrugged and waved a hand dismissively. The pyramid would never be complete.

Bai lit a cigarette with trembling hands. Huang's gangsters hadn't taken any part in the executions. None would meet his eye.

He began to realise the whole exercise had been about incrimination. Fiori and the KMT had drawn the Green Gang into this horror. After such atrocities the communists would never forgive them. The Green Gang had no choice but to ensure the KMT won.

Shifting loyalties had finally been set in stone.

"Evil work," said a voice from the shadows.

Bai had thought he'd been alone. It had been a long walk back from the docks to Huang's compound but he had waved away the rickshaw drivers plying their trade on the bridge across to the French Concession. Even at this early hour, trade was brisk, bringing wealthy Europeans and Chinese back from the dens and the brothels.

The oil lights on the ends of the high, curving handles of the passing rickshaws provided weak and occasional illumination. Electric street lighting had come to the Concession many years before but the bulbs were easily shattered by drunkards throwing stones. In these long, dark sections between high glass-topped walls, the footing was uncertain.

He was near to Huang's mansion and whoever had spoken must have been waiting for him. Bai slipped his gun from its holster, keeping his movements as unobtrusive as possible.

"I mean you no harm," the stranger said quickly and Bai saw two lighter shadows move apart at eye level. Bai guessed more than saw that the man was showing him two empty palms.

The voice was deep and its accent was not quite right, a Shanghai accent but modulated by another accent he could not place. That told him it was the old man from yesterday at the teahouse.

Bai thumbed the hammer back on the Webley, making no attempt to soften the sound.

"I am your friend," the man said. Despite the click of the hammer, a chilling sound to anyone not holding the gun, Bai could hear no anxiety in the man's voice.

That was even more worrying.

"You're not my friend. Let's move to where a street light still shines. I want to see your face. Who are you anyway?"

The man laughed. "A ghost."

The park lay a little way back from the street. During the day, grey-liveried Chinese nannies would push perambulators larger than themselves, armed bodyguards following discreetly behind. Benches around the park were where they would sit. They'd gossip about their masters and mistresses amongst the palms and the ferns and the purple flowers of a plant he'd heard Fiori call bougainvillea. The French had brought it with them to China where it had flourished. The park was a place of intense colour but now it was all washed away in the yellow street-light.

The bench was well lit and reassuringly long. Too long for the man to lunge at him before Bai's first bullet punched a big hole through his chest.

Despite this threat of instant death, the man sat easily, his hands open on his lap. He made no sudden moves except to swat at the moths and insects that buzzed around their ears and neck.

"What is your name, ghost?"

The man tried to smile but the sides of his mouth hardly moved, as though he were terribly weary. He gave another wet cough. Bai could make out deep creases on his forehead and saw how the skin hung low on the jaw, yet around the eyes it was swollen.

"One favour, young Bai?"

"Don't call me that! I don't know you and you have no right to use my given name."

"Ah. We'll come to that. But please, take your finger off the trigger. It would be unfortunate if what I had to say caused you too much of a surprise. The gun is cocked and I'm an old man and not as fast as I once was."

Bai eased his finger off the trigger but let it rest ready on the trigger guard.

The old man smiled again, even more grimly than before. "My name is Hu Jun."

141

Anger flared and Bai's finger twitched on the trigger guard. The old man had been right.

"Dong Lei lied," said the man. "It was some other unfortunate the mob hacked to death on the docks. I escaped to London and have lived there ever since. He covered for me, protected me. Then he took my wife as his own."

This was said so bitterly it sounded genuine.

The man stared him straight in the face. "He also took my son."

Bai looked more carefully. At the high cheekbones, at a jaw less rounded than most Han, at ear lobes a shade less generous. The heavy forehead and deep-set eyes were not his but suddenly he saw the other resemblances. He couldn't help blinking in surprise.

Hu Jun caught this and sat back, satisfied.

"Nonsense!" said Bai as peremptorily as he could. "What do you really want?"

"It is simple. I want to give my son a present. Let me reach into my jacket pocket. I will do it slowly."

Bai's jaw clenched so hard he could feel the skin move over his own high cheekbones. Ostentatiously, he moved his finger back onto the trigger.

The ghost was as good as his word. A hand with only two extended fingers dipped into a side pocket and emerged with a bundle of paper. This he deposited on the seat between them.

Reaching out, Bai raised the first piece of paper so he could see underneath.

Monochrome white, and with writing on only one side. Bai had seen these before when Huang had done business in the combined British and American Concession, though European currency was also used there. If this really was a British five-pound note then…

"One thousand pounds," said Hu Jun. "A fortune in Shanghai. Take your woman and run like the wind." He laughed. "There are steamers now, not like in my day. Straight through the Suez Canal. You could travel in the sort of luxury only Huang and his mistress are familiar with. She will not object."

Bai clenched his jaw again. Such knowledge was heavy with danger.

The man shrugged. "I've seen you with her. You are too obvious. Sooner or later even your foolish boss will notice. Get her out now or you will both die by Huang's hand."

"Where did you get this money?"

The ghost shrugged. "Opium, to begin with. Perfectly legal until 1920 and then suddenly it wasn't. Luckily I sold everything before it became very illegal and instead bought property along the Thames..." He hesitated. "That is a great river, like the Yangtze, but in Britain."

"So I've heard."

"I became wealthy. Once I heard your mother had married Dong Lei, I ceased feeling guilty for deserting her. That black shadow had become such a part of me I wasn't aware of it until it was suddenly gone."

Bai's finger went back to the trigger guard. "Why did you come back?"

Eyes as fathomless as the Yellow Sea met his. "You are dying," Bai found himself saying.

"The Middle Kingdom is in our blood, as you will find when you leave it. I never smoked my own opium before but now... the pain. Dreams come and at their heart lies this great beast." He waved a hand to take in Shanghai and the lands beyond. "One day all the world will come begging to its door."

He laughed again. "Or maybe just in my opium dreams!"

The way he said it, it was if something weighty had settled within him.

"You're staying? If Fiori finds you're alive and within his grasp then he will kill you and me and Dong. Surely you must return to England?"

Hu Jun shook his head sadly. "At the bottom of the sheaf of bills is a letter. It has the address of my lawyer back in London upon it. Take your woman and go there. Tonight, if you can. Dong and I... we'll take our chances."

Perhaps only a man who had left China could say such a thing so lightly. To Bai it was inconceivable. Britain and all the other countries were merely the Earth. Their only connection with heaven was through China—Chung Kuo, the Middle Kingdom. China was already half way to heaven. Why descend from halfway up the mountain?

"Are you seeking revenge on Dong Lei for what he did?"

"For saving the lives of my wife and child? No, but my feelings towards him are... complicated, for what I lost he gained. Bitterness and gratitude war within me." The ghost smiled sadly.

They looked at each other in silence for a very long time.

Then, Bai carefully uncocked the hammer and put the pistol away.

11. Baoding, China

The Son, Benny Hu, and the Guardian Angels

Benny's running shoes slapped down too loudly on the hard-packed earth. Sometimes, the winding path straightened for longer stretches through the bamboo and Benny would catch a glimpse of Fu. The man wasn't a natural runner so Benny kept having to slow down until he was safely out of sight again.

Now Benny stopped completely and made as if to adjust his backpack so he could glance over his shoulder. The path behind was still clear

It was early evening and elsewhere workers were already home or hurrying back for the evening feast. All around him unfamiliar birds cheeped from the bamboo, getting ready for dusk and the night.

No signs of drones or circling planes, though the bamboo covered most of the sky. Jiang should be waiting, further into the forest. He'd be scanning the heavens too, ready to text if he saw anything. Between them they were covering several hundred metres behind and ahead of Fu.

Fu was so out of shape Benny sometimes had to drop back almost to walking pace. Surely the man's wife must be getting suspicious by now? All these supposed runs yet the guy still looked like a sack of shit.

Some of the bamboo trunks were thick as his wrist and taller than a double-decker bus. Far above, the leaves swayed as the wind played over the tops. It was like being at the bottom of a green ocean, looking up at the wave-dappled surface.

The snail's pace run seemed to have been going on forever. The man was in no real hurry and Benny began to suspect he was tiring of his mistress. Nevertheless, he should soon be getting to where Jiang was waiting, off the main trail on the little path that would take Fu to the apartment complex of his paramour.

Benny glanced back once more and was startled by something darting across the sky, but it was only the flickering of a little bird.

Just for a second, he remembered other spies, other times. Aftermath pictures, some so old they were in black and white, of what had happened when the Guoanbu pounced. Bloodied corpses, fingers and noses, genitals and breasts missing, the proud calling cards of an implacable, conscienceless enemy.

He took a deep breath. How had he got used to taking such ridiculous risks?

The path was now following the last slow sinuous curve before interception. As he got to the end of the curve, he looked back one last time.

Still nothing.

Increasing his pace, he felt the blood surging through his body. Jiang should already have ambushed Fu just fifty metres ahead.

Benny cut right on a diagonal into the bamboo. As the path disappeared behind him, he heard raised voices ahead. He slowed, then tiptoed forward, peering around each trunk until he could make out the two figures in the shadowy world.

Jiang was looking fierce, pointing with his finger at Fu's chest. Fu was cowering before the younger, fitter, harder man. Jiang was speaking quickly and Benny could only catch the odd phrase... lives at risk... useless pile of shit...

Benny, creeping forward, kept searching around for movement, for anything that looked out of place in the jade gloom.

"I was there filming you, at the teahouse back in Taiwan. Spilling your guts to a foreign spy. We have you cold and yet now you dare to fuck with us!" There was a loud crack as Jiang slapped Fu hard.

Fu staggered back, tripped and fell. Jiang stepped quickly forward, fist cocked but already Fu was drawing himself in like a foetus.

Benny knew just what Jiang would be feeling. They were both hunters, both warriors in their way. Shows of weakness only angered them, made them do things they shouldn't.

As fast as he could, Benny came out of cover and sprinted towards them before Jiang could do any real damage.

Jiang leaned down to grab Fu by his hair but the man broke away, hands and feet pedalling backwards under him. He kept looking up at Jiang, terror in his eyes.

Jiang's body tensed like he was going to attack. A twig broke under Benny's feet and Jiang spun round, a moment of alarm giving way to relief when he recognised him.

Benny almost missed it in the shadows. Something, perhaps that bird again, dropped down towards Jiang's head.

Benny pushed forward hard, diving the last few steps, his shoulder catching Jiang in the midriff.

Crack.

It was like someone with warm breath had coughed across his neck, then he was tumbling head over heels, his arms and legs tangling up with Jiang's.

Extricating himself, he staggered to his feet, scanning. Something skittered around amongst the dried leaves from last autumn. Whatever the drone had fired had unbalanced it. He leapt, crushing it underfoot, its plastic carapace and little rotors crunching into fragments.

"Jesus fucking Christ! Above you!" Benny heard something like awe in Jiang's voice.

Without thinking, without looking, Benny swept his arms above his head. Something slashed at his wrist but by the time he looked up it was gone.

The sound of something big crashing through foliage made him spin look around but already Fu was out of sight, running for his life into the bamboo.

"We need to get the fuck out of here!" yelled Jiang.

"Wait, we…" Benny began but Jiang was already running into the bamboo forest, away from the track.

"Stupid fucking…" Benny muttered as he scanned the little glade, unhitching his backpack. If the other drone had moved slowly, he might never have seen it. Instead, it darted at him. He brought the backpack swinging round, just catching it, sending it somersaulting into a bamboo trunk. It fluttered to the ground like a stunned bird.

Benny stomped on it, again and again, triumphant.

"I got it!" he yelled.

But there was no response. "Jiang!" he shouted as loudly as he could.

Stupid asshole! he thought. Apart from this little spur to the mistress's apartment complex, the path was a circuit. Outside it was bamboo forest, some of it so dense you might easily get lost.

Not a good idea if the Goo were after you.

Benny started running in the direction Jiang had taken. Most of the bamboo was mature with thick trunks but ahead he saw what appeared to be a thick curtain of the younger stuff. He saw the broken stalks where Jiang had crashed through.

Something made him slow down and that saved him. He had just enough time to grab the slender bamboo when his leading foot came down on nothing but space.

He fell, but for a second the bamboo held, and he smacked back against the side of the ravine.

Then the bamboo came away he was falling again.

Too late he saw Jiang's outstretched arm right below him. He came down on it hard and heard the bone snap like a twig.

The impact compressed him like a concertina, making him knee himself in the jaw, driving the breath from his lungs.

Stunned, he toppled over.

For a second, he lay looking up at the narrow tree covered ravine and the hole through which he and Jiang had fallen. It took a few seconds before he could manage: "Sorry, mate!"

But Jiang said nothing and didn't move.

This time it was fear that drove away Benny's breath as he slowly pushed himself upright and turned to look at him.

The drop couldn't have been more than five or six metres but Jiang had landed head first on the hard ground. His head was at sickening angle to his body. Benny could see one wide-open eye. He put a trembling finger to the side of Jiang's neck but already knew what he would find.

There was only one stone-cold certainty in Benny's future. He had to run, had to escape the hell that was sure to descend.

Yet still he hesitated.

What would happen to Jiang's body? Dumped in an unmarked grave most likely, or incinerated in a furnace, his ashes discarded.

Would Jiang have cared either way? Was he religious? Did he have a close girlfriend who would miss him?

Jiang had been right. How little he'd known him, this man who was the closest thing to a real friend that he had.

There was nothing he could do for him. Gently he touched that absurd quiff, flattened now by the hard ground.

Already he could feel the first tendrils of guilt easing their way around his heart.

No time for that. Not yet.

He stood up and looked around. A little further down the ravine the land dipped. It was a bit of a struggle but he managed scramble out. Taking his bearing from the still visible hole in the bamboo, he set off in a direction to bring him back onto the path. Fu lived in the nearest thing Chinese cities had to a suburb. Benny and Jiang had carefully studied the maps, so he knew that beyond the bamboo forest was farmland growing sorghum and millet. The fields were threaded with small tree-shaded roads.

The plan had been to simply follow the circuit back onto town if the meeting with Fu had gone to plan. If it hadn't, their back-up was to make for the northern extremity of the circuit and cut through the last fifty metres of forest and onto those farm roads.

So that's exactly what he did, finally breaking out of the forest and onto a rutted dirt track.

He squatted down in the shade of the forest's edge and allowed himself a moment for thought. The drones, tasked to follow Fu like guardian angels, couldn't have been programmed to kill just anyone who got close to the man. Dead Chinese citizens every time Fu went for a jog was too high a price even for the Goo.

No, they must have been loaded up with pictures from the clothes store security cameras. Somehow the Chinese had become suspicious and set up the drones to kill anyone who looked like them if they tried to make contact.

If the Chinese had been really suspicious, they'd never have let Fu out in the first place. Unless they'd loaded this bamboo forest with operatives, in which case Benny would already be in handcuffs.

There may not be a surveillance squad waiting in ambush, but the drone would have squirted out its alarm once it got a match with Jiang. Somewhere in the city a Guoanbu crash team would be scrambling.

He had to get out of the vicinity as fast as he could. However, the first thing to do was take off his make-up, turn his face into something the drones and AI wouldn't recognise.

He pulled off his running shirt, now sorry he hadn't broken much of a sweat. He scrubbed away at his face, spitting on the cloth to dampen it. From his backpack he took out tee-shirt and trousers and quickly put them on. He buried all his running gear under earth and leaves.

Then, hands in pockets, out on a casual stroll, he followed the dirt road, taking the first fork north. Meanwhile his mind was racing, trying to work out what to do.

Nothing big like a car or bus would be coming down this dirt track any time soon. Could he use back roads and tracks like this to walk all the way back to Beijing?

Someone coughed and Benny almost soiled himself. The sound had come from a field to his right. Benny crept over to the untended bushes that divided up the land. Parting the leaves, he saw an old farmer barely five metres away. He was stooping, staring myopically at the feathery end of a sorghum stem and fingering it absentmindedly.

Then, something of far greater interest caught Benny's eye.

He moved along the bushes to a small gap to get a better look. There, resting on its side was a bicycle that had been old when Benny was still in nappies.

He stepped through the gap and cleared his throat. The old guy turned round, mouth open in surprise. The city was barely a kilometre away but the Chinese weren't renowned for taking walks in the country. Strangers here would be rare.

"Hello, old father," said Benny affably, giving him a friendly wave.

As the old guy had turned towards him, Benny realised the man's stoop was permanent. Years of sun and a hard life had etched lines deep into his face. Quiet country life must also have deprived him of his tongue for he didn't answer and just continued to gape.

"Harvest time?" prompted Benny.

The man looked stupidly back at the sorghum. Benny noticed that years of perspiration had produced dark patches on his straw coolie hat that rose almost up to the pointed top.

The man turned back. "No," he said.

The seconds stretched, the full range of conversational possibilities apparently exhausted.

"Nice bicycle!" and Benny pointed at the black rusty old wreck.

"Really?" said the old man, the first signs of intelligence returning to his eyes.

"I'd like to buy it."

And now the eyes narrowed; when it came to haggling the man was on firmer ground.

"How much would you take for it?"

"It was my father's," said the old man, though that would have made it a penny-farthing rather than a modern bike. "I could not part with it."

Benny reached into his pocket and pulled out a roll of cash. He kept aside a few thousand yuan and offered the rest, an astronomical sum for such a pile of shit.

The old man's eyes widened but then the look of calculation crept back.

"No!" said Benny firmly. "That's it."

The old man hesitated but then shrugged and took the money.

"One other thing," said Benny.

The bicycle clacked and rattled like an old hand-loom, each rut driving the barely covered springs of the seat up into Benny's crotch. The reek of ancient sweat ingrained in the old man's coolie hat was almost intolerable.

Benny could only imagine what he looked like. He hoped with all his heart that, somewhere, Jiang was laughing.

12. Shanghai 1927

The Grandfather, Hu Bai, and the Tiger's Bloody Stripes

Even in a city as sprawling as Shanghai, night brought the sounds and scents of the jungle. All around Huang's estate, colonial villas nestled amongst small forests bearing mango, peach and bananas. Cypresses and happy trees, dove trees, hibiscus and violets grew among the numberless flowering plants the Europeans had brought from around the world to be nurtured by the rich soil. These, and the less pleasant but also jungle-like smells from the hutongs, all wafted through the bedroom window, caught on the breeze from the Yellow Sea.

With these heavy, sweet and rotten odours came noise, the beating of a million tiny wings, the sounds of countless leaves being gnawed. Some insects made ceaseless clicking sounds like a child working a light switch.

All this was interspersed with the death cries of smaller animals caught by rats and cats, and the squeaks of bats so high-pitched they walked a tightrope between reality and imagination.

Bai and Jingfei lay in each other's arms, the fine cotton sheets tangled and sticking like a new skin to bodies wetted by passion.

"Do you love me, Bai?" A hard nail ran across his ribs.

So used to this question that he had come to ignore it, he looked out at a three-quarters moon and tried to imagine a faraway land.

"Jingfei..." he began, but hesitated. So much hung on what he said next, danger and promise in a brief, giddy equilibrium.

"What, my dearest?" Used to making love in the deepest dark, tonight the moon framed in the window allowed him to make out eyelids heavy with sleep. He reached out and cradled her cheek in his hand.

"There is..." But again the words dried in his mouth. He was trying to grasp an idea that was as awkward and sharp as a curled-up hedgehog.

"My father is alive," he blurted, immediately cursing himself for his weakness.

"Alive?" Half asleep, her surprise was muted.

"He came back and I saw him. He is rich, he gave me money." Her eyes were wider now.

He told her the story, put his life and his father's and Dong's in her faithless hands. She kept silent. In the moonlight, he found it difficult to read her expression.

She lifted herself up on one elbow and looked down at his pillowed head. "He wants you to go to England?"

"With you, yes."

"Me?" In her surprise she sounded like a child.

"Yes. We would live in London. Not as well as this..." and he indicated Huang's palace, "... but we would live free. I would not have to do Huang's evil work and you would never again have to share his bed."

Her eyes narrowed. "How would we—?"

"Escape?" he interrupted eagerly. "Steamship. I'll get tickets for one that departs early one morning. We could slip away from Shanghai before Huang even wakes up and realises you are gone."

"How would we get out of this house in the early morning?"

"The guards walk around the outside but don't pass by the gatehouse. I will... take care of the gatekeeper. We can slip out through the gate, find a rickshaw..."

"That early?"

"If need be, I will steal a rickshaw and hide it nearby then pull you to the docks myself."

He couldn't be sure but was she smiling? Did she think this was a game of make-believe?

"But how would we get out of this house without waking the servants?"

"The same way I get in. I will tie knots in the rope. You will be able to climb down."

Now her smile was clear. "And my luggage?"

He groped for her hands. "No luggage, you take only the clothes you are wearing."

Her head reared back as though she'd suddenly found herself sharing a bed with a snake. She pulled her hands from his and slapped his chest before turning away from him.

"Idiot!"

"What do you mean?"

"Leave all my clothes and jewellery behind? Are you crazy?"

He grasped her chin again and pulled her head around so their eyes were inches apart. "This is our chance to escape."

"Not without my things."

"I'll buy you more."

"Not like these, not unless your father is as rich as Huang."

He struggled to marshal his tumbling thoughts. "How long do you think this will last? How long before Huang tires of you?"

"I have my ways to keep him interested. You of all people know that."

It couldn't have hurt more if she'd scraped her nails across his face.

"You really are a whore," he said before he could stop himself.

A hand darted out, clutching the hair at the back of his head, pulling it back. "You bastard. I've had nothing all my life, nothing I could call my own until now. If I have nothing then I'll be nothing again, to be bought and sold like an animal."

"You won't have nothing. You'll have me!"

She tugged his hair harder. "Just moments ago, you said Huang would tire of me. What about you, Bai?"

He grasped her hand and pulled it away and winced as it took a bunch of hairs with it. "I will never tire of you because I love you, you silly bitch!"

She opened her mouth wide, to say what he would never know, for he quickly slapped a palm over it. Things were already far too loud.

Perhaps she realised this too, for she froze. Both listened through the insect noises for the creak of foot on wood.

But no sound came. He took his hand from her face.

They lay regarding each other in silence as the moon drifted out of the window's frame and a deeper darkness fell.

How could he be surprised when they came for him? Since Hu Jun had slipped back into his life, he'd been expecting the worst. Fiori would find out about Hu Jun and exact revenge for a long-dead Frenchman. That or the veil would fall from Huang's cuckhold eyes.

Jingfei had not been able make up her mind, trapped in this life of luxury with a man she detested. At times he hated her attachment to mere things, at others his heart bled at the fear and insecurity that was its source. Tempting her out of this life was like coaxing a frightened kitten out of a sheltering box.

Arguments had gone back and forth. They all came down to how much she could take with her. Already she had bid him up to a suitcase for her most precious clothes and a large handbag for her jewels. Still hesitating, she hoped to strike a harder bargain.

As for Hu Jun himself, Bai had heard no more of the man. Perhaps he had died or returned to England. Dong too had disappeared, an unpleasant surprise to Huang after so many years of loyal service.

Now, as he and Jingfei lay asleep in bed, some faint noise, the creak of a chair or the scrape of a shoe, gave the men away. Enough warning for Bai to be struggling up from sleep just as a blow almost sent him straight back down into its depths.

Stars whirled around the darkened room as rough hands grabbed his legs and arms. He felt the bite of ropes on his skin. He heard Jingfei's cries of outrage receding as men held him down and tied him tighter.

Bai felt himself lifted. He and the two men holding him were half way out of the bedroom door just as his vision began to clear. The two men's feet thudded down the stairs and someone else opened the door onto an estate coming alive with lights.

Carried along, face down and only inches from the grass, he smelt its early morning wetness. To the east, sullen rainclouds were obscuring the first faint flush of dawn.

They swung away from the house, and he realised they were heading towards...

He heard the tiger give a wet, puzzled grunt as though it too had just been roused from sleep. Bai lifted his head as much as he could. Ahead, in front of the tiger's cage were lamps and the shapes of several people. He saw a fist raised then smashed down and heard Jingfei moan.

At last, he began to struggle, jerking his knees to his chest then kicking them out. The two men lost their grip and he flopped to the grass. He struggled to his feet but a boot came flying out of the gloom and kicked him hard on the jaw. His head spun though a half turn and he crashed down. Boots and fists thudded into his ribs and abdomen and groin.

This time they just took one leg each and dragged him, his face sliding over the wet grass then scraping over the gravel of a path. He heard Jingfei scream in agony.

"Leave her alone you whoresons!" he yelled. They stopped pulling and a heavy foot smashed down onto his right kidney. His lungs emptied and black shapes whirled in his eyes.

He felt himself lifted again, then turned over and dropped. He crashed down onto the solid wood of a table, his head lolling over one end, his lower legs over the other. He felt ropes being untied then retied but had not the breath to move or resist.

When, finally, he managed to lift his head up, he found himself spread-eagled, his legs and arms bound to the legs of the table.

Above him Huang's face hove into view. Europeans often said that the Han Chinese had impassive faces. A race long used to oppression learns to hide its feelings. But then one day, when it all became too much, when the pressure deep inside could no longer be borne, there came an upwelling of dangerous madness, and all restraint was lost.

Bai saw in Huang's face this ancient, boundless cruelty and knew that before the sun rose both he and Jingfei would be dead.

Huang pointed at his chest. "Cut away his clothes!" Then he turned and shouted, "Bring her over!"

Jingfei was trying to hold down her horrified sobbing. Two men were pushing her forward, her arms behind her back, her beautiful silk night gown torn and smeared where they had dragged her across the ground. Blood was dripping from the side of her mouth and her right eye was red and swelling from a brutal blow.

Knives were already cutting into his clothing. He turned back to Huang who was grinning down at him. "Why are you doing this?"

Huang gently pushed away a lock of Bai's hair that had fallen over one eye. "Because you are fucking my woman. Why else?"

"No, I have never." Even to Bai it sounded so lame.

Huang leaned over and spat in his face. Bai could smell and taste the bitter tea.

The cutting done, he felt all the clothes being torn from his body, the sudden coldness of the air shrivelling his scrotum.

Helpless, terribly exposed, Bai began to plead as someone handed a dao to Huang who then put it against his throat. Bai felt his skin part where the cold metal touched.

Huang barked: "Closer, I want her to watch!"

And now she and Bai were barely inches apart. He could not bear the pain and misery etched in her face. She looked at Huang, her expression fierce. "What is wrong with you?"

Huang jerked the dao up to strike her and Bai was sure she nearly died there and then. Instead, voice trembling, Huang said. "He stinks of you and you stink of him."

He grasped Jingfei's chin in his free hand. "Let us see what happens to your lust when your lover dies the Death of a Thousand Cuts. Or at least, my own version."

Huang turned back to Bai who lifted his head, fearful of where the blade would strike. Huang laid it along one of Bai's ribs then drew it slowly towards him, his eyes rapt as the blood welled up. The blade was so sharp that Bai hardly felt a thing. It was only when Huang made a parallel cut, barely an inch away from the first, that he felt the first icy fingers of pain.

"I beg of you..." Jingfei was saying as Huang made two smaller cuts to join the parallel lines, delineating a strip of flesh a foot in length. He placed the blade back into one of the smaller lines, worrying at the skin until a flap lifted. Grasping it, he turned to look back at Bai.

Bai saw the muscles in the man's face twitch and braced himself. The strip of flesh came away with the sound of ripping silk.

Shock brought Bai's supper back up into his mouth. He turned his head and spat out the acid vomit. All he could feel was the savage stinging of the newly exposed muscle.

Jingfei, horror written across her face, looked as though she too would be sick. He sought her eyes but she would not meet his.

Huang took his time, making more cuts with the dao. As the third strip of flesh was ripped away, Bai found himself moaning unashamedly. Still, he sought Jingfei's eyes, still she looked away. Too numbed to cry, her cheeks were dry.

By the time Huang had exposed three sloping tiger stripes of red on either side of Bai's ribs, darkness was again crowding his vision.

"Hold his head!" Huang commanded. Jingfei let out a piercing shriek. Huang punched her in the side of the head. Her eyes grew dull and the men holding her struggled to keep her upright.

Rough hands pulled at his hair while others grasped the sides of his head. The dao came towards his face, its size magnified by his terror. This time when the flesh was torn away, the billowing clouds of darkness claimed him.

Cold water smashed over his face, stinging his exposed flesh and hooking him out of the dark waters like a fish hauled from the depths. Huang was still above him, his head tilting from side to side as he admired his handiwork.

"If only you could see yourself, Tigerman," he whispered.

Bai searched for signs of life in Jingfei's swollen face and half-closed eyes but could find nothing.

"You loved her, but she never loved you," Huang said. "Me neither. That's why this..." and he waved the dao over Bai's face and body, "... disfigurement is not quite satisfying. Hurting you does not hurt her, except for her fear that I will do the same to her. Perhaps I can't hurt her heart but I can hurt yours."

From the corners of Jingfei's swollen eye the first tear appeared. Huang grasped her chin and brought it up to lock his eyes with hers.

"The foreign spies have taught us much about torture, dearest Jingfei. The Russian Cheka especially. Do you know they shove high pressure hoses up women to blast out their insides? Imagine a government doing that to its own countrywomen. Barbarians!"

He stroked Jingfei's hair. "Not for you, my love."

He turned to Bai and winked. "What can I do to reach her, make her understand how I feel?" He clicked his fingers and Jingfei was wrenched away. Bai twisted his head and saw men grasping her arms and legs, carrying her towards the tiger cage. She was screaming and kicking but the men were strong and determined.

They stopped a man's length from the cage. Bai could see the tiger sitting back on its haunches. It seemed uncertain. Uneasily, it kept glancing away from the group of humans and then back.

The men began to swing Jingfei back and forth. She was shouting but her words were hurried and her tongue too numbed with fear. He could not understand a word but knew she was pleading for her life.

Back and forth she swung, her body reaching as high as the men's shoulders. One of the men began to count. "One... Two... Three," and then Jingfei was sailing high into the air. As she cleared the top of the open cage her exquisitely decorated gown billowed out and for an instant she looked like a beautiful bird in flight.

The cage was high and Jingfei's fall was long. She struck the ground with a dreadful sound. The tiger shuffled back in alarm.

Time shuddered to a halt. Jingfei did not move and neither did the tiger or the men. Finally, impatiently, Huang strode to the bars and gestured angrily. "Eat her, you mangy sack of shit!"

The tiger slunk as far back as the cage allowed. Huang slammed his hands against it in anger. He turned to the men. "Fetch sticks, poke the fucking thing!"

Jingfei had still not moved by the time the men got back. Bai found himself wishing she was already dead.

The bamboo poles from the gardeners' shed were long and thick and the tiger roared in pain as they jabbed at its ribs. It slunk around the cage, stepping carefully over Jingfei.

Huang looked like he would burst into flames. "Poke her, you abortions!"

A pole jabbed her midriff and Jingfei gasped. The tiger froze. Bai had time for two startled breaths and then it was upon her. A heavy paw slashed across her belly, parting silk and flesh.

Bai jerked his head away but Huang grabbed his hair, twisting his head back around, his fingers clawing open his eyelids. Bai struggled and tried to bite but Huang's grip was fierce.

Suddenly Jingfei's screams cut out and he heard the men's grunts of disgust. A stench washed over him and he knew the tiger had opened her and she was dead. He stopped struggling and let his eyelids be forced wide open.

"What the fuck is going on here?" roared an outraged European voice from away towards the gate. Bai heard a scurrying of feet and Huang let him go. Bai turned his head and saw the gatekeeper approaching, hands together, head bowed.

"I could not stop them, Master."

Behind him and out of the darkness, loomed two Concession policemen. They were real Frenchmen, not the usual Vietnamese coppers from their Annam colony.

Both stopped mid-stride as they caught sight of what the tiger was doing in the cage. They both drew their guns.

Huang stepped forward. "I am..."

"I know who you are," interrupted the more thickset of the policeman. His tone was brisk, authoritative but Bai could see the fear and uncertainty in his eyes. "All I want to know is what the hell is going on here."

The man's eyes went from the cage where the tiger was worrying at the bloody pile of rags, to Bai's splayed body and the blood dripping from his chest and face.

"Deuxieme business!" said Huang. "Talk to Fiori, your boss. Our boss!"

Bai could not stand the look of horror in the policeman's eyes. It revealed all too clearly how awful his flayed body must look. Instead, he looked away towards the gate where a single light at the gatehouse showed the policemen's car.

A flicker of shadows to the side caught his eye. Two figures slipped by the car and into the grounds of the mansion, then were swallowed by the darkness.

Had they been real? He couldn't be certain anymore. Surely this was a fever dream? No thief would be stupid enough to break into Huang's lair.

The policeman was struggling with what to say next. "This is a decent neighbourhood. It's bad enough you keep a tiger that's always roaring its fucking head off, but now... the screams of the woman..." Again his eyes strayed back to the cage.

"There will be no more noise. Our business is done."

The other copper, younger, leaner, angrier, stepped forward. "This is disgusting, Huang! We can look away for some things but you've turned this place into an abattoir."

The older cop placed a restraining hand on the younger man's chest.

Huang smiled. "Fiori pays me to deal with the Chinese. That's what I'm doing. There are no Europeans here, except for yourselves. How do you think this all works? There are so many Chinese but only a handful of you. You need me and my men to make sure my countrymen behave. Without us..." He waved his hand.

"I'm going to talk to Fiori. You've not heard the last of this!"

"Good luck finding him. There are so many whorehouses in Shanghai. But he is coming here for lunch tomorrow. Come and join us both then!"

The older policeman looked wretched, perhaps a decent man trapped in a terrible world. His eyes again found Bai's. "Help me!" Bai groaned.

The man hesitated but then his jaw clenched hard and he turned and walked stiffly away. The other followed but not before giving Huang a daring look of the deepest contempt.

Huang watched them leave then looked down at Bai. "Nobody to help you now. We'll let you watch while we scrape up what's left of poor Jingfei."

He turned away and walked over to the cage. As he did so, Bai heard the police car start up and reverse back out over the gravel. Turning his head, he saw the gate man hurrying back to close it then stand there holding the bars and watching the retreating car. Light from the car's headlights dimmed rapidly as it raced away from this place of horror.

Then shadows moved and Bai saw a figure step up behind the gate man and run something across his throat. The two men struggled then a third figure emerged from the shadows and grasped the struggling gate man's legs. He was bundled off into the darkness.

From far away he heard a wet, suppressed cough.

Huang's men were poking the tiger away from the cage door. The tiger roared but seemed to have had enough of this evening for it turned and retreated as far as it could. It lay down and began to lick Jingfei's blood from its paws. The blood splashed back over its face looked like the exaggerated lipstick of a demon.

The men still hesitated to open the cage door and Huang had to scream at them.

As the door was opened, three of the men pushed into the cage, poles extended towards the tiger while a fourth man squeezed between them, dashing to what was left of Jingfei and dragging her corpse back out.

The tiger snarled but did not move.

After the cage was secured again, the men looked at Huang. "Chop her up and shove her in the furnace!"

Huang was turning towards Bai when he stopped and turned back to his men. "Get the furnace going before you put her in. There's too much blood. You'll never get it started if she goes in first."

Huang watched the men drag Jingfei away. He pointed at the darker trail they were leaving behind on the lighter gravel. "And get buckets of water to wash that away."

He came back to Bai, gazing over his face and torso. "It almost seems a shame to kill you. I'm tempted to make you live your life looking like that. You were always a little too pretty, Bai. I should never have trusted you with her. A pair of trousers would make her wet."

Bai tried to spit at him but his mouth was as dry as desert sand.

For several more seconds Huang stood admiring his handiwork. He opened his mouth to say something else but the crashing of gunfire froze him. His face flickered with the light of muzzle flashes as though from far away lightening.

A figure emerged from the shadows. It strode quickly forward and Bai could see the pistol glinting in its hand. From further away came four more shots, separated and achingly deliberate.

"Who the hell are you?" shouted Huang, sounding startled but not yet fearful.

Bai's father, now almost within touching distance, raised his pistol and shot Huang through his eye. Huang's head jerked back and he flopped to the ground as though all his bones had dissolved in an instant.

Hu Jun stepped in closer and put a bullet through his other eye. Behind him, Bai saw Dong come out of the shadows, loading shells into his revolver. Both men came over and looked down at him. Again, he had to look away from the horror in their eyes.

He felt his bindings being cut but he had been so long with his arms and legs pulled hard back that he could not move. It was as though his limbs had turned to stone.

The older men took his arms and legs and began to carry him towards the gate. Bai could see the pain and effort in his father's face. "Hold me under the arms," he said. "I can take my own weight."

It wasn't true but at least he could take some of the load. The three of them staggered over to the gate and they laid him down against the guard hut.

"I'll get the car," said Dong. "You open the gate."

Bai felt suddenly dizzy and feared he would black out. Every single movement was agony. Looking down he could see the damage the dao had inflicted. Huang's work had been more meticulous than Bai might have expected. Three almost uniform tiger strikes cut diagonally down across each side of his rib cage, leaving bright red muscle exposed. Here and there, bits of yellow fat still adhered.

From so far off it was still just a faint tinkling, Bai could hear a police car's bell. Hu Jun quickly dragged open the gate as the heavy engine of the Citroen started up and the headlights of the gangster's car lit up the mansion.

The car came crunching over the gravel and stopped beside them, Dong reaching back to fling open the back door. Hu Jun grasped Bai and wrenched him up off his feet, making his skin burn as though drenched in acid.

He was slapped down on the leather upholstery and Hu Jun clambered in after him, pulling the door shut. The car took off in a spray of gravel that pattered over the guard hut.

Bai felt it skid as it turned sharply into the road, fish-tailing several times before Dong regained control.

Then the car roared liked a tiger as Dong floored the accelerator.

Bai lay sprawled on the soft green leather of the back seat of the Citroen as it bounced over dirt track roads. The plains of Anhui gave way to more uneven country as they crossed over into the green hills and mountains of Jiangxi. Hu Jun had wisely taken a longer westerly route, though better and more direct roads ran south through Zhejiang and Fujian and straight down to Hong Kong. The Green Gang would be after them but its writ did not run in more westerly provinces.

The mess of skirmishes between the old imperialists, the KMT, the warlords and the other gangs had left the telegraph network in tatters. The nascent telephone system had been laughable at the best of times. Even if the Green Gang had known who to alert, they didn't have the means.

If the three of them kept off the main roads they might stand a chance but they had the problem of petrol. Dong had loaded the rest of the back seat and footwells with cans of the stuff that Huang had stockpiled but it was nowhere near enough to get them to Hong Kong. With gasoline almost unheard of in the countryside, sooner rather than later they would have to risk cutting back to the big cities on the coast.

Bai could not bear the sight of his wounds but he had little choice. Cloth touching it was unbearable. Even so, as they passed through towns and villages, Dong had to throw a coarse tartan car rug over him. Once seen by any locals, his wounds would never be forgotten and his track would be too easy to follow.

The fibres of the rug, coarse and uncomfortable even upon healthy skin, now scraped like the metal wool used to scour oil-blackened woks.

The pain drove him into delirium.

When he began to rave, Hu Jun reluctantly stopped the car in what passed for a town in this part of the country. Inquiries of stunned locals, their eyes full of wonder at the car, soon yielded directions to the one they sought.

The old apothecary's eyes opened wide when Hu Jun brought him out to the car and he looked down at Bai, naked, splayed out and sweating on the back seat.

"What devil did this?" the old man croaked. He plucked nervously at his monk's robes.

Nobody answered. The apothecary hissed in disgust and shook his head, then turned back towards his little shop, beckoning Hu Jun to follow. As Bai waited, the blue sky above him spun and birds swooped down in crazy spirals, intent on plucking out his eyes.

Then someone was grasping the back of his head, lifting it so other hands could drip a bitter tea into his mouth. Up close he could make out the remnants of a long-ago dao slash across the old apothecary's forehead, a sickly white scar against his ruddy complexion.

Tepid water was splashed over his chest and abdomen and Bai moaned as something coarse was rubbed over his skin. Then a soothing cream was plastered over his wounds.

"The four herbs," said the apothecary. "They will stop suppuration but someone should sit with him and brush away the flies. Cover his wounds at night, no matter how much he protests. If you see maggots then the wound must be cauterised."

"Will he live?" he heard Hu Jun asking anxiously.

The apothecary turned weary old eyes to him. "The wounds are not deep, except the one to his heart."

"Heart?" Hu Jun looked down in surprise at Bai's chest.

"This man, is he your son?"

"Yes."

The old man nodded. "Your son is in shock. It is the memory of what has happened that troubles him. I have no medicines that can help with that."

Hu Jun reached into his jacket, now dirtier and scruffier than back in Shanghai. The twisting movement seemed to loosen something for he bent suddenly and hacked up a gout of blood. Bai could hear it splash onto the road.

The old apothecary looked at Hu Jun soberly. "Lung knot kernal," he said. "I can treat that."

Hu Jun seemed unconvinced. "How?"

"The smoke of thirty-six charms."

Hu Jun shook his head. "I have lived abroad for a long time, apothecary, in a place where your Taoist beliefs hold no water. I have come to see that charms will do me no good."

"And how do the people there cure this illness?"

Hu Jun breathed out. "They don't."

"Then the charms would not hurt."

"Thank you, apothecary, but we have no time."

"You lived on the other side of the world, did you not?"

"What makes you say that?"

The old monk smiled. "Your clothes look European, British, I think. Though dirty now they were clearly expensive. Yet your disease that we call the 'destroyed palace' is mostly of the poor. This makes me suspect you have taken up the filthy British habit of drinking milk!"

Hu Jun smiled. "Perhaps."

"It carries disease. Why do you think we Chinese stopped drinking it long ago? Westerners still do not understand this."

"Whatever you say, old father," said Hu Jun handing over a generous bundle of cash.

Hu Jun got back in the car. Despite the pain, Bai managed to lift himself up enough to watch the old apothecary waving sadly until he disappeared from view.

Later, when his wounds came to burn less and the world no longer held only pain, he listened to Dong and Hu Jun arguing as the coast slid by. There were things his father could not help worrying away at.

"Did you love her?" Hu Jun asked once, unable to hide his anger.

"I grew to love her."

"And did she love you?"

Bai, still lying on the back seat, was looking up at the back of Dong's head which shook in irritation. "Perhaps. She never stopped telling me she thought you a fool." Dong turned to look at Hu Jun. "And that's what I think as well."

Hu Jun kept his eyes on the road. "Then we all agree."

"Why did you gut that Frenchman?"

"I've thought about little else for many years. The only answer I can give is that he deserved to die."

"It wasn't your job to execute him."

167

It went silent again, as it always did when the past reared up. This time the silence stretched for several miles. Above Bai's head the tops of the katsura trees whizzed by, the speed too great to make out the oval shapes of their green summer leaves.

Finally, Hu Jun spoke like a man giving voice to his deepest fears. "Where you good to her, Dong?"

"You worry at this like a dog at a bone. Marrying her was the only way I could save her. The Green Gang wanted their revenge. By defending her I put my life on the line."

"I know, I do know. And my son has paid for my foolishness."

"Stop indulging your self-pity! He was indentured but he had a good job. He would have been fine if he hadn't stuck his cock where he shouldn't. It seems the Hu men make a habit of getting into trouble when it comes to whores."

Bai kept quiet, too weak and tired to spring to poor, dead Jingfei's defence. Soon he fell into the numbness that only sleep could provide.

At night Bai slept where he lay on the back seat while the old men lay down in the dirt by the roadside. One morning, after a week on the road, Bai heard Dong calling his father's name, each time sounding more and more urgent. Bai was recovered enough to ease himself out of the car and was just in time to see what happened next.

Hu Jun, finally roused from sleep by Dong's shaking of his shoulder, turned his head and coughed a gout of blood onto the grass. Then he was consumed by a paroxysm of coughing, blood spraying out like spittle.

The sun had risen high by the time Hu Jun was well enough to travel again. Now it was Hu Jun lying in the back seat, and Bai watching drops of sweat drip down the old man's forehead, the skin over his temple like parchment. Bai had seen people die like this before. Not for nothing did some call this the corpse disease. Some sufferers simply faded away but those who brought up bloody phlegm went much faster and usually in one final catastrophic haemorrhage.

He searched hard, but could find little in the way of feeling for this ghost. Hu Jun had saved his life, it had to be said, but Bai was still grieving deeply for Jingfei and her terrible fate. The pain was so great he wished the old man had never bothered.

"Both of you sit up! Bai pull that blanket over your shoulders!" Dong said.

Bai did so, wincing as the material grated over his body. He heard Hu Jun grunt as he pulled himself upright. Ahead was a barricade and beyond it were several huts. Two Chinese men in unfamiliar uniforms with brown leather holsters on their belts stood either side of a horizontal pole blocking the single lane.

As the car pulled to a halt one of the men came over, appraising each of them in turn and finding it hard to hide his surprise at what he saw. One European clad Chinese, another one clad like a coolie and a third with startling facial scars. This was not part of the usual routine.

"Hello," said Hu Jun in English.

The uniformed man looked startled. He was in his forties with a fat, well-fed face.

"Don't you police speak English?" asked Hu Jun in Mandarin.

"Some, but I usually leave that to him," and the policeman pointed a thumb over his shoulder at the huts. Bai realised one of the uniformed men there was a European in a khaki shirt and shorts with a diagonal strap across his chest. He was smoking a cigarette and, judging by his distracted gaze, his mind was on other things.

Hu Jun turned back to the Chinese policeman. "No need to bother him."

"Convince me!" The man's Mandarin was accented. Cantonese would be his first language.

Hu Jun eased a single piece of paper from his breast pocket. He unfolded it and Bai caught a glimpse of a photograph stuck to it. "My passport."

A Chinese with a British passport! The policeman's day was getting stranger and stranger. He glanced back uneasily at the

European before looking more sternly at Hu Jun. "And what about these two?"

"My servants."

"Are they British too?"

"No, I hired them while I was in China. I am unwell and I need them to accompany me."

"What happened to that one's face?"

"He stuck it where he shouldn't. Between the thighs of someone else's wife."

Again, the man looked back at his superior who was absorbed in the process of lighting a cigarette. Hu Jun coughed lightly and as the man's head swung back, he opened a palm to reveal a small bundle of white notes. "Your boss is busy. We should not trouble him."

Hesitant up to now, the policeman took the money in one smooth motion and signalled to his colleague on the other end of the pole. It swung upwards.

Dong pulled gently away. Bai could not help looking back. The policeman was managing to look both confused and immensely gratified at the same time.

Hong Kong was not unlike Shanghai: plenty of modern buildings but here, where space was much more limited, they were building upwards. The rickety-looking bamboo scaffolding rose to prodigious heights, clinging to the skeletal steel structures like ivy. The streets were just as bustling but the language was unfamiliar and the accent that went with the Cantonese sounded barbaric. Rats the size of cats hurried hither and thither. Back in Shanghai the stray dogs would have made short work of them.

Hu Jun's money found them swanky accommodation in a hotel overlooking the bay. Bai slept between sheets of fine cotton. Luxurious, expensive, comfortable but all too reminiscent of those on Jingfei's bed.

In the long sleepless nights when his mind wondered like a ghost through the graveyard of his hopes, he alternated between contempt that she had not escaped with him while she could, and the rawest yearnings for the warmth of her body and the taste of her lips.

During the day, as they traipsed from one government office to another, Hu Jun mopped at the blood seeping from the corner of his mouth. The language spoken now was English and was as incomprehensible as the Cantonese. At well-appointed offices, steaming in the humidity and heat, the white people would look at Bai's face with an alarm that could not hide their morbid interest.

Bai let himself be led around, biddable, as if he had the corpse disease himself.

Bai's picture was taken and he signed documents he could not read. Sometimes the officials wore rumpled linen suits, sometimes they wore khaki uniforms. One swanky old man, holding himself like an emperor, his dark uniform jacket speckled with ribbons and medals, had signed something with the most grandiose of flourishes.

At every meeting bulging envelopes were exchanged, the officials pocketing them as though this was the most natural thing in the world.

The pain lessened and Bai's health improved. Now he could wear loose-fitting silks, the only material that slithered rather than dragged across his abused flesh. Even so, he would have preferred to just lie on his hotel bed. Hu Jun never explained why, but Bai's presence seemed required at these interminable meetings.

Finally, one night in a restaurant overlooking Junk Bay, Hu Jun revealed his plans.

The junks covered the bay like a carpet, many strung with gay red lanterns. It looked beautiful, heavenly, but Bai knew that the reality was far more pungent. It was not uncommon for families of twenty to live on one small craft, all shouting, fighting, cooking, eating and loving. The numberless fleet seethed with emotions soothed not at all by their world's gentle bobbing.

Hu Jun no longer ate but he seemed to find pleasure in Bai's returning appetite.

Bai was picking away at a plate of prawns, some in a bland white sauce, some in a slightly spicy red one, the two laid down like a yin and yang symbol. Idly, still not really caring, he asked what they had been doing for the last week. Hu Jun looked thoughtful and sipped at a glass of the white poison that the old apothecary had blamed for his disease. It certainly looked revolting to Bai's eyes. What's worse he'd noticed in so many of the offices that the British officials poured it by the gallon into their tea. Savages!

"I have been smoothing your way, son. Dong's too. You are now both British citizens with passports that are being prepared. I have written a will and signed it before a judge. You now have birth certificates, expensive forgeries, of course, detailing your births in Limehouse in London. With these we will go to a bank, one that operates back in Britain as well as here, and open accounts for you both. I will transfer money and you will be able to use that to buy tickets when the time comes."

"Tickets to where?" asked Dong.

"London, where else? My house will be Bai's. He will take care of you, I am sure. He loves you as a father." For once there was no bitterness in this and Bai found himself swallowing away a lump in his throat even though what Hu Jun said wasn't really true. Dong had always managed to be there for him but had somehow remained distant. Bai had never really thought of him as a father.

"Aren't you coming with us?" he asked.

Hu Jun looked at him sadly. In the brief weeks they had been together they had been through so much but they were still strangers.

"My lungs are paper thin and they fill with blood. I will not survive an ocean voyage, no matter how well appointed the cabins."

Bai frowned. "So, we are to wait here until you recover?" he said, though knew he was being foolish.

172

Hu Jun shook his head. "I will die soon, no matter how many burning charms I inhale. I would like you to stay until I die but... you may leave when you like."

"We will stay," said Dong earnestly.

"Of course," said Bai.

"Good, then there is nothing more to say."

"Should we take your body home?"

Hu Jun looked around at the bay and the lights of Kowloon across the water. "China is my home."

"This is not China."

Hu Jun gave a laugh, which turned to a cough. When, finally, the paroxysms had abated, he was still left with a weak smile, though a drop of bright red blood gleamed from the corner of his lips. "This is as much China as Shanghai, though the British do not understand this. This is where my bones will rest and it as good a place as any in the Middle Kingdom."

From the deck of the ocean liner as it left the city, Bai could see the little hill and the crowded cemetery where they had laid Hu Jun to rest. He kept watching as the whole country disappeared in the humid haze, leaving behind the bodies of his only lover and a father he had never known.

13. London

The Son, Benny Hu, and the Unsentimental Whore

Cash might be dying away but taxi drivers were never going to turn their noses up at it, so the notes disappeared in a flash. Benny was too weary to ask for change. Local government's losing struggles to repair crumbling roads had made the journey in from Heathrow like a slalom and the guy deserved a tip.

His ground-floor flat had an entrance several steps up from the pavement. At the top step he paused, turning to survey the street, like a traveller relieved to be back in familiar surroundings. There were cars he had never seen before but that was no surprise. Residential streets across London were crammed with parked cars; if you found a space within half a kilometre of your home it was your lucky day.

Vans were what he worried about. It was well after six o'clock so there shouldn't be any workmen around, but there was one battered old white van fifty metres down on the other side of the road. Nobody in the front seats but he couldn't see if anyone was in the back. He'd take a stroll later, get a closer look.

For now, he turned his attention to the door. As soon as he'd moved in, he'd had it changed, harrying the poor carpenter until it fitted so snugly it wouldn't rattle even with the sharpest gust of wind.

Putting his bag down, his body blocking his movements, he felt the hinge side of the door.

Nothing.

He stood up, reaching into his pocket for the keys, exhaling slowly and deliberately. The little piece of clear plastic he had wedged in the cleft had gone. Someone had opened this door while he was away.

He hesitated. The flight had been long and economy class. Even if a Guoanbu assassin was waiting for him behind the door, he needed his bed too badly. Besides which, Six would almost certainly be responsible for this intrusion. Deniables though they may be, the service did not take casually the loss of any of them. If Jiang had been betrayed then the finger of suspicion would inevitably be pointing at Benny.

Even so, he put the key in the lock and turned it as quietly as he could, slipping through and closing the door gently behind him.

He waited in the dark, listening intently. Sometimes, if one waited quietly, all senses alert, one just knew if someone else was there.

Nothing.

He turned on the hall light. Bending down, he found the little bit of plastic on the inside of the door where it had fallen.

Double-locking the door, he dumped his bag on the bed and headed into the lounge-cum-kitchen. He closed the curtains, poured himself a malt, and fired up his laptop. He put in the address for the secure server and typed in his user name.

Not recognised the laptop told him.

Too tired he thought, then carefully retyped the name.

Not recognised, the laptop told him again.

He sat back, crossed his arms over his chest. A third attempt would lock out this laptop until the sun turned to a cinder.

So what the fuck now? he thought.

Had they ditched him? Surely not! At the very least they would have demanded a debrief. Uncomfortable notions wormed their way into his brain. If they thought he was a traitor, would they kill him?

Benny took a deep breath. Six might play fast and loose in the Far East but they were more circumspect in the West, let alone in the UK itself. Prison, solitary for the rest of his life, would be more the ticket. And the first sign of that would be a policeman knocking at his door.

Numbed by jet-lag, he sat looking at the room. Bare floor boards, utilitarian sofa, TV. No pictures on the wall. The place was as barren as his life.

Jiang had got on his nerves in so many ways but at least they had been able to talk, up to a point. Long nights staking out people and places had led to a strangely profound but stunted version of friendship for both of them.

Benny didn't like it, but he had to admit they'd had something in common. Jiang's relentless womanising, Benny's search for his mother, both seeking an intimacy they'd never experienced.

Inevitably this brought his thoughts to Lea. If Six were withdrawing from his life, was he now completely alone?

He had always known that one day he would have to start another life. Something more real than Jiang's bullshit about buying his way into a Triad. Benny had hundreds of thousands stashed away but would that be enough? He also had a couple of passports in names that Six knew nothing about.

Not that Six would be surprised by that. Every spy had to have a way out.

Perhaps he should just forget Lea, go abroad, settle somewhere else, force himself to be open-hearted, make friends. Find a wife, produce some kids.

For a few fleeting seconds, he bought into it. Believed he could do it. Believed that with one bound he could be free.

But then he was back in the barren little room, the hollow he had made for himself. Something would always be missing, somewhere in the deep core of himself.

He reached again for the laptop and opened his mailbox. Her email address was all she'd ever given him. He didn't even have her phone number.

We need to meet. Anytime, anywhere he wrote.

Then he poured himself a malt and waited.

The doorbell shrilled its way through a dream of drowning in an ocean of bamboo, leaves filling his mouth and nostrils, stems piercing his heart. He opened his eyes to find the laptop still open. Beams of light through chinks in the curtains illuminated a star field of drifting dust motes.

He struggled upright and staggered into the hall, putting one eye to the peephole. Lea's frowning face filled it. He hesitated, trying to remember if she'd replied to his email.

He opened the door, blinking in the clear light. She planted a hand on his chest and pushed him aside, then grimaced. "You smell! Haven't you even changed yet for fuck's sakes?"

"Lea, I..."

Palm open and upright, she chopped the air between them. "Shower!" she ordered.

After the shower, cold because he had forgotten to fire up the boiler before unconsciousness had claimed him, he stumbled into his bedroom, hoping against hope he'd find her in his bed. He'd have settled for a cuddle but he doubted even that was to be had, so he dressed quickly in denims and a checked shirt.

He found her in the kitchen brewing coffee. Her back was to him and it was a superhuman effort not to put his hands on her slender waist. An effort he wasn't quite up to but, even as he was reaching for her, she turned and pointed imperiously at the kitchen table. "Sit!"

By the time he'd settled down, she'd clumped a pot of smoky coffee on the table. "Are you hungry?" she asked.

He tried to work that out but decided in the end that he wasn't. "No."

She found two mugs and filled them. Neither took milk but she reached into her bag for sweeteners and put two into her mug.

"Miss me?" he asked.

The look on her face made him feel sick, his worst fears realised.

"God!" she said. "Could you be any more of an arsehole?"

They sat in silence waiting for the coffee to cool. She let him take a few good sips, let the coffee start to work its magic. "The house is clean," she said.

He searched her face for a suggestion of guilt for the intrusion, or even a hint of regret, but all he got was a cool, appraising look.

"So, we can talk?"

"We can talk."

She was telling him that Six had broken into his house and, amongst other things, they'd checked for bugs. Previously they'd done regular sweeps of his place but only by arrangement and at his convenience. Clearly the time for such niceties had passed.

Without preamble she asked: "How long have you been working for the Guoanbu?"

177

"Give me a break!"

"Why?"

"It wasn't my fault!"

"Then whose was it?" She'd never been gentle but now her voice was hard enough to crack a walnut.

"I don't know. It could have been anyone or anything. Fu for a start. Perhaps he took fright and rolled on us. Or maybe the whole thing was a counter-intelligence setup to smoke us out. Maybe you should be looking at whoever put Six onto him in the first place."

"Right, so it's our fault your partner, the guy you recruited, the guy you trained, whose back you were there to protect, winds up dead."

Benny struggled to contain the flash of anger and caught himself before he licked lips that suddenly felt so dry. It would only make him look more guilty. He had to keep calm. "Or maybe they caught onto us when we were following him. Maybe they checked the cameras in the clothes shop. It was Jiang who picked up Fu's bullshit message about the Uighurs. The drone that tried to kill him must have been loaded with his image, a guardian angel programmed to strike if Jiang made another appearance."

"Jiang was killed by a drone?"

"Not directly, but it drove him to it—the fall that killed him, that is. Why, what's the Chinese version?"

"Road traffic accident. I've seen the pictures. His own mother wouldn't recognise him, even if he had one."

Benny felt sick but kept going. "Any RTA would have been post mortem. No, a couple of drones tried to kill us both. One shot jobs, like wasps."

"Really? And you didn't spot the drone operatives? Wouldn't that have been your job, Benny?"

"There weren't any. The damn thing must have been autonomous. I mean, come on, autonomous drones aren't exactly science fiction anymore."

"True, but the idea of allowing a lethal drone to operate all by itself within China is a bit of a stretch."

"Not according to Fu. They've been using them to take out some of the more troublesome Uighurs and Falun Gong for years."

"On the peripheries of the country maybe, but not in the heart of the Middle Kingdom. Not in Baoding."

He shrugged. "The Chinese want control of everything. Like I say, the idea of a trap makes the most sense. Fu was the cheese, the drones were the mousetrap."

"Again, that doesn't quite add up. Jiang was worth more to them alive than dead."

"Jiang knew nothing."

"Oh, come on!" she said with real anger. "We may have held him at arm's length but he knew what ops he was on. He knew who we'd turned. Why would they kill him so... off-handedly?"

She was right, it didn't ring true. Trouble was, he didn't know the answer.

A silence fell, though there was so much he wanted to ask. Finally, "You and me... where are we?" As soon as he said it, he cursed himself. Too clumsy, too needy.

"What do you think?"

"You can turn it off, just like that?"

"I'm not a robot. That level of intimacy..." She waved a hand in the direction of his bedroom.

"Even so it's all a bit... whorish."

Her delicate features composed themselves into a cold smile. "With you it was more like being a foster mother."

He was too tired for that stiletto to do much damage. "You're married, aren't you?"

"So what?"

He didn't know what to say. He realised she'd pledged herself to this double existence. She was impervious to anything he said.

He sat back resignedly. "Why are you here, what's going to happen to me now?"

"Well, for a start, I need your passport. You're going nowhere until this is all cleared up."

"Why should I give it to you."

She leaned forward; a sharp red nail pointed at his chest. "We could have arrested you at the airport but we're choosing to play nice. We're giving you the benefit of the doubt. For now."

She held out her hand, palm up.

Benny stood up, his limbs heavy. He went to the bedroom and fished the passport out of his hand luggage. Back in the kitchen she took it from him and slid it into a side pocket of her handbag.

"You're going on a little trip into the country. I'll text you when and where. Don't go out until then!"

"How do I get to this place?"

"Drive!"

The security services had houses dotted all over the country where they could interrogate spies and debrief defectors. Such places weren't noted for their splendour. He imagined some ramshackle old house with dingy rooms full of ancient furniture, the walls hung with carefully positioned mirrors. Whatever happened there, it wasn't going to be pleasant.

The fear was that it would be only a stepping stone to darker, bleaker venues. Places from which he might never return.

Then again, what Lea had said had been right. If they really thought he was a double they'd have nabbed him at Heathrow and he'd be eating cornflakes in the terrorist-hardened confines of a London nick.

She swept her hair back, a sign she was getting ready to leave. Despite everything he still wanted her to stay.

"When you leave, do so late in the morning so you'll miss the rush hour. Don't go trying to lose your tail because it'll be us."

"Not even a hint of where I'll be going?"

"The end of the world," she said. "In more ways than one."

14. Southampton, England 1970

The Mother, Mary Hu, and the Dissolute Don

It had been a rainy day, fat raindrops crawling down the window pane. This room in her student flat, crammed with books and piles of dirty clothes, had already been small enough. Now, with two of them heaped on the single bed, it felt difficult to breath.

James wasn't an old man, she kept telling herself, but even though barely forty his skin was subtly looser than that of the boys of her own age. Pinch the skin of his chest and then let it go, it didn't spring back to flatness quicker than your eyes could follow. Instead, it subsided in what she liked to think was a more elegant fashion.

Pinching his flesh was a habit she couldn't break, like probing at a painful tooth with your tongue. Though his bright, clear eyes would smile every time she did it, she knew he didn't like it.

Suddenly oppressed by the foetid smells of recent sex and unwashed clothes, she eased her way off the bed and stepped to the window. Though he should be satisfied enough for a while, she knew his eyes would be following her naked bottom. She tugged up the warped old sash window with its peeling white paint and peered out through the drizzle. Between buildings slick with rain, she glimpsed the grey waters of the Solent.

Even in the best of weathers there was something depressing about Southampton. A port city, once upon a time it had been jumping like Liverpool or Glasgow, but then the Luftwaffe had bombed the theatres and bordellos to buggery. As an operation to exorcise the spirit of a city with high explosives, the enterprise had been an unqualified success.

"God, but you're a wonder. So beautiful!" she heard him murmur as though to himself. There followed the click of his cigarette lighter and then a long draw on his cigarette.

Beautiful? Of that she had no doubt. Out on the city streets men always looked at her. Always. An exotic flower growing through cracks in the concrete of this drab country.

"There's something I wanted to talk to you about," he said casually, but for once he didn't hit quite the right note. For an instant she was back in his office with three other students. His tutorials always seemed so informal, such was his charm, but everyone knew their place.

This had the same ring. What was he going to teach her this time? She turned to face him, the cold damp air from the window raising goose bumps on her back.

"What are you going to do when you get your degree? You're not going to do research, are you? Not going to become Doctor Hu?"

She snorted, partly at the tedious old joke, partly at the notion of becoming an academic, of pouring over endless papers, of becoming po-faced, self-absorbed, boring.

"Didn't think so," he said, taking a self-satisfied draw on his cigarette. "You're far too flighty for that."

"Flighty!" And she was upon him. He had to hold the cigarette out of harm's way as she scrabbled at his armpits. Ticklish, he batted her arms away with his free hand. "I apologise unreservedly! Allow me to withdraw my boorish comment!"

She nestled into the crook of his arm, her bottom hanging precariously out over the edge of the narrow bed. "What's this all about?"

He shrugged. "Your future. This is your last year. What then?"

"God, you sound so fucking old." Like my father, but she kept that uncomfortable thought to herself.

She had chosen Chinese Studies for her degree through sheer laziness. She'd expected the course would be easier because of the dribs and drabs of Mandarin she'd picked up from her father, and the robust Cantonese she'd got from her more down-to-earth mother. And she'd been right. Not having to work as hard as other students left her plenty of time for singing and dancing and drama. Those were the subjects she would have preferred to study but this had been growled away by her otherwise reticent and gentle father. Taken aback by the strength of his feeling, she had complied, to both his surprise and hers.

It was only later, when she'd been doing the course for over a year, at one Christmas break back in London, she had finally teased out why he was so adamant. He felt women who danced and sang and acted were whores.

Something must have happened in his days in Shanghai, something that seemed to have emptied him out, though good luck ever getting him to talk about it! Not that she ever pressed. Stray into any subject that might impinge on his disfigurement, and he retreated like a snail into its shell.

The memory of Hu Bai's reaction made her smile to herself. James wriggled a little as she pulled at some straggling hairs around one of his nipples. "When I finish college, I want to dance and sing and act."

"Really? I would never have guessed you had a flair for drama."

She slapped his chest. "How about I throw all your clothes out of the window? Would that be dramatic enough?"

He pushed himself up on one elbow and turned to look down at her. He wasn't smiling and, for a second, she wondered if he had taken her seriously. He avoided scandal at all costs. His wife was another lecturer in the same department and poisonously adept at academic in-fighting, by all accounts. Not someone to get on the wrong side of if at all possible. Even Mary, hardly a shrinking violet who cared what other people thought of her, found her intimidating.

Mary didn't like the way he wasn't saying anything. "What?" she asked

"I might have a job for you."

"I'm not interested..."

"No, not at the university. Not at any university."

What the fuck was he talking about? Did he want her to au pair for his brace of mewling brats? She waited, tensing. If that was his game, having her on tap while she skivvied for him, she was going to bite him, hard enough to make a mark he'd have to spend weeks hiding from his harridan of a wife.

He leaned over her and stubbed out his cigarette in the ashtray on the tiny bedside table. Then he leaned back and this time his eyes were narrow and searching. "Hong Kong," he said.

"What?"

He pursed his lips as though reflecting. She suddenly realised the look was manufactured, rehearsed. For the first time she begun to wonder how much of all this had been an act.

The draught from the window was making the room cold enough but now there was a whole new level of iciness.

"What do you feel about Britain?" he asked.

She shook her head in annoyance. "It's okay." What was his point and would her ever get to it?

"Yes, but what does Britain mean to you?"

She shrugged. "It's home. What else?"

"Is it home? You're one hundred per cent Chinese."

"I've never even been there. My family—"

"Your gangster family."

She froze, mouth still open. Nobody knew about that. Hell, it had taken her years just to get a hint out of her father.

Without thinking, she pulled up the sheet to cover her nakedness.

"You're the daughter and grand-daughter of Shanghai gangsters. Men who turned against their bosses, who fled into far exile. Where do your loyalties lie? It's a reasonable question."

Suddenly and unexpectedly cornered in her own little room, she lashed out. Though the slap raised ugly red finger shadows on his cheek, he hardly flinched.

"I more than deserved that," he said. "Please, hit me as much as you want."

She did, but only once and then there seemed no point.

The affair had been going on for only a few months. Dark-haired, lean-bodied, charming when he wanted to be, he was attractive enough but was there more to it? Were daddy issues at play? Her own father, beaten down, reserved and wounded had always been stern and distant. James was much younger, but still not too young to be her father. He had given her affection aplenty, though at first only indirectly through sarcasm and irony. He had made her laugh, something she realised her father had never done.

The clincher, however, had been that she sensed something else in him. Charming but bland would never have been enough for her. This other hidden thing had intrigued her enough to sleep with a married man, despite a vow she had made to herself.

She had begun to wonder recently if James' secret had merely been regret. Wife, two kids, good job, secure pension, yet he gave off the air of someone who had lost something, again like her father. Disappointment was not attractive in a man, other than the first impulse one might have to give the wretch a hug. After that, it was difficult to hold off a feeling of contempt.

Perhaps James had sensed that in her. Perhaps he was afraid he was about to lose her. Perhaps he had realised it was now or never.

"Why did you sleep with me?" she asked.

The question seemed to take him by surprise. He sighed. "Because I shouldn't have. Because I'm married, because you're my student and because I'm supposed to be doing something else with you."

"What?"

"Recruiting you."

She laughed in surprise. "Recruiting me for what?"

"The British government. For security work."

She laughed again, this time more loudly.

He put a finger over her mouth. "I'm serious."

They looked at each other in silence for long moments. He didn't crack a smile, his eyes didn't narrow.

"Why the fuck would you want to recruit me?" She wasn't sure if she believed him or was just playing along with his joke.

He lit another cigarette and lay back, looking up at the lumpy white polystyrene tiles covering the ceiling.

"China's in a god-awful mess. Mao's fucking things up like there's no tomorrow. Tens of millions are being starved or executed. Yet the Chinese are smart and industrious. A billion of them could be a threat to the world, economically, militarily. Mao, through his incompetence, keeps them contained. But Mao won't live forever. Once he goes all might change. We need to keep tabs on China, not least because of Hong Kong."

He stopped talking. No joke after all.

She reached over and grabbed his jaw, wrenching it around towards her. "What the fuck are you talking about."

"The Chinese Security Services are nothing like in your grandfather's day. However, they learned their lessons from the Cheka and the Deuxieme Bureau. And they did all that, incidentally, in Shanghai when your grandfather himself was there, though he was trying to stop them. That's where it all started, but since then the Chinese secret service has grown beyond belief. Nowadays, half a million agents work for the CSS, though usually they're just spying on their own people."

Sometimes he was like this in his lectures, skulking round the edges of something, approaching at tangents, defining the boundaries but never probing deeper.

She leaned in, teeth bared. "But recruiting me for what and why?"

He edged away a little, one shoulder now against the thickly textured anaglypta wallpaper. He held out his bare forearm so it was alongside hers. On his was revealed the whiteness of a disappointing English summer, on hers the ages-long kiss of the sub-tropical sun.

"You see, my dear, that people like me can pass as Russians, or Poles or East Germans, provided we take care learning the language. But Chinese? Not a chance."

She couldn't help blinking in stupid, naive surprise. "And where better to recruit British Chinese than in a Department of Chinese Studies? Fuck!"

He didn't answer.

186

"A spy! James Bond, Harry Palmer and now me. You've got to be joking!"

He sat up again on one elbow and turned so their faces were close.

"On the contrary," he said. "You're perfect for the job."

And, before she could stop him, he kissed her.

⊕

Most of her training was in a Nissen hut surrounded by woodland inside an Admiralty base in Teddington, west of London. That the Admiralty would settle in a place a good thirty miles from the sea was an enigma she tried to crack, exercising the skills she was developing to charm people into revealing what the hell the navy was doing here.

One thing she found out was that some of the odder shaped buildings held huge tanks of water for testing new ship and torpedo designs.

She liked to take strolls. Walking around the site was hardly condoned, especially when you were Chinese, but her Ministry of Defence security pass, rock-solid East London accent and, most of all, her looks seemed to disarm even the most hard-arsed of military policemen.

She soon found other drab olive green Nissen huts hidden away within little stands of trees. MI5 seemed to do a lot of its training here but it hadn't taken her long to realise that the Hong Kong section was like the appendix, a tiny organ that was forgotten about until it started to complain. All the money and resources coalesced around the more glamorous work of foiling Russian agents operating on British soil. After all, Russia was the threat, not poor struggling China where the rulers seemed intent on either executing or starving their own people to death.

Britain had ruled HK for well over a hundred years, a dreadful imperial complacency settling over it like a shroud even though the lease agreement on the New Territories with China was running out. With that gone, HK itself was unsustainable for the British so it too would go. However, some doubted such a handover would ever take place, the argument being that China was so hungry for hard foreign currency that an extension was inevitable.

Others, showing some vestige of paternalism for the natives, were trying to stir up concern about what would happen to the Hong Kong Chinese once the mainlanders got a grip on the place. The portents weren't good. China treated its own people disgracefully.

One good thing about being in the HK section was that for some of the training she rubbed shoulders with trainees from MI6. Firearms and unarmed combat training weren't really Five's thing. Pretty much all their agents, except those in the HK section, operated in the UK where a shit-load of back-up was but a telephone call away.

Not so in HK, and so she needed the same skills as agents for Six operating abroad, from where it was accepted that some would never return. Meanwhile, her Five trainers had boasted that they had never lost an agent in service. When she probed deeper, asking if that was for the UK only, they had grown reticent.

Hong Kong may have been an enigma, fitting uneasily into the British security hierarchy, but Six still looked with envious eyes upon it. Whichever way you cut it, it was definitely abroad so why leave it to poor old stay-at-home MI5? As the deadline approached for the handover this turf war was warming up but, for now, only Five operated in HK.

Six was used to sending its agents into far-off lands to lay their lives on the line. This made their agents a lot more interesting. Part of Six's training was to squash this down, make them appear less dashing, more normal, more easily overlooked.

You can dress a wolf in sheep's clothing but it'll still be a wolf. And bad boys had always been a weakness of hers. Hells Angels, ex-cons, they'd all come chapping at her poor old father's door asking for his daughter. She'd liked their edginess; the Angels riding their bikes like fiends, trying to frighten her, the hard-men ex-cons who didn't give a fuck about anything, who never thought through the consequences of their actions. All of them living inches from disaster.

It didn't need the appalled and disappointed looks from her father to make her realise how fucked up she must be.

A couple of weeks training with guys from Six, in their charming, arrogant company, and she'd soon forgotten bland old James. One chap in particular had caught her fancy. Hard-bodied, darkly handsome, with a look in his eye that spoke only of the worst of intentions, she'd lured him into a clump of ferns during a stroll in Richmond Park.

Wild though she was, she'd always drawn the line at anonymous sex. Nevertheless, that they'd never know each other's real names made it even more delicious.

"It's so easy for you, Su-Lin" he said afterwards, drawing a finger across her flat belly. It was early autumn, and now that their hot and heaving battle had finished, she wouldn't be waiting much longer before sliding into her clothes.

"What is?"

"This!" He waved a finger over their naked bodies. "You can get what you want, just when you want it."

"Huh! Look who's talking! I'll bet you've never lacked for girls."

He shook his head. "I'm not in your league."

He seemed serious and she tried to hide her surprise. Barely four years ago she had been in school, an ungainly fish-out-water Chinese girl in a London comprehensive school. Perhaps that had given her a certain mindset, for she still felt an instant of surprise when men found her attractive, common though that was.

The truth was she relished the sense of power her beauty gave her. It was sometimes a struggle not to let it go to her head.

She looked up at the beech tree whose reddening leaves hung low over the ferns. "I wonder where we'll be in a year's time."

"Fuck knows, for me anyway. It's obvious where you're going."

"Oh yeah?" Certainly, she'd never told him but she wasn't surprised he'd worked it out.

He sat up and started putting on his shirt. There wasn't much hair on his chest, the only disappointment, though he could be delightfully brutish in other ways. "Yeah. Watch yourself. The Sovs can be bad enough but they don't hold a candle to the chaps you'll be up against."

"So, it's all Yellow Peril and Fu Manchu with you? Really?"

He smiled. "Maybe. Maybe I've watched too many old movies. But one thing is true, if we're ever caught, neither Russia nor China are going to treat us gently."

"Getting cold feet?"

"Sometimes. Who wouldn't?"

When she didn't respond he frowned at her. "Come on! I've been honest, although that's completely against my better judgement. Don't tell me you don't feel the same way."

She didn't bother to answer but instead sat up and started to put on her shirt.

"Seriously? Never a moment of doubt?"

"Put it down to Oriental fatalism."

"Bollocks! You're more British than I am." He shook his head but she sensed a reluctant admiration. "You're my wild girl, sure enough."

She did up the last button of her blouse and then put her lips to his. Right at the end of a long lingering kiss, she took a spiteful nip at his lower lip.

He jerked back in surprise, bringing fingers up to his blood spotted mouth.

"I'm nobody's anything," she murmured to herself, not caring if he heard or not.

Tradecraft and firearms training were fine and so was unarmed combat, with no shortage of Six boys willing to grapple with her. Tall even for a white British girl, she was strong enough to hold her own against some of them, some of the time.

Not bad, but the trainers taught her well in subtler, dirtier, more evil blows against groin and windpipe and eyes. Incredibly, they'd made up a rubber head and torso with eyeballs you could scoop out. These even had little cords as a stand-in for optic nerves. She learned to whip out the eyeballs as easily as an epicure would scoop out an oyster from its opened shell.

Cantonese was a bitch, her trainer an austere white academic whose own pronunciation was faultless and who was impervious to her charms. He drove her crazy with that ridiculous sing-song language.

He was good, though. Despite his own expertise, he didn't teach her faultless Cantonese as that was the last thing she needed. Apparently, her cover wasn't really a cover at all. It had her as English of HK extraction. It would mark her out as a foreigner when she got to HK, and earn her a few patronising looks, but that was all to the good.

Her biggest problem was with her drama teacher. Where the hell Five had found her, Mary had no idea. A blousy woman, too stout and never pretty enough to be a leading lady, it was clear she resented Mary's looks.

Mary had been in plenty of am-dram productions at school though she was inevitably chosen for more decorative roles. There were few parts for Chinese in school plays and the idea of her playing a white lead just wasn't countenanced.

Spying was about pretending to be something you weren't so acting lessons made sense, at first. Soon, however, it became clear that she was not being taught for that reason at all.

When Miss Simon was unhappy, she clapped hard, stopping Mary in mid-flow. "Stop trying to be Steve McQueen! I don't want you underplaying things. Here, less is very definitely not more."

Miss Simon, though that would not be her real name just as Su-Lin was not Mary's, brushed her aside to take centre stage at this end of the Nissen hut and turned to the imaginary audience.

"Such will *never* be the case," she intoned, head back imperiously as she slashed the air with the side of her hand on the 'never', the half-cylinder of the building ringing with her declamation.

Mary didn't bother to hide her annoyance. "People don't say things like that in real life and certainly not in that way, not this century at least."

"Of course they don't, my dear." Miss Simon deployed the 'my dear' like it was a weapon.

"Then why are you teaching me this?"

Miss Simon tapped a finger against the side of her nose. "Can't say. You know that very well, my dear."

"But this is all so over the top."

"Precisely! Try it again!"

This time Mary pushed Miss Simon aside and whirled around. "Such will..." she roared, her hand tracing a huge sweep, palm raised, "...*never* be the case," and then crossed her arms across her chest, the mighty empress having spoken.

Miss Simon nodded her head. "I suppose that was... okay."

"But I was taking the piss!"

"That's as may be, but melodrama is what we're aiming for."

"Melodrama?"

"As near as dammit, yes."

Five liked Teddington because they had control within its fences and so Miss Smythe had to come to her. Every day she rattled in on her bicycle, mud spattering her Laura Ashley dress, far too grand to be fazed by the guards and the guns and the occasional body searches by tough-looking Wrens.

Feeling like a fool was bad enough, but Mary's anger steadily grew as time passed and she finished all the other courses yet still this bullshit with Miss Simon continued. Her failure to perform to the woman's satisfaction was holding her back.

And that was a big problem.

Mary had stayed at one form of school or another for almost twenty years, though on a number of occasions it been a close-run thing. Seducing the music teacher when she was sixteen had almost ended her schooldays, as well as his career. Things had been looking bad but then Hu Bai had come down to the school for the one and only time. Flayed-off skin never entirely grows back and the tiger stripes across his cheeks had shocked the headmaster. What had shocked Mary was her father's suddenly hard cold eyes. The menacing man that day in the head's office was not the person she knew.

In the end the school had dropped the whole matter, officially for lack of evidence, but really because it had all become just too weird and scary.

She'd come straight to Teddington from university without even a summer vacation and she'd now been here for six months. She was gagging to get out into the world and experience some excitement but this old witch was holding her back.

And still there was all this declamatory bullshit. It made no sense. Finally, stupid though this all was, she bent herself to pleasing the silly old woman.

Mary never coped well with bottled-up anger and as the weeks wore on, she felt like a pressure cooker on full heat. As ever, when badly wronged, she needed to strike back.

Finally, Miss Simon was, if not satisfied, at least appeased. On the last day as she came in to sign the final paperwork, Mary had followed her out to her bicycle smiling with gratitude. "Thank you for everything, Miss Simon," she said, leaning in to kiss her on the cheek.

Miss Simon seemed taken aback. Three solid months of butting heads and suddenly she seemed to have turned the girl around. "My pleasure," she said. "Best of luck, Su-Lin."

Mary watched her cycle away. 'Now that was acting, you old boot,' she thought to herself, fingering the pliers in the pocket of her jeans.

❀

Even Mary had been relieved when Miss Simons' altercation with the security Landrover caused no fatalities. The vehicle had been coming towards her on a narrow road between the trees. She'd veered to the side and braked, succeeding in the first but not in the second. Off the road and into a ditch she went, flying over the handle bars and thudding headfirst into the loamy soil.

Miss Simon left the base soiled and bereft of dignity but with no broken bones. A perfect result as far as Mary was concerned.

Revenge, as ever, tasted so sweet.

15. Foulness, Essex, UK

The Son, Benny Hu, and the Field of Reeds

The tail had been so subtle that even though he had been watching carefully, Benny had begun to wonder if it was there at all. They were certainly taking no chances. Serious surveillance on anyone in a car might involve ten vehicles and twenty people if you didn't want the tail being discovered.

He was far out of London, almost at Southend, before he spotted a car he had noted when he'd set out that morning. This soon disappeared again and it wasn't until he was beyond the seaside town, and had caught his first sight of the Thames estuary, that he saw it for a third time.

The car was the tip an iceberg and it showed that Six wasn't messing around.

That was scary all by itself. Lea's assertion that Six were giving him the benefit of the doubt must be so much bullshit. This amount of manpower was to make sure he couldn't run.

Thinking of her brought another surge of anger. Right from the start she'd played him. He hoped she'd be at the meeting. He'd been endlessly, bitterly rehearsing what he would say. She wouldn't find it to her taste.

Meanwhile, as Benny's old BMW effortlessly ate up the miles, the landscape around him was slipping back into the past. Fields of reeds stretched serenely to the horizon, waiting to be harvested by farmers in smocks and floppy brimmed hats who had gone to their graves centuries before. No more than thirty miles east of London, this was a different world. Miles of mud flats and the meandering maze of creeks that locals claimed were still haunted by the ghosts of a Dickensian cast of smugglers, convicts and highwaymen.

Foulness was an island that had been owned by the military for nearly two hundred years. Used for artillery testing, the roads and buildings had remained unchanged from Victorian times.

Benny had been here before. A keen walker, he was fascinated by the notorious Broomway. Until a bridge was built, it had been how people got to the island on foot – and then only at low tide. Running for six miles along the Maplin Sands, with the mists and the outlines of the Kent coast across the estuary easy to mistake as the Island, over a hundred walkers had been lured to their deaths there over the years. The tide came in fast over the mud flats and, once the shingle path disappeared under the water, it was all too easy to stray into the mud. The fine silt would suck at your feet as you struggled towards the mirage only to be swallowed by the hungry Thames.

Once a month the MoD opened the Broomway for serious walkers. Benny had been a couple of times, had gone so far out into the mist that disorientation had set in and a delicious tang of fear had blown away the cobwebs of London life. Once he had even closed his eyes and spun himself around until he really had lost all sense of direction.

He had savoured the confusion of his senses, not sure which way led to safety, which way to a watery grave.

He had reached into his pocket, taking out his phone with its digital compass. All he had to do was glance at it to tell which was which.

Instead, he almost threw the phone far out into the water.

That kind of behaviour had disturbed even him.

Strange that Six had chosen this same place to meet. It had to be coincidence.

His destination wasn't on Foulness itself but close enough that he could see the bridge and the military comms masts on the Island side. He headed north out of Great Wakering, the nearest little village, on a single-track road. The tide was out and he could make out the tilted-over masts of a couple of small fishing boats beached on the creek mud. He found the farmhouse after five hundred metres and at the end of the track. Surrounded by creek and reeds, a muddy sign advertised it as being a fishery as well as a farm.

He pulled into the yard and parked between two stacks of creels. When he opened the door the pungent smell of salty mud and fish rolled into the car. Gusts of wind off the North Sea stroked the reeds like the fir of a much-loved pet.

He got out and put his hands on his hips and turned to survey the flat Essex landscape. Far away to the north, beyond what he knew would be the River Crouch, church steeples dotted the gently rising ground.

The land that time forgot he thought.

He turned back to take a closer look at the ramshackle farm-cum-fishery-cum-what-the-fuck. Many of the roof slates were missing. Perhaps that explained the little weather-stained caravan lurking in the building's shadow. It was big enough to sleep two uncomfortably.

Six could be cheap, as his endless battles to reclaim legitimate expenses had proved. But even by Six's low standards this had to be the shittiest interrogation centre ever. So much so that it was hard to...

His stomach shrank to a ball. This wasn't an interrogation centre at all.

Disposing of a body amongst all these reeds would be so easy.

Suddenly he felt trapped. Perhaps he should get back in his car, barge his way through the legions of cars following him. Back to

Southend then north into the back roads of Essex, driving like a madman to shake them all off and get clear.

Too late! He heard the gentle drone of a car's engine coming down the single-track road. Over the top of the reeds he saw its black roof moving like the fin of a shark.

No room to get past it without his wheels sinking into the mud. He was bottled in.

Then he heard another motor approaching. Frantic, he searched around for a weapon and saw a handy looking metal pipe sticking out between a couple of rusted oil drums. He rushed over and was reaching out for it before he realised what it really was.

It was the barrel of an assault rifle and it was pointing dead-centre at his chest.

Behind him he could hear the first car pulling into the yard. Looking round he saw men beginning to climb out. As they did so he heard the vicious crack of a far-off high velocity round.

"Get down, you stupid prick!" Lea was suddenly beside him, pulling at his arm. She had a gun, a small automatic, and she was pointing it at the men in the car. All around, camouflaged figures were rising like spectres out of the reeds.

And in all that confusion, something caught his eye, something stupid, almost comedic. One of the guys getting out of the car was struggling to pull a gun out of his shoulder holster. It came free but he'd been concentrating too hard. His foot caught the sill of the car and he pitched forward.

Suddenly Benny was living a lucid dream, real life moving with glacial slowness while his thoughts sparked like lightening. The gun in the man's outstretched hand was pointing at them and about to hit the ground.

Benny had put his arm across Lea's body and swept her behind him.

The gun went off.

Someone shoved a lance into Benny's side, sending him pirouetting away, arms flailing, one foot catching on another. One hand slapped the ground as his face smacked into gravel and dirt.

There was thump to his right as an overbalanced Lea tumbled down. There were other sounds, halfway between coughs and sighs.

Turning his head, trying to make sense of the spinning images, he could see, over at the car, a thicket of arms being raised. Camouflaged figures were splashing their way out of the muddy reeds.

He felt Lea's hands roughly grab him, turning him over. She tore at his shirt, then bent low to get a closer look. He felt her fingers touch his flesh. Far above them all a lonely little cloud rolled across an ice blue sky.

Lea was wearing a nicely cut black suit but it didn't stop her sitting back heavily on the dirt. She put her hands on her knees and nodded her head in what looked like relief.

"It doesn't look bad," she said. "In and out, barely grazed you."

"Well, it doesn't feel that way," was what he'd wanted to say but it didn't come out right and she frowned in puzzlement

Over her shoulder he saw camouflaged soldiers clustering round the car. Several were pointing their assault rifles down at the guy on the ground. He wasn't moving. Two other Chinese guys were on their faces in the dirt, hands behind their backs and secured with cable ties.

A guy in a green pullover, clearly the officer in command, had appeared and was now talking urgently into his phone. Then he gave a nod and put the phone away. He strode over to them, looking down at Benny's exposed flesh.

"How is it?" he asked.

"He'll live," said Lea, getting to her feet and dusting herself down.

This was enough for the officer. He turned to face Lea. "Got another three carloads in the village. Nobody injured."

"The shot?"

"Just a warning, calmed down our Chinese friends no end."

"The other cars?"

"Heading back to London lickety-split, but we'll get them before they even reach Southend." Then, as though having second thoughts, the officer squatted down beside Benny.

"Ambulance is on the way."

Message telegraphed, he stood back up and marched off.

Lea was looking down at Benny, hands on her hips. "It really isn't that bad. You could probably stand up."

The world had begun to revolve, the little cloud circling like a stacked plane over Heathrow.

"Not right now," he managed to say and this time it came out all right.

Lea raised her head and looked around, her expression troubled. She took a deep breath. "If you hadn't..." But then she stopped. She looked down at him again. "Fuck you!"

"You're welcome."

She shook her head. "I don't owe you anything." But it sounded like she was trying to convince herself.

Benny ventured to lean over on an elbow and push himself upright. Steeling himself for the worst, he glanced down at his wound.

Lea was right, the bullet had ploughed only a shallow furrow across his side. A centimetre or so deeper and it would have punctured the cavity containing all his guts. Peritonitis would have been an issue. As it was, a dab of antiseptic and a few stitches was all that lay in his future.

He still felt too wobbly to stand. Instead, he looked back up at her.

"Don't give me that look!" She sounded so annoyed.

"What look?"

"The sick puppy thing."

"I wasn't."

Those high oriental cheekbones he loved so much were ticking at her skin as she repeatedly clenched and unclenched her jaw.

"Bollocks!" She knelt down until her face was close to his, her dark eyes fierce.

"Jade Forest," she said then stood back upright, turned on her heel and strode back into the farmhouse.

16. Hong Kong 1972

The Mother, Mary Hu, and the Hidden Treasure

Arms folded across her chest, Mary looked out over the steaming tropical city. Her cool, air-conditioned apartment, high up on Victoria Peak, commanded views across the harbour to bustling Kowloon. Beyond that, in an easy day's walk, lay China.

She'd never been there, but she'd helped plenty who'd fled the place. Like swallows presaging the momentous changes of spring, the refugees were signs that the Great Beast was stirring.

Thinking of the refugees made her think of her father and grandfather. She'd learned little about either from her father, who hoarded his secrets like a miser. Now in Hong Kong, she'd seen MI5 files that brought their lives into startling focus.

Both had made names for themselves, however reluctantly. They'd become urban legends, cropping up in interviews with fleeing dissidents and politicians, gangsters and spies. Decades ago, they'd appeared on the radar of domestic intelligence. Searching background checks had been made.

She'd never known her grandfather so when she found out he had murdered a Frenchman a zillion years before, it had been little more than mildly intriguing. However, there were other, later, reports and she had real trouble equating the man in those with her shy, gentle, broken father.

One thing the investigations had cleared up was the mystery that had intrigued and horrified her for her whole life. Once, returning from her school (one of the better private ones in East London) and desperate for a slash, she'd barged into the bathroom. Her father, usually such a careful and cautious man, had been taking a bath but had left the door unlocked.

Unable to halt her momentum she was right up to the bath before she could stop. His arms came up, not to hide his soapy genitals but to cover the mutilations of his chest. With cold, drenching shock, she realised that those alien, almost tribal markings on his face, extended further down across his body.

The facial scarring, on the few occasions they had seen them without disguising make-up, had intrigued her twittering school friends. Tall and lean and rangy, he would have been a good-looking Chinese man but his disfigurements gave him a dangerous allure which took him to another level in their eyes. Usually, fathers were considered old and sexless but sometimes she had seen her empty-headed friends casting him looks of frank and not unfavourable appraisal.

Until she had come to Hong Kong, she had not known how to answer their incessant questions and speculations as to why he had been so butchered. Now she knew the answer.

The gangster Huang Jinrong had a voluminous file, much of it devoted to his assassination and the massacre at his home. One of Huang's men had somehow survived a finishing shot to the head, though he was forever blinded. The French secret service man, Fiori, had interrogated him on his hospital bed.

The Deuxieme Bureau had held the information close to its chest for many years until it was shared in a moment of détente with MI6, one imperialist war-monger to another. In the following years, in an equally uncharacteristic gesture, Six had finally shared the file with Five.

Mary couldn't recognise her father in what was written about the gangster Hu Bai. A participant in the Shanghai massacre of 1927, the lover of the mistress of a dangerous Triad boss, horribly mutilated by said boss while he fed his mistress to a tiger! Mary was hardly a sheltered innocent but it made her head spin.

Her father was such a quiet, contemplative man. A moderately successful property developer who still spoke his careful English with a Shanghai accent. He had not married until his fifties; perhaps it had taken that long for enough skin to regrow over the parts that had been torn away. Perhaps he had felt too mortified to inflict himself on a woman.

Not that it would have mattered to Mary's no-nonsense mother Lin. When they met, she'd been working as a nurse in a general surgery ward and would have seen far worse.

Mary fingered the sumptuous curtains that betrayed her European tastes. Rather than the propitious reds and golds so loved by the Chinese, she preferred understated fawns and off-whites. Rather than heavy dark wood for desks and tables she went for blond Scandinavian furniture. Her Chinese actress friends thought her apartment insipidly furnished; she thought theirs garish.

One of her understated pieces of furniture was much more exciting than her friends could imagine. A solid white desk, it lay against one wall. From her airing cupboard she took three small pine boards and laid them just to the front and side of three of the legs.

A western diet and upbringing had made her far less dainty than the Chinese starlets. Her firmly muscled body was a source of fascination for producers, not to mention for her lovers. It gave her an edge in casting for certain parts, usually the overbearing but beautiful villainess.

It also meant she could easily lift the desk, pivoting it around the fourth leg, until she could ease the other three legs down onto the pine boards. This would leave no telltale indentations on the carpet when she lifted the desk back into its usual position.

She went around the back of the desk. She slid back an artfully disguised panel and pulled out some files.

The papers were in the usual tatty old brown folders that MI5 loved so much. They looked earnest, worthy and heavy with the authority of a labyrinthine officialdom. Files like this crossing desks back in Whitehall would carry with them with the sense of permanence and certainty that Hong Kong was safely under British control.

She knew all too well that it wasn't. The place was a hotbed of espionage heaving with double and even triple agents, their betrayals so common that some lost track of who they really served. It was a city where everyone was superficially open but inwardly guarded. A city now deeply in denial about the time soon approaching when the Great Beast would reclaim its orphan child.

She took out a folder and flipped it open. She brushed her long black hair from over her eyes so that it cascaded over her shoulder and down her lean frame. Every inch the actress now, each theatrical gesture was for the benefit of an imaginary camera.

Miss Simon, it turned out, had taught her well. Nothing that Mary, now calling herself Jade Forest, did nowadays was knowingly underplayed. As far as Hong Kong film directors were concerned, if you underplayed a part then it showed you could not act. Once, when Mary had tried to introduce some nuance into a reaction shot, that of a shop girl betrayed by her rich lover, the director had lifted up his megaphone and screamed: *If I want no acting then I get any bitch off street!*

The potted history at the beginning of the file she knew too well. Mao, the man her father had failed to eliminate (such an opportunity wasted!) had gone on to lead a brutal civil war against Chiang Kai-shek and the right wing KMT. The KMT had previously made a good job of ridding China of the warlords who before them had filled the vacuum left when the monarchy had fallen. In 1927 the KMT had had the communists in their sights and the Shanghai massacre had been just the start. The KMT had gone on to wipe out 300,000 of them in the following year.

That said, even in his early days, Mao had been pretty good at massacres too, including 700,000 Hakkas in the mountainous provinces of Jiangxi and Fujian.

Deaths in China were on a scale Mary could not comprehend. The numbers were absurd and always had been. A quarter of a million killed in the 1920 earthquake, for example, but her own ghastly favourite was the 700,000 who had constructed the First Emperor's tomb. To show his gratitude he had them all executed and entombed with him.

But Mao had come to triumph over these piddling death tolls, even surpassing the twenty million or so killed by the Japanese when they invaded China before the Second World War. As a taster, he oversaw the murders of four million landlords and wealthier peasants before masterminding the agricultural changes in the Great Leap Forward that saw around forty million starve to death.

No wonder the peaceful people of Hong Kong were in denial that this monster was due to reclaim them in less than twenty years. Doing anything to fend that off, or at least cushion the blow, was the right thing to do and left Mary with no doubt that her work was important.

In the end, Chiang and his KMT fled to Taiwan, where they had been a thorn in China's side ever since. The mainland, Hong Kong and Taiwan made three sorts of China. The Great Beast was hell-bent on making sure there would be only one.

Grandfather and father Hu's Green Gang, so out of favour with the communists after the Shanghai massacre, blotted their copybooks still further by collaborating with the invading Japanese even before the Second World War. When the communists finally came to full power, the few surviving gang members fled to Hong Kong. However, the heroin refineries they started there were soon taken over by local Chaozhou gangsters and the Green Gang had been wiped out.

So much for the background history. Mary now got to the part of the file she dealt with; the little people victimised by it all. She liked to be prepared for her work so she concentrated on their details before taking the file back to the desk. Before she put it away, she reached into the hidden space and pulled out her little black Beretta.

She plucked out the magazine then drew back the slide to make sure no bullet was chambered. She pulled the trigger and the gun gave a satisfying, well-oiled click.

She lay the gun and magazine down on a coffee table, eased the file back into its hiding place, closed the panel and then carefully manoeuvred the desk so the legs were exactly over the indentations they had made in the carpet. She picked up and hid the little wooden boards.

Returning to the coffee table she slid the magazine back into the pistol. She placed it in her fawn leather handbag, covering it with a gaudy silk handkerchief.

When she put it on, the little bag was heavy on her shoulder. She stood in front of her full-length hall mirror and practised putting it on and off her shoulder, increasing her familiarity and ease, making the bag look lighter than it really was.

Finally, she checked herself in the mirror, turning to make sure the dress showed to advantage her hard little breasts and buttocks.

She re-applied her lipstick and eyeliner, the black lines emphasising the shape of her eyes. It hardly mattered, though. In her experience it was the unearthly jade green of her pupils which transfixed most men, sometimes reducing even the high and mighty to tongue-tied schoolboys.

She might turn heads but she was still a long way from the dainty perfection of the big Hong Kong stars. She had just enough beauty for supporting roles: star's best friend, gangster's moll, evil conniving whore, wicked demoness. She'd played them all.

She was already on borrowed time. She was approaching her thirtieth year and one day the producers would lose interest.

But not just yet!

17. Somewhere in the UK

The Son, Benny Hu, and the Morgue for Forgotten Things

Grey walls, locked cells, barely edible institutional food.

Now this, thought Benny, was an interrogation centre.

They'd taken everything away, leaving him only some green scrubs and white slippers to wear. No TV, no newspapers. Thick airport thrillers were the only things to read. Sooner rather than later, he was going get really sick of Wilbur Smith.

The days were long and the nights even longer. Once a day, they'd take him for interrogation. No water boarding or bloody noses for him, just relentlessly polite questioning going over, again and again, events that had become fiction even to him after so much repetition. Soon, like his interrogators, he had come to doubt everything that had happened in China.

Refusing to answer their questions would have meant prolonging this monotonous hell. He hadn't been charged, hadn't even been arrested. That he was here at all would appear on no record, enter no statistical tabulation, would never furrow the brow of a concerned politician or social worker. There were no family to miss him, no friendships deep enough to register real concern at his disappearance. Certainly not for someone who disappeared for long stretches anyway.

Ludicrously, melodramatically, he had taken to marking the passing days on the wall. Over each week, and with just his fingernail, he scratched six lines like a picket fence with a final diagonal flourish to kiss the week goodbye.

He was scratching a line in the nearly completed fourth fence when he heard footsteps on the polished floor. He got up wearily, bracing himself for another day's interrogation.

His cell had no natural light so the trips to the interrogation block where a treat. At one point, a single window looked out onto a couple of oaks by the gate. Redness was creeping into their leaves, harbingers of an early autumn. It must be getting cold out there but inside some ancient beast of a boiler huffed and puffed to keep the temperature high and the atmosphere stuffy. The place felt like a care home, only adding to his sense of confinement.

Out there, soldiers would be prowling the grounds but inside nobody wore uniforms. No suits either, just casual jackets, sometimes even just shirts and ties. Once he'd noticed one of his interrogators wearing comfortable looking corduroys.

He slouched after the man leading him to his interrogation. The guy was tall and slim, his stride verging on the jaunty, like he was heading for a hot date. When he got to the door, he held it open and with the other hand waved him through like a maitre d'.

But this time, rather than some grey, nameless apparatchik from Six poring over files, he found himself looking into Lea's unfaltering gaze.

"Take a seat, Benny." Her voice was so much cooler than the centre's overheated air.

He hadn't seen her since the farm. She was wearing the same black suit. Well cut to her slender form, it was more a fashion accessory than work gear. She looked good.

They stared at each other across the cheap wooden table, its legs firmly bolted to the floor in case of a surfeit of emotion. Each waited for the other to break the uncomfortable silence.

Over the last few weeks Benny had become used to a lack of comfort so he won easily. She grimaced a little then asked: "How's the wound?"

Benny lifted up his greens. The stitches had fallen out and the bruising had faded. The scar was still visible but it wouldn't be for much longer. Anything he was left with would only be noticeable by a lover or under the harsh lights of an autopsy table.

He couldn't help smiling at the memory of how the medics had acted at Southend General Hospital. Gunshot wounds were a rarity in Essex and it had been like all their Christmases had come at once.

"What's so funny?"

He wasn't in the mood to share. "That I should catch a bullet meant for you." He waved an arm around to encompass the grim little room. "And that you would be so grateful."

"I am grateful, Benny. I've done nothing ever since but spend my time checking out your story. Hoping we could resolve this as quickly as possible, one way or the other."

"And will it be one way, or will it be the other?"

She sat back and crossed her arms. "We believe you. On balance."

Benny couldn't help but laugh.

"What?"

"Etiolated, as in the weak growth of plants in the absence of light."

"What the fuck are you talking about?"

"You, the way you said that. It sounded feeble."

Creases appeared in the satin smooth skin of her forehead. "You really need to grow up, mate. Nothing's certain in this business. 'On balance' is the best you could hope for."

She was right but he wasn't here to make her feel better. He'd suffered agonies of guilt about Jiang when alone in his cell. He had to take it out on someone. "So now what?"

"Well, whichever way you look at it you're fucked. Even if you were working for them, the Chinese aren't going to forgive you for leading them into our little trap. We netted fifteen of their operative, plus we now have eyes on a shitload of their associates."

"A counter-intelligence coup. Nice idea, by the way. Making it all go down in the arse end of nowhere. No chance of collateral damage, no chance of the Goo disappearing into the crowds."

She nodded slightly, apparently not caring any more about his opinions. "Want a cup of coffee? Good stuff. This place isn't just for bad boys like you."

He believed her. Even now somewhere, in another wing, a defector was probably being treated like royalty.

"We might be able to rustle up some cakes as well. May as well go for it. We've got a lot to talk about."

"Like what?"

She smiled, though not warmly. "Your new life, such as it will be."

There are still internet cafés around if you take the trouble to find them. Usually within immigrant ghettos where people sleep ten to a room. This one was in the back of a deli selling what were probably Romanian delicacies. The only things he could identify were massive pigs' trotters immersed in a clear jelly, and parcels of meat and rice wrapped in cabbage.

Five quid and the price of an instant coffee bought him unlimited time on one of the grease-smeared PCs in a dingy backroom. Only one other guy was there, eating his food and sniffling with a cold as he watched what looked like a travelogue of a hilly, heavily wooded country. Tinny wailing music leaked out from his headphones. The man was absorbed and didn't even turn to look when Benny came in.

One benefit of this place was that it didn't have a wireless internet connection, everything was hardwired into a box which was hardwired into the phone network. Even if they had managed to follow him, there was no wi-fi signal to tap into. Even so, he'd ducked and dived his way through alleys and shops and the underground, switching connections only when a train was on the opposite side of the platform. He'd made so many changes even he didn't know what station he would wind up at. From there he'd taken a taxi to this place.

So, when he logged on he was as sure as he could be that Six weren't going to know about it.

His own place was out of bounds forever. The hostel he'd been dumped in would be monitored. Six were setting up an identity for him somewhere up north and he was staying in the hostel until they did. He'd be starting from scratch all over again.

He began searching the net. There certainly were a shitload of Jade Forests but they were pretty much all about a huge virtual location in a popular video game. It was also the name of a beautiful Belgian model who didn't look remotely Chinese. The name was actually Foret and he assumed that was French for forest, though in the event it turned out to mean 'drill'.

The search algorithm was big on similar spellings. Jade Forrests included a management consultant and an equestrian, neither of whom seemed in any way relevant to him. Then, whatever convoluted algorithms the search engine was using revealed there was indeed a Jade Forest in Hezhou in China. The place must be pretty obscure because it hadn't provoked a single comment on Tripadviser.

Deeper and deeper into the search results revealed a tonic water and a martial arts training group.

Away to his right the man gave a massive snort followed by an explosive sneeze that pattered mucous across his screen. Benny held his breath, hoping the cloud of water droplets loaded with germs would sink to the floor before he had to breath in again. The man dug out a tissue and made a half-hearted attempt to wipe his face clean. One more sneeze like that and he was going to get a broken nose for his troubles.

Benny sat back and folded his hands across his chest. Lea had been at her most vulnerable when she'd given him the name Jade Forest. It must be a tasty morsel of truth and therefore something she must bitterly regret mentioning. The way she had treated him had been appalling, and he hardly felt he owed her anything. At the interrogation centre he'd been tempted to ask outright about Jade Forest. The listeners would have heard and she'd have been in trouble.

And that might have been gratifying, but then Six would have known that he knew about the mysterious Jade Forest. What might they resort to in order to stop him looking into it further?

Just like he was doing now.

He paged on. A spa, a road in Missouri, a design of wallpaper, all of them buried amongst the mountain of hits for the damned video game.

Something to do with Tai Chi, a Houston apartment complex, a Chinese film star...

He smiled to himself. Just about the one thing he remembered about his mother was that her nose was a mess. Hardly film star material.

He was bringing his finger down to page on when the hairs on the back of his neck stood up. The hit was for a website devoted to Hong Kong cinema of the 70s and 80s which at least would be the right time period. An actress called Jade Forest had appeared in a film called Bloody Killer Demons from Hell which the fans had rated based on the body count and the gallons of blood spilled.

Yu Lin was the translation of Jade Forest but his search engine didn't seem to be able to cope with the accented vowels indicating rising and lowering tones. It drew a blank.

He found a Chinese website claiming to be an encyclopaedia of HK film. Putting in the Chinese name brought up a picture of the actress, a tall slender beauty, fine-featured and with smouldering, devilish eyes.

He forgot to breathe.

For the first time in over thirty years, he found himself looking at his mother. Not the one he had known but a glitzier, far handsomer version. He peered more closely. He knew well enough how make-up could be used as a disguise but there were limits. He realised that his mother had once had a perfectly formed nose.

The site had a filmography and this brought up a whole bunch of films, none of which he'd heard of. Then again, the only films he knew of from HK were the Bruce Lee chop-socky stuff. His mother's films had names like Tortured Singer, Slaughtering Chef, Sold into Slavery, Ninja Apocalypse. The movie posters showed knives, guns, blood splatter and semi-naked women. Thankfully, none of those were of his mother.

He found a section devoted to actors' bios. Some had many pages of text but his mother's ran to just three lines.

Jade Forest. Born London 19??, moved to Hong Kong in 19??, worked for Shaw Studios 19??—19??. Appeared in 54 films, her height precluding her from leading roles. Usually played scheming mistress/ villain. Suffered disfiguring accident and retired in 19??

Hong Kong films had always been a joke, being ridiculously gory and incomprehensible. Films consigned to the notorious HK Category III were the worst. Films where a man might lose his penis and have a horse's cock transplanted in its place. Where real animals were hacked to pieces, where a cat might be trapped in a cellar with a horde of starving rats. Movies where disembowelling was mere punctuation rather than a devastating moment around which the whole plot pivoted. Films where every attempt at gratuitous semi-nudity was resorted to, where any women with (for Han) an uncharacteristically generous cleavage was forced at every opportunity to lean forward, spending entire movies as if they were hunchbacks.

The afternoon slipped away unnoticed as he ferreted through his mother's past. Not much of the new information was welcome. Jade Forest had had her own fans and they were more than happy to write slash fiction involving characters she had played, usually sick dominance fantasies. Perhaps it was Mary's height but this fan fiction usually ended up with her driving the tip of her high-heeled shoe into the helpless protagonist's crotch or eye socket.

One gossipy website linked Mary with an actor called Tang but, in the end, after Tang had been busted for public indecency in a gents' toilet in the 90s, the author had downgraded their relationship from red-hot affair to fag-hag friendship. Film-wise Tang had dropped off the radar after his arrest but as far as Benny could glean from other fan sites, he was still alive and living in Hong Kong.

Why had Mary made HK her home before she had given birth to Benny? Perhaps she'd gone back there after she left him. Lea claimed that she'd not been on a mission when she'd disappeared, but that meant nothing. Even Benny knew that HK, sitting cheek-by-jowl with the Great Beast, had been an espionage Mecca back in the 70s. It was an obvious place to send an operative of Chinese extraction.

Why would she have returned to the place? Lea had now gone completely dark and would be of no help anyway. The only way he would ever see her again was if Six came looking for him, in circumstances that were unlikely to be to his benefit.

With Lea gone and Jiang dead he had nothing left here in the UK. If he started a new life in Gateshead, or wherever, then he would be back to zero. All he had left was this central mystery that had dogged his life. Who was his mother and why had she vanished? Where had his whole family come from for that matter, and what had happened to them?

If he was ever going to answer these questions then now was the time.

❁

The storage facility was in a run-down industrial estate in Croydon. On one side, single-floor cinder-block buildings held the offices and workshops of plumbers and mechanics. On the other side, beyond the chain-link fence, a crumbling housing estate peeked through a line of scrappy trees. Everything looked drab and woebegone under an oppressive leaden sky.

The facility had been a long walk from the station; the days of using his car for anything but the most mundane chores were now gone. Face recognition might still be challenging for AIs but when it came to number plates the issue had been sewn up years before. At least on foot he could duck and dive through shops and arcades.

The storage facility had cameras. There was a fair chance they'd stopped working years before. Even so, he was wearing a baseball cap with a priapic brim that cast a shadow across his whole face.

The attendant, a moody well-dressed Sikh who gave every indication of having a job well beneath his station, hardly glanced at Benny as he took his card. He thrust a form across the desk. "Sign!"

Benny did so and the man compared it with something on his screen. Finally, he looked up. "You have the key?"

Benny fished it out of his pocket.

"Ring when you want to leave. The button is down by the right of the door. We close at five. "

Benny nodded and the man bent down and pressed something below his desk. There was a buzzing sound and the door clicked open. Inside, strip-lights flickered to life, revealing two rows of roll-up shutters.

The interior was broken up into a grid of corridors and Benny made his way through them, wrinkling his nose at the stale, metallic smells and the lines of dust bunnies becalmed where walls met floor. He imagined each unit full of old toys and dirty clothes.

Pulling up the metal shutter made a terrible racket in this morgue for forgotten things.

His unit contained only a couple of cardboard boxes full of old paperback books, a bounty too crap for even the most desperate thief. He dug through until he found John Grisham's A Painted House and lifted it clear. Opening it revealed a hundred pages with their centres cut out. Inside this cavity nestled two passports and a debit card. False identities and an account built up carefully over the years.

Traitors or not, every spy needed a way out. Just in case you were burned, just in case regimes changed, just in case a monstrous fuck-up meant scapegoats had to be found. Situations where suddenly you were the fall-guy.

He rolled down the shutter for the last time. It took a few rings of the bell but finally the grumpy Sikh buzzed him out.

Benny waved him a final goodbye.

18. Hong Kong 1974

The Mother, Mary Hu, and the Blue-Haired Dogs

Already in mid-air, her scarlet robes flapping like wings, Mary saw the sword slicing straight at her face. She jerked her own sword up, attempting to deflect it.

Above all, she tried desperately not to flinch.

Steel met steel with a clang. Tang's sword was driven upwards, hacking through her straw hat. Their bodies collided, kicking the wind from Mary's lungs and spinning her through the air. The harsh studio lights spiralled away.

She made herself go limp in the nick of time, crashing down onto a mattress, one flailing foot hitting the concrete floor. Far away she heard a solid thud and realised Tang had not been so lucky.

Pandemonium. Everyone was shrieking, not least the director. Extra film for retakes came out of his salary. Tang was wailing like a little girl and the wardrobe woman was already grabbing up the destroyed coolie hat and cursing. Mai, Mary's hairdresser, was looming over her, brandishing a powder brush and scolding her loudly.

Mary batted Mai's hands aside and sat up to nurse her foot. The filthy mattress, one of a job lot imported from a US flophouse twenty years before, stank like a whore's crotch, or so she imagined. Every time an actor landed on it, it would puff out the rotten fragments of skin from drunks long dead, the richness of their odours having steadily matured like rank cheese under the hot studio lights.

Her foot hurt like hell but at least nothing seemed broken. Mai was reaching in again so Mary slapped her away, and this time was less gentle about it.

She got to her feet and limped over to Tang, who was lying on his back and weeping freely. Mary would have booted him in the ribs but that would have meant putting her weight on her bad foot.

She realised the sword was still in her hand. The edge was blunt as buggery but it would still smart. She raised it above her head but was tackled by a bunch of quick-thinking crew members who prised it from her hands.

"You fucking amateurs!" the director was yelling. "You move like fucking elephants!"

"I hit my mark just right!" Mary found herself shouting back. Oriental arguments started explosively but soon petered out if left alone. She should have kept quiet but this had been a bastard of a day.

Tang was looking up at her plaintively. "I'm sorry, Jade. My foot slipped. I hit the trampoline off-balance."

Tang was such a wimp that at times like this he always made her feel like a bully. With his long floppy hair and elegant movements, he was like a throwback to the Hong Kong cinema of the sixties. In those social dramas the audiences loved heroes who would have looked bookish and effeminate to Western eyes.

When HK cinema had swung towards Kung Fu, the lead actors had had to get a whole lot tougher, even Tang. The fight sequences might end up looking balletic, but were bone-crunching to produce.

The reason Tang got jobs was that he excelled in 'the look'. Before every fight, deadly male adversaries would glare at each other in a decidedly homoerotic way. After that they'd fight in what, to Mary, looked like classic sublimation. Homosexuality was forbidden, but was always lurking under the surface in this strange culture.

"Sound's gone!" someone shouted. "We'll need to check it out."

Mary didn't need to be fluid in Cantonese and Mandarin to know what this meant. Nobody had a clue what was wrong but it would take a while to fix.

The director, a thin, driven man who smoked constantly, stamped his feet and seemed to be trying to tear his hair out. He looked up at the ceiling of the big sound stage and screamed.

"Come on!" said Mary, reaching down. "Let's get some tea."

Tang grasped her proffered hand and she pulled him to his feet. Supporting each other as best they could, they staggered away from the unconvincing stand of bamboo where the fight had been taking place.

Mary, as usual, was playing the villainess, in this case one who had poisoned Tang's beloved. This was the scene where Tang would have dispatched her before shoving his sword up her husband's arse. In the penultimate scene Tang would have cut the arms off her dying warlord husband, an oblique oriental reference to castration, before killing himself by ritual disembowelment.

In other words, your basic Kung Fu tragedy.

It made the Carry On films look subtle.

They both collapsed into canvas chairs and the tea lady quickly brought them the brackish tea Mary still had trouble appreciating.

The film, like just about all of them nowadays, was in Mandarin for audiences in Taiwan and for the Chinese diaspora, particularly those in the States. Once China closed its markets to HK film, local audiences were too small to keep making films in Cantonese.

Once upon a time all Hong Kong films had been in Cantonese but those days were long gone.

People still spoke the language, of course, so she and Tang switched to it.

"You slipped?" said Mary, arching an eyebrow heavily accentuated with powder. Make-up was never understated, especially if you were playing a bad guy.

Tang's head was bowed and his big lick of black hair slid down over one eye. He brushed it back in a gesture the girls here loved. Come to think of it, it might work back in the UK as well. Tang could have filled his life with beautiful women just about anywhere in the world but his tastes were for rougher trade.

"I was distracted. I think Wei is seeing someone else. If he left me, I don't know what I would do without him."

Wei was the son of a small landowner cut to pieces by jealous neighbours whose savagery had been given full reign by Mao's brutal dictates. He was just the sort of unmannered country boy that got Tang's juices flowing. Mary had also been interested in him at first, as she was in all the fleeing Chinese who wound up in HK, but the boy had no intelligence information to offer. Her gentle probing had simply left him confused.

Actors in genuine pain tended to take facial expressions to whole new levels. Tang looked like he was living his last moments in exquisite agony. "Where does it hurt?" she asked wearily.

"My back. Could you make sure I still have one?"

Without waiting for a reply, he stripped off his shirt in one graceful movement. Mary had time for only a glimpse of a hairless chest and well-defined abdominal muscles, and then he turned to show his long, elegant back. Before Mary knew what she was doing she was gently touching a red discolouration just above the swell of a hard buttock peeking over the top of his black trousers.

"Ow!" he said but did not draw away.

"That's going to leave a nasty bruise." Close up she could smell his sweat from the running and the jumping under hot lights. Mary just hoped she smelled as good as he did.

"Maybe if I put some face cream on it. Cool it down a bit."

Tang snorted. "Thank you, Doctor, that sounds just right."

"Got any better ideas?" Mary had heard that in Hollywood you couldn't move for doctors and nurses on film sets, but the Shaw Brothers in HK took quite a different view. In their Clear Water Bay facility there were eleven stages plus fifteen permanent sets, almost all in continuous use, but few, if any, qualified persons to tend the sick and injured.

The make-up ladies could be called on in a pinch. From bitter experience, she and Tang knew their Chinese remedies for bruising consisted of one part cayenne pepper to five parts Vaseline. Both knew it was ineffective except if your skin was broken, in which case it was very effective at promoting pain.

"Any shirts-off scenes?" asked Mary, sitting back down. She took films one scene at a time and couldn't remember from her single complete read-through. Why bother when the plots were usually more similar than a litter of puppies?

Tang also tended to take a pragmatic view of his low art. As he pulled his shirt back on, his smooth brow was creased with thought. "I don't think so, not on this one. And the other, over on Three, I don't think I take my shirt off there at all. Got to do some ballroom dancing though." He rubbed his back. "That's not going to be easy."

"Wind, snow, flowers and moon," said Mary wryly though, as with so many other HK expressions, she had no idea where it came from. It meant that this other film would show opulence and decadence. HK was still a society in transition. The older generation, many of whom had swum to freedom over the Pearl River Delta, had known little but starvation and poverty. They were cautious, conservative and steeped in Confucian paternalism where the older generation were supposed to be respected as they were always right.

The lifestyle examples of rich Westerners were existential threats to that life, counter-examples to this way of thinking. They also showed too sharp a contrast with the conditions most

Hongkongers lived and worked in. They toiled for ten hours a day, six days a week making textiles and plastics. Eight thousand were crammed into every square mile in slums where single-bed spaces accommodated three families, all sleeping in rotation. They were second-class citizens, with no democracy, no civil rights and ruled by an indifferent parliament in a country half a world away.

No wonder the kids rebelled, no wonder they took to drink and drugs and juvenile delinquency. To counter this, heavy handed 'youth' films were produced. Parables where some youngster was seduced by the bohemianism of the rich, lost all filial piety and then promptly came a cropper, being used and then spat out by rich Westerners and the Chinese HK elite. The youngster would return to the family, where they would be welcomed back, though not without a final 'I told you so' homily from the father.

That Tang was keeping his shirt on meant he wasn't being seduced by a rich woman in this other film, another common trope. Perhaps it was his screen sister who was being seduced, in which case he would wind up administering the homily to her gravestone.

It was all nonsense but the strange thing was, and this sometimes made Mary dizzy with incomprehension, this crap somehow helped keep the lid on the boiling dynamite stew of HK. It was a mystery to her why everyone didn't go berserk.

"You drifted away for a second there, Jade. New lover?"

She looked up to find Tang smiling down on her. "If it was, you're the last person I would tell."

He laughed and then flexed an arm and winced. "I hope they never fix that damned sound. Want to get something to eat?"

"Like I can afford to put on weight. I'm nowhere near fragile enough as it is."

He put his hand on her shoulder. Annoyed with herself, she felt something within her stir. As ever, she wanted the unattainable. "You have your own beauty, Jade," he said solemnly.

"My own...? Fuck you, Tang!"

He gave her an airy wave and, laughing loudly, walked away with beautiful, fluid strides. That had been a bad fall, but he was a good enough actor to still make his movements look easy, when he wanted to.

"Break for lunch!" the director roared belatedly through his megaphone.

Apart from mounting consternation around the sound equipment, the stage fell silent. Silence in HK was to be savoured and Mary indulged herself, though her stomach rumbled and the thought of those stodgy dumplings that Tang would soon be slurping down nagged at her.

The big space smelt of dust, much of it face powder, but this was cut with the coppery reek of overheating electrical equipment. The fierce lights were always kept on. A Run Run Shaw dictat held that these frightening things were more likely to explode if turned on and off too frequently.

She pretended she did not hear the soft steps approaching, too timid to be those of a self-absorbed actress.

"Mistress Forest?"

Mary spun round as though surprised.

"I'm sorry, I did not mean to startle you." The woman was middle-aged and she wore the apron of the kitchen staff, though Mary noted her hands were finer, less coarse and wrinkled than those hard-working women. The skin fold extending from her nose to eyebrow, so common in Han Chinese, was even more exaggerated and it was as though her eyes were being submerged. It would be difficult for this woman to look alarmed for she would not be able to open her eyes wide enough. Nevertheless, it was clear from her bowed posture and the wringing of her hands that she was in distress.

"What is it?" Mary decided to remain seated. If she stood up, she would tower over the tiny woman and that might be enough to send her scurrying away.

The woman bowed even lower. "It is said... sometimes you help..." She seemed to lose her nerve and turned as though to flee.

Mary quickly placed a gentle hand on the shoulder of her worn tunic. "Please, tell me what is troubling you."

The woman looked at Mary with her buried eyes. "The blue-haired dogs."

Suddenly the big space was too quiet.

"Come with me!" Mary commanded, taking a firm grip on the woman's arm. She led her through the shadows of the back screens to a side door and out onto the road running between the stage and Clear Water Bay.

Hong Kong meant fragrant harbour but today, and indeed most days, it was quite the opposite.

The hazy sun was casting insipid shadows but Mary found some behind one of the large packing cases that littered the site. She bent down a little, trying to meet the woman eye to eye.

"What's your name?"

"Mei Lung."

"When did you get here?"

"A month ago. Myself, my husband and my daughter. She is only twelve."

"And why would the blue-haired dogs be interested in people like you?"

The woman shook her head, not giving that away so easily. "I do not know you, Mistress Forest, but we have heard that you may be able to help people like us."

If ever there was a double-edged sword then this was it. Blue-haired dogs was a rather old-fashioned term for the Chinese Secret Service. If they were interested in someone then that person was just the sort of target Mary was after. On the other hand, if her activities were too well known then that would excite the interest of the deep water fish, Chinese agents under long-term cover in the colony. Sometimes called cleaners, they would occasionally be activated to kill a fleeing traitor, but they could so easily be sent after counter-intelligence agents like Mary. It wasn't for nothing she had been given a gun and why, even here in the studios where the costumes were too tight to hide such a weapon, she had a thin but evilly sharp knife strapped in a leather sheath to her inner thigh.

Mary took one seemingly casual look around. Horned devils, bloodied warriors, white haired monks, garishly made-up courtesans, all ambled by on their way to and from the canteen, stages, make-up and changing rooms. Here it was the ordinary that would be out of place.

She decided the only threat might be from Mei Lung and she didn't look threatening at all.

"Tell me your story!" she said.

19. Hong Kong

The Son, Benny Hu, and the Bamboo Cocoon

As the plane touched down at the airport in Hong Kong, Benny could almost feel the sudden transition from Second World to First. A feeling only reinforced when the ultra-high-speed train rocketed him along the shore of the South China Sea. Far away, he could see the elegant soaring steel and glass towers of Hong Kong. Once, not so long ago, this was as modern as China got. Now cities like this were commonplace; indeed HK was starting to look just a little bit old-fashioned.

Until not so long ago these colossal skyscrapers were constructed by men scrambling up bamboo scaffolding that clung to the rising buildings like ivy. It gave the glass and steel a ramshackle air. Only when the bamboo was taken away did each harshly beautiful building emerge like a butterfly from a cocoon.

Nowadays, the big towers were put up using steel scaffolding, health and safety finally coming to take-no-prisoners China.

Just inside the Tropic of Cancer, HK sweltered in the humid heat of late summer. Rumpled after his long flight in cattle class, then emerging into the moisture-laden air from the fiercely chilled rail station, had felt like getting a hot towel slapped in his face.

Now that everything was on his own dime, it was all so expensive. The hotel he had booked was a tall thin building that looked like it was being squeezed by raggedy apartment buildings on either side. Down below at ground level in the narrow street it was as though the shops had exploded outwards, merchandise piled on tables blocking the pavements.

After a brief nap, which was all his confused body clock would allow, Benny eased his way into the tiny bathroom and renewed his make-up. It was safe to assume his make-up-less photo had made its way up the Guoanbu's priority list.

He took a taxi out to Aberdeen, to the southwest of Hong Kong Island. It had once been a fishing village, just like Dubai. Against the onrush of time and money, such identities had long since been obliterated.

There was certainly money here, as there was everywhere in this place, but look more closely and some of the tower blocks betrayed their poverty. The one he finally found, surrounded by tiers of others and far back from the waterfront and its glittering floating restaurants, was one of them.

There was no doorman and the entrance was locked. Benny ignored the panel of numbers and names and little buttons, instead making sure the brim of his baseball cap was low over his eyes for the sake of the inevitable camera. He waited until the first person came out, an elderly man with a cane and a stoop. Benny grabbed the door before it closed. By the time the poor old arthritic soul had stopped, steadied himself and managed to turn around to remonstrate, Benny was in the lift and the doors were closing.

The fifteenth floor smelled of cabbage, just like in Eastern European apartment blocks, though overlain with the scent of sesame oil. Benny's stomach rumbled; like his biological clock it was still in some confusion. He tried but failed to remember what he had eaten on the plane.

He took a deep breath and shook his head to clear it.

The corridor was featureless but was at least swept clean. Someone here had some pride or sense of civic duty.

Though there was no name; Benny recognised the correct red door by its number.

He stopped for a minute, marshalling his thoughts, yet to decide even at this last minute what exactly he was going to say and what level of falsehood to employ. Giving up, and deciding to wing it instead, he pushed the little buzzer beside an empty bracket for a nameplate.

Benny could see that a window must be directly behind the peephole because it showed a single little disk of bright light. After a few seconds this was eclipsed as a dark object filled it. Benny put his hands together and bowed low.

Nothing happened for a few seconds but then he heard the lock turn and the door opened just a little. A rather watery eye topped with a carefully trimmed eyebrow peered out.

"Hello. It's Mr Tang, isn't it?"

No response, though the eye narrowed slightly. Benny noticed a little bolt chain dangling in an arc just below it. Shouldering his way in wasn't going to work unless he charged in hard, knocking the old guy flat and alerting the whole block in the process.

"I am sorry to bother you, sir, but I am here on a family matter. It is to do with Jade Forest."

The eye opened in frank alarm. Benny was sure the door was about to be slammed in his face. He leaned forward quickly. "Please, Mr Tang, you're my only hope." Not hiding the urgency in his voice.

The eye disappeared, the chain fell away and the door opened. Automatically, Benny checked the corridor either way to make sure it was still empty. He stepped through the door, glancing warily at the man holding it open, just in case something heavy was about to come crashing down on his head.

The apartment was light and airy and there were flowers in a large vase on the hall table. Tang pointed to a doorway and Benny went through into the lounge. Everything was neat and tidy but the chairs and sofa were of worn, scuffed white leather. Another gesture from Tang had Benny sitting down on one of the chairs. He smelled a chemical odour and guessed that though the sofa was old, Tang worked hard to keep it clean.

Tang hovered indecisively but oriental manners eventually triumphed over curiosity. "Tea?" he asked.

"Thank you." Benny watched as the man walked out of the room, across the corridor and into what appeared to be the kitchen. According to the film bios, Tang would be in his seventies but he moved like a younger man. Though it was late in the afternoon he still wore a silk dressing gown with the rich deep yellow of old gold.

As he waited Benny, glanced around. More flowers sat on a little coffee table. Pictures, some in black and white, showed scenes from some of Tang's old films. Assassin, punk, prince, floppy-haired intellectual, Tang had played them all. A couple showed lean young men, barely clothed and in the dignified, tasteful poses of high-end erotica.

As it sometimes did, his subconscious worked faster than his thoughts. Even before he had consciously recognised the figure in one of the pictures, he had got up and walked over to get a closer look. Mary and Tang, dressed as peasants, stood posing, hands around each other's shoulders and grinning. A convoluted ragamuffin-to-riches movie was Benny's guess, but this shot was less glossy and studied than a studio promotion. This one had been taken just for them.

He heard Tang return and put something down on the coffee table. Then the man came to stand beside him.

"Scary woman," said Tang. "Lovely but scary."

Tang's cologne was a little too heavy, perhaps in an attempt to disguise his old man's smell. Today's film bios were considerably less circumspect than the old studio-generated PR stuff. His few remaining fans took it as read that Tang was gay and nothing in this flat hinted at the contrary.

"You were friends?"

"Yes, we were friends." There was no doubting the sadness. Benny found himself abandoning subterfuge.

225

"I am..."

"I know who you are," said Tang. "I saw her in you right away."

"Really?" Benny turned back to the picture. "I never thought so."

"Perhaps because you only knew her after her... accident. It disfigured her. It hardly made her irredeemably ugly but for a movie star..." He gave a dismissive wave.

Benny went back to the sofa and Tang poured a drink from an exquisite little teapot. His movements were delicate, almost dainty, something he must have strained to disguise in his more heroic movies.

They took a few sips. The tea was bitter but refreshing.

"Why are you here?" asked Tang eventually. Perhaps weary from age, as Benny was weary from travel, he seemed disinclined to be politely oblique.

"She left when I was five. I want to know what happened to her."

"That was so long ago. Why have you waited until now?"

Benny put the tea down and sat back. "I heard the name Jade Forest for the first time less than a month ago."

"Hah!" Tang gave a little smile. "What strange games your mother played. All women have their secrets, but Jade..." He tailed off, his silence eloquent enough.

Benny reached into his little backpack and got out a pen and pad of paper.

Are you being monitored? he wrote and showed it to Tang.

Tang blinked in surprise but then waved a hand. "Unlikely. The Guoanbu, or Gonganbu as they were known in those days, were all over me when the British left but that was over thirty years ago. When my star faded so did their interest. Once upon a time I used to live high up on the Peak, you know. So did your mother."

Without thinking, Benny looked around and Tang gave a grim little laugh. "It was a long fall. When the Chinese took over, they wanted tough heroic peasants in their films. Not my strong suit."

Benny nodded to the window and the concrete towers. "I thought everyone was monitored now."

"It was the young who made the protests, and it was they the Guoanbu went after. They did it slowly, carefully, one disappearance or demotion at a time. Like a creeping ivy that slowly strangles a tree. No, they had strangled me many years before that."

Benny doubted Tang was au fait with modern surveillance techniques. "Do you mind if I check?"

Again, Tang seemed a little taken aback but he gave another wave.

Benny couldn't hope to do a full sweep without equipment but at least he could check the basics. Smoke detector and electric sockets all looked normal when he prised off their covers. He found the main fuse box and glanced back at Tang who had been following him around. Benny raised his eyebrows and after a second Tang shrugged in defeat. Benny turned off the power then went to check that all the lights had winked out on the wi-fi box.

That would just have to be good enough.

They went back to the little lounge. Benny's tea had grown cold but Tang didn't seem inclined to brew some more.

Benny sat forward. "Did you know she worked for the security services?"

Tang shrugged.

"How did you know?"

"She told me."

"You were close?"

"Women often get on well with men like myself."

Times had certainly changed in HK. Tang felt confident enough to make such an admission, albeit rather obliquely.

"When was the last time you saw her?"

Tang's eyes unfocussed as he made calculations. "Towards the end of the seventies," he said finally. "Yes, I was working on Snake Thief at the time. How could I forget? We were working with real snakes. Jade would laugh at me when I came back to my apartment, still shaking with fear."

"She stayed with you?"

"I had a big apartment then. I entertained many friends in those days." Benny could guess what that meant.

"And after she stayed with you, what did she do? Where did she go?"

Tang put his hands on his knees and leaned back. Benny noticed the fingernails were manicured to perfection. Even in genteel poverty Tang attended to what he must regard as the finer things in life.

The silence stretched. "Why do you want to know?" asked Tang finally.

"Because when she left to come back here and stay with you was the last time I saw her. She never returned to the UK."

"What happened to you?"

"I had no father, at least none that I knew about. My grandfather and great-grandfather had left before I was born, also to China. They too never returned. I had a grandmother but she died soon after Jade disappeared. That left me as an orphan so where else would I go but to an orphanage?"

Tang looked politely concerned. "I am sorry to hear that. Was life difficult?"

Benny shrugged. "I suppose my treatment was... humane." It was the best he could do.

Tang nodded. "Humane but little love. Such a sad story." It sounded like he meant it.

Benny felt a catch in his throat which he quickly coughed away. "So, this is why I am here. You were the last person to see my mother, at least the last I know about."

"You say your grandfather and great-grandfather also never returned from China?"

"Yes."

"Do you know why they did not return?"

"No. By the time I was old enough to ask questions my mother had gone and my grandmother had died."

"Didn't they have friends who might have known?"

"Again, by the time I was old enough to look for them they had gone, the few they had. The neighbours where I used to live had moved and the new occupants had never heard of my family. There were a few friends I was able to track down via a local Chinese association but they turned out to be more like acquaintances. It may be that my family had no real friends at all, at least none close enough to share their family secrets."

As he had been saying this Tang had appeared to be growing more and more concerned. "So, I am the only friend that is left?"

Benny shrugged. "Well, there are others she worked with at the Shaw Studios who I might be able to track down. Perhaps they can help but... yes, as far as I can tell you were her closest friend. If anyone knows what happened to her then I guess it has to be you."

Tang sighed and shook his head. "Just to make this clear. Your great-grandfather comes to China and disappears, your grandfather comes to China and disappears, your mother comes back to HK and disappears. The hand of fate lies heavy on your family. A less cautious man than yourself would not be out here now."

Benny leaned forward. "My circumstances have changed and left me with nothing, less than nothing. This mystery has been with me all my life, a shadow that has never left. I have nothing to lose by ending this."

"Except for your life. With that kind of history, anything I say may lead to your death."

"I'm willing to take the risk."

"Yes, but am I? I loved Jade, in my way. Why should I pave the way for her son's self-destruction? Give this up! Go back home, meet a girl, start a family! Live!"

"I can't."

Tang shook his head again. "Well at least I have a choice in this matter. I need to think about this."

"Think about it?"

"Yes. Come back, the day after tomorrow. Say 6pm. I'll cook a meal."

Benny tried to hide his annoyance. Only later, head down and baseball cap lowered to mess with the AI, did Benny realise he had forgotten to ask Tang if he knew who his father was.

20. Hong Kong 1974

The Mother, Mary Hu, and the Cut Sleeve

Ormeroy's tiny office stank of cigarette smoke. A corpulent man, he perspired freely in the humid, fuggy air. His thin grey hair, carefully side-parted, lay plastered across his head.

He let Mary's inexpertly typewritten report drop from his fingers to fall amongst all the clutter on his desk.

"It's probably a come-on," he said weightily, as though this was news.

Mary suppressed a grimace. Ormeroy held all the strings. He was her boss in a condescending service in a far-flung colony under paternalistic rule.

But she was an actress and knew how to play this part.

"So, what do you think we should do, sir?" she asked brightly.

He shrugged. "This is what you're here for, my dear. It's why the British government put pressure on Run Run Shaw to hire you in the first place. It wasn't just your acting skills that got you the job, you know."

Somehow this happened every time. The man loved putting her in her place. Colonial boss—Chinese coolie. The old Far East hand who thought he knew it all.

Even worse, he often did.

Playing the subordinate was one thing but that didn't stop her speaking up when she had to. "I do have concerns, sir. Perhaps we've been too successful. After Mao came down on the entertainment industry it's been like Piccadilly Circus here, a Mecca for fleeing artistes, their friends and families. We helped them and in return they've told us what's been going on. But now..."

Ormeroy held up a hand. "But now word has gotten back to those still in China that we can magic them away to lives of wealth in the UK or the States. The place has become a magnet for all the dissidents."

"The papers made too much of Chow. If they hadn't mentioned where he worked..."

Ormeroy shook his head. "We still don't know how that got out. Xinhua probably. I don't know why the hell the governor doesn't just shut them down. Why in the name of God allow a Chinese press agency here in the first place? Freedom of the press, my arse! Excuse my French, my dear."

Chow had been a mid-ranking Gonganbu official who had fallen foul of the latest purge. He'd produced sickening accounts of millions slaughtered during Mao's Cultural Revolution. Up to then, the occasional actor or intellectual fleeing persecution, torture and death had brought tales of murders and even massacres, but it had all seemed so piecemeal. The West had had no idea of the extent of the carnage until Chow. The Gonganbu had learned much from their old Cheka trainers, including diligence in their accounting.

Poor Chow. He'd had a brother who was a lighting electrician for Run Run Shaw. Mary, her ear exquisitely attuned to gossip, had heard of Chow's arrival in HK. She had made the first approaches. What she found was a broken man cowering in a HK slum. The Gonganbu had tried to arrest him when he had been visiting the southern city of Dongguan, perhaps convinced he was about to flee. He had shot his way out and had escaped in a police car then abandoned it and slogged through the porous New Territories and down to HK.

And all the time he had known exactly what the dog beating squads would be doing to his family back in Beijing. The families of traitors were almost always killed, but not before torture was used to extend their agony. Typically, vinegar would be forced down their throats, smouldering incense applied to their armpits. Then the torturers would begin to cut.

The Gonganbu were more than capable of reading between the lines. They'd have seen Five's hand behind Chow's revelations and they wouldn't have liked it. What they didn't like they would try to stop, by any means necessary.

Mary had made her point and it was up to Ormeroy to say something more. She kept quiet until he gave another heavy shrug. "What can I say, Mary? You're on the front line. We've trained you, we've armed you. If you think it's too much..."

She shook her head slowly. "No, but you don't know what it's like to be out there on your own."

Ormeroy smiled drily. "Don't I? Anyway, you're not on your own. Half of Shaw's staff are on our payroll."

This was bullshit but she let it pass. "Has there been any chatter? Any signs of deep-water fish stirring?" MI5 and the Royal Hong Kong Police had the HK population under mass surveillance. A surveillance infinitely more intrusive than would ever have been contemplated back in the UK. This Orwellian level of scrutiny was aimed not only at Chinese agents but also at HK citizens wanting to turn the place into a democracy. Mail was intercepted, phones tapped and moles embedded in a wide range of organisations. A democratic HK was the very last thing the British nabobs wanted.

Ormeroy spread his hands. "It's all still bubbling away as usual but nothing of note has broken the surface recently."

Actors spent much of their free time looking in mirrors, perfecting their expressions. She knew that her single, infinitesimally raised eyebrow would show how unconvinced she was.

"We have a test." Something in his voice made her sit up. Perhaps the name Mei Lok, Mei Lung's husband, had rung alarm bells amongst the burrowers in MI5's archives.

"It turns out Mao unleashed even more mayhem than he intended when he set the Cultural Revolution in motion." Ormeroy was stirring his finger around on his desk top, a habit he had when he was reciting a speech he'd already prepared. "He just wanted to shut down the artists and teachers and intellectuals who might have been able to articulate opposition to his sweeping changes. He unleashed the Red Guards and they went nuts. Job done, intellectuals either dead, banished to the wastes or imprisoned in the laogai, their gulags.

"But that's not all that happened. Mao let loose those hounds to do all the winnowing out but he hadn't wanted the security services touched as they were under his control. However, some in the intelligence services found the process too useful a weapon and used it to settle their own scores, or eliminate rivals. They wound up killing thousands of their own as well as sacking or imprisoning tens of thousands more. Our friend Mei Lok was one of the victims."

Ormeroy nodded his head, agreeing with himself. "He was right up there," and he lifted a hand above his head, palm flat, "so don't bother asking him or his wife about the small fry, we want to know the names of the disgraced heads of the committees and, more importantly, the names of those who have replaced them."

Mary didn't often smoke, she hated the scratchy feeling at the back of her throat first thing the next morning, but sometimes the actions of retrieving and lighting a cigarette gave her time to think. She waited until the cool menthol-flavoured smoke was swirling around her lungs before looking directly at Ormeroy; then she tilted her head back and directed a plume of cigarette smoke at the ceiling.

"If this is a test then you must already know the answers."

"I can't comment, obviously." His fingers flicking this away.

There were always defectors, men who had fallen out of favour, and there were always small-scale purges of corrupt branches of the intelligence services. That was the bread and butter of intelligence gathering, that and bribery and blackmail, but this was beginning to sound like it was on a different level.

Sometimes it was easy to see the Chinese secret state as monolithic and impenetrable. The Gonganbu were so secretive that many of the half a million of them didn't even know who their bosses were, at least more than couple of rungs higher up the ladder. If MI5 had the information to corroborate what Mei Lok said, then they must already have a well-placed mole.

Neither of them seemed inclined to break the silence. Perhaps Ormeroy was giving her a chance to think this through.

Mary took another draw on her cigarette. The Chinese played the long game and it occurred to her that it was quite possible the supposed mole had remained one of theirs, a triple agent feeding MI5 false information. Perhaps Ormeroy and MI5 were wanting to use Mei Lok's information to verify the loyalties of this highly placed source.

Or perhaps Mei Lok had been sent in by the Chinese to test if there was a highly placed mole in their midst. If MI5 accepted his story too readily then that would tip them off.

Or perhaps Mei Lok and the mole were working together to establish the mole's quite false credentials.

It was like staring into two mirrors that faced each other. Deceits, like the reflections, bounced back and forth before fading into infinity.

Stuffy old intelligence apparatchiks like Ormeroy liked understatement. It's all they had for humour.

"So," she said, "I guess we've got to be careful about this one."

He opened his hands in affirmation but said nothing.

Ormeroy's seedy offices were not far from the Kwun Tong Typhoon Shelter. It was raining, so with her rain hood and umbrella she was able to keep her face hidden as she dived down alleys, sometimes retracing her steps to surprise any tails.

Tradecraft could be irksome, especially when times were quiet. Now she applied the old tricks with newfound enthusiasm. Actors may have exquisite control of their own features but their reading of the expressions of others was nowhere near so reliable. Even so, she had sensed an excitement under Ormeroy's studiedly paternalistic exterior.

She came out onto the harbour front. Before catching a bus back to the Shaw studios, she stopped to watch the hair-raising spectacle of flights arriving at Kai Tak. The airport's single runway thrust like an erect penis far out into Kowloon Bay. The big new Boeing Jumbo jets had recently started to land here and the effect was always breathtaking. Planes approached from the north-west and skimmed just above the roofs of the high rises. On Mary's last landing she swore they had been so close she'd been able to make eye contact with a Chinese guy smoking on a roof. Once the jet hit the runway, reverse thrust was applied to the max to bring its shuddering mass to rest before it reached the end of the runway and became a poorly designed boat.

It was always entertaining and she stood for quite a while listening to the roars of the jets, like the bellowing of wounded beasts, as they tried to rid themselves of their momentum before it was too late.

She was on one of the infrequent days off granted to second-tier stars. Usually, she'd spend the day gossiping with actors and extras, technicians and make-up artists, with porters and canteen staff, with Shaw's harried office workers and script girls.

Normally this would be a general trawl for intelligence about new arrivals, but now Mei Lung would be the only game in town.

Film making, like war, was made up of long intervals of boredom interspersed with short but intense periods of action. People had to be available for when everything burst into life, but otherwise all they could do was stand around and gossip and drink tea. Everyone knew everyone else's business. Mei Lung's arrival might just be a minor background detail, but nevertheless she'd have been noticed by many.

When she got back to the studios, she started to dig. Unfortunately, the only extra piece of information came from a lowly porter who reckoned he had seen her in the Walled City. That was a no-go area even for the Royal Hong Kong police. Dreadful even by HK's condensed living standards, everyone there lived a life of not-so-quiet desperation.

Having skirted the subject and found nothing of use, she headed over to the canteen and Mei Lung herself. The woman was hunched over a large sink rinsing out bowls. Mary was struck by how absorbed she appeared in her task, almost as though she were taking refuge. As Mary touched her shoulder, she jerked round in alarm.

Mary wasn't the best actor, but she had worked with some really good ones. None of them had made fear look so genuine.

Around her the canteen staff bustled furiously. Mary in the deliberately low-class clothes she was wearing today merited little of their attention.

"An hour, where we first talked," Mei Lung said quickly and turned back to her tasks.

Mary had no choice but leave.

With no work there would be no tight costumes today, no being fussed over by twittering dressers with only the haziest concepts of personal space. Mary could carry a gun without fear of discovery. Mei Lung seemed no threat but in this world of ruthless people doing desperate things, nothing was quite what it seemed.

She was worried enough that as she waited, five cigarette stubs accumulated around her feet, usually a whole day's worth for her.

The sun was setting over Junk Bay and its carpet of boats. Their multi-pointed fin-like sails were furled, leaving the masts sticking up like a denuded forest. Cooking smoke drifted lazily away towards the setting sun.

Burning fuel and wood could be a deadly combination and junks caught fire all the time, always a major diversion for those standing around between takes. A crowd would gather on the western side of the studios to appreciate the spectacle. Little figures would swarm over the tied-together junks like ants, using buckets and basins and whatever was to hand to extinguish the fire before it could spread. Some of the older hands at the studios reminisced dreamily of fires that had burnt up scores of junks in a single afternoon.

Mei Lung was light on her feet, even though she seemed burdened by the weight of the world, but Mary had been listening intently for her approach. She gripped the gun in the pocket of her raincoat more tightly.

The woman's deeply shrouded eyes were looking up at her again. "You wanted to talk, Mistress Forest. Has there been any word from your superiors?" The woman was trying to keep it together but there was a tremor in her voice and Mary wondered why a strong man like Mei Lok would have married a mouse like this.

Then again, after political in-fighting all the live long day, the last thing someone like that would want when they got home was a tongue-lashing from his wife.

Mary glanced around. It was the end of the day but not for Shaw studios. Shooting would continue until whatever scenes that had been scheduled were finished. Even so, some people were heading home and a steady stream of them was passing by.

She leaned over to speak in Mei Lung's ear, her voice low. "Anyone can claim they are married to Mei Lok. Why should we believe you?"

The woman froze and Mary almost laughed. The battle scenes in Kung Fu films were so kaleidoscopic in their action that in order to help the viewer work out was happening, anyone killed would suddenly freeze. This drew the viewer's eye.

Mei Lung hadn't been killed but from the look on her face she might as well have been. The deep folds meant she couldn't open her eyes further, but Mary was astonished to see her pupils literally widen in alarm. The woman began to knead her hands and a big fat tear rolled down one cheek.

"Calm down!" she found herself saying. She'd hooked plenty of fish in her time. A couple had been actresses, ex-mistresses of important government officials who had been dropped when Mao's edicts against popular theatre and cinema come hammering down. Even women like that, naturally florid in their responses, had never produced a reaction like this.

The woman's world seemed to be ending before her eyes. Mary had hoped to put the woman on the back foot. Instead, it was like she had shoved a knife in her guts.

"We have some questions," Mary told the stricken woman quickly. "Take them back to your husband and get him to provide the answers, then bring them back to me. That's all you have to do."

Mary had a feeling the woman had to fight an impulse to grab her hand and shake it in wild gratitude.

"What do you want to know, Mistress Forest?"

The questions were detailed and there were many. Too many for even a more together person than Mei Lung. Mary handed her the two pages of foolscap, the questions laboriously translated into pinyin, the Chinese written language. The woman didn't even look at them before sliding them into the pocket of her apron.

"You live in the Walled City, don't you?"

Mei Lung looked like she had been struck and held a hand to her mouth. Though she made no answer it was hardly necessary. At least this saved Mary the effort of trying to follow her home undetected. The Walled City was a rabbit warren of twists and turns and narrow, branching alleys. Following someone unobserved there would be impossible. On top of that the inhabitants were more like cornered tigers than burrowing rabbits.

Mary watched Mei Lung scurry back to the canteen. Defections were never simple, never straightforward. Even so, Mei Lung's visceral but clearly genuine reactions had been far too over the top.

Something wasn't right.

⊕

Sound stage 4 was the usual warehouse full of harsh lights and highly strung actors. It had been an intense day off for Mary but nevertheless she found herself on the other side of the cameras watching Tang give the foppish performance he was born to.

Wardrobe had him aping the British with an absurdly heavy tweed jacket. Large black spectacles framed his pretty eyes over which his black cowlick would repeatedly fall so he could flick it away with artful insouciance.

Tang had complained enough about this part that she knew the plot all too well. Delinquent Girls was probably the Shaw Brothers' last gasp attempt at a film aimed primarily at the HK market. A young girl from a rich but inattentive family was living the high life of glitzy nightclubs and drug-fuelled days gambling at the Happy Valley Racecourse. Casual acts of delinquency involving cataclysmic fight sequences bring her to the attention of the police who, refusing all bribes (putting the film in the same league as Disney's Fantasia for cinema vérité) dump her into a youth rehabilitation centre. There she crosses swords with two young whores who come from the wrong side of the tracks, having also gone bad through poor parental control.

After one balletic fight scene which would have reduced real people to heaps of torn flesh and broken bones, the three lightly bruised teenagers are brought before the head of the youth centre, played by Tang who had spent literally hours bending Mary's ears about how he was far too young to play the part.

Tang's character was there to provide the paternalistic stabilising Chinese influence on their lives that the girls lacked. Suddenly enlightened and realising that it was their fathers who were responsible for their turning away from Confucian norms, they set out for revenge. Cue more gruesome killings after which one whore kills herself, the other goes mad and the rich girl winds up bowed before Tang saying how sorry she was for rebelling.

Mary had few pretensions when it came to textual analysis but even she could see what this film was all about. Poor and rich both go wrong, not because of being spoilt by obscene wealth or because of the unremittingly grinding poverty and overwork of the poor. Goodness, no. It was clearly the fault of the parents who did not exercise proper paternalistic Confucian control of their children. The rich girl's kowtowing to Tang at the end is simply showing how wrong it is to go against the Chinese sense of order.

Sometimes the capacity of the oriental mind to deceive itself set Mary's own mind reeling. Young people found these 'youth' films an unsophisticated joke. No wonder they were in terminal decline.

Tang had been playing a scene with the three girls and, when it ended, Mary made her way across the stage.

"Hi, Jade" said Yuk-Jing, one of the actresses playing a whore.

"How's it going?" The four other actors had stopped talking as Mary caught up with them. Mary had made herself popular by passing on all the gossip she collected. No doubt they hoped she had some juicy new titbits.

"Well," said Yuk-Jing, "the director hasn't got the faintest idea how to direct, the wardrobe mistress is too busy fucking the producer and nobody gives a shit about the whole damned thing."

"Not only that," said Xia Ping, who was playing the little rich girl, "but Tang can't keep his hands off us."

Everyone laughed. "You just don't have what I'm looking for," said Tang haughtily but with a smile.

"So, what's new, Jade?" asked Yuk-Jing. The wardrobe mistress might have her mind on other things but she had managed to outfit the three girls in dull reform school uniforms which were nevertheless form-fitting enough to still made the actresses look sexy. They clustered around Mary, eyes avid for salacious detail.

"Run Run has ordered a new Rolls Royce. Jade green apparently."

The girls nodded thoughtfully. Tales of conspicuous consumption were second only to sexual peccadilloes when it came to piquing their interest.

"He's already got ones in gold and red. I guess green was inevitable," said Yuk-Jing judiciously.

Mang Wa, the third actress and the only one who possessed even a shade of shyness, chimed in, "Always a generous man, always giving away his money for education."

They all nodded, Run Run Shaw was the ultimate father figure in this industry.

"Shame he produces such crap," said Tang.

Just for a second there was a shocked silence. A lifetime of Chinese compliance struggled to hold its ground, but then they all laughed except for Mang Wa who continued to look scandalised.

"Oh, come on Mang Wa," said Tang trying to tickle her under the chin but she slapped him away.

"Some of these films are important. Delinquent Girls is important. You go too far, Tang."

Tang brought his hand across his mouth, literally wiping the smile from his face. He bowed down low. "My apologies to Run Run and to you Mang Wa."

"Shameless!" she said and flounced off, the other two actresses following after, hands over their mouths to hide their smiles.

Mary looked at him. HK leading men were never tall and so with her own height they were almost eye to eye. She couldn't discern an iota of regret on his smiling face. "The British have a saying," she said. "Never bite the hand that feeds you."

"Where's the fun in that?" Tang put her hand in his and started off to his changing room. "I've been slapped down by everyone at one time or another. Why not do a bit of harmless biting?"

"Ah, yes, the sad tale of a homely, starving young boy raised by poor roadsweeper parents, bravely hiding his lameness and stammer from a cruel world."

"Very funny, Jade. Yes, I may have had many advantages..."

"... such as a rich father..."

"...such as a rich father, but it's never easy being a man who likes other men in this country."

"Perhaps it would be easier if you didn't make so much of a fuss about it. Half the men in this studio are... you know... but they keep quiet about it and they don't get into trouble."

"*You know?* Can't you even say it, Jade?"

"You mean like one who indulges in the passion of the cut sleeve. I don't even see how that means what it's supposed to."

"Jade, Jade, you look so much like one of us and you speak our languages so well, but you're as Chinese as a British bulldog."

She didn't even try to hide her annoyance and slapped his shoulder with her free hand.

"Ouch, that's still sore!"

"Serves you right! So, you want me to call you a cut sleeve?"

"Forget bulldog, you're as British as fish and chips wrapped up in the Daily Mirror, with a dab of tomato sauce and all washed down with Tizer." Tang had travelled to Britain as a child with his wealthy parents and sometimes he could still surprise her with his knowledge of the country.

They had arrived at the drab plywood cabin making up one of the many changing areas that littered the site. Tang opened the door and looked around quickly. "It's empty. Come on in and I'll try to explain in words a poor cockney like you might understand."

The room was strewn with costumes. Kung Fu films were sweaty affairs and the room stank. Mary realised the room was 'empty' only to Tang's lofty gaze but in fact contained a wardrobe mistress collecting up some of the soiled garments. Eyes that had seen it all glanced their way just once, then she went back to her business.

Tang took off his tweed jacket and started to unbutton his shirt, taking his time. He loved talking and was clearly going to enjoy himself.

"Passion of the cut sleeve comes from the ancient tale of an emperor who was sleeping with a favoured male servant. The servant was apparently lying on the sleeve of his robe. The emperor had to go for a piss in the night, or something, but rather than disturbing his bed mate, he cut the sleeve off his robe."

"Riiiight...?" said Mary.

"You see, it shows the tenderness between the men. It shows the love of one man for another."

Mary had to admit, if only to herself, that that was much more elegant than 'gay' that had recently become the favoured word back in Britain. "Any other expressions?"

"Plenty. Easily the most common are homosexuality illness or just plain hooliganism, though as you can guess, those are ones I have no fondness for."

Tang carefully removed the shirt and Mary gasped. The purple bruise covered almost all of one side of his back. "Are you sure you haven't broken a rib?" she asked.

"I don't think so. I once saw an extra get hit with a stave by mistake. He really had broken ribs and he started spitting up blood. No blood with me, just soreness. I've probably just cracked them."

Mary moved closer and gently brought a hand up to touch the discoloured area.

Tang shivered. "Your hands are so cold!"

His skin felt warm and buzzing under her fingers. "Can I put some ointment on this or would it hurt too much?"

He looked over his shoulder at her. "Not all hooligans are delicate flowers, Jade."

"I don't like to see you in pain," she found herself saying. Then, to both their surprise, she leaned forward and placed a gentle kiss on his bruised flesh.

21. Hong Kong

The Son, Benny Hu, and the Revenge Against a Dog Beater

The skyscrapers of HK, their glass sides like facets of colossal jewels in the setting sun, looked like doorways into tomorrow. However, they led only to a darker time for beneath the bright, shiny facade, Benny knew all too well that the Guoanbu's icy tendrils burrowed deep and penetrated everywhere.

The odds were stacked against him and he cursed the madness that drove him. Why try to find connection with a mother who had abandoned him, who had disappeared like morning mist?

Yet here he was following her. China was like a black hole, his family like planets caught in its intense gravity, consumption by fire their fate.

Further along the road the apartment blocks began to grow smaller, greyer and dirtier and, in the shadows where sunlight never struck, he could see faint green stains where microscopic life had found a purchase.

With so many back alleys, so many crowded streets, it was easy to shake off any tail. Finally, he was forced to concede that either a full team of a hundred or more were following him, or there were none at all.

Tang's apartment building came shyly into view between the others that hemmed it in. This time there was no need for subterfuge, Tang buzzing him through the security door.

He was waiting as Benny emerged from the elevator. The older man was wearing another brilliant yellow creation decorated with the tropical plumage of fabulous birds, though whether it was a dressing gown or kimono was hard to say.

As Tang hustled him into the apartment, Benny noticed how he moved. He still had the fluidity of a trained actor with complete control of his body. Considering his age, the word sprightly came to mind though Benny doubted he would want to hear that. Did Tang still have boyfriends? Was he an elderly philanderer still chasing the young?

Tang sat him down at a dining table next to a window. This gave a candid view of the apartment on the opposite side of the air-well. A child's face, mouth sticky with what looked like plum sauce, was pressed against the window, peering back.

Benny looked away in embarrassment. Tang's furniture and pictures and ornaments were all old though well-kept. An old philanderer would need money but there was little evidence of that. Perhaps Tang's star status, or his roles which had been as camp as seventies HK mores allowed, were enough. Perhaps it was the young men who bought him drinks.

Meanwhile Tang was clattering away in the kitchen and Benny could hear a spatula scraping across a wok and then the wuff as Tang tipped it and the oil ignited. Whatever he was cooking was heavy with garlic and ginger and smelled delicious.

244

Benny looked back across the air-well. He was still the subject of the child's intense regard, though the kid was presently excavating a nostril with a finger. Behind the child a woman suddenly emerged from the shadows in the other apartment and grabbed it from behind. When she looked up, her eyes met Benny's and a grimace of disdain distorted her mouth. She turned quickly and swept the child back into the shadows.

Benny, suddenly feeling like a catamite, had seen on her face no element of surprise at a younger man's presence in Tang's apartment, though it was clear she didn't approve.

Tang emerged from the kitchen carrying an enamelled tray holding two small dishes. When one was placed before him, a brief look of disappointment must have crossed Benny's face.

Tang chuckled. "Yuk sung. Commonplace, I know, but just taste it!"

Little curved lettuce leaves cradled the minced pork which was speckled with chopped spring onions, carrots and chillies. Benny lifted his chopsticks, their intricate designs beautiful but fading with long use, and pincered a chunk of mince.

HK food was aromatic, it had to be for people to taste it in the numbing humidity. He'd eaten this dish a hundred times before but somehow Tang's version was richer, deeper, more exotic. He looked across at Tang with new respect.

The older man swept his hand across his own dish. "Don't even ask how I did it. I'll take the secret to my grave. An old man must keep his enticements to himself otherwise..."

Benny was glad he left it at that.

They ate in silence while Benny savoured his meal.

Concentrating, trying to grasp the last little bit of fragrant meat, he sensed that Tang was observing him and he looked up.

Tang chuckled. "It's good to know I can still cook."

Benny sat back, still hungry and wishing that had been a main course and not just a starter.

The smile left Tang's face. "Were you followed?"

Benny glanced across the air-well. On the window opposite all that remained was a smear from whatever the kid had been eating. "Can we pull the curtain? I think the kid over there can read lips."

"The kid over there hasn't got a brain cell in his head." Nevertheless, Tang got up and, with only a trace of a grimace to betray the pain in his old bones, pulled down a paper blind.

Benny took a sip of iced water. "No, not unless they were making a Broadway production number out of it."

They looked at each for a few beats. Benny put down his chopsticks. "Have you decided how much you're willing to tell me about my mother?"

Tang studied his carefully manicured fingers. "I am used to my life," he said quietly.

"What does that have to do with anything?"

"It has everything to do with it. I'm an old man gently declining. There's no shame in that. In fact, it's comforting. I don't need shocks, disturbances. But that's all you are, isn't that right? You're someone who looks for trouble. You're just like your mother."

"Is that so bad?"

"It is if it gets you killed."

"And do you think she's dead?"

"Probably. Better that than mouldering away in some prison, in the cold of the far north or in the hot deserts of the west. Death or jail, it would have to be one or the other. If it hadn't, she'd have come back for you."

"Are you sure about that?"

Tang remained silent, disinclined to defend Mary's maternal instincts. How would he know if she even had any?

"Why did she come back to Hong Kong?"

Tang sighed and lifted one knee across the other, fussily making sure the strange hybrid garment he was wearing did not slip to reveal his old man's flesh. "Revenge, I suppose. She was a bitch if someone riled her."

"Revenge for what?"

"Something a dog beater once did. Hong Kong was a hunting ground for their squads long before the British left. People fleeing Mao and his terrors were their targets."

"So, this person was working for the Guoanbu, or Gonganbu or whatever they called themselves in those days? Again, what did he do? Was he the one who disfigured her? Is that what this was all about?"

Tang smiled. "She was an actress and all actresses are vain. There was also a terrible betrayal."

"So, she came back to HK to kill this man, this dog beater."

"She didn't put it so bluntly. I'm reading between the lines. Getting her own back was a weakness of hers. At the time, she had not known this man's name, indeed all she would tell me was that he had a strange triangular-shaped face, like that of an elf. Such features are not unheard of amongst the Han but they are unusual. Still not much to go on."

"But she managed to find him?"

"Later, with the help of her friends at MI5. His name is, or was, General Chen."

"Was?"

"I think her MI5 bosses had some notion of getting him to defect but I imagine Mary had other ideas."

"You're saying she was still working for MI5?"

"Maybe, maybe not. I think other things mattered more. Revenge was certainly an ingredient in this broth, but so was danger. She needed the tension, the adrenaline, the buzz as they say nowadays. For such people as your mother, this gives their lives savour."

"So, she chose this thrill, sweetened with revenge, over me."

Tang's eyes twitched in discomfort. "She was... without fear. Overconfident. Perhaps it was her downfall. Perhaps she was sure she would come back to you.

"The other actresses hated the fight sequences. We rarely had stunt men or women in those days. They weren't sharp but those swords and spears could take your eye out. Your career would disappear with your looks. Even so, your mother relished all that nonsense. She nearly took my eye out on a few occasions."

Benny couldn't keep a horrible thought to himself. "This General Chen, did he rape my mother, is he my father?"

Tang frowned and held up a hand, palm towards Benny. "Calm down, young man. She never said anything like that. I don't think any of that's true."

"Who is my father then?"

Tang looked weary. "I have no idea. There were many handsome young actors that we worked with, not all of them gay. Your mother was eye-catching, even in an industry full of beautiful women. She had many admirers."

Benny didn't try to hide his disappointment. Tang nodded sadly. "I am sorry. The actors... well, we're all a silly, insecure bunch. You wouldn't want one as your father anyway."

That was easy for Tang to say, he hadn't been brought up in a cold, draughty orphanage full of damaged kids taking their abandonment issues out on each other in all sorts of terrible ways. Where the nights were filled with the sounds of friendless little boys weeping into their pillows.

"So, what did happen between this General Chen and my mother? What did he do that was so terrible? I think you know more than you're letting on."

Tang nodded, it seemed in resignation. "If I tell you, will you leave?"

"So you can do back to your life of gentle decline?"

"Exactly."

Benny nodded. "Fine. Tell me and you'll never see me again."

It was never wise to trust the expressions of an actor but just for a second the man looked unsettled. What game was this old ham really playing?

Tang looked away at a wall full of pictures. "I suppose Chen will be long dead, perhaps at the hands of your mother, perhaps from old age. I guess it doesn't matter anymore so, yes, I will tell you."

And he did, after a fashion.

22. Hong Kong 1974

The Mother, Mary Hu, and the Overgrown Schoolboy

Mary had never seen Ormeroy so silent for so long. The cigarette smoke in the room was almost as thick as the pea-souper smogs that had often smothered London back in the fifties.

She was dressed as a businesswoman today, Ormeroy insisting on her looking as different as possible on each visit. She crossed her legs and checked her stockings for runs, then smoothed a black skirt that did not need smoothing.

In the early days, Ormeroy had had her tailed from her home to this dingy office, checking that her counter-surveillance techniques were sufficiently robust. That had ended, as far as she knew, when she'd realised she was being followed. The thin, sallow man had been wearing the black tie, white shirt and black trousers of a nondescript clerk. She had lured him down an alleyway, waited for him at a dog-leg turn then shoved a gun in his face.

By then she'd played enough villainesses to know how to be convincingly fierce. She'd watched a dark stain spread over the crotch of his trousers as the man, hands in the air, had babbled about working for Ormeroy.

Shaking off surveillance in HK was easy. So many crowded markets, so many underpasses, so many alleys to duck down if you didn't mind sharing them with the enormous rats.

Since Mei Lok had appeared on the scene, she'd been even more careful. So much so that coming here today she'd managed to lose herself at one point, as well as any tail. Ormeroy had raised an eyebrow when she finally turned up flustered and late.

He must have read through the sheet of paper in front of him a dozen times. The paper was flimsy enough that she could just make out the red 'TOP SECRET' stamp on the other side.

She took advantage of his absorption to look at him closely for clues. An old Far East hand, he treated her little better than the Chinese: politely but never revealing more about himself than he had to.

Ormeroy didn't wear a wedding ring and there was no telltale white band where it would have been. His single state was affirmed by his thin, greying hair which, though it had a distinct parting on the left for comb-over purposes, was just a little too scruffy. A wife wouldn't let him get away with that, if only because it would reflect badly on her. A wife might also have pointed out the patch of stubble under his chin that he'd missed when he'd shaved this morning.

The office was full of files and contained nothing of a personal nature. Apart from a calendar showing scenes from China there were no pictures anywhere to liven up the drabness.

He was her only MI5 contact in HK and it made her existence here feel even more precarious. If she was caught and captured then all she could ever tell anybody about was this office and a man she didn't know at all. Even the name she knew him by would be false.

He finally put the page down on his desk, though not before turning it over so she couldn't read it.

"This has certainly put the cat amongst the pigeons."

He was looking at her with such frank appraisal she found herself saying, "What?"

"This bit about wanting to meet your superior, about wanting face-to-face reassurance. That would never happen. If anyone's going to meet him it'll be you."

She shrugged. "He's just bargaining, sir." She pointed at the paper on his desk. "Anyway, this is all coach before horses. Is he worth it to begin with?"

Ormeroy nodded.

She waited but nothing more was forthcoming. She'd been expecting him to say something, to modify or qualify.

"So, he gave us some high-ranking names and they checked out with the intelligence your highly sourced mole in the Gonganbu gave you," she prompted, fishing.

He gave a slight smile and shook his head. "Who said anything about a mole? All you need to know is that we're interested."

"So, I've got to go into the Walled City. Alone?"

"I can't make you go."

Not that he had to. The idea of going into that terrible place was stupid, crazy but so exciting. Not that Ormeroy needed to know how she felt.

Ormeroy broke the silence that had descended. "All you have to do is gain his confidence, tease him out. Besides, there are precautions we can take."

"Like what? Level the place with a nuclear strike?"

"You'll see." The first meeting with Mei Lung had been two weeks ago and since then she and Mary had been exchanging increasingly heated messages at the studios. Mei Lok wasn't coming out of the Walled City until MI5 made some sort of gesture.

She sat forward a little. "You do understand, sir, that this could well be just a ruse to get someone from counter-intelligence into the grasp of the Gonganbu. If they're in there then they're untouchable in the Walled City. Even the Royal Hong Kong police absolutely refuse to enter the place. If Mei Lok is still Gonganbu and this is a trap, once they have me there, they could hold me forever and do whatever they wanted."

"Bringing in a defector always has a risk." He waved a hand over the paper. "On the face of it, this risk may be worth it. Perhaps I need to gently remind you that this is the nature of your job."

"There's got to be limits."

"Not when push comes to shove, my dear."

The police station in Wan Chai on the north shore of Hong Kong Island had the usual imposing colonialist facade with tapering two-storey-high columns, the bases of which didn't even start until the second floor. Red and white metal scaffolding supported an antenna perched atop the building. It gave the place a queasily anachronistic look.

Perhaps somewhere inside were wood-panelled boardrooms and restaurants for police grandees, but so far all she'd seen were cramped and dingy offices. In HK there was usually no room for anything else.

Mary sat uncomfortably with Ormeroy. This was the first time they had ever appeared together in public and it felt odd. In any other milieu it could make their lives forfeit.

They made no small talk as a single table fan sluggishly stirred the hot air. Black-and-white pictures of squads of coppers, all of them white, hung on the walls.

Ormeroy was puffing away on a cigarette and using an ashtray that had been half full before he started. The room smelled of smoke and leather and meaty, Western man-sweat. Mary had caught sight of a few secretaries, all mousy white women, as they'd made their way through the corridors, but otherwise there was no question this was where serious men went about serious business. Or so they thought.

"Sorry to keep you waiting," said a voice that clearly wasn't. Mary turned to see a slender man entering with a file under his arm. He was wearing the summer uniform of the police, off-white shirt and shorts, long socks up to the knees and patent leather shoes. A Sam Browne belt across his chest was completed by a gun belt holding what Mary knew would be a trusty Webley revolver.

Mary could never get used to grown men wearing shorts. It made this man look like a kid on his first day at a particularly tough primary school.

The man caught sight of her and the corners of his mouth turned down in calculating appreciation. He had blue eyes that were perhaps a shade too close together and his hair was short and of a nondescript brown.

He held out a hand and, as she rose to take it, he kissed the back of it.

"Enchanté," he said, though he seemed a little surprised when he realised that at five feet eight inches she was as tall as he.

"You must be Miss Forest."

"I suppose I must be."

"Ormeroy," said Ormeroy, extending a hand.

"Marshall," said the man, looking glad to move away from the awkwardness Mary had created. "Please, take your seats again!"

He walked around the desk and cast the file down onto it as though it hardly mattered. He took a seat and sat forward eagerly, both forearms on the desk. "Cards on the table?" he asked.

"Not our forte, Inspector" said Ormeroy, smiling.

Marshall seemed taken aback until he finally got Ormeroy's little joke. "Sorry, forgot who I was talking to."

Marshall would be in his late twenties but already knew it all. Mary had read in the papers, though she could barely believe it, that in order to get white recruits, the Royal Hong Kong Police advertised at universities back home. Any wet-behind-the-ears recent graduate who showed the slightest interest was shipped half way round the world. Instantly they were made an officer, given a gun and put in charge of a squad of ten experienced Chinese coppers who really did know it all. It tended to go to the ex-students' silly heads and it made these men-children dangerous for they had no sense of their limitations.

But he was a man, white and British, so Ormeroy's usual condescension vanished. "I can't go into specifics, but we have a target, inside the Walled City. We need to get in and then lead him out."

"Yes, you said as much on the phone. Will the target be willing?"
"Yes."

"Then why not meet him at the racetrack, or the Star Ferry, or even here?"

"He's reluctant. He needs reassurance."

Marshall's brows knitted in disbelief and for the first time Mary wondered whether he might not be entirely clueless. "That doesn't sound right," he said.

Ormeroy shrugged. "It may be worth the risk."

The copper sat back in his chair and steepled his fingers on his chest. "Hong Kong's a rum place by anyone's standards, and we in Special Branch see it all, believe you me. You can hardly move here for spies. We extend courtesies to all our allies and so we wind up doing all sorts of very odd favours for them. We can arrest people and lose them in the system for a while. We can close a wh... brothel, raid a drug den, search a ship in the harbour. We do our best, especially for our colleagues in MI5, but we do have limits. Limits about the risks we're willing to expose our men to."

Mary didn't believe him for a second. The Force played fast and loose with everybody and everything. The Hong Kong Police had got the 'Royal' name for suppressing the communist uprising of 1967. Bearing in mind the carnage happening on the mainland, Mary was ready to concede that that had been a good thing. Unfortunately, this was also the only good thing the people of HK had to say about them. Their pay was poor, even for the white officers but especially for the Chinese men. Every stallholder in the colony paid 'tea money', also known as 'hell money', to a Chinese copper. Every drug den and brothel, every smuggler and every hustler paid kickbacks.

In turn, to ensure they could continue with this low-level extortion, the Chinese coppers kicked back money to their white superiors.

Whenever someone complained about the police back at the studios, even the women would spit with relish.

Then again, corruption was so endemic here that even the motto of the fire service was 'No money, no water'. After the money was paid and the fire was out, they'd keep pumping water into the smouldering building until they were paid a second time to turn it off.

Marshall crossed his legs. This pushed up his starched shorts and Mary found herself looking at a straggle of pubic hair protruding out of the side of some white underwear. She looked up at the man's face, wondering for a second if this had been deliberate but, judging by his frown, he seemed to have weightier matters on his mind.

"Look, whoever your target is must know something important about our friends across the border, the government or the Gonganbu. I hate to be indelicate, but does Six know about this?"

"That's not really your business," said Ormeroy mildly.

"Oh, it definitely is, if it's about the mainland. You may have carte blanche in the colony but otherwise it's MI6's purlieu. If they feel they've been kept out of the loop then they'll certainly complain to the British government who then haul my masters in the colony over the coals. They in turn take it out on poor coppers like myself."

"I can assure you that our friends in foreign intelligence will be fully informed in due course," said Ormeroy smoothly.

"This assurance is duly noted," said Marshall and even went so far as to scribble something on a piece of paper. This seemed to satisfy him and he sat back, not saying anything more.

"The Walled City," prompted Ormeroy.

"Dreadful idea. I mean meeting there, you couldn't have chosen a worse place."

"It wasn't our idea at all."

Marshall didn't seem to hear him. "We can't go in, you realise that. If you run into trouble then it's up to whoever's going in to make it back to the entrance. And I mean entrance, singular, because there are scores of them and we can't station men at every single one. Whichever entrance this person goes in, then that's the one they've got to come back to.

"If they're being pursued, we'll have enough men there to cover them. But I repeat again, if they don't re-emerge then we can't go in to rescue them. Even if I had a thousand coppers, I wouldn't attempt it because half of them would never make it back out."

"We don't know which entrance it'll be yet. And, by the way, the person going in will be this lady beside me."

Marshall did a double take. "Wouldn't advise it. Not for a second. Where's James Bond when you need him?"

When neither she nor Ormeroy dignified this with an answer he licked his lips and nodded. "I'll follow you in myself and wait for you at the entrance. Where will you meet your contact?"

"At the studios," said Mary.

"The Walled City's only a few miles from the studios, as the crow flies at least. I'll follow you in my own car. It's a green Ford Cortina. I'll give you a note of the license plate so for God's sake don't try and lose us."

"How many others?" she asked.

"Five and they'll be stationed nearby."

"Is that enough?"

"We'll all have sterling submachine guns as well as pistols. If you do stir up the hornets' nest in there then it's knives and perhaps a few pistols you'll have to worry about. Provided you get out of the same place you got in, then your pursuers aren't going to tangle with us. We could mow them down by the score."

Mary had sometimes seen the white coppers patrolling while cradling those lethal submachine guns. She'd thought it the height of arrogance because if they ever cut loose with them in a densely packed place like HK then many innocent people would die.

Colonial imperiousness, the underpinning of everything in HK.

"Again, I have to be blunt. The lovely lady here... well she might pass though she's rather taller and more healthy looking than the usual females in that place. You'll have to try and disguise that as much as you can. Very brave of you by the way, Miss Forest."

Mary clenched her jaw but kept her mouth shut. Male chauvinism was a term increasingly being bandied around back in London but this was a world away and would mean absolutely nothing to this man. Indeed, it would be quite beyond his comprehension. There was not a thing she could say or do that would make him think more highly of her. She was Chinese and female and that said it all as far as he was concerned. Normally she wouldn't care but her life may well depend on this jumped-up little arsehole.

Marshall took a buff folder from a drawer. "I hope you'll humour me in one matter."

He took two sheets of foolscap from the folder and gave them to Mary and Ormeroy. "It's a waiver. Had our lawyer, good chap, came from Eton, give it a once-over. I'm afraid he made a bit of a meal about the possible consequences of your little foray, just to make sure there's no doubt what you're letting yourself in for. I just need you both to fill in your details and sign at the bottom to signify that despite all the horror stories, you don't give a damn."

Mary glanced at the densely typed text. The lawyer had muddied it up with enough legalese that there were whole sentences she couldn't understand. However, the subtext was clear: abandon all rights ye who enter here.

Marshall leaned across the desk offering her a fountain pen.

She took it and signed her life away.

23. Urumqi, China

The Son, Benny Hu, and the Stars Sparkling in Sunlight

Far away across the arid plain rose the jagged, icing-sugar-dusted peaks of the Tian Shan, the Mountains of Heaven, poking up into crystal-clear skies.

Urumqi, according to the guide books, was the city in the world furthest from any sea. Benny could believe it as the dry desert air nipped like a wire brush at the lining of his throat.

Around him soared minarets predating anything the Han had constructed here, but they were dwarfed by the Han-built skyscrapers surrounding the little enclave. The ancient Muslim quarter was hanging on by the skin of its teeth, drowning in the tidal wave of the Chinese century.

Benny caught a glimpse of his reflection in a shop window. Hide in plain sight was always a good strategy. From his fawn Timberland boots to his Marks and Spencer checked shirt, he looked the part of the Westerner. Fearless, confident, he let his gaze dwell on anything a Western tourist would find exotic.

Right now, an old Uighur, thickly bearded with a heavy jacket and doppa, a square embroidered skullcap, was pushing a cart stacked high with bulbs of garlic braided together like a maiden's hair. Even just his heavy beard set the old man apart from the wispy affairs that older Han still sometimes favoured and were the best they could grow.

The old man was painstakingly steering his cart in and out of parked BMWs. He seemed like a ghostly echo from a distant past.

The tour had first met in a mid-range hotel in Xian. He had excited little curiosity among the rest of the group, many Brits of Chinese extraction being lured here by the magic of the Silk Road. The others in the group were a German couple, tall, athletic and earnest, as well a trio of adventurous Scots girls in well-seasoned hiking boots.

It was to be a shoestring trip from Xian to Urumqi, then through Kyrgyzstan all the way to Tashkent before finally flying home. Six tourists, a driver and a guide all crammed into a tiny Toyota minibus. Every night they had stayed at little run-down inns where cockroaches and mice were plentiful and Western toilets were but a dream.

Stop-start, stop-start, the minibus had disgorged them at every historical site along the big busy highway. Once there had been real minarets and mosques, castles and keeps but they'd long since been chipped away by the brutal desert winds or bulldozed to oblivion by the Chinese. Now, ersatz versions had been hastily re-imagined in painted ferro-concrete.

Back in 2013 the Belt and Road Initiative had been little more than a notion of President Xi Jinping, but now, barely a decade later, it was a surging artery of trade with vast highways and rail-lines stamped down on the desert; all bringing the West into the embrace of the East.

And with the re-emergence of the Silk Road, or at least the modern coked-up, steroidal version with its thundering fleets of tankers and trucks, had come a resurgence of interest in its history. With that came tourist dollars. Now, hordes of little minibuses zoomed down these new highways, stopping to click away at the fake historical marvels.

This made the tour good cover. Tourists had to go through all the usual security checks but the whole apparatus was geared towards people coming into China, not foreigners going the opposite way.

Urumqi was the last stop before the real desert began. He had chosen this tour because it stayed almost two full days here, with side trips to the Grand Bazaar and Tian Shan Mountains.

The tour guide had been very sad to hear that Benny had felt unwell at breakfast. A young Han girl whose English was surprisingly good, she had been solicitous when he told her he had to pull out of the day's activities. He assured her he just needed some rest, not medical attention. He was confident he would be well enough when they set off again at four this afternoon.

Even before the minibus had reached the end of the street, Benny had left by the back entrance of the squat little brick inn, the big satellite dish on its flat roof the only sign of modernity.

Red baseball cap over his eyes, garishly decorated knapsack on his back, he hadn't been trying to blend in.

Now he was approaching the cafe. It was on the edge of the city and next to a Uighur neighbourhood. Tensions between the Uighurs and the Han weren't as bad as further south in the state but had been simmering for generations. All the Uighurs he saw on the streets had a beaten, downcast look. All-seeing TV cameras perched on tall aluminium poles were shining harshly in the sunshine, as plentiful as straws in a harvested wheat field.

He was using his last false identity. He'd constructed it years ago, before face recognition became such a big deal. The only dispensation he had made to looking different had been a shaved head.

Even if he hadn't been wanting to make the face recog cameras task more difficult, he would have needed the baseball cap just to stop his skin turning ripe tomato red in the desert sun.

He took a table out front and sipped sweet tea. He kept glancing around but always his eyes came back to the nondescript apartment block across the road. It was made of concrete with rows of small windows and minuscule balconies over which brightly coloured clothes and mattresses dried in the sun. It looked straight out of communist times, hardly the place one would have expected someone like Chen to retire to unless he had done something very bad.

Behind the apartment block was the Touton River, though more in imagination than reality. But for the snaking furrow of what might in another season contain water, it was almost impossible to distinguish from the endless desert that stretched away to the west.

He wondered what it would be like for Chen, living on the edge.

Once again Benny found himself out on a limb. If Chen told of his visit, and why wouldn't he, then they'd be able to pick him out from all the images taken by these legions of cameras. Four hundred kilometres of desert lay between here and the border with Kazakhstan, the nearest place his UK passport might afford him some protection. Would that crappy little minibus, with or without the other passengers, get him there before the AI matched those images with the photo on his tourist visa? It seemed unlikely.

He'd done what he could to delay pursuit. He'd found the ubiquitous tracker on the tourist minibus and had hidden it in another vehicle, hopefully sending the Guoanbu hustling off in the wrong direction.

It wasn't enough, but he couldn't see how he'd get another chance to do this.

He opened his back pack and dragged out an Alibaba delivery box he'd retrieved from a waste bin at another apartment block.

Rising, he tossed some greasy bank notes down on the tabletop. The Han waiter gave him a disapproving look. Even this far from Beijing, cash was a rarity. Throughout China everyone paid by phone.

He started across the road, tiny dust devils whirling at his feet. The dark little windows of the apartment block loomed up over him, and he imagined a sniper at every single one. He turned the Alibaba box so the logo was visible.

Twenty buttons at the entrance but only one for Chen. Whether it was the same Chen was another matter. Back in HK, Tang had only been able to tell him about this apartment block but that was all that Mary had mentioned getting from Five's files. A shabby apartment block just where the Tunqiao Road crossed the Toutun River. It wasn't much but Tang had felt Mary was being more forthcoming than usual. He'd got the impression she'd wanted someone to know where she was going.

Benny hit the buzzer and it seemed like a long time before the speaker gave a little click.

"Yes," said a croaky old voice.

"Delivery for Chen."

"I'm not expecting anything."

"Chen, apartment..." Benny quickly checked the number, "... twelve."

"But—"

"Do you want this or not?" Peremptory, but it was how people here talked.

The lock buzzed and Benny pushed his way in. A quick glance back but nothing much was happening in the dusty street.

A sign by the stairs indicated Twelve was on the first floor. The building looked better inside than out. The floors were bare but well swept. As he walked up the stairs, he ran a finger across the inside of the banister, a place few fingers reached. There wasn't a trace of the otherwise ubiquitous desert dust.

Chen's door was plain but there were pot plants either side, their broad green leaves seeming to flourish in the low light coming from windows at either end of the long corridor.

Benny hesitated at this sign of domestication. Did a woman live here as well?

There was a bell and he pushed it once then flattened his ear against the door. The occasional car might be passing by outside but the glazing in the building was good and he was able to hear the shuffling of feet and the clacking of a cane.

The door creaked open. Benny saw the strange triangular face and he pushed his way in, his shoulder unbalancing the old man. Benny grabbed him before he could fall and forced him back against the wall. He kicked the door closed.

Chen's eyes widened as Benny's hands probed into his armpits and groin. The old man was wearing some sort of shell suit, the material so insubstantial that Benny could feel the thin legs trembling as he ran his hand down them.

"What...?" was all the old man managed in slurred, phlegmy voice.

"Is there anyone else here?" Benny hissed in his ear.

The wrinkled face, one eye cloudy with cataract, looked at him with shock. The mouth hung open, the narrow jaw revealing densely packed yellow teeth. Benny was so close he could smell the tainted breath from a failing digestive system.

Benny pulled one of the man's shoulders away from the wall then got behind him and pushed him forward, a human shield.

Some shield—the old guy collapsed at the first step and Benny found himself carrying him.

The little entrance hall opened into a lounge-cum-kitchen. This was empty so Benny took the old man first through the door into a tiny bedroom then through another door into the bathroom. The place was so small it all took just a few seconds. Nobody else was there. Spartan, a little dingy, no decorations. No woman lived here after all.

By now the old guy was whimpering. Benny took him back into the lounge and lowered him onto a raffia chair. Chen didn't seem to favour anything soft. Even the bed, a thin mattress on the hard floor, had looked uncomfortable.

With dismay, Benny saw a tear rolling down Chen's face. The man wiped it away with a skeletal hand.

"I am a poor man. I have nothing worth robbing." The slurring was so bad Benny struggled to make him out. One side of his face hung lower than the other and Benny realised he'd had a stroke.

Benny dragged across another chair and sat down opposite him. "I'm not here to rob you."

The old man's head nodded back in surprise. His eyes strayed over Benny's clothes.

"You're not even Chinese!" Benny had heard less fierce accusations in East London pubs after a pint had been spilled. Chen seemed genuinely affronted. "Go back home, you robbing piece of shit!"

"I just want information, you evil old bastard."

"Information? What information?"

"Hong Kong. Talk or I'll kill you."

"Good, kill me!"

"What?"

"I'm eighty fucking seven and I wear a nappy."

"What does that mean?"

"You'll never live long enough to find out."

"Look, I just need you to tell me something. If you do, then I'll be gone."

"And if I don't?" Chen didn't seem much interested either way.

Had he already forgotten what Benny had said? "Like I say, I'll kill you."

"You're going to do that anyway."

"Not necessarily."

The old man seemed to relax into his chair and for a second Benny thought he had believed him. But then, losing interest, Chen's eyes strayed away to the view out of the window. Was he senile?

Benny snapped his fingers. "Hey!"

The old man's eyes refocussed on him. "Who are you?"

"That doesn't matter. I'm here to talk about Mary Hu." Not a flicker crossed the old man's face. "Jade Forest."

This time something did show. The old man's eyes had sunk with age and were overshadowed by heavy folds. Even so, Benny thought he saw the faintest narrowing.

"The bird!" said the old man triumphantly. Perhaps remembering things was a game he rarely won nowadays. "The bird that could not fly!"

Tang had told Benny of Mary's fall and it was all he could do not to grab the scrawny old neck and squeeze the life out of it.

"What happened to her?"

The old man lifted his fist and smacked it down onto the palm of his other hand.

"Not then. I'm talking about thirty-five years ago."

Chen looked at him blankly.

"She came to see you. Here!"

"Here?" The old man looked genuinely puzzled.

"She visited you here in Urumqi."

"Why would she do that?"

"To kill you," said Benny grimly. He made a fist and pushed his knuckles against the man's left eye.

"No, she didn't."

Benny went over to the little kitchen. He started opening cupboards and drawers until he came to some cutlery and other kitchen utensils. A big pair of scissors with red handles caught his eye.

Chen watched disinterestedly as Benny returned and knelt down beside him. Benny lifted the old man's wrinkled little finger and fitted it between the two blades. Chen winced at the applied pressure and the sharp edges cut grooves in the brittle skin. He grunted as drops of bright red blood pattered onto his trousers.

Benny looked into the old man's eyes. "Ten fingers, ten toes, a cock, a nose, two ears. This is going to be a long and painful afternoon."

The old man grinned. "Are all British people so charming?"

Perhaps Benny would have cut his finger off, but he was never to find out. The door of the flat was hit so hard the lock sailed by Benny's ear. A figure, unbalanced with too much momentum, came staggering in. Benny saw the pistol in the man's hand and reacted without thought. He straightened his legs, launching himself like a missile. The top of his head caught the reeling man full in the face. The gristle in the man's nose was pulverised with a crunching sound.

Benny twisted the gun from his grip.

Another face appeared at the door. Benny fired before he'd got the gun fully seated in his palm. The bullet kicked fragments out of the lintel above the door. The head jerked back.

Out in the corridor men, many of them, began to shout.

Benny stole a glimpse at Chen who didn't seem to know what the fuck was going on.

Suddenly the glazing in this place, double or even triple to muffle the night's cold desert winds, was his enemy. He sent a bullet through the pane of the nearest window to weaken it, then dived at it, head first. Just for an instant he found himself falling in a cloud of stars sparkling in the sunlight.

Then the impact on hard-packed earth drove the air from his chest. Managing to roll onto his back, he sent a couple of bullets back up at the broken window.

Still unable to breathe, he somehow scrambled to his feet and lurched off across the street towards the shops and the coffee bar. Behind him he heard an engine rev up and tyres screech. Glancing back, he saw an SUV, windows tinted black, swerve out from the kerb.

Air began trickling back into his lungs as he barged through the door of the cafe. A woman carrying a tray of drinks went spinning as his shoulder caught hers. He heard voices raised but these were drowned by the SUV screeching to a halt outside.

He stormed through the kitchen at the back then out of the open door into an alley. Waste bins littered it like an unruly mob, giving him cover as he jinked his way through.

The alley opened onto another road. Moving too fast to look, he lurched across it, a car swerving to miss him. Then he was into another alley between single-storey houses. Vaulting a fence, he found himself amongst more apartment buildings.

To his right a minaret, real not make-believe, rose into the sky and he realised he must have entered the Uighur enclave. As he kept running, modern brick houses gave way to adobe buildings looming over twisty alleyways.

It was just what he needed. Within a few minutes the sounds of pursuit vanished.

He found himself in a lane lined with little stalls selling wrinkled vegetables. The stallholders were all Uighur, as were the customers. He slipped the gun into his waistband and stopped for a second to catch his breath. He wasn't surprised that everyone was looking at him, an out-of-breath Han would be rare in this little market.

Then he realised they were all staring at something over his shoulder. That's when he became aware of the faint buzzing.

He whirled around but the air suddenly felt like cloying honey. He flipped up his shirt and dragged the gun from his waistband.

Slapping a bracing foot down to stop his spin, he found himself staring straight at a drone. It hovered at eye level a few metres away.

Benny brought the gun up just as something in the drone fired, the sound like a firecracker in the enclosed alley. The recoil kicked the drone backwards as something stung his cheek.

Reflexively he took one hand off the gun and touched his skin, his finger catching on something. Wincing, he pulled it out of his flesh. It was the size of an old-fashioned domestic fuse. The metal needle at the end glinted evilly in the sun.

He grasped the gun again with both hands and took aim at the drone. Behind it, he saw shapes diving to either side as people in the alley sought cover.

The drone was already rising. The first bullet, and his best chance, was a miss. He fired more shots as the thing accelerated upwards. Then a bullet caught the drone, kicking it over and sending it fluttering down.

Benny turned and ran, the lane ahead now clear of people, though he was aware of stallholders crouching beneath their tables.

Out of the alley and into a thoroughfare, he raced across two lanes of squealing traffic and into another alleyway. Twenty metres in he came to a fork and took the right one. The alley got narrower and people ahead quickly flattened themselves against the sides as he barrelled by.

He felt a sudden pain in his mouth and wondered if he'd broken a tooth. He tried to relax his clenched jaw, just as searing pain radiated along it. He felt the muscles on one side of his neck spasm, pulling his head down. Unbalanced he bounced off a doorway and barely managed to keep to his feet.

The pain advanced like a wave, washing down one arm, making his fingers and palm grip the gun so fiercely he could feel ever tiny furrow in the gun butt. Molten metal felt like it was pouring down the inside of his leg bone.

The leg gave way and he smashed into the ground forehead first. His leg spasmed, kicking him over onto his back. His jaw was clenching so tightly he heard a tooth crack and he felt it crumble.

His eyes were wide open and he couldn't have closed them if he'd wanted to. The sky above the alley was only a slit but even this quickly narrowed into total blackness.

Then, somehow, the total blackness got even darker.

24. Hong Kong 1974

The Mother, Mary Hu, and the Rout of the Imperialists

Sometimes, in her rare reflective moments, Mary wondered whether her wildness sprang from a lack of imagination. By the time she really understood what her rashness had got her into, it was usually too late to do anything about it.

Tales of the Walled City had always intrigued her and she'd known that sooner or later, by herself or alone, she would explore it. Now, at last, it rose before her like a decrepit mountain out of the shacks of Sai Tau Tsuen village, and she realised that, once again, she had bitten off more than she could chew.

She stopped the car, a rental hired under counterfeit credentials, where the village petered out before the looming monstrosity. The village itself was misnamed, for it was just as much a part of the densely packed city as any other district.

Mary glanced over her shoulder and could see Marshall's Cortina pull into a side road behind them. She turned to Mei Lung beside her. The woman had looked increasingly stricken as the day had progressed.

Mary had fitted herself out with grubby black tunic and trousers and battered coolie hat. Supposedly a peddler, her shoulder bag held Chinese candies of every description.

"You go first, Mei Lung, and I'll follow. We'll keep around five yards apart."

Mary made a mental note to remember every step of the way. If things went bad, she had to make it back to exactly the same point they went in. Get lost in there and she'd had it.

Mary gave herself a final once-over to check she looked her part, then she signalled for Mei Lung to get out. Mary gave it a beat then followed.

For the life of her, Mary couldn't work out how they would get into the Walled City. The medieval walls that had given the city its name had been demolished by the Japanese during the last war. Thirteen- and fourteen-storey buildings had risen in their place. They were so closely packed that from this distance she couldn't see where even a cigarette paper could slip between them.

It was no wonder the inhabitants called it the City of the Dreadful Dark.

The Walled City had grown like a benign tumour on the site of a thousand-year-old salt trading outpost that had first evolved into a fort. With the influx of Chinese fleeing civil wars and purges, the tumour become malignant and fast-growing, one makeshift storey being added haphazardly to another, many built crookedly right from the start, others made crooked by failing concrete. In some buildings, the concrete gave out after just a few storeys and rickety wooden shacks perched precariously one on top of another. Built without foundations, all these skyscrapers might collapse at any time, taking their closely packed neighbours with them.

According to the guidebooks (after exhortations that tourists never go to the Walled City under any circumstances) it was pointed out that in Europe a density of a thousand people an acre was considered gross overcrowding. Here it reached ten times that.

Mary flinched as a huge shadow swept across the street and a 747 thundered by overhead. The plane looked close enough to touch and she had to force herself not to duck. Though the noise was ear-splitting, those on the streets seemed not to notice. The plane disappeared from view to the south-east then she heard the frenzied shriek of its reverse thrust as it touched down at Kai Tak barely eight hundred yards away. Mary belatedly realised that the Chinese guy she'd made eye contact with when she last flew into the city had been on a roof in the Walled City.

The city was made up of hundreds of buildings all squished together in a raggedy square. It looked pretty solid but small spaces cut right down to the ground in a few places. Even so, according to Mei Lung, sunlight never penetrated directly to the bottom except for on one or two precious days a year.

Not many people were coming in and out of the Walled City so it was easy to keep sight of Mei Lung. All of the passers-by looked poor; illegal, downtrodden masses making their way to and from the worst jobs HK had to offer. On the approaches, peddlers had set up their wares on the steps of little broken-down single-storey shacks. Bruised fruit and rotting meat baked under the hot sun. More heartbreaking, battered rejected toys from the endless little factories that supplied the world with poor quality plastic playthings lay scattered on blankets like dismembered corpses on bloody battlefields.

Somewhere in this hellhole that was the Walled City were children. Children who might rarely, and only by craning upwards, ever see the light of day.

As they got closer to the looming edifice, Mary was at last able to make out something wider than a slit in the facade. It was about five feet across and people were funnelling into it. She noticed that five or six storeys above, one building had tilted to the side, healing the slit from that point upwards, and only being held up by the building it was leaning against.

Abandon all hope ye who enter here, she thought as she plunged into the gloom. She couldn't stop herself taking one last glance back at the outside world.

There was electric power, here on the ground level at least, but this showed only as infrequent strip-lights casting uncertain and flickering illumination on the dirt-blackened and broken concrete floor, and on the heavily barred windows. Overhead, swags of cable carrying stolen electricity hung tethered, branching out to make a cat's cradle across the narrow spaces.

Delving deeper, and skirting the end of another leaning building, she caught a glimpse of unfiltered daylight fifty or so yards above her head. Each place where a building ended, little alleyways opened to the left and right, most too narrow if you carried too much weight.

Further in, and already too far for even the bravest police snatch squad to penetrate, little stalls appeared in doorways or makeshift caves where the walls had been hammered away. Mary had seen plenty of drugs being surreptitiously used at the studios, but here they were displayed in wanton profusion. Sprays of heavily budded marijuana, tied like bunches of parsley back home, vied with thick blocks of brown and black cannabis for the customers' attention. Bowls of heroin in all shades from white to brown jostled balls of opium and garishly painted phials of God-knows-what. Other stalls specialised in drug paraphernalia with piles of pipes and bongs and spoons and used syringes.

She could smell the fumes from little factories opening onto the thoroughfare. Some doorways revealed food being prepared under filthy conditions. In others, weavers toiled under weak light over ancient looms.

Whores, garishly painted to show colour even in the gloom, lurked in doorways. In others, pimps dressed like birds of paradise beckoned.

Meanwhile, the smell was getting worse. A small stream was making its meandering way along the alleyway through tilts and breaks in the cement floor. This would be rainwater, percolating down from the world above, but she smelled urine too. At least the smell of shit wasn't as oppressive as she'd expected. There were no sewers here so whoever collected the night soil must be doing a good job.

Sure enough, as they turned a corner a little man struggled by with a bucket full of shit. She was wondering how they disposed of it when they suddenly emerged from the alleyway and the sight she saw literally took her breath away. She found herself looking upwards, mouth open like a fool.

This was an entirely new world. A world where buildings and vegetation had somehow become one. They were in one of the Walled City's modest internal squares. Sunlight streamed in from high above but, even though it was near midday in a city flirting with the edge of the tropics, it could not penetrate all the way down to the depths. Large areas were left in perpetual shadow.

Jungle mosses and even vines clung to crumbling masonry, in some cases covering it entirely.

Beneath the green, she saw balconies overcrowded with objects of every description and hung with washing of all the colours of the rainbow.

The sheer complexity looked so organic, as if the Walled City was a living organism. And a deeply fucked up one at that.

Most of the balconies had awnings of ripped cloth or battered corrugated metal; some had no cover at all. Some apartments had windows, glazed and unglazed, some didn't. Most window openings were covered by bars.

Even though the square was open to the air high above, the stench was apocalyptic. As her eyes adjusted to the higher level of light, she realised that on one side the lower floors of the apartment blocks were submerged by a gentle brown wave that rose in a steep curve almost to the second floor. On this tsunami of night soil, objects were scattered like flotsam and jetsam: bathtubs, boxes, bicycle wheels, soiled mattresses, scraps of clothing.

Her mind reeled. This must be a collection point for night soil before it was taken away for fertiliser. It couldn't be taken away that often as there seemed to be a hell of a lot.

Mary realised she was acting far too surprised. She glanced around to see if this had been noticed.

Her heart sank. Ahead, a group of men were looking at her frankly, almost greedily. They wore the usual raggedly tunics and trousers but they were hanging on more healthily nourished frames.

The men reached into their pockets and knives began to appear.

Mei Lung screamed in fear and desperation. She tried to grab Mary, stop her leaving but she pushed the woman away and headed back into the alleyway.

Mary ran as fast as he could, people scattering as she raced towards them.

She fumbled the Beretta from amongst the candies in her bag and risked a glance over her shoulder.

Six or seven men were only a few yards behind. She hurled her bag at the first but he batted it aside. Still running she fired back but high, the gun giving a mighty crash and a startling muzzle flash that lit up the alleyway. The men all stopped and crouched, hands over heads.

She gave all her attention to running. She'd carefully memorised every twist and turn they had taken. Her feet slapped through the puddles and she felt the wetness of the filthy water seeping up through the fabric of her trousers.

A bent old woman didn't get out of the way fast enough. Mary caught her almost full on and sent her flying. A whore, lipstick engorged lips open in a startled 'O', had her legs scythed from under her by the old lady.

Mary didn't dare look back at what became of them.

The entrance wasn't far ahead now but the splashing noises behind were getting closer. This time when she flung her arm back, she didn't go high. She aimed at the nearest man, right at his sternum, but she missed. The shoulder of a guy a few yards behind him kicked back and he went down, flailing arms and legs taking down more of the pursuers.

Mary stopped and turned round fully. The lead guy was still coming but this time when she aimed, he dived to the side and took cover behind a stall.

She turned back and started running again, her lungs already aching.

And then, suddenly, she was in bright sunlight. Mary searched frantically through the glare for Marshall and his men.

Through the glare she could make out a single white man, a sterling cradled in his arms. Marshall!

Then, stupidly, comically, her heart slumped again. His submachine gun was pointed right at her.

"Drop the gun, Miss Forest!" Marshall sounded like he was amused.

"You bastard!" But she didn't drop the gun. It was all cocked and ready to go. Dropping it might make it fire. She bent down and placed the pistol gently on the floor.

"Good girl!" said Marshall.

Hard hands grasped her upper arms and then she was being dragged backwards into the Walled City. Darkness closed over her like she was being swallowed, Marshall still framed by the closing mouth.

He waved. "Enjoy yourself!" he shouted.

The alley was now deserted. Whores and pimps had melted away into the shadows and the little stalls, so overflowing with goods, had been stripped in an instant, the wares hustled to safety.

She was yelling but the sound just echoed away.

Her backward momentum slowed and she realised they were stopping by the man she had shot. He was lying on his front groaning, the raw red crater of the exit wound in his back was plain for all to see.

A man came around and stood in front of her. "Bitch!" He drove the breath from her with a punch to the gut.

They started dragging her backwards again and she felt a sandal pulled off. Her bare heel scraped over the broken concrete but she was suddenly too tired to lift it up.

It seemed to take an eternity before they re-entered the enclosed square. They dragged her across it to the shit heap side and she realised trenches had been dug through the ordure and rubbish so people could get to a little entrance. The tops of the stinking trench rose to either side as they dragged her through it.

The Walled City was like an anthill constructed by mad ants, every new view showing something detailed, intricate but utterly crazy. On the opposite side of the square she saw leaky piping of every size and colour running down from some of the lower floors. Again, there was something organic about it, the pipes so irregularly placed it was like the glistening veins and arteries of some terrible monster.

Her heels dragged through black water seeping out of the middens. To the right she caught sight of the tail of a massive rat disappearing amongst a pile of bloodied surgical wrappings.

Again, she screamed for help but not a single curious face appeared on the stacked balconies. Most were hung with tattered awnings offering some protection from rubbish and ordure raining down from the apartments above.

The light cut out suddenly as they entered a dark stairwell. They clumped up steps whose edges cracked against her heels, forcing her into a crazy sort of back-peddling motion. It was like she was helping the men carry her upwards to her own destruction.

What where they going to do? She thought of her father and his tiger disfigurement, of death by a thousand cuts, of the exquisite tortures accumulated over thousands of years by the longest lasting culture on earth.

For the first time since she'd been a child, she thought she was going to cry.

They rose through one filthy landing after another. At one point a dirty faced child in a soiled nappy looked at them with wide-eyed surprise, a sticky rice ball held motionless before its open mouth.

Six, seven, eight floors? She should have counted. Finally, and in desperation, she tensed, intending to kick hard, overbalancing the men holding her.

They were too quick. One of them grasping her arm shifted a hand behind her elbow, the other hand shoving down. Arms weren't meant to bend back like that and the pain made her roar like a demon.

Behind her, she heard a door creak open and she was dragged through into a blackened, fire-damaged room. In one corner a little girl cowered, one eye black and closed by a terrible bruise. A pattering of feet from the stairwell made Mary look back and she saw Mei Lung emerge on the landing and race into the room. "Chun!" she cried when she saw the little girl. She ran to her, kneeling down and cradling her in her arms. The girl began to sob.

Mei Lung looked up at Mary. "I am so sorry," she said.

"Me too." Mary swung round in surprise. Squatting on the floor, hands on head, was Ormeroy, as out of place in this world as a saint in hell. A Chinese man stood over him, holding a gun to his head.

"What..." she gasped.

"Bastards grabbed me right outside my own home. That bastard Marshall betrayed us."

"No kidding!"

Perhaps to keep her quiet, one of the men punched her again in the gut. Her legs gave way and she hung between their arms.

They all seemed to be waiting for something. Mary cast a bleary eye around the room. Scorch marks climbed the walls and darkened the ceiling. The window frame had been burnt out, any glass in it falling to the midden below. Some light was coming in but it was sickly and tinted green, reflecting from moss and mould and vegetation on the walls of the little square.

The men holding her let go just as her legs were kicked out from under her. Her head banged off the soot-black wall and sent the room into a spin.

When the world settled down, she realised Ormeroy was squinting at her, his brow creased.

"Oh, my dear," he said. "I'm so sorry." Usually professional, often condescending, not above berating her when it came to tradecraft, there was a softness in his tone that scared her more than anything that had happened in this dreadful place.

Now that her vision was settling, she found the room full of the solid shapes of six men all looking down at them. There was something controlled, something military about their bearing. Something about the way they stood, at ease with each other but contemptuous of her, made her think they were a single unit. Ex-Peoples Liberation Army, probably.

Another figure strode into the room. His movements were less measured and he lacked the compressed feeling of physical control the others exuded. If he was military, it had been a long time since he'd trained. He was nearer Ormeroy's age, fifty or so.

Faces, both Asian and Caucasian, tended to be oval or circular. However, some Chinese faces took a more triangular shape, very wide brow tapering to a thinner, almost pointed chin. This and the man's amused eyes reminded her of a terrifying goblin from an old nursery book. It wasn't that his face was ugly, rather that it was just the wrong side of odd. As with his soldiers he was dressed in the soiled tunic and trousers of almost all the men in this terrible place.

He spread his hands. "Mr Ormeroy, Miss Forest, your situation is grave. There is no hope of rescue. Do you understand this?"

"Who are you?" Ormeroy's tone was gruff but steady.

The man bowed just a little. "Your enemy, I suppose."

"What do you mean enemy? I didn't think I had any."

"Deny, deny, deny," and the man laughed. "Let me show you that we are beyond that."

The toe of his boot slammed into Mary's nose.

She heard the crack as it broke. In agony she slumped down like a rag doll, her vision blacking out.

When she came to, she found her nose blocked with blood and snot. She had to breathe through a mouth full of a coppery taste. Looking down she saw what looked like a red napkin over her black tunic. She'd never lost so much blood in her life, even that time she'd come off a Hell's Angel's motorbike during a bash at Brighton.

"You piece of shit!" she heard Ormeroy say. "If..." but his voice faltered, "If you want information then you'll be disappointed. We're very low down the pecking order."

The man nodded. "Miss Forest, certainly. You, Mr Ormeroy? Not so."

Ormeroy turned to Mary. "It's not just information they want. They're setting an example." He sounded so sad. "They'll get what they can then they'll kill us. Kill us as horribly as possible. It'll make the service think twice the next time someone with real information comes along."

He turned back to the man. "Does it ever make you wonder why so many Chinese flee the place? Do you ever think twice about the starvation, the purges, the endless suffering?"

The man smiled and waved this away. "We'll start with a list of all your contacts, Mr Ormeroy, their functions and their current status."

"Go to hell!"

The man nodded. "I see you intend to make this as unpleasant as possible. Well, so be it."

He walked over to a corner of the room. Mary had been too dazed to notice the wooden box the size of a small suitcase. The man opened it and turned it around so the metal instruments glinted dully in the green submarine light. Ill-lit though it was, she could make out the triangular teeth of a saw.

"You can scream all you like. Nobody will ever come. You, Mr Ormeroy, from what we can tell, you've been in the wars. We can only guess at some of the unpleasant things you had to do in Africa and Malaya. The British were never gentle with people who simply wanted them out of their country.

"We'll get all we want out of you, but you're probably quite resilient so that would take time and I'm not a patient man. That's why we'll start on Miss Forest, just to give you some incentive."

"She doesn't know anything!"

"But you do, Mr Ormeroy. What is this charming young woman to you? On the one hand she is Chinese and so a lesser being..." He held a hand up to quell Ormeroy's objection. "In your paternalistic eyes she's like a pet or a child. Perhaps you even feel affection for her, after a fashion. And, as she is a lesser being, you feel responsible for her, for her welfare, for her protection. Like slave owners, some at least, who felt responsible for the welfare of those they exploited."

In one quick movement he reached forward and dragged Mary to her feet, pulled her across the room so she was looking down on Ormeroy's squatting figure.

"Look at her, Ormeroy! She's your weakness, your colonialist's Achilles Heel. Are you really going to sit here silently as we slowly cut her into pieces?"

Ormeroy opened his mouth as though to say something, then closed it again.

He shook his head as though to clear out all the nonsense. "If I tell you all you want, will you let her go?"

"Of course. But, as you understand, we still need you as an example."

Mary realised that this was the point she should be yelling 'No, don't tell him anything!' but that really wasn't how she felt at all.

"What do you want to know?" Ormeroy's voice was heavy with resignation.

"Who is your immediate superior, and where does—"

Despite all his weight and ungainliness, Ormeroy came up from his crouch like a tiger, cannoning into her and the goblin, sending the goblin spinning away. Propelled backwards by Ormeroy's mass, she felt her feet leave the ground. His face pressed so hard against hers she felt the slickness of his sweat. The broken window ledge caught the back of her knees and she pivoted over the side.

Above her, she saw only sky.

Then she was falling.

25. Urumqi, China

The Son, Benny Hu and the Paralysing Venom

She came to him like a ghost in the night. It was dark or he had the dimming eyes of a dying man because her features were hidden. Where once she had been lean, time had made her thin and had given her the faintest of stoops. Even so she still moved with an actor's controlled grace.

"Benny..." she said in his dream, but then words seemed to fail her.

Maybe he was dying for he could not move, could not speak.

"Are you sure he's alright?" She had turned and he could just make out two bulky figures looming behind her like guardian angels.

Why would a ghost have guardian angels?

"He's definitely not taking it well. Must have had a bad reaction." The voice was gruff with the heavy accent of the desert lands.

The ghost turned back to look at him and all was silence again.

"Leave us," she said finally and the guardian angels faded away.

The next thing he knew she was stooping over him. "Poor little Benny." She sighed. "I don't know what's wrong with me. The truth is... the truth is that I looked down into your crib and felt... nothing. I'm no better than my father when it comes to affection. Perhaps what we went through scared the love out of us."

She turned and began to pace back and forth, pulling the terrible truths from her depths.

"And I so wanted revenge. Getting even had always been my way, a weakness. But after I'd left you, after I'd set out to get it, I realised there was far more to it than that. I'd kidded myself I was out to avenge Ormeroy and myself. But even before I shattered that bent copper Marshall's skull, I'd known it would solve nothing.

"Revenge as displacement activity, something to take my mind off the shameful sense of relief when I left you and England behind. I'd given it all up for the thrill of living life on the edge.

"My one true addiction and I had precious little time for another.

"I hope you can hear all this, Benny. Don't make my mistakes. Listen to what these people have to say and do what they want. They still won't trust you, and they never will entirely, but in time it will get better. You just have to prove yourself."

How and to whom? he wondered.

"You can make a life here, settle down." Her earnestness was painful to listen too. A penitent who had much to make up for but never could.

Then why didn't you try it yourself? How he wished he could have said that out loud!

"I'm sorry. I really am." A hand reached out. Perhaps she touched him but he could feel nothing.

"Goodbye…" And then she was gone, unable even now to say the word son.

A pale hint of light found its way through the black waters. With it came the first faint pins and needles of returning sensation. Enough for him to realise that one side of his face felt like it was being held in a vice, locked in a spasm that was crushing his upper and lower teeth together. The eye above it was jammed shut.

When at last the sight in his open eye fully returned, he found there was not much to see. He was lying on his back. Above, a single recessed bulb was the only feature on the grey ceiling.

He lay there for what seemed like hours, paralysed and groaning with the returning pain and trying to remember his strange dreams.

Suddenly he felt his forehead go cold as his stomach fell sickeningly away. He vomited, gobs of puke erupting but then subsiding back into his mouth. Unable to tilt his head, he desperately tried to push the vomit out with his heavy, ungainly tongue.

Anything but draw it all back into his lungs.

Perhaps it was the strangled gargling sound that saved his life. There was a clunking sound then heavy footsteps and rough hands were turning him over, thick fingers probing into his mouth. He saw the bile green puke cascading to the floor. The men shuffled back to avoid getting splashed.

He felt them adjust his position. They weren't gentle. "Puke over the side, dick!" said one.

Like he had a choice. At least now lying prone on the rough blanket, his head over the side of the bunk, he could get rid of the stuff. Had these idiots never heard of putting unconscious people on their sides?

They watched him puke until all that came out was water, then they left.

A fly buzzed across his face and alighted on the tip of his nose. Its big eyes stared back at him and it rubbed its front legs together as though in anticipation of a feast.

Benny blinked hard with his one good eye and the fly disappeared.

Returning sensation was like a mass of fire ants crawling over his flesh.

Several years later, or so it seemed, the pain began to recede but left behind an unpleasant buzzing sensation suffusing his muscles. It was like a hundred tuning forks had been implanted in his flesh.

For the sake of experiment, he tried to move a finger. It was sore as hell but at least the damned thing twitched. More experiments with more muscle groups and he was finally able to sit upright in a world that was spinning like a top. Satisfied, he allowed himself to subside back down.

His work for the day done, he closed his one good eye and made ready for a week or so of quality sleep. Then he heard the door open again and two guys in blue uniforms strode in. Behind them came a third pushing a wheelchair.

"Back in the land of the living?" The desert winds had given the man a wrinkled weather-beaten face. Benny watched stupidly as they clamped rough hands around the tops of his arms and hauled him upright. The second man grabbed his legs and he was lifted off the bed and dumped into the wheelchair like a rag doll.

"Fucking traitor!" said the first guy and slapped him hard.

"Cunt's winking at you," said the second guy. "He wants to fuck you."

"Fuck this," said the first guy and slapped him again.

"If I could open this eye I would," said Benny but, with a tongue made of lead, this came out as all sorts of wrong.

"What did he say?"

"Fuck knows."

They all stood there, hands on hips, looking down at him like he was a dying dog. Something of interest but not necessarily worthy of pity.

"Should we clean him up first?" asked the wheelchair guy.

The other two turned to look at him.

"Shit!" said the wheelchair guy. "Why do I get all the crap jobs?" He turned and stalked out the door.

"Where am I?" Benny tried.

The first man rolled his eyes and stuck his tongue out of the side of his mouth. "Bleugghhh." Making fun of the handicapped was clearly his party piece.

The second man put his hand on Benny's shoulder. "You'll soon be able to talk again. And that's when the fun really begins."

The wheelchair man came back with a bowl and cloth and started to dab at Benny's face. He stepped back to admire his handiwork. "Fuck, this cunt's more Han than we are. And still he betrayed us."

The first man waved a finger at him. "The blood of the great Khan runs through our veins, Aiguo. You ought to be proud of it."

"I am! I'm just saying." To prove his patriotism, he slapped Benny but this time on the numb, spasmed side of his face.

"Fuck!" Aiguo shook his hand. "He's solid as a fucking rock."

The first man snorted. "It's the juice they gave him. Muscle spasms where it hits, that's all." He rapped his knuckles against Benny's unyielding cheek. Then he did the same on the other side. "But this side's soft as shit. The main thing is that it knocks them out but without fucking up their breathing. Much."

"What did they give him?"

"A mixture of cobra venom and werewolf piss, for all I know. Stitches 'em up good, though."

The second man looked puzzled. "You've seen this before? Since when?"

"It was when I was working down south. They test this sort of stuff out on the Muslims. They test everything out on those bastards."

The other two nodded sagely.

The first man prodded Benny in the chest. "Say hello!"

Benny hesitated and got another slap but this time on the feeling side of his face.

"Huthuurh," he managed.

The first man shook his head. "Naah, he's not done. He shouldn't still be as messed up as this. It must be his Western upbringing, it's made him weak as water. We can't take him to Shihong yet, she'd have our balls for breakfast—too busy for this shit. Waste of fucking time. Strap him in and give him another couple of hours."

Wheelchair man produced cable ties and soon the tops and bottoms of his legs and arms were strapped to the chair.

"So long, wanker," said the first man and they all left.

Sensation was now quickly returning. With what he was sure was to happen next, it was the last thing he needed.

26. Hong Kong 1974

The Mother, Mary Hu, and the Paint-Filled Balloon

Ormeroy's impact bent her body back, her knees catching like a hook on the fire-damaged masonry of the window ledge. She swung over the edge, her back slamming down against the outer wall.

Ormeroy's momentum carried him over her and out into the void, his arms and legs flailing.

She felt a hand grasp at her leg. Impulsively she kicked it away, anything rather being pulled back into that room. This dislodged her other leg and then she was falling.

Almost immediately she smacked into something metallic and her legs flipped over her head. She came off the corrugated awning feet first and was able to grasp onto the railing of the little balcony below.

Secure for an instant, she stole a glance over her shoulder just as, far below, Ormeroy's big body struck the ground, exploding like a paint-filled balloon.

She turned and looked back upwards. The goblin and one of the soldiers were leaning far out of the window and looking down at her. The soldier raised a pistol and took aim.

In panic, she let go and was falling again. The metal railing of another balcony shot by before she could reach out to grasp it. She caught the edge of the next balcony but it almost wrenched her arm out of its socket. She held on only for an instant, enough to pivot her under the balcony so her body crashed into the wall below.

She was falling yet again. She landed awkwardly on another metal awning, toppling over the end head first before she could stop herself.

In that split-second she saw no more balconies, no more awnings, nothing to break her fall. The ground, four floors below came flying up at her. Instinct made her curl up like a foetus, turning her in mid-air, crashing her down backwards into the mound of filth.

Black slurry exploding upwards then came pattering down around her.

She lay struggling for breath. Lying deep within the impact crater was like staring up out of her own grave. She started thrashing, trying to find purchase to haul herself out.

Undermined by her frenzied movements, the walls of the grave fell inwards, blinding and smothering her. She panicked and scrabbled away, losing her sense of what was up, what was down, worried she was digging herself deeper.

Then the filth parted and she tumbled out, rolling down the soft black slope.

Groggily she looked around, her eyes flicking away from the mound of shattered flesh that had been Ormeroy. Twenty yards away one of the furrows in the filth led to an alleyway between buildings. She stumbled towards it, every limb aching like it had been fed through a mangle. From far above she heard gunfire and bullets made little fountains in the muck around her.

She began to weave. It should have been too far for an accurate pistol shot. Even so, a bullet kicked up masonry a few inches to the side of her face just as she got to the entrance.

For once the darkness of the Walled City was a blessing. She followed twists and turns, her bare feet splashing through the filthy water running down the centre of the alleyway. Some people, the few for whom this life had not extinguished all curiosity, looked up from their looms or their stalls or their pimping as she stumbled past

The alley wormed its way between the ramshackle buildings. Her life now depended on her sense of direction. She kept to the broader alleys, where several people could have walked abreast, but now her senses told her she needed to squeeze down a much narrower space, barely eighteen inches across.

She slid sideways along this for twenty yards and then found it curving as though the whole side of one building was bowing out. For a second, she imagined it collapsing on her, entombing her in this filthy city a world away from home.

Then she saw a line of light and her heart skipped a beat. Sure enough, ten more yards and she was out into daylight. It felt like waking from a nightmare.

Across the narrow street was another slum, one- and two-level shacks with narrow thoroughfares between them. She staggered across the road before diving into the maze of little streets.

※

The apartment block, just like the buildings in the Walled City, had many floors. However, it gleamed pristine white in the direct light of the sun. It wasn't hemmed in on all sides by more of its kind, rather it kept a respectable distance as it rose from the tropical vegetation of Hammer Hill.

Mary sat across the street at a bus stop, partly sheltered by an ill-tended bougainvillea in the garden of another apartment block. Its leaves and purple flowers cascaded over the roof of the bus shelter.

She'd found a stand-pipe in the slum and had washed as much of the filth and blood off as she could. She had no mirror but it didn't matter. Even when shop windows had started to appear as she got clear of the slum, she'd avoided her reflections. Shoeless, clothes still deeply soiled, her face... she didn't like to think what her face must look like. As she washed the blood off, she'd felt the swelling. Her nose, already smaller and more demure than a Westerner's, now felt flattened out of existence.

Even amid her pain and shock she felt the flowering of pure hatred. Marshall and the goblin-faced man would pay for what they'd done.

From the blossom-draped bus shelter, she could watch the little reception desk and the uniformed guard. She'd been here often enough before at parties to know how the residents complained of the man's frequent absences. They reckoned that if he really pissed that much then he certainly needed a doctor.

After half an hour, sure enough, he stood and walked rapidly out of view. Quickly, she stood and shuffled across the road and through the door. She pushed the elevator button and one set of doors immediately opened. As the elevator rose, she leaned back and closed her eyes. The walls of the elevator were mirrored to give it a less enclosed feel, but they were no friend today.

The doors opened on the tenth floor and she stepped gratefully out onto the thick red carpet. For the first time in hours her bare feet didn't hurt.

Even so, everything else did and the nearer she got to the apartment door, the greater her pain. She'd been living on adrenaline and a beast-like determination to stay alive. Darkness and unconsciousness lurked at the corners of her vision.

She rang the doorbell, her eyes sliding over the whorls in the fine timber of the door. One of these seemed to spiral down and she felt herself going with it, being drawn into the door's wooden depths.

But then it swung open and Tang was looking at her.

She saw immediately that he didn't even recognise her. She saw annoyance, then disgust, then even a hint of fear.

"What..." But then he stopped. His lower jaw dropped wide open. For once he didn't look handsome.

"Jade! Oh my God! What happened?"

27. Urumqi, China

The Son, Benny Hu, and the Besuited Functionary

Benny must have fallen asleep because he awoke to find his shoulder being roughly shaken.

It was the man called Aiguo. "Say: I am from Shanghai and am the son of a sailor."

Though this was in Mandarin there were still plenty of s sounds. Benny did his best but produced so much spittle the man stepped back. It sounded like he had a cleft palate as deep as the Grand Canyon but at least what he said was comprehensible.

"You'll do," said Aiguo, coming around behind him and giving his wheelchair a push. Stockily built, he had a bald head and slightly vacant eyes. Hardly officer material.

Out of his cell, Benny found himself in a grey corridor with doors on either side. There were no bars but he caught glimpses of signs giving instructions regarding 'detainees'. Stuff about food and drink and toilet facilities. The latter was too late for Benny; at some point the toxin had made him void his bladder and the urine had soaked its way into his clothes.

"Where are we?" he asked.

Aiguo snorted. "Seriously? What are you, fresh out of the box?"

More corridors, more rooms. Occasionally, men and women, many holding folders, passed by but seemed entirely incurious about an evil-smelling man bound to a wheelchair.

Not one scrap of decoration, not one ailing pot plant broke the tedium of the place. There were more and more signs, some about fire alarms, some exhorting people to dress smartly. Several signs prohibited loud talk but the only sound Benny had heard was from the rubber tires of his wheelchair on the linoleum.

They stopped before one door indistinguishable from the rest. Aiguo opened it and shoved him through. A desk, a chair and a lamp. No window, no terminal, no signs.

Aiguo bent down to check the cable ties were still doing their job and then he stood up and ruffled Benny's hair like he was a child. "Best of luck, wanker!" And then he left, closing the door gently behind him.

With no clock on the wall, or sun to look out at, Benny lost all sense of time. All he knew was that he sat there for what felt like ages.

This and the lack of anything to look at began to work on him. He imagined himself lost in some bureaucratic labyrinth, only to be found in the far future as bones strapped to a rusty wheelchair when a bulldozer was levelling the place.

The drug must still be messing with him because a big fat teardrop made its slow, stately way down his cheek.

He shook his head, determined to keep it together. They were going to kill him, sure enough. Deniables: the clue was in the name. No outraged embassy official would make protestations to the Chinese government. No support group would band together and camp out at the Chinese embassy in London. Only the Guoanbu knew where he was and they certainly weren't going to tell anybody.

"Was anybody ever so fucked?" he asked himself. Then he wondered if he had said it out loud.

He shook his head again, hoping to clear it like the teardrop that he had flicked away. It had hit the wall and was even now making its unhurried way down to the floor.

Even the walls were crying for him!

He almost shed another tear.

He'd been keeping as still as he could because the cable ties were tight. The skin around them had turned bright red. If he moved, they'd start to bleed.

Nobody would miss him, not even Lea. His handler, she'd even shared his bed but not her heart. His cover blown, he was an embarrassment to her and to Six.

Why hadn't he dropped this mad quixotic quest? Why hadn't he just forgotten a mother he hadn't known anyway, got a decent job, married a pretty girl, settled down and had kids like everyone said he should?

The truth was he was just too damaged. Perhaps all abandoned children were. He'd never have been able to trust anyone enough to spend his life with them. He would always have been too afraid they would be wrenched away, leaving a hole in his heart that could never again be filled.

He'd made his bed. There was nothing left to do but lie in it.

He heard a door open. Whoever came in smelled of soap and shampoo.

Though strangely fragrant, at least his torturer was clean. That would be a comfort when they shoved a sliver of bamboo up his urethra.

As she walked by him, the first thing he saw of his interrogator was her high heels. Not stilettos exactly but hardly the usual flat soles of women who worked for the Chinese government. His gaze followed the nylons up to a black skirt and jacket.

Not even looking at him, she took a seat behind the desk and started poking and flicking away at a tablet she'd brought with her. She gave him plenty of time to get a good look.

At least she wasn't some horny-knuckled old interrogator who'd knocked out more teeth than they'd eaten hot dinners. The unsettling news was that she looked so young, barely thirty at a guess. Was she all he warranted?

Thick black hair swept down to her shoulders. Her features were perhaps a little broad but there was something about the way her intense brown eyes were so absorbed in whatever was on the tablet that made her quite attractive.

Mao's revolution had promised greater equality—women hold up half the sky had been a slogan—but, as with so much else, the promise had been hollow. Men still held the lion's share of senior positions. That's why he couldn't take her seriously.

She finally looked up at him, comparing what she saw with something on her tablet.

"Hello, Benny Hu," she said in American-accented English. Was she a personal assistant, sent to make sure everything was shipshape before someone big and snarling arrived, heavy fists swinging?

She looked at him with frank disinterest. Back home, a clerk at a post office counter after a very long day would still have put more feeling into it.

"Going to see Chen was a big mistake, Mr Hu. You must have been desperate. Once you stuck your head above the parapet, we had no trouble nailing you for the Fu Chonglin business in Baoding. That silly make-up only works with routine AI surveillance. Lower the thresholds for matching and bring in a human to look at the results that get through and... well, you know the rest."

"I don't know what you're talking about. I've never heard of those people. My name is—"

Her hand shot up so quickly he hesitated. "Don't waste my time!" she said. "The real question is how long you've been doing this. With your general physical description and the MO you used for the Boading job, we're checking through all the main defections going back twenty years. Even as we speak hundreds of people are poring over your pictures. We're pretty sure we've already found matches for cases in Taiwan and Thailand, Africa and Australia. Even here on the mainland."

"I'm just a tourist," he said wearily.

"No, Mr Hu, you are not. You are an MI6 operative, though one they hold at arm's length. Deniable is the expression your esteemed colleagues use. How must that make you feel at a time like this?"

"MI6! Come on!"

Did she give the slightest of smiles or was that just his imagination?

"I want to see someone from the British Embassy," he said firmly and turned his head away as though that was the end of the matter.

"You'll see no one. Nobody you want to see, anyway."

He kept silent, not looking back at her.

From the corner of his eye, he could see she was holding up the tablet.

"Everything you want to know is in here. Your mother Mary Hu, otherwise known as Jade Forest, Hu Bai your grandfather, and Hu Jun, your great-grandfather.

"It's all in a name. Your mother abandoned the Chinese tradition of putting surname first. She switched her names round to make it more Westernised. Then she gave you a name that did the same. How demeaning, how disgraceful!"

"What are you talking about? My mother was born and bred in the UK so of course she switched them round. Why not?"

When she didn't answer he stole a glance. Her eyes were narrowed and she shook her head almost imperceptibly.

"You're talking like my mother was a traitor just because of that. She was British, not Chinese."

"She may have had a British passport but she betrayed China and not just with the name. Like you she was a spy, though for MI5." This time the smile was genuine. "The British thought they owned Hong Kong so they used their domestic security services. Sometimes their arrogance was beyond belief."

"Not that you're arrogant."

The smile got broader. "Oh, we're arrogant. Why wouldn't we be? This is the Chinese century, Mr Hu. In barely forty years we've gone from a poor, developing country into the world leader in robotics, AI, space travel and cloning. People in the West have no idea how far behind they've fallen. However, MI6 knows and that's why it sends ticks like you to steal our blood one drop at a time?"

"I am not a spy."

There had been something about the authority in her tone that made him realise he had got it all wrong. She wasn't a clerk or some assistant. There would inevitably be a hard-knuckled bruiser somewhere in the background but he'd do what she ordered, not the other way round.

China really was changing after all.

"Who are you?" he asked.

She did not answer but instead began poking away at her tablet.

"Your thugs said your name was Shihong."

She said nothing but again he saw a tiny narrowing of her eyes. Aiguo et al were going to be in trouble.

"And your father?" she said, looking up. "Would you like to know who your father is? He's still alive, FYI."

"I'm more interested in my mother." His voice was wavery but it could just have been the traces of the neurotoxin.

"What do you mean?"

"I haven't seen her in forty years. Is she still alive? Do you know anything about her?"

Shihong seemed surprised. "You saw her last night. You talked to her... well, after a fashion."

Benny swallowed so hard he almost threw up. No dream after all!

"Are you alright Mr Hu?".

Struggling to assimilate what she had just told him, he could only nod his head. "Is she still here?"

"No. We tried to get her to stay but she was having none of it. We had to order her to come in the first place. She's a tough cookie."

"She works for you?"

"Has done for years. Ever since her abortive attempt to kill Chen. She'd gone rogue. I mean, killing Marshall like that! She'd burned her bridges with MI5 and had nowhere else to go."

"Killed? Who's this Marshall, anyway?"

"This is getting tiresome, Mr Hu. You know well enough what she did to him. And she came here to do the same thing to Chen but realised it was better to let him live so he'd suffer longer. Chen was in disgrace. He'd captured a senior counter-intelligence figure, then lost him."

She must have sensed his disbelief for she held up her hands. "Chen was lucky he didn't get a bullet through the back of his neck. Even so his debriefing was too... strenuous. He suffered a terrible stroke. The wreck you saw the other day was after forty years of improvement."

"Is my mother coming back?" He cursed the weakness in his voice even as he spoke.

Shihong licked her lips. "Motherhood is not for every woman," she said finally. From her frown it seemed she realised just how lame that sounded.

Benny needed time to work out how he felt about this—perhaps years. In the meantime, and more for the sake of form he said, "I don't know anything about this spying business. I don't know what my mother got up to in the last forty years."

Shihong put the tablet down and spread her hands across the table, wiping the slate clean, going for a new start. "We have ample evidence that you are a spy. Not that it matters. There'll be no trial. We're judge, jury and executioner. We can do what we like with you and nobody would ever know."

"So, what do you want?"

"We want you to work for us."

He knitted his brow, an innocent tourist trying to feel his way through a labyrinthine maze. "So, assuming I am a spy, you're wanting to turn me into a double agent?"

She shook her head again, unimpressed by his performance. "MI6 will never have you back. You were well blown after the Baoding fiasco and what happened in that place east of London..." she leaned forward and stroked the tablet, "... Essex. That whole thing was a setup, a trap baited by MI6 with you as cheese. How do you think we got onto you? A source we trusted named you for Baoding. MI6 must have got to them and they blew them too for the sake of a counter-intelligence 'coup'. And I have to admit it was a good one.

"But anyway, as far as they're concerned, you're finished. You've got nothing to lose now, so we want you to tell us all you know of MI6 and then we want you to work for us catching people just like you."

"However you cut it, you want me to betray my own country."

"Not primarily. MI6 is a minnow. Britain is a minnow. America may be a bigger fish but its influence is fast declining. The EU, if it had a single cohesive intelligence service, might be a problem but they don't. They have more than twenty agencies, all guarding their own secrets fiercely. That's what intelligence services do."

"So, whose spies do you want me to catch?"

"All them, of all the nations, but especially those from India."

"India?"

She shrugged. "Where China leads, India eventually follows. Both countries have over a billion people, so we each have more geniuses in our countries than America and Europe combined. That's why we are already so far ahead of you, but only India has the potential to catch us."

"I don't know anything about India."

"But you have an array of tricks and tools. Both you and the Indian secret services learned your trade from the British. Setting a thief to catch a thief is a strategy as old as time."

"I am not a spy."

She picked up the tablet again. "Hu Jun: West section, plot 214, Sai Kung municipal cemetery, Hong Kong."

"What?"

"Where your great-grandfather is buried. I've already given you your mother and this is another gesture of my good faith, Mr Hu. Now it's your turn."

Benny blinked in genuine surprise. "I've got more significant gifts from Christmas crackers." For a second, he wondered if she'd know what he was talking about, but then he remembered that though they didn't use them, it was the Chinese who made all the world's crackers.

"I am a generous woman, Mr Hu. Ask me anything about your great-grandfather. If I know, I will tell you."

He said nothing and the silence stretched. Without the distraction of her talking, Benny again became uncomfortably aware of the cable ties cutting into his wrists and ankles.

She shrugged. "Your great-grandfather was a gangster in Shanghai over a hundred years ago, Mr Hu. Opium, that was his business. He murdered a Frenchman then fled. Ran an opium den in Limehouse in London. He left his son behind in Shanghai, even though that son would almost certainly have been the subject of retribution. It seems your family has always been..."

She let it hang. Traitorous? Criminal? Dangerous? Prone to desertion? If Hu Jun really had been some sort of Fu Manchu and had been pushing opium in Limehouse, then Benny hardly felt inclined to spring to his defence.

"Tell me about your handler. We're probably going to find out who that is before the day is out anyway. This is your chance to get ahead of the game."

Still he said nothing. She shook her head, "I give, you take. It's hardly fair."

She tapped the table a few times with her forefinger. "Hu Bai, your grandfather, who your great-grandfather so disgracefully abandoned in Shanghai, was also a gangster and murderer. He murdered his boss and some of his men. He did this with the aid of your great-grandfather who had at last returned to Shanghai to help him. Hu Bai and Hu Jun then fled to Hong Kong. Hu Bai had been mutilated. Strips torn off his face and torso so that he had the patterning of a tiger."

Horrible but no surprise. Tang back in Hong Kong had told him something similar. It had explained why he had found no photos of his grandfather in the meagre possessions Mary had left behind.

Thinking of Tang suddenly linked two other betrayals. That's how the Chinese had known he and Mary were going after Chen! The old bastard had always been working for them.

"Hu Jun managed to get the injured Hu Bai onto a boat back to Britain but he died in Hong Kong and was buried there. Chinese may leave, but their heart remains in the Middle Kingdom."

Benny laughed. "Now that was something you'd find written in a Christmas cracker."

"Perhaps. Maybe we Chinese have a romanticised view of our country. Nevertheless, your great-grandfather returned and never left again."

She spread her hands. "I'm shown you my good faith. Tell me about the work you did for MI6!"

He shook his head and sighed.

Shihong shrugged. "Despite what you think, we can be generous. I'm going to tell you what happened to your grandfather, tiger-striped Hu Bai. To cut a long story short, he flew to Hong Kong to try to find your mother when she disappeared. It was too much for him. After the terrible thing that had happened to him in Shanghai, he had faded from the world. Such a difficult life, the walls of his heart were thin as paper. He died in Hong Kong still looking. He left behind a wife in England, Mary's mother. Unfortunately she too died, perhaps the loss of her husband and daughter too much, and you were given into care."

Information he had been looking for all his life but administered too quickly. He shook his head. "I haven't a clue what you're talking about."

Shihong could not be happy with the way this was going but she was still game. "Tell me about your handler."

Benny laughed. Genuine and uninhibited, it came out too loud for the little room.

She flinched but then nodded, as though in agreement. "Perhaps you are still very angry about what happened to Jiang. That was a mistake. We would rather have taken him alive, of course. He seems to have been even more out on the limb than you but he still had valuable knowledge about your operations.

"You were both unlucky. Fu Chonglin had recently come to our attention because of his associations with dangerous Uighur dissidents. It was those we were trying to catch, but instead you and Jiang stumbled into the trap. Setting up lethal autonomous drones to monitor Fu Chonglin was unwise. There are factions in the Guoanbu that favour automation over humint..."

She smiled slightly at Benny's frown, "...of course, not being a spy, you would not know that stands for human intelligence.

"The argument, of course, was cost. We would have needed thirty men at least to surveil Fu 24/7. Instead, we could do it with just four drones, two lurking, waiting to follow him when he left home, two recharging on a nearby docking station. Makes sense, except when people like you turn up and there's no flesh and blood operatives nearby. The drones can't arrest, all they can do is kill.

"So, I want to tell you that we are genuinely sorry." Shihong somehow made her apology sound like she was the one being magnanimous, like she was somehow rising above some tawdry dispute.

"If you wanted to take this Jiang chap alive for what he knew, why didn't you want to do it for any Uighurs?"

"Ethnic-based terrorists are the worst. They believe with all their heart, something neither you nor your mother nor your friend Jiang could claim. Interrogating fanatics like that is a waste of time. I mean look at Guantanamo; the Americans got nothing useful from their prisoners even though they tortured them for years."

"What a strange world you live in."

He knew all too well that the more Shihong told him the more certain it was that he would be killed. The stuff about the drones alone pretty much sealed his fate. With no hope of survival, he had absolutely no motive to play along.

She nodded. "Perhaps in the circumstances further evidence of our good faith is required." She went back to her tablet.

With her head down, Benny had a chance to study the parting in her black hair and could just make out two thin white lines either side. With Chinese, age was always difficult to estimate but that she dyed her hair meant Shihong wasn't as young as he had thought.

At least that made some sense. More so than this topsy turvy interrogation where the inquisitor was providing all the information.

She set down the tablet and leaned back. "When did you start working for MI6?"

Was she serious? Did she really think any of this would buy his cooperation?

"Even if I really was a spy, and even if I had something to tell you, you're going to kill me anyway. Why should I say a damned thing?"

"Times have changed, Mr Hu, and you are definitely on the wrong side of history. Now that we have the power and the money, we have no need to indulge in the excesses of men like Chen. We are softer, gentler in how we exercise our power."

"Tell that to the Uighurs!"

"We are re-educating them and, yes, to do that we have... constrained their freedoms. But we haven't massacred them, something the Chinese have been doing to each other for thousands of years. China is changing, Mr Hu."

"The imprisonment of a million people as a sign of social progress. Now I really have heard it all."

"It is refreshing to have someone of your ethical stature take such a high-minded approach to my... our... country."

Benny looked around. "This is not my country and you are most certainly not my fellow countryman."

"This could be your country. It should be your country. It seems to me your entire family is like the corn caught between the grindstones of East and West. You at least have the chance to escape their fate.

"In any case, the past is the past, Mr Hu. Put these ghosts to rest, for your own sake. China's future is glorious. Give yourself up to it."

"And if I don't? Torture, imprisonment, death?"

She stood up, reaching into the breast pocket of her jacket and bringing out a card. She picked up her tablet and came around the table again. She poked the card into the pocket of his trousers.

Closer now he saw the tiny wrinkles around her eyes. She looked down at him with a mixture of sympathy tinged with irritation. "No, Mr Hu. We are letting you go. My phone number is on the card. If you change your mind, when you change your mind, then call me and we will welcome you home."

"You're going to let me go?"

"Not me personally. I don't trust you not to attack me. The guards will do it. I would advise you not to take your anger out on them. This is a hard part of the country and they would certainly beat you badly."

"So, you're giving me back my passport and credit card and phone."

"We're giving you nothing, Mr Hu. Why should we when you've been so uncooperative."

"How do I get back to the UK?"

"We'll let MI6 know we're releasing you. They can decide where we hand you back. I'm guessing they'll choose somewhere at the border with Kazakhstan."

Benny knew this meant that all he was going to get was a bullet in the back of the head. "You mentioned my father. Who was he?"

"I have told you so much and you have given nothing in return. If you want to know then come back to us, of your own free will. But if you do come back, then do it for other, more substantial reasons than finding out the identity of a father you never knew."

And with that she was gone.

28. Hong Kong 1974

The Mother, Mary Hu, and the Fateful Kiss

Tang wanted to call an ambulance and the police. He wanted to alert the press and Run Run Shaw and the Governor of the colony himself.

The only way she could stop him was to tell him the whole truth.

But first she persuaded him to let her take a long bath. When some of the aches had been soothed away, she had steeled herself for a glance in the misted floor-length mirror. Her nose, now squashed almost flat against her face, had left air-slit nostrils too narrow to breathe through. The goblin's boot had also raised black eyes, making her look like a panda.

The rest of her looked even worse. Large areas of evil-looking purple bruises covered much of the milky coffee shade of her skin. Her fall had been so frightening she'd hardly been aware of the impacts but now she felt the aftermath in every atom of her body.

As well as the storm-dark bruising, scrapes and cuts patterned her skin. It looked like a sheet of paper molested by a small child with a red crayon and far too much time on its hands.

One day she would find the goblin and make him suffer as no man had suffered before.

Her nose had to be dealt with first. Sitting down, her back hard against the porcelain bath in case she fainted, she laid both hands flat against the barely raised sides of her nose.

Even that hurt like hell.

As gently as she could, she brought the sides of her hands together, trapping what was left of her nose between them.

Then she pulled.

There was a horrible crackling sound. A flash bulb went off right in front of her eyes.

Her screams brought Tang banging at the locked door.

"Go away!" she yelled.

301

Sitting up, she crawled unsteadily back to the mirror. The flesh around her nose was so swollen it was still difficult to see if her manipulation had worked. At least her nose didn't seem quite as squashed as before and was more or less perpendicular to her eyeline.

She got Tang to fetch her cotton wool. Then she packed her nose out, hoping that would hold it in place long enough to set.

Finally, she sent him for ice and she wrapped it in a dish towel and pressed it against her face, driving herself through the pain until numbness smothered it.

All the time she was thinking of Marshall and the goblin-faced man, her boiling hatred helping her deal with the agony.

Her nose had just been for starters and now she had to attend to the rest. So many of the cuts and scrapes were inaccessible to her suddenly achy, weary body. In the end Tang had to help. She lay naked on his bed while he dabbed the wounds with antiseptic and used up every plaster in his bathroom cupboard.

He'd had plenty on hand; they were handed out like candy after fight sequences back at the studio.

"This is crazy," he kept saying. "You need a hospital. And the nose—if you don't get it treated, you'll never work in film again."

"There are plenty of ugly old women roles. Now all I need is to grow old."

"Oh, Jade!" His voice caught and she realised he was on the verge of tears.

After all the dabbing and soothing they sat together on his white leather sofa, before them a bottle of Johnny Walker's Red Label whisky that she was working her way through steadily. This and the Chinese medicine he had given her were submerging the few remaining sharp pains into a generalised, gnawing ache.

Like her own apartment, Tang's was light and, with the balcony windows open, it was airy. Spotless and immaculate, it was the apartment of a woman, though one more tidy than Mary had ever been. Part of her wished for a used sock poking out from under a chair, or even to find a single errant pubic hair on his toilet rim. A hint of man sweat, or some scuffed plimsolls would have been nice.

There was nothing. He was a better woman than she was.

He could even be a good listener when he tried, so good she occasionally glanced at him to check he was still breathing. When she got to the bit about Ormeroy taking her with him on his swan dive out of the window, his jaw had dropped open, just like when he'd opened his door to see her standing broken before him. It was an expression so simple, so unaffected she felt she had caught a glimpse of the little boy he must once have been.

When her tale ended at his apartment door, he sat back and said nothing for a long while. Then: "So why can't we call the police or take you to hospital?"

Mary took a sip of her Red Label. "Think about it. What would happen?"

"You get medical treatment, your nose gets reset and that Marshall copper spends the rest of his life in jail."

She put the whisky glass down. "This isn't Run Run's latest crime drama. This one has no happy ending."

"What do you mean?"

"It's Marshall's word against mine. Who do you think they'll believe? Anyway, once they had me in custody, he'd make sure I'd be dead before morning. Money talks in the police. It's an orchard of bad apples."

His eyes flicked away. Every HK resident knew well enough they lived at the bidding of their British masters, but it was always annoying to be reminded of how corrupt they were. HK citizens kept their heads down and pushed such thoughts carefully aside.

"There's evidence..." But he didn't finish the sentence.

"Goblin face and his men are long gone. Ormeroy is dead. Mei Lung and her daughter... well, who knows what happened to them."

"So, she wasn't the wife of this... this secret service chief."

"Again, who knows? Perhaps she was just another refugee whose child they held to ransom to get her to play her part."

Tang took a sip of his lemonade. Like most Chinese, even those in HK, he'd never really gained an appetite for alcohol. "What about your bosses? Can't you just go straight to them?"

She sighed. "My only boss in HK lies splattered all over the floor of the Walled City. I operated out on a limb, for circumstances just like this. In case one of the defectors I was bringing over was a double agent. If they captured me there wasn't much I could tell them, except about Ormeroy."

"That's a stupidly dangerous job, Jade. What the fuck made you do it in the first place?"

She flinched a little at the anger in his eyes. "The money was good," she said, defensively.

"Stop it!" he said as fiercely as he'd ever said anything in real life. "Stop acting! I've played too many scenes with you. You can't fool me."

"But it's true! The money Run Run pays us is crap." But she could hear her voice getting higher, sounding petulant.

"Money's got nothing to do with it! You don't care about money. It's the most un-Chinese thing about you."

Taken aback, she found herself at a loss for words. Perhaps if she tried...

He held up a hand, palm flat towards her in warning. "Don't do it!"

"What!"

"You were going to say it's all about loyalty, weren't you? Loyalty to your country."

He was right but she wasn't going to admit it.

"Seriously? Loyalty?" he said scornfully. "After the way your scummy British pals run this place?"

"It's better than what the Chinese would do!"

"You may know that now, from talking to plenty of refugees. But that's not it. When I first met you, you were a little girl on a big adventure. And you know something, I don't think you've changed one tiny bit. You like the danger, don't you? I mean look at you now. You're a wreck but I haven't seen a single tear."

All her life Mary had heard people talking about themselves and it always soon became clear they hadn't a clue what they were going on about. Perhaps she was no different in her self-deceit.

He crossed his arms on his chest. "So, MI5 here aren't going to help you and you reckon the police would kill you. What are you going to do?"

"I need to figure that out. Can I stay here until I do? " She found his eyes. "Will you let me?"

"Of course, Jade, I wouldn't be much of a friend if I didn't."

"Nobody must know I'm staying. That means no bringing your other friends back here."

He clearly hadn't thought of that. For a country that prohibited homosexuality, there were an awful lot of gay males and Tang attracted them like flies. It had been both lucky and unusual to find him here alone today. Calculation wrinkled his brow.

"I suppose I can make alternative arrangements."

"Thank you for being so kind to me, Tang."

"You're acting again!"

She slapped him but very gently.

"Okay, so you can stay here while I wait on you hand and foot. Then what?"

"Hopefully the swelling will go down in a week or two. I'll need to change my appearance as best I can. My new nose will help but I'll trim back my eyebrows, widen and thicken my mouth with lipstick, cut my hair back. That sort of thing. You can buy me stuff to hide my face: floppy hat, sunglasses. Then at least I can start to venture out."

"Then what?"

"I'll let you know."

But, even then, she knew that she wouldn't.

The worst thing of all was getting the cotton out of her nose. She waited a week, hoping that was enough for it to set. She did it after Tang had gone to work so he wouldn't hear her moans.

First, she cut out little sections of the cotton with nail scissors. No matter how careful she was, every little cut pulled agonisingly at cotton fibres that had merged into the clotted blood.

Tang had been unsettled because she'd never cried but he should have seen her now. Her eyes, still surrounded by fading purple, became waterfalls.

Finally, when she'd got most of it out, she pressed her nose gently. It hurt abominably but held. Full on in the mirror it didn't look too bad, if a touch squinty, though it was definitely flatter than she remembered. Han noses are flat, more than those of Europeans, but this took it too far. Before she'd thought her face verged on being beautiful. But now...

With great trepidation she picked up Tang's hand mirror from his immaculate but beautifully kitted out dressing table. She took a deep breath and held the mirror sideways so she could see her profile in the dressing table's mirror.

She groaned. She hadn't packed the cotton far enough up her nose. It now rose to form a definite bump in the middle. Hardly remarkable for a white person but absurd amongst the ski-slope profiles of Han noses.

Later, she had waited for him, lying face down. They had got into the habit that when he returned, he would massage lotion into her bare back. The bruising was fading but she loved the way his gentle hands moved across her skin.

Tonight, his hands were especially gentle. After a while he said. "Turn over and I'll do your ribs."

She must have tensed and he felt it.

"What?"

She cursed herself as tears came to her eyes. She'd been vain about her looks, what actress wasn't, but she'd prided herself as not being as bad as the others.

"I've taken out the cotton and I'm ugly."

"Really?" He sounded more interested than appalled. If she hadn't been lying on her front, she'd have punched him for real.

He grasped her shoulders and pulled her over and up. He gently grasped her jaw and tilted her head, studying her profile before turning it back.

Their faces were inches apart and she could watch every expression. Assessment, disappointment, hope and even, finally, acceptance.

"You're still pretty," he said.

A big, fat schoolgirl teared rolled down her cheek.

He looked taken aback. Then, wonder of wonders, he kissed the tear away.

Then his lips found hers.

✦

All the long nights she and Tang spent together, they talked about their lives and her work. It was a relief to tell someone about life in the service. Tang found her tales of Five endlessly amusing, spying being a ridiculous game for overgrown schoolboys from an era being washed away by the surging tides of a new world.

Sometimes on those long nights they even made love, but usually not. That Tang could occasionally love her at all was a dispensation, a fleeting but unpredictable gift from a god not always kind to lovers.

As time passed, the danger mounted. The Gonganbu would still be looking for her, as would Marshall, if he hadn't already fled. Even if he had left HK there would be others in the HK police who were in the pay of the Chinese. She was putting Tang in danger; the only surprise was they hadn't got onto him already. She shuddered to think how he would fare under their interrogation. She loved him dearly but he was not a strong man.

One day, without warning, and to save him, she simply slipped away while he was at work.

The bank clerk in Kowloon gave her the slightly embarrassed look that everyone would give her for the rest of her life. Her signature was at least intact and she still had the safe deposit key.

All her bras had been altered to hold it and thankfully she'd put it in for the Walled City expedition. Just in case.

Now alone in the chill of the vault, she used it to open her security box. Inside was money but nothing else. She should have got her own fake passport years ago. The MI6 guys she'd trained with had boasted of theirs. Stupidly, she'd never dreamed she'd need one in a British colony.

The fishing boat had the upswept bow more redolent of a pirate ship. What looked like washing lines were strung across it. Even though no sharks' fins hung like pennants to dry in the sun, the boat reeked of their ghostly presence. The paint was peeling, scraps of rope lay strewn across the deck and the gangway had holes big enough for an incautious foot to drop through.

The old captain, sunburned and face deeply lined from peering out at endless glittering seas, looked at her blankly as she strode on board. His eyes lingered over the tightly fitting black trousers and plum coloured tunic that Tang had bought her.

A younger man, perhaps the captain's son, was sitting cross-legged at the bow and cutting rope with an evil looking knife. He at least looked surprised.

"Business good?" she asked.

The old man gave a grim little smile. "Wonderful."

"Are you busy now?"

"What the fuck do you want?" asked the younger man.

"I want to hire you and your boat."

The captain looked around in surprise. "We don't do pleasure trips."

"This isn't pleasure, this is business." That was one word in HK that got everyone's attention.

The captain's suddenly broader smile revealed yellowed teeth spotted with black decay. "What did you have in mind?"

"Taiwan. One way. Right now."

The captain nodded because, with Mary's fugitive status now revealed, everything was explained. Her fate now rested on a knife edge. If these were good, honest fishermen and respecters of the law then she was fucked. Even if she could get away from them, they could raise a hue and cry and she'd never make it off this poxy dock.

She tensed, ready to make a dash for it anyway.

The captain looked her up and down again and said the word she had most wanted to hear. "Expensive!"

She glanced around. "This isn't the QE2."

The captain grimaced. "Long trip. Nearly two days for you, but four for us. Have to be back for my niece's wedding on the tenth. No time for fishing so the whole trip would be just for you."

She'd divided her cash into two bundles and she threw one onto the deck at the old man's feet.

He picked it up with oil-smeared fingers and counted it.

"More!" he said.

"Don't be ridiculous!" She was already in his power. No need to seem weak as well, even though she didn't need all the rest of the money. If they got her to Taiwan then all she had to do was reach the British embassy in Taipei. Even if they dropped her off on the far south of the island, she wouldn't need a lot of money for a bus.

"You sleep on deck, you eat what we eat."

Mary tried not to smile.

✦

She'd never been seasick but the Taiwan Strait was choppy. Far out at sea, perhaps the two men might have tried their luck with her but at least the vomiting kept them away. When they dropped her off at a rank little fishing village on the west coast of Taiwan, there were no fond farewells.

It was little more than a hundred miles to Taipei but it took five little buses and two whole days of travel.

Not having a passport, convincing the doorman at the embassy that she was British had been difficult. She was finally shown into the presence of someone who called himself a press attaché but was obviously MI6. His manifest disbelief vanished when London immediately responded to his cables.

When it became clear she was telling the truth, he listened with relish to her tale of just how much MI5 had cocked things up.

To her great relief, they didn't send her back to Hong Kong. Instead, they hustled her aboard a British Airways flight to London via Bombay.

She had thought it was the sea trip that had upset her stomach, that or the bony fish stew the captain had given her to eat. But now, a week later and after decent food, her stomach was still unsettled.

Finally, thirty thousand feet over the Bay of Bengal, and after yet another trip to the toilet, she realised she was pregnant.

29. The Gobi Desert

The Son, Benny Hu, and the Road Leading Only Eastward

Carefully, trying hard to disguise what he was doing, Benny strained at his bonds. He was in the back seat of a BJ80, the Chinese army's off-roader of choice that looked like it had been carved out of granite. It was making its noisy, ponderous way down the highway, the desert either side broken up by the rippling heat of the late morning.

His life depended on getting free. Once Shihong had left, Aiguo and the first guard, whose name it turned out was Bingwen, had frogmarched him to the BJ80 and to his certain doom.

What was going to happen next ran on an endless loop in Benny's mind: the kneeling down in the desert, the bullet through the back of his head, the sand on his lips his last sensation.

For the sake of his sanity, he tried to think of other things.

He started by concentrating on Bingwen, whose name meant 'master of the arts'. Sometimes, the poorer the family, the more elevated the names that Chinese parents came up with. Bingwen's coarse accent, plus the fact that every few kilometres he wound down the window to hawk noisily out, betrayed lowly beginnings. Slightly plump with a round smiling face he didn't seem to have a care in the world.

Bingwen didn't command his attention for long and his thoughts quickly swung back to his fate. Didn't the Goo have a more elegant system for disposing of bodies? Were grave diggers or furnace operators expensive? Was it really going to save them much money by leaving his corpse to desiccate in this desert? To be like the old Bactrian camels whose lonely bones were strewn all over the place? Left abandoned by their owners after a lifetime of wearisome service.

He concentrated on the cable ties, brutal things to bind a man with. The thin plastic had already bitten off several layers of skin. If he pulled hard enough, he might be able to get one hand free, though at the expense of degloving it, stripping the flesh right off.

But even if he managed to do it, then what?

They'd pinioned his arms behind his back and bound both his legs together. Then again, maybe he didn't need to get out of the ties. Could he bring his feet up and kick the driver, an old guy in a dowdy uniform, in the back of head? Perhaps send the car spinning off the road and crashing. Hope he would be the only one to emerge still conscious from the crash. Perhaps he could kick the three men further into unconsciousness before finding something to cut his ties.

No! The seats in the Mazda had high, broad headrests, protecting the men's heads. It was all stupid, wishful thinking anyway.

Fear was making his breathing harsh. Even this scrappy desert was too enticing a place to leave forever. Perhaps if he pleaded, they would let him live, let him escape into the wasteland, let him restart a life hidden from men.

The car kept passing through small towns that made a living supplying food and drink and fuel to the trucks and minibuses streaming along the G312 highway, known in China as the Mother Road but elsewhere as the Silk Road. The towns looked deserted, their dwellers hiding from the wind and the dust and the sun.

Why hadn't they interrogated him properly? Shihong had taken only a few half-hearted stabs at it. Though she'd complained about it, she hadn't seemed unhappy to tell him things he didn't know. Things that meant so much to him that she should have bargained away carefully. Instead, she'd just blurted it all out.

A reverse interrogation. What were the Chinese up to?

Now another tiny town came into view, a place called Todok that drifted northwards from the road. Somewhere nearby there must be a river for there was cultivation on that side of the road, fields of straggly corn rising upwards with the ground. The south side of the road was pure desert with only a few tufts of scrub amongst bleakness.

"When are we going to get back from this, old father?" said Aiguo, "We've got a barbeque for the in-laws tonight. Wife'll fucking kill me if I'm not back on time."

The old guy, who had never stopped smoking, turned a weary eye to him. "Late."

"Why do you put up with all that?" said Bingwen from the backseat where he was sitting next to Benny.

Aiguo turned to look back at him. "I like an easy life. Three meals a day and a leg over regularly."

Bingwen nodded reluctantly. "I suppose it has its compensations."

Time passed and the cab became filled with the old man's smoke. He kept looking in his mirror back at Benny like he wanted to say something. Whatever he did for the army, he'd spend a lot of time in the open air for his skin was very dark and wrinkled. Far ahead a hideous confection was growing out of the desert and soon they were almost upon it. "Korgos," said the old man suddenly. "This town..." and he indicated the skyscrapers and the huge cranes and the giant video screens waxing lyrical about the glories of the New Silk Road, "... this town wasn't even a village only a few years ago. There were no bars or restaurants and people shat in the street. Now look at it! But it's still a border town full of people that'll kill you soon as look at you."

The old man opened the window and chucked his cigarette stub out before immediately lighting a new one. He sniffed at the dry desert air. "Smell that?"

Nobody answered.

"The future!" he said. "You spend a lifetime travelling through desert and steppe, you learn to see far. You learn to see through the glitz and the shit..." and again he indicated the town, "... to what's underneath. This place, with its road and its railway and its pipelines and its fibre optic cables, it's an artery. And it all leads back there." He pointed eastward.

Aiguo turned to look at him in frank disbelief. "What the fuck are you talking about?"

"This young man needs guidance. He's clearly lost his way."

"And what, exactly, has that got to do with you?"

"I'm old, near retirement. It is the job of the old to offer their advice to the young."

"Your job is to drive us out into the desert. Are you sure you can even do that?"

The old man nodded his head. "I was brought up around here."

He looked in the mirror again and Benny found himself staring into wise old eyes. "My point is, son, you're going the wrong way."

"There's no harm in seeing the world, old father."

The old man looked at him more carefully, one eye slightly closed by what looked like a recent insect bite. "I think you've seen enough of the world, son."

"Thanks for your advice. May your luck be as immense as the Eastern Sea."

"And may your future be as brilliant as embroidered cloth. And it might yet be if you don't waste your strength fighting the tide."

Aiguo slapped his hand down on the plastic dashboard. "Are you two finished?"

The old man shrugged and went back to driving and smoking.

Korgos was now so near that, for a moment, Benny's heart rose. They wouldn't take him all the way to a city to kill him. However, just as they approached the city limits, the old man took a turning to the left so insignificant it took Benny a moment to realise it was even a dirt track. Hardly used by anyone, the desert winds were inexorably covering it in dust.

The dirt road breasted a small rise to reveal a massive hollow full of discarded plastics. It was over a hundred metres across and looked like a trashcan for the gods. Full to the brim, the pit must be waiting to be covered with sand, though Benny suspected it might wait forever. Getting rid of rubbish generated money but covering it over when the pit was full didn't. China might have smartened up its central cities but here on the periphery the desert had always been a receptacle for all that people didn't want.

A few hundred yards beyond the pit, tufts of scrubby grass showed where desert was yielding to steppe. The blue of the sky had taken on a red tinge as evening drew near with a couple of early stars appearing.

They bounced down a shallow depression into what looked like a dry river bed. The old man suddenly stopped and shut off the engine. They were nowhere and there were no witnesses.

Benny struggled not to empty his bowels. The sky, hazy with dust had never looked more beautiful. The off-roader's plastic covered seats suddenly smelled more fragrant than anything he remembered.

"Are you sure this is the place?" asked Aiguo.

"Welcome to the border," said the old man.

Bingwen and Aiguo both got out and came round to his door. They opened it and heaved him out, letting him smack down on the packed dirt of the track. Aiguo reached into a pocket of his jacket and Benny found himself yammering. "I'll talk. I'll tell you every fucking thing you want to know."

Bingwen leaned in close and Benny smelled the bitterness of his breath. "Too late dipshit! You had your chance."

"But I know things. Names, places, operations. I know procedures, operating instructions, drops and codes, tricks and a hundred and one ways to fool face recog. I even know how to fool gait and heartbeat analysis. I know about—"

Bingwen slapped him hard. Then he pointed a finger at himself. "Is this the face of a man who gives a fuck what you know."

Meanwhile rather than a gun, Aiguo had pulled a knife from his pocket. He flipped it open to reveal a long, forked blade, deeply serrated on one side. He held it close to Benny's eye.

Benny felt urine dribble down his thigh.

"You're a fucking traitor." Aiguo waved the blade around, doing little feints, driving the blade at Benny's eye. "Once we'd have tortured the fuck out of you. But now...," and he looked around, as though scanning an unfamiliar horizon, "...it's a new world."

"Why don't we just do him anyway?" said Bingwen. "What would be the harm?"

They looked at each other, then both laughed. "Dream on!" said Aiguo.

He reached in with the knife and shoved it between Benny's wrists. He began to saw away, Bingwen taking a firm grip on Benny's upper arms.

As the cable tie parted, the relief was little short of orgasmic. Aiguo now sat on Benny's legs and cut the cable tie around his ankles. The two men exchanged nods then jumped back, out of kicking range.

But Benny wasn't for kicking anyone. He lay there, holding his hands clear of the dirt, his wrists too sore even to rub.

Aiguo pointed at the ground. "Stay right here, wanker! You're being watched." Then, without another word, the two men got into the car. The old man waved to him through the window then reversed the car back down the road, kicking up a cloud of dust that the westerly wind quickly dispersed.

Benny lay there as the same wind laid a dusty skin on his old one. He lay there so long that carrion birds began to circle high above him. The fear that had cramped his stomach and bladder began to ease and his muscles, clenched in dreadful anticipation of imminent death, began to slacken.

Now all that remained was to work out what the fuck had just happened. How to explain why the Goo had captured him, provided him with information he craved, had made no serious attempt to get anything in return, and then had just let him go?

That said, he had no money and no credit card and no phone so getting back to the UK wouldn't be exactly easy.

At least he was still breathing.

Standing up he could just make out the dustbowl over Korgos. Like Las Vegas, the place was a glittering abomination rising out of the desert and the lights were starting to come on.

Should he start moving? Why had they wanted him to wait here? Nothing was making any sense.

The old driver's words niggled away at him. The West was losing in every way and China was winning. China was becoming the only game in town and nowhere was this more evident than here where the Belt and Road Initiative was made form. Propaganda for it was everywhere in these western reaches. It wasn't just the new roads or the railways, there was a maritime Silk Road under construction with ports and harbours and airports and railways being built with Chinese money all across the Med, the Indian Ocean and the South China Sea. There was even a polar Silk Road for Arctic shipping, and a digital Silk Road of undersea cables. It all formed a vast web drawing Europe towards Asia. And nestling at the centre of the web was Beijing.

China was on track to invest six trillion bucks in the enterprise, making the Marshall Plan to re-invigorate Europe after World War Two look like chump change.

For a second Benny had the image of China as a black hole, bending space itself so that everything funnelled down into its maw. He could almost feel the desert dust tilting under his feet, sliding him back towards Beijing.

Other unsettling thoughts tugged at his attention, and particularly about Tang. Before venturing into mainland China both he and Mary had been to see him. Mary had stayed with Tang for months after the Walled City debacle and had had no choice but to confide in him. By getting her to talk, Tang would have succeeded where Chen's brutal methods had failed. When

316

Mary came back on her quest for vengeance, Tang would have tipped off the Goo and they'd have been waiting for her in Urumqi.

Then, forty years later, Benny rocks up at Tang's door, looking for his mother. Tang just has to point him in the same direction. The old bastard!

Then he thought of his grandfather. The poor old guy had returned to the East only to die, just like his father before him.

Hu Jun had died protecting his tiger-striped son. The son had died trying to protect Mary. And now Benny had risked his life searching for her. All in the name of love.

Tang deserved to die but Benny found he had no taste for killing the tired old man. Lust for vengeance was something he hadn't inherited from his mother.

Why would Tang have worked for Chinese intelligence? He'd come from a wealthy family. Perhaps their excesses had appalled him. British spies like Burgess, Philby, Blunt and Maclean had also been from well-to-do backgrounds, public schoolboys who turned traitor. In a way, Tang was less to be despised than the British spies. They had turned against privileged white imperialists just like themselves. Tang, on the other hand, had rebelled against white imperialists who had no business being in his country in the first place.

Why was he offering excuses for Tang? What strange mirror world was he now in?

He tasted dust and realised a harsher desert wind had sprung up. The first few stars grew hazy. Above Korgos, the lights reflected off the dust in the air, forming an inverted brown bowl over the hidden city.

He heard a car approaching from the other side of the invisible border and he saw the rising dust from its wheels. It pulled up and three figures got out and approached him. There were two bulky men either side of a tall, slender woman. A few more metres nearer and he realised the woman was Lea.

Stupidly, ridiculously, his heart leapt. "Jesus!" he heard himself say.

"Hello, Benny," said Lea.

Benny shook his head, trying to clear it. "How did you know..." He pointed around at the empty desert.

Lea was looking sick, ill at ease. Exposed. "That you'd be here for the handover. The Chinese told us, obviously."

She must have seen the puzzlement on his face. "We're here to take you home."

"Why?" he asked.

"You know why," she said.

"Six washed its hands of me. Why wasn't that the end of the story?"

Now they were closer, Benny could get a better look at her two companions. Broad-browed with hard, cruel mouths and eyes, they looked at him as though from a higher reality, like scientists peering at an insect through a microscope. All three were wearing suits but the two men looked uncomfortable in theirs. Already they'd pulled out and lit cigarettes. He guessed they were just a couple of Kazakh heavies. Lea's hair had fallen forward to make a long curtain over one eye and she pulled it back over her ear with her free hand. "We don't want the Chinese to have you. You know too much."

"Do I? Six kept me at arm's length my whole fucking career."

"Come home, Benny."

He'd never seen her look so out of control. Benny realised this mission was a form of penance for her. She had to prove her loyalty, atone for her mistake of telling him his mother's new name. And it would cost her because she was exposed if the Chinese were watching. And why wouldn't they?

"I don't even have a passport," he said. "They took everything away."

"You don't need one," she said, just a shade too quickly.

And suddenly it all fell into place. They thought he'd been doubled by the Chinese, or perhaps that he'd worked for them all along. They weren't going to take him home, they were going to take him to a cobbled together black site here in Kazakhstan.

Maybe just an isolated hut in the desert. And then they'd work on him, drill down to what he knew about the Goo, try and turn him yet again, like a hog being spit-roasted.

And, if they couldn't be convinced that they'd turned him, then why take him home? Who might he spill his guts to next?

Death in the desert would seem such an attractive alternative.

He searched her face for a trace of softness towards him but all he could see was regret. "I don't work for the Chinese," he said as earnestly as he could. "How many successful ops have I run against them?"

"Of course, we know you don't work for them."

He didn't believe her for a second. This whole thing was a learning experience the Chinese had orchestrated for his benefit, to show him that he couldn't go back.

He had to get out of here. Where, though? He couldn't just wander off; he was in a desert and night was falling. The only thing he could see out there was the buzzing, blurry sin hole of Korgos.

Without another word he turned and set off towards it.

"Whoa!" Lea shouted.

There was so much alarm in that single word that Benny had to turn. He saw one of the men had already pulled out a gun.

Benny heard the evil, visceral crack of a high velocity round, and the man fell backwards.

Suddenly, Lea and the other man were caught in a cat's cradle of thin red beams. Two ended in the centre of the man's chest. One ended over Lea's heart and it was joined quickly by another.

Benny slowly turned all the way around to see if any of the red lines were touching him but there was nothing.

Lea and the other man slowly raised their hands.

"You bastard! You set us up!" said Lea.

Benny looked at her for several seconds and was surprised to find himself laughing.

And he was still laughing after he'd walked a hundred metres and had turned to take one last look at her. She was still there, arms raised, entangled in the cat's cradle of sighting beams.

Then he stopped laughing when he realised he was caught in his own cat's cradle.

He trudged on towards the jazzy lights, still not sure what he was going to do next. No passport, no money, no credit cards, no phone. The Chinese wanted him alive, but they clearly weren't intending on making that life easy. This too was penance.

What scared him most was the way they had handled this, with such confidence that they would win and, perhaps, not caring that much if they didn't. He found himself admiring their terrible arrogance.

The sky was now almost black and the illuminated bowl of dust over Korgos was a bright yellow.

Korgos was a notional frontier town on a Chinese frontier that was in reality moving inexorably westwards. The Middle Kingdom had never invaded other countries, it wasn't really in its DNA, but they did demand fealty. Instead, a new virtual frontier was expanding, not through soldiers and guns but through technology and money. So many of the endless miles of this huge Eurasian continent was already theirs, in effect if not in name.

And this was happening everywhere. The rug was being pulled from under the complacent West. Its fall would be hard, its future only that of subservience.

The ship was sinking and everyone on it who he had cared for was dead or had rejected him.

Did he have any real choice? He faced re-birth, but knew that whatever struggled out of the cocoon would be hard and cold beyond recognition.

Reluctantly, but inevitably, he began his long walk back to a road that led only eastward.